About Darry Fraser

Darry Fraser was born in Victoria, Australia and spent part of her childhood around her beloved River Murray. Her novel, *Daughter of the Murray*, is set there. She is the author of several works of romantic and women's fiction. Her books are heart warming and at times funny and reflect her love of a good story. Darry currently lives, works and writes on an island off the coast of South Australia. Visit her website www.darryfraser.com or drop her a line at darry@darryfraser.com. She'd love to hear from you.

Daughter of the Murray

DARRY FRASER

First Published 2017
Second Australian paperback edition 2018
ISBN 978 1 489 25118 3

Daughter of the Murray
© 2017 by Darry Fraser
Australian Copyright 2017
New Zealand Copyright 2017

This is a work of fiction. Names, characters, places, and incidents are either the product of the author's imagination or are used fictitiously, and any resemblance to actual persons, living or dead, business establishments, events, or locales is entirely coincidental.

Published by
Harlequin Mira
An imprint of Harlequin Enterprises (Australia) Pty Ltd.
Level 13, 201 Elizabeth St
SYDNEY NSW 2000
AUSTRALIA

® and TM are trademarks of Harlequin Enterprises Limited or its corporate affiliates. Trademarks indicated with ® are registered in Australia, New Zealand and in other countries.

Cataloguing-in-Publication details are available from the National Library of Australia www.librariesaustralia.nla.gov.au

Printed and bound in Australia by McPherson's Printing Group

MIX
Paper from
responsible sources
FSC® C001695

Good things come to those who keep trying.
To Dane and Georgina — we made it! Sorry it took so long.

One

There was no escaping this day, no matter what she did.

A vibrant sun dawned over Mallee country and the bedroom lit up. 'For goodness' sake, Ruth. Keep the curtains shut.' Georgie buried her face under the threadbare bedsheet.

'Now, come along, Miss Georgie. You love the early morning.' Plump Ruth bustled about. She drew back the other heavy curtain one-handed before she thumped a breakfast plate of bread and jam on the dresser beside Georgie's bed.

Eucalyptus scented the shimmering heat and it drifted to Georgie even under the bedclothes. 'If you're going to tell me one more time that Mr Dane is coming home today, so help me, I'll—'

'You know Mr Dane comes home today.'

'I know it, Ruth. You've told me a dozen times.' Georgie pushed the sheet away. 'I can't stand the man and yet I've never met him. All I ever hear is Mr Dane this, Mr Dane that. Mr Dane, so handsome. Mr Dane—' She sat up, yawned and flexed her back, flinging her arms above her head. Her fingers splayed then she relaxed bonelessly onto the pillow with a long exhale. She'd

1

heard it all before. 'The poor man has no clue he's coming home to this.'

'Oh, he's not a poor man, miss. He's a rich young gentleman now. And I remember him well when we was in the schoolyard; I was only a year younger. He was fine to look at an' all, even back in them days.'

Georgie pulled a face. 'If he looks anything like his father, I certainly can't imagine you'd call him fine to look at.'

Ruth cast her a quick glance and swiped a hand over her untidy mousey brown hair. 'No, miss. He *doesn't* look like Mr Tom—'

A screech outside the room interrupted her: Elspeth wanting her hairbrush.

'Oh God. My cousin intends to wake the dead this morning.' Georgie swung her legs to the floor.

'Miss Georgina, blaspheming. And where's your nightdress?' Ruth fussed about the bed like some hen pecking at corn kernels. Her backside wobbled under her dress as she bent to rummage through a pile of linen under the wash-stand.

'It's too hot for a nightdress, Ruth.'

'Hardly, and you shouldn't sleep like it.' Ruth found the discarded nightdress on the floor and held it out.

Georgie tugged the worn shift from her and wriggled into it. She padded barefoot to sit on the stool in front of a plain timber table with a small mirror on it. A fresh bowl of hot water and a hard scrap of soap waited for her. 'And why are you here, anyway? God knows we can't pay you.' Georgie rubbed her face with bare hands. 'Bloody depression coming, says Uncle Tom.'

'You shouldn't speak of that either, Miss Georgie. Mr Tom will pay—'

'Don't talk foolishly, Ruth. The whole district knows he'll drink it away before any bloody depression gets here.'

'The devil will come get you with talk like that, that's a fact.' Ruth huffed and puffed as she blew hair out of her eyes. 'And what if Miss Jem was to hear you say that?'

'The devil is welcome,' Georgie said and Ruth crossed herself. 'And my Aunt Jemimah won't hear of it. All she cares about is her son coming home.'

'He is your cousin, Miss Georgie, he's family and—'

'He's not my family, Ruth. He's my *step*-cousin.' Georgie pulled her hair back from her face. 'Now, would you please do my hair for me?' Her thick dark hair was only ever plaited, and that was how she preferred it. 'You do it so well.'

'Miss, I'm not to dilly-dally here. With Mr Dane coming, Miss Jem and Miss Elspeth want their hair attended to, and yours being so simple you can do it yourself, they said that I—'

'Bloody Mr Dane has been coming for nigh on the four years I've been here and I haven't seen hide nor hair of him yet. What makes today so bloody different?'

'Oh, and gutter talk. The devil *will* come, missy, right here, to the good Queen's colony of Victoria. You make no mistake.' Ruth shook her forefinger and bustled out.

Georgie smiled into the mirror. *The devil will come ... To our River Murray landing, no less. What rubbish. I'm sure the devil has better work to do.* Some said God had forgotten the Australian colonies years ago, the devil even earlier. She dragged the brush through her hair in long strokes, bringing back the gleam after its tousling on the pillow.

Bloody Mr Dane will get a shock when he arrives.

From the furtive whispers and heated arguments in the dead of night when no one thought she could hear, Georgie would wager bloody Mr Dane, the mighty son and heir, knew little of what had befallen Jacaranda since he'd been gone.

Even Georgie's stepfather, her Papa Rupert in England, hadn't believed her. She'd confided her suspicions by letter but he'd not answered them. To the contrary, he'd chided her for her lack of charity, implied her imagination was still quite rich and that she should try to be more tolerant of the family's ways.

There'd been nothing but silence from England since, and that had been well over a year ago.

She was nearing twenty-two ... so old and unmarried *still*. And with no prospects of a good life ahead of her if she remained with the MacHenrys, she reasoned it was her right to fend for herself. When Uncle Tom slurred and slurped his way into rum-addled unconsciousness, she'd ease a few coins from his pockets and secrete them away to a cache under a floorboard in her room. She hadn't scraped together nearly enough to pursue her chance at life, though.

If only Uncle Tom had taken her up on her offer to handle the books for him. At least that would be something she could do. She was good at sums; she preferred them to needle work and cooking. But he remained adamant to the point of belligerence that she would not attempt such a thing, 'being a woman and all'. Tom's books were under lock and key. A key he never left around.

However, there was Conor Foley. Her Conor Foley.

She smiled as she thought of him. Only three weeks ago, his riverboat, the *Lady Mitchell*, had docked at the landing on the MacHenrys' property to deliver the goods Jemimah had ordered from the city. Conor brought the much anticipated newspapers from Swan Hill that Georgie read line by line, hungry for the world outside.

Conor Foley.

His soft Irish brogue, the gleam in his eyes, the deep auburn hair, the broad shoulders. A man who towered over most men, weighty and solid. He was much older than the tiresome boys of the neighbouring homesteads, well past his thirties; he had been to war in South Africa.

Conor Foley offered her a new life with just a glance of mystery and intrigue.

Ruth burst back into the room. She grabbed the hairbrush in Georgie's hand, apologising as she did so.

'What are you doing?' Georgie held fast to the brush.

'Please, Miss Georgina. There's such a commotion today. Miss Elspeth's misplaced her brush. Please let me have the brush. What with Mr Dane returning ... He's been away far too long, wouldn't you say?' Ruth had her firm grip over Georgie's hand on the brush.

Georgie wrenched the hairbrush free. 'Since I have never met him,' she said sternly, 'his absence has hardly bothered me. But his homecoming is sorely testing my very good manners.' She thrust the brush into Ruth's hand, sending the woman back a pace or two.

Clutching the brush to her chest, Ruth disappeared as loudly as she had arrived, muttering something that sounded distinctly like 'Good manners, my arse. You'll get yours, my girl.'

Georgie sighed long and hard, then set about plaiting her hair.

Impatient with having to be modest, especially now she was alone, she hoisted the nightgown off. Once naked again, she washed in a hurry, and dried with the threadbare towel. The drought meant deep, long baths were rare, so a quick but thorough wash with a flannel and basin had to do.

She stood in front of her wardrobe, an open box built of river gum. It contained hand-me-downs from neighbouring ladies. Georgie hadn't received new clothes for years, even though she had requested some in her last two letters to England. She'd grown out of the last set of clothes her stepfather had sent from England and they'd been altered long ago for the much smaller Elspeth.

Hands on hips, Georgie stared at the four dresses. A bleached day dress, one light blue dress, one dark blue and a faded pink one. None of them suited her today. No, today was a good day for a long ride along the banks of her beloved river. She needed to escape the madness of today.

She knelt by her bed, flipped up the thin, lumpy mattress and dragged out a pair of men's trousers, an old shirt and a checked piece of cloth. She took the cloth, a piece of wide fabric torn from an old bed sheet destined for the horses for rubdowns, and wound it around her chest to flatten her breasts. The shirt went on over the top, the trousers pulled up over bare legs and arse, drawn around her waist by a slim leather rope she had borrowed from the tack room. She faced the little mirror again, coiled her long, black plait atop her head and stabbed some pins into it to hold it there.

Then she reached for her flat-heeled riding boots, the only thing she had left from England. They were the colour of burnt caramel, laced to mid-calf, the leather supple and soft after years of loving care. She pulled them on, tied each lace firmly, let the pants drape over them and stood tall.

She grabbed the thick slice of bread left by Ruth, shoved it into a small calico bag then picked up a hat lying under her bed. She sidled out the door to the veranda. A quick look to the left, then the right, and she marched across the dusty yard to the stables. Nobody would be bothering her this morning, all too busy awaiting his lordship's arrival.

Joe, the stocky, barrel-chested contract stableman, and Watti, an Aboriginal man with a shock of wiry grey hair, were in the stall with the black stallion, MacNamara. Joe crooned as he swept the brush powerfully over the horse's flank and back. The horse swung his head to stare at Georgie, but waited patiently as his groomsman prepared him for the day. Watti polished the big saddle as it hung over the rail.

Georgie leaned on the stable doorway. She watched Joe as he whispered in MacNamara's ear, rubbed his nose and plied him with soft Irish compliments, the lilting murmur music to her ears. Joe ran his hands over a glossy flank, down to a fetlock and back, and the horse stood nodding his proud head. Joe would camp in the stalls on the days he spent at Jacaranda, for MacNamara was a prized possession, and Tom MacHenry dared not neglect him.

MacNamara stood sixteen hands. Georgie could just see over his withers. He was eight years old now, past the silly stage, and he had responded well to her training. She'd fed him and groomed him as a younger horse, cleaned and oiled his saddle, looked after his teeth and, when he got too big for her to look after his hooves, Joe had been called in to keep the horse in top condition. She loved the horse. Joe knew it, the horse knew it.

Joe was also the one who made sure Dane MacHenry himself would foot the bill for MacNamara's upkeep, and for the other two horses: Douglas, a gentle roan, and Brandy, a chestnut. Left to Tom, the horses wouldn't survive. Georgie knew that well enough.

She pushed off the doorway and walked into Joe's line of sight, reaching up to scratch MacNamara's forelock. 'Morning, Joe. Morning, Watti.'

Watti mumbled something as he nodded, his dusty black face sombre, eyes averted.

Joe lifted his chin at her. 'Morning, Miss Georgina. In your ridin' clobber today, I see.'

'I thought to take myself away from all the gormless softheads for a while.'

Joe snorted a laugh.

'Is Mac ready?' Her hands ran down the horse's neck and slid across the muscled chest. How she loved that sleek, hard body and its power. Mac was a dream to ride, obedient to her lightest command. They would tear through the paddocks together, whatever the weather, and end up exhausted and exhilarated.

'Mr Dane's coming home and Mr Tom wants the horse ready for him. Sorry, miss. Not MacNamara today.' Joe kept his gaze on the horse. 'Mr Dane comes straight to the stables when he comes home. Wouldn't be too good if Mac were gone with you.'

'That would be your opinion, Joseph O'Grady.'

Joe inclined his head. 'It would be that.'

Georgie inhaled with a low hiss. That blasted Dane MacHenry again. 'Comes straight to the stables, does he? Since when, in the last four years?'

Joe studied her. 'Believe me, Miss Georgie, it wouldn't be worth the trouble.' He returned to his brush work. 'Besides, miss, I doubt you'd want to see Mrs Jemimah out of sorts over it.'

Georgie shot a glance at Joe. 'No, of course I wouldn't. I know Aunt Jem is looking forward to his return.' She tapped her foot. 'Then it looks like I'll have to take Brandy.'

Joe dipped his head and kicked the dirt with his boot. 'Miss Elspeth wants to ride Brandy today.' Georgie lovingly looked after Brandy, Elspeth's mount, too.

Georgie's eyes widened. 'Elspeth? How extraordinary. That poor horse.' She paused. 'Do you think the donkey would be available, Joe, or is he also engaged to ride with the rest of his kin?'

'If we had a donkey.' Joe gave her a smile. 'Douglas here is rarin' for a good run, miss. He's in good form and no one to ride him. Take Douglas. He's a good boy.' Joe tethered MacNamara and unlatched the next stall door. He stepped inside and ran his hand over the muzzle of the roan. 'He's a good boy,' he repeated to the horse.

'He is at that.' She loved Douglas too, he just wasn't MacNamara. But her mood lifted. 'All right. I'll saddle him up, but not with one of those stupid women's things.'

Joe threw a blanket over Douglas's back. He knew better than to assist further, so he watched Georgie heft the saddle onto Douglas. As she tightened the girth, she muttered.

He cupped a hand to his ear. 'What's that? Did I miss some of your colourful language?'

She stepped into the stirrup and threw herself astride the horse, then beamed at him. 'I said, let the blasted devil come for his horse. But not a word of that to anyone, Joseph O'Grady.'

''Pon my Celtic soul, as usual, miss.'

She gee-upped Douglas into the yard, stooped gracefully to unlatch the gate and swung it open. Joe would latch it behind her.

Two

Dane MacHenry gripped the seat of the rough cart, his knuckles white, as his father drove, bouncing over a track pocked with large holes. They rounded the corner and there was Jacaranda, sprawled a hundred yards ahead.

My family home ... Good sweet Jesus, the place is a mess.

What had happened to the proud young Murray pines that flanked the road into the property? He'd planted them at the same time his father had added on to the house to give Elspeth her own room. Only a straggly few remained.

They bounced through the gate ... or what had been the gate as Dane remembered it, now only broken timbers, left to rot where they'd fallen. The entrance archway had disappeared, no trace of it left. He eyed the sign: *Jacaranda*. It lay flat on the baked earth just inside the boundary fence, which may as well have been non-existent.

And the house. When he stared at the veranda, the sagging roof gave him a jolt, though the timbers and stones of the walls looked sturdy enough. As they drew closer he saw the window frames were crumbling, eaten away, and in some the glass—so very carefully tended by his mother—was missing: there were boards covering a window on the far left.

All this in just over four years?

'Jesus, Pa. What the hell's happened here?'

Tom shook his head, grim and frowning. 'Much to talk about.'

Dane stared at him. It didn't seem long ago that his father was a great bear of a man. He'd had a thatch of coarse, dark blond hair, shaggy eyebrows and a quick grin, even in times of trouble. His big hands were capable of anything, from cradling a newborn lamb to thwacking a log with his axe.

The man Dane sat beside now was a shadow of the man he remembered. The hair had receded, thinned, greyed. The lines on his face were more than just age; they were worry and perhaps ill-health. It was his father's eyes that disturbed Dane the most: wild eyes, bloodshot and furtive, like that of a cornered cur.

The cart jumped and banged its way to the house. The neglect of the family property showed years of disregard, not just a few lax months.

Dane knew six years of severe drought had decimated the Mallee, Victoria's northwestern district. But the rains had returned and rich grassy plains grew from ruddy red dust. Why was Jacaranda still so browned off and shrivelled?

This was neglect, pure and simple.

One more year had been his plan. One more year in Sydney. After that he'd return to work the farm, to take over. To put in place new ideas for cropping, perhaps citrus or grapes and irrigation. He'd learned much, and still had much to learn, but now his job looked like a completely different task.

Damn me, I should've have returned a year ago ... 'Pa, what the bloody hell has happened?'

Tom swung the cart to a halt, dropping a wheel into another deep pothole at the steps of the veranda. Both he and Dane swore loudly.

———

Inside, Tom was impatient for everything at once. 'Yes, yes. But where did you get enough money to buy that place? Surely a hotel is not an easy thing to come by? Where did the money come from, son? Where?'

'Money?' Dane asked. He stopped short. His mother straightened in her chair. Elspeth, his sister, was oblivious to anything but what was on her plate.

His father nodded and pushed a forkful of fried egg and bread into his mouth.

'I didn't buy the place. I won it. At cards.'

Tom erupted into a coughing fit, his mouthful spilling over his shirt front. Elspeth looked at her father curiously between shovelfuls, and Jemimah jumped up to thump his back and help him mop up. The silence while Tom tried to control his choking was thick. Jemimah stood stony-faced behind him, thumping him again. Elspeth ate on.

'You all right, Pa?'

'Went down the wrong way.' Tom slurped a dish of tea and swallowed audibly, clearing his throat. 'You won it at cards,' he wheezed.

'It was a run-down brothel—sorry, Ma—and this fella challenged me while I sat at his table.' Dane didn't mention it was his good friend and business partner, Reuben Cawley. 'We played cards for it and I won. Simple.' He began to eat his breakfast.

'Pa plays cards, too.' Elspeth's mouth was full. 'He plays with Charlie Rossmoyne and that riverboat man, Conor Foley, who—'

'That will do, Elspeth,' Jemimah cut in. 'Come with me. It's time to leave your father and your brother to talk alone.'

'I'm not finished.' Elspeth forked the last scrapings from her plate into her mouth.

Jemimah glared at her daughter. 'Where are your manners?'

Elspeth burst into tears. 'I have manners. I have manners!' She rushed out of the room, dragging the tablecloth in her hurry.

Jemimah drew her lips into a thin line, and left the room.

Dane stared after her. He remembered his mother as healthy and vital, but now she seemed bowed, and not quite her old self. Her dark blonde hair had bleached and looked brittle, and she was thinner than he recalled. But her eyes still held a spark of life. She'd fussed a little over him, kept holding his hands and hugging him quickly, smiling broadly. Then she'd release him and moments later return to hug him again but the broad smile was a shadow of its former self.

He turned to his father. 'Things are not good.'

Tom rubbed a hand over his mouth. '*Things* have been neglected here of late.'

Dane frowned. 'An understatement, I would say.'

'It has been ... difficult. Debts. Bad weather. Upkeep of a family. Elspeth is at an age—'

'Clearly.' Dane knew Elspeth would be about sixteen now, and old enough to be brought into society. But she would not have wrought this havoc of disrepair on the place. Elspeth still seemed a child, untidy in her dress and her hair, which looked as if she'd never gotten a brush near it, let alone pins and a cap. She was tall for her age, but ungainly. Her big doe eyes, hazel and haunting, reminded him of someone who knew life was going to be hard.

The silence grew. Dane continued to eat. He decided his father could do some more talking.

Tom pushed his plate away, stood and reached into a cupboard behind him. His hand emerged gripping a bottle and two glasses. He filled one, swallowed its contents in one gulp and poured two more.

Rum, and it was barely ten in the morning.

'It's the girl, Dane. This Georgina, your mother's step-niece.'

'What of her?' Dane had read in Jemimah's letters of the girl coming from England to live with the family, but he hardly thought much of it. He had dutifully sent five pounds more each quarter. The letters from his mother had stopped a year or so ago. Perhaps he should have wondered more about that.

As Dane hadn't touched the proffered glass, Tom took it back and swallowed the rum. 'Her father is to blame for why I've got no money, son.'

Dane stared. *He* sent money, regular payments each few months. Money he had expected was feeding the family, building capital in the place, waiting for him to return. 'I send you—'

Tom waved him down. 'Your mother's brother, Rupert, is the girl's stepfather. He's accrued big debts, gambling and whoring, and I've been … sending your money back to England to cover his arse.' His father rolled the rum tumbler as it stood empty on the table. 'He'll go to debtor's prison unless I can pay off his debts. So, for your mother's sake, I send drafts to him.' Tom shook his head slowly. 'It would be a shock to you, I know. Your mother wasn't to tell you before now, wasn't to worry you.' He kept his eyes downcast. 'It's been going on for a while and as you can see, the place is deteriorating, too fast now. I need your help, son. I need more financial assistance.' He reached across and poured himself another tot.

'How much more?'

'They want to foreclose. I'll need—'

'Foreclose?' Dane exhaled loudly. 'Why didn't you get me to come earlier?'

'I needed what you were sending.' Tom hesitated. 'You do have more money, don't you, son?'

Dane shook his head to clear it. Jacaranda was in jeopardy because of his uncle's transgressions in England while his daughter was supported here? At least in that regard the girl was safe with his family and not forced to beg in the streets—or worse—but was his family safe now? 'How much?'

'Five hundred pounds.' Tom's speech slurred.

'Five—!' Dane leapt to his feet, knocking the rum to the floor. 'That's a bloody fortune.'

Tom gurgled as he rushed to retrieve the bottle.

Dane kicked it out of reach. 'Leave it, Pa. I send you twenty pounds a quarter. Why has that not been enough?' He glanced about the house, aware his mother and his sister—and the help— would be nearby, and lowered his voice. 'There is more to this story, and I will hear it. We'll go out and ride. Now.'

Tom still would not meet his eye. Instead, he bent to pick up the nearly empty bottle.

Dane stalked out of the house.

He reached the stable long before Tom.

Joe greeted him warmly. ''Tis good to see you back again, Mr Dane. You're a welcome sight, you are.'

Dane gripped the other man's hand. 'Good to see you're still here, Joe.'

Joe shrugged. 'We only come back an' forth these days. Some-one's got to do the heavy work for me horses.'

Watti made his way over from Douglas's stall. 'Mista Dane.' He took both Dane's hands in a shake. 'Good on yer, fella.' He beamed at Dane, one tooth missing from the top row.

'Good on yer, fella, Watti. Good to see you, too, old man.'

'Look at MacNamara now, Mr Dane. Just look at him.' Joe beckoned Dane to MacNamara's stall.

'Jus' look at him, that one, that horse.' Watti leaned over the stall rail.

'Just look at him,' Dane repeated. His gaze roamed over the big horse. 'He looks very fine.' MacNamara's black coat glistened, his eyes were wide and clear, and the smell of his breath was clean. Inside the stall, Dane ran his hand down a foreleg. 'He's still a beauty, Joe. I've sorely missed him.' He glanced around. 'And the stables, man. They look better than the house. You've done it proud. All thanks to you two.'

'Not entirely me and Watti, Mr Dane. We're only here now for the heavy work, as I said. No, sir, not all us.'

'I'll lay a bet it isn't old Tom yonder.' Dane hitched a thumb towards his father as he stumbled in through the stable doors.

''Tis the young lady, Miss Georgina.'

'Is that so?'

'She's in here mucking out, scrubbing the place, oiling the timbers. I bring her fresh hay and she spreads it, she feeds them. Never seen a lady work like that before.' He turned to stroke the big horse's neck. 'And she's rubbed all them horses down, talks to 'em all day an' night.' He shook his head. 'She rides MacNamara like she was a part of him and they whip through them paddocks like the wind itself. He gets a good run from her, and well he needs it, too.'

'A good thing for the horse.'

'It is that.'

Dane turned to his swaying father. 'Can you ride in that state?' he asked.

'Coursh I can.'

'Joe, will you change that sidesaddle—' Dane indicated Brandy, '—and saddle up for Pa?'

'I can do it meshelf.' Tom leaned on the stall door.

Joe handed MacNamara's reins to Dane and then reached into Brandy's stall. 'Mr Tom, perhaps you would hand me up your saddle?'

Dane led MacNamara out of his stall. The big horse shied and as Dane swung up onto the broad back, the horse danced under the unaccustomed weight. Dane barely touched him with the stir-rup and MacNamara was off.

'Jesus,' he yelled and managed to halt ten yards from the gates. 'I'd forgotten how keen he is.'

Joe laughed behind him. 'He's lost none of his fire. It's Miss Georgie keeps him at his finest.'

Dane grudgingly admired the girl if she could handle his pow-erful horse. He trotted back to Joe, waiting for his father to steady himself.

Joe gave the older man a leg-up into the saddle. Tom gripped Brandy's mane as he thrust his feet into the stirrups. He pitched forward to remove his foot from a stirrup twisted by his careless-ness then tried to replace it. It proved difficult.

Watti stepped up to grip Tom's ankle and pushed it into the stirrup.

Dane leaned down to Joe. 'He has been paying you, Joe?'

Joe nodded. 'He has, Mr Dane. 'Tis in his best interests.'

Dane lifted his chin towards his father and spoke quietly. 'How many people know of this?'

Joe glanced at Tom, who still concentrated on the stirrup though Watti had stepped back. He hesitated only moment. 'About everyone in the district.'

Tom trotted past them. 'Come on, then, lad. Don't keep your old dad waiting on yer.' He rode with one foot lolling out of its stirrup.

Watti threw his hands in the air.

Dane wheeled MacNamara and followed his father out.

About everyone in the district.

He didn't have five hundred pounds, dammit. He'd have to sell his tavern for that sort of money, and it was too early yet. There'd have to be another way. Then he'd have to find funds on top of the debt to re-stock, buy seed ...

He would forestall the bank, speak to his business partner.

They cantered out of the home paddock. 'Tell me everything, Pa, right from the start.'

Tom bumped in the saddle, at odds with the horse. 'I'll tell you one thing: he's ruined me, and your mother, and Elspeth,' he wailed. 'The damned game he plays, he's too good … and I lost my head. All that money.'

'My uncle?'

Tom frowned then shook his head. 'Yes. I mean your uncle.'

'You don't sound like you know who it is you're talking about. Sober up so I can get sense out of you.' Dane rode west to look over some of the property. It would give Tom time to clear his head.

Keeping the river on his right, Dane took them through a couple of paddocks. He leaned down from the saddle to unhook the gates and shut each behind them as Tom came through.

Tom swayed atop Brandy. 'Wouldn't bother wi' that. There's no stock.'

'I can see. There's no feed here for stock, either. Place is as dry as a chip.' Every direction Dane turned a barren red landscape stretched before them. The dust of the land disheartened him. His heart thumped. This degradation, in just over four years. Why had Jemimah not written and informed him?

'Do the windmills still run?' Dane stared at a silhouette in the distance. He remembered the excitement years ago when his father first purchased one from the engineer, Mr Alston, in the Western Districts.

'When I need them to. I haven't let sheep out here for a year or more.'

It wouldn't take much to fix this paddock. A few good men, some tools, weekly maintenance, unless otherwise required. Small stock levels to begin with … fence off a few paddocks to sow seed …

He swung MacNamara and looked east towards the river banks lined with trees. 'Let's head to the river.'

'Good idea. I'm hot as hell.' Tom wiped his forehead with his sleeve, which came away damp.

Sweat ran down Dane's back as the sun rose higher. He headed for the shade of the mighty river red gums, and for the cooler air lifting off the water.

They stopped on the bank, overlooking a bend in the river, one of Dane's favourite places as a boy. He gazed across the slow flow of muddy water then dismounted and walked to where the river lapped the dun-coloured bank. His past leapt back to him.

Tom said, 'I'm right now, son, but for a big headache. If you don't mind, I might piss then have a smoke.' He slid off Brandy and stepped to the nearest bush.

Dane tethered the two horses then sat on his heels staring at the river. 'I don't have five hundred pounds, Pa,' he called over his shoulder.

'Can you get it?'

'You'd better tell me all of it.'

Tom returned buttoning his pants, sweat gleaming on his face. He slid down the trunk of a sturdy gum and sat heavily, pulling a pouch from his pocket. He rolled a smoke. 'It began just as soon as the girl arrived from England, not long after your last visit. Your uncle, Jem's brother—you only met him when you were two or three—bit toffee but all right, I suppose. Er, back then.' He scratched a match to light his smoke, took a draw and looked at Dane. He'd gone as white as a sheet. 'Lad, can you get me a cup of water? Cup's in Brandy's bag.'

Dane opened the rawhide bag slung on Brandy's saddle and pulled out a tin pannikin. He took it to the river, dipped it and returned to Tom.

Tom swallowed the water. 'He married a widow in Melbourne. The girl is his dead wife's daughter. When the wife died, he went back to England, took the girl with him. Schooled her there for ten years, thereabouts. His new wife came along and she didn't want a young unmarried colonial around, especially a step-daughter. He begged Jemimah and me to take her and said he'd send money to … ' He shrugged, and stared at the ground. 'God alone knows how, at eighteen, the poor girl … ' His voice drifted off again.

'And she's been living here ever since? You should have put her to work.' Dane sat beside his father, picked up a pebble and hurled it into the water.

'Your ma hoped we'd find a suitable husband, but no one around here's good enough. Georgina was a bit above us all when she first arrived, but not so much now. Still, these days she has some damned notion about the vote for women. That'd scare any man off.' Tom held up a hand to Dane's querying glance. 'Anyhow, your mother's repaid a good deed, trying to help her brother, who'd helped her when no one else would.' His lip curled; he hawked and spat. 'But let that story be for now.'

'Story?'

'It's your mother's to tell. Not important now.'

Dane shrugged that off. So, the girl was living here while the family struggled to pay her father's bills. *A breath of fresh air*, his mother had written long ago, and certainly nothing since. Elspeth had written, *at the very least I used to get her old dresses* … And in Tom's letters, only a fleeting mention.

'Pa, something doesn't sound right. I've sent you money. You said it went to England, for Rupert.'

Tom looked as if he were thinking. 'Not all your money, now I recollect. Some to pay off loans here.'

'What loans?'

Tom lifted a shoulder. 'I borrowed from the lads. The neighbours.'

Dane stared at him. 'Are they paid back? You've kept careful books?'

His father shrugged again. 'No point now.'

'No point—? We will pay them back once I see the books.' Dane rubbed his face. Things were going from bad to worse. 'If I went to our solicitors in Melbourne with papers, and with financial backing, would the bank still foreclose?'

Tom closed his eyes and leaned on a tree trunk. He flicked the rolled smoke away from him and crushed it with his boot. 'I don't know, Dane. Can you get anything?'

'I can try. I can't get five hundred pounds, perhaps one-fifty.' He thought for a moment. 'You need to be relieved of the girl's care.'

His father looked up, blinked into the light then squeezed his eyes shut. 'It has already been—'

'She will have to go elsewhere. To work as a governess, perhaps, or some such thing.'

'Perhaps.'

'I will think on a solution.'

Tom's eyes remained closed for a moment longer. 'You do that.' He didn't look at Dane when he said, 'Until then, not a word to your mother.'

The sound of an approaching rider interrupted them. A young, reed-slender youth on a big roan crashed through the light scrub and burst onto the banks of the river close to the tree under which Tom slumped.

'Uncle Tom,' the rider shouted, and the huge horse wheeled about, narrowly missing Dane as he leapt out of the way.

'You bloody idiot,' he yelled.

The rider jumped from the saddle, rushed to the older man sitting under the tree and squatted beside him, laying a hand on Tom's shoulder. 'What happened, are you all right?'

It was a girl.

In two bounds, Dane was by her side. He gripped her wrist and she stood, resisting. 'You damned fool. You could have killed me.'

She faced him, her eyes flashing. 'Don't be a daft bugger. I wasn't *aiming* for you.'

His heart banged against his ribs, his breath caught as if his windpipe had closed. In those few moments, her face etched onto his memory. The shape of her chestnut brown eyes, and the proud set of her full mouth. Freckles spattered her nose. His gaze flickered lower, but the loose shirt hid the curves he expected to see.

He tipped the hat from her head and she scowled at him. A heavy plait fell to her shoulders. It was as thick as rope, black and glossy with blue highlights that shimmered and weaved through it.

'And keep your hands off me.' She snatched her arm from his grip. Suspicion narrowed her eyes and her nose crinkled. She bent to Tom at the base of the tree. 'Are you all right, Uncle Tom? What are you doing on the ground?'

He nodded. 'I'm all right,' he said and struggled to his feet, pushing himself up against the tree trunk. 'Dane, this is your step-cousin, Georgina Calthorpe. Georgina, this is my son, Dane James MacHenry.'

The girl was clearly not about to be conciliatory. Dane finally dipped his head at her.

She maintained her glare a second or two longer, then held out her hand.

He gripped it. 'You're dressed as a stable lad.'

'I am dressed for riding a horse,' she spat.

His grip was harder than it needed to be and he held it until he saw a faint gleam of contempt in her eyes. He let her remove her hand. She stared stonily at him then turned her back.

He watched her every move as she marched to a patient Douglas, who was nipping tufts of dead grass, and bent to take up his reins. She touched a hand to her throat, scratching at dust, then wiped her face with the tail of her shirt. She mounted and turned the horse.

Astride. Dane stared anew. He hadn't noticed because he'd assumed she was a youth.

Erect in the saddle, she walked the horse towards him. The riding quirt was in her hand and she slapped it gently on her leg, now almost under his nose.

He stepped back as she pushed the horse further towards him. The breath of air from the slap of the quirt fanned his cheek.

He grinned and grabbed her ankle.

Enraged, she flicked the quirt close to his face and whipped Douglas around so tightly he reared, too close to Dane. 'I'm going home, Uncle Tom,' she shouted. She wheeled again and fled, the horse as anxious to move as she, and then they were gone, leaving a trail of dust and leaves in their wake.

Dane wondered at her skill, for the quick sting of the riding quirt had barely touched his cheek.

—•—

Georgie galloped all the way home, threw herself off Douglas's back and, under protest from Joe, furiously rubbed the horse down, muttering all the while to herself.

The devil will come.

Georgie finished with the horse, marched back to the house, yelled for Ruth to help fill a bath and strode into her room. There she collapsed, shivering at what she had done.

She'd nearly struck him with the riding quirt. Her rage had been reflexive—he should not have grabbed her ankle; the steely grip of his fingers had dug deep.

She took a couple of breaths and ran out to help Ruth as she lumbered in with the bath then followed her out to lug buckets of warm water, one after the other, until the bath had just enough to sit in. Ruth took her leave.

Georgie stripped down and climbed in, grateful they still had water close by. She scrubbed her face and neck, soaped her underarms and between her legs, and then sank into the warmth of the water, allowing it to soothe her nerves. She wished she drank rum ... it seemed to help Uncle Tom sometimes.

She stood and stepped out of the water, dried herself off and shivered again. The shiver, she knew, was not from the cold. Still his face would not leave her memory, burned there as much by her anger as by his. She sat at the little armoire, wrapped in her house gown, and tried to finger comb her hair, her brush still not returned to her. Knots entangled what was usually a cooperative mass. She willed herself to undo every snarly little one, but she gave up in frustration.

Choosing her light blue dress, she slipped a chemise over her head and stepped into the dress without bothering with her corset. She pulled on an old pair of drawers and jiggled until she was comfortable. The unsettled feeling in the pit of her stomach and between her legs remained, but she resolved to be calm.

Her stillness was short-lived. Elspeth burst into her room, a nervous Ruth behind her.

Georgie spun around, prepared for bad news. 'What is it, Elspeth, what's the matter?'

'I saw you ride off sitting with your legs open on that horse,' Elspeth shouted, as though she'd been shot in the foot.

Georgie, relieved, rolled her eyes. 'Oh, that. Don't be bloody tiresome. So what?'

Elspeth gasped. 'I'm telling Ma.' She flung herself out of the room as quickly as she'd come in with Ruth in tow once again, throwing her hands in the air.

Georgie knew then that trouble could not be avoided. The last time Aunt Jem had seen her riding astride, she had ordered Georgie to her room for three days. And if Elspeth told her of Georgie's language, the confinement would surely be longer.

Then there was the altercation with Dane.

Her heart thudded again. She stamped her foot. 'Oh, bloody, bloody, bloody,' she said aloud, though not too loudly. She dared not say any of her favourite profanities just in case she could be heard.

Josephine, a servant from her stepfather's house in England, was to thank for the language education. Georgie spent more time sneaking around downstairs with Josephine and learning from the stablemen—their talk as well as their horsemanship—than she did upstairs.

She hurled a thin bar of soap at the wall and flopped on her bed.

By late afternoon and with no shrill demand from Aunt Jem to present and explain herself, Georgie emerged cautiously from her room, via the veranda door, to take a short, dignified walk to the big gardens at the back of the house. There, by the remnants of the orange orchard, was a large swinging garden bench. She took a seat. An involuntary bubble of laughter found its way to her lips as she replayed the scene with Dane and the riding quirt again.

And then there would be dinner. *Oh dear.* It hadn't occurred to her that she would have to face him at the dinner table. Well, she would have to cross that bridge when she came to it. She was determined to deny her action if he were so ungentlemanly as to bring it up, though she doubted he was a gentleman, the way he looked at her.

She sat there until nearly dusk, admitting to herself she was a little wary of returning to the house in case she accidentally met Dane without anyone else nearby. But she knew she'd have to go in soon.

Sliding off the swing, Georgie turned to face the house. The sight of a figure just ahead startled her and she cried aloud and stepped back.

'There you are.' Dane dipped from the waist only a little. 'I believe we're expecting you at dinner.'

'Oh.' He was so close. So close she could see the pores of his skin, the tufts of beard stubble where his razor had missed its mark. The hairs on her neck prickled, and a peculiar heat flushed her face. 'I ... I'll be along in a moment.' She stood her ground, hoping he wouldn't approach any closer.

'You'll be along right now.' He stood taller, then indicated she should walk back towards the house. 'We don't wait on you.' It was softly spoken, the words barely audible, but his eyes glinted as a frown furrowed his brow.

Heat bloomed in her chest. 'I did not mean—'

'You are here only because my parents are sympathetic to your plight. Do not make a mistake and continue to take it for granted.'

'Don't mistake me for a servant,' she bit back.

'You should be no more than that.'

She chilled at the unspoken threat. 'What utter nonsense.' Georgie marched three paces towards the house before he caught up with her.

'Let me escort you to your room, where you can freshen yourself.'

'I have no need—'

Dane took her elbow and strode with her to the veranda, steering her towards her room. He dropped his hold and shouldered the door open, letting it crash against the inside wall. He glanced at the room in the low glow of dusk. 'Hardly a palace for our resident princess.' He scrutinised her as she stood shaking. 'Is that fear or rage?'

'You're not balanced in the head,' she snapped. 'Why should it be fear? I'm not some timid ninny.'

He shrugged. 'Rage, then.' He stepped closer.

Her stomach dropped away but she willed herself to stare back at those blue and depthless eyes. *So fierce. So fierce ... but why?*

She dropped her gaze and focused on his chest, the black hair wispy and curling out from the opening of his shirt.

'There is much to discuss at dinner.' His breath was cool on her face. 'All thanks to your stepfather's indulgences.'

'What has happened—?' Her voice caught. Fear clutched her throat. She stared into intense blue eyes and tears welled up at the mention of her stepfather. He was so far away.

'Be at the table in ten minutes.' He stepped towards the door. 'And I haven't forgotten the incident this afternoon.'

Georgina didn't watch him go. She sagged against the wall, sucking in a breath the moment the door clicked shut behind him.

Three

My God. What an absolute little actress. She acts as if she doesn't have any idea what I'm talking about. A neat trick with the tears. A brat. But quite the loveliest brat I've ever seen.

He strode down the lengthy veranda to the dining room.

Dinner was a strained affair. Elspeth slurped her food, Jemimah's eyes were red, Tom gazed owlishly at his food and Georgina merely sat with her head high, totally ignoring her plate.

Exasperated, Dane leaned forward. 'What has gotten into everybody this evening? I come home and look how I'm greeted.'

His mother lay her hand on his arm. 'Your father and I have some worries, as you know, and Elspeth … '

Dane looked at his sister. She had her mother's colouring, pale creamy skin and sun-lightened wavy blonde hair, which she had styled to emulate Jemimah's. Elspeth was tall like her mother, but still had a certain childish pudge about her, which had the look of his father's side. She had yet to learn Jemimah's calm and grace.

Jemimah followed his gaze and looked at Elspeth, whose elbows rested on the table, a fork suspended halfway between her open mouth and her dinner plate. There was mess on the tablecloth where she'd spilled some of her meal. 'Oh my dear,' she said to her daughter. 'Try to be a bit more careful.'

Elspeth reddened and stood up. Her bottom lip quivered, a splash of gravy under it. 'I couldn't help it. I was—'

Dane pushed his plate away. He rested his hands on the table. 'Ma, they are my worries, too. We have some grave problems to sort out.'

Jemimah looked askance at her son. Then she stared at Tom, who wouldn't meet her eyes. She sucked in her cheeks. 'Elspeth, pick up your dinner. You will finish it in the kitchen.'

'What?' Elspeth stared at her mother.

Tom slapped an open palm loudly on the table. Everyone jumped. 'Do as you're told.'

Elspeth burst into tears and fled from of the room. Georgina glanced at Jemimah.

Tom edged forward. 'Dane, I don't think this is the time to—'

Jemimah spoke hastily to her niece. 'Georgina, you are excused from the table. You're to meet me in the parlour. Now.'

Georgina shot out of her chair. Jemimah followed her, telling her husband and son she would be back when the mood and manners at the dinner table improved.

'What a good dinner,' Tom remarked drily, and pushed his plate away. 'Dane, I have to ask you not to involve—'

'That girl knows she's involved in all of this.'

Tom shook his head. 'We will have to deal with that as a separate issue.' He chewed his lips, tried to steady his shaking hands, and looked towards the cupboard housing the rum. 'The first task is to send you to our solicitors. Take a paper stating your ownership of Jacaranda. At least that will give me some time to—'

'Is that all it would take?'

Tom shrugged. 'I don't know. But I have to do something.'

Dane shifted in his seat. 'I'm not sure how that would work. If I was to inherit this place, and if it is under insoluble debt, I don't know that I can stop the banks with a solicitor's paper.' He glanced at his father. 'I hope there are no bank notes over Jacaranda guaranteeing Rupert's debts.'

Tom frowned, hesitated. 'None.'

'Good. Ma mustn't send any more money to him. And Georgina must leave here.'

'That's what your mother is talking to her about, now. But I can't remove her, I've no money to send her away.'

Dane watched him for a moment. This was all out of balance. 'I can't fully grasp what has happened in these last four years—I'm surprised you didn't call for me earlier.' Tom only thinned his lips. 'But as for Georgina, I can to take her to Sydney after I return from Melbourne.'

Tom gave him a startled look.

'With a chaperone, of course, Pa.'

'To a brothel?'

'It's not a brothel now, I told you.'

Tom snorted. 'It might as well be. Even if I am a weak bugger where money and drink is involved, I will not see Jemimah's niece at some tavern, trotting along behind you.'

Dane raised his brows. *Where money and drink is involved* … 'If you are indeed a weak bugger, she might be better off.'

'Don't smart mouth me, boy.'

'I'll see she's well looked after. I could even find her work as a governess there. That can wait a week or so. The more pressing matter is my going to Melbourne. I can ride tonight if we draft something quickly.'

'Tonight? Yes, of course,' Tom conceded. 'The sooner the better. It'll be hard on you, lad.'

Dane nodded. 'Not anything compared to losing the place. Let's get to it. And Pa, we'll forgo the rum, I think.'

———

Georgie sat, clasping her shaking hands in her lap, and waited for Jemimah to speak.

Jemimah sat opposite, sighed and raised her eyes to the ceiling. 'My dear, this is a very hard conversation for me to have with you.'

Georgie's heart pounded and her ears hurt with it. 'Aunt Jem—'

'Oh, I know about the riding astride. Elspeth could not wait to inform me.' Jemimah looked down at her own hands. 'That's not what I need to talk about … although you know I don't approve of that, no matter that a new age is coming.'

Georgie dropped her chin and sighed inwardly. It was her aunt's favourite saying of late.

'Your Uncle Tom and I have had to make some hard decisions for ourselves. Considering as best we could the heavy burden of the homestead, the loss of income because of the drought and, of course, an economic depression certainly coming … '

Georgie sat motionless. *What is this?*

' … we are going to have to send you away for a period of time.' Jemimah looked across at her and frowned. 'We are yet to decide where, and to whom, but we find we can no longer support—'

'My Papa Rupert supports me,' Georgie cried, but then a chokehold gripped her throat and words would not come.

Jemimah shook her head. 'Not for a long time, Georgie. I don't know what has happened to him, he doesn't answer my letters. I don't believe you've had any from him in the last year or so either.'

Georgie stared wide-eyed at Jemimah. 'That cannot be so,' she forced out. 'How could he not—'

'Tom has had to send him funds so he could avoid debtor's prison … '

Georgie shook her head. 'No—I don't believe that!'

' … and we are now at the very last of our own reserves, pitiful though they were to begin with.'

Georgie's chin puckered. Speech had retreated. Her heartbeat pounded against her throat.

'We have to prevail upon Dane to support us, and Elspeth, until we can find her a position, of course, but for you, I'm afraid we cannot ask him—'

Breath blurted out of Georgie. 'Where am I to go?'

Now Jemimah shook her head. She blinked rapidly. 'It would only be for a short time, my dear, I'm sure. I could not ever—'

'Aunt Jem.' Georgie's eyes filled with unshed tears.

'I am so sorry. We will have to make arrangements soon. It breaks my heart, Georgie … '

Georgie leapt to her feet. 'Aunt Jem, I don't want to leave you. Not you, not the one person who took me in—no, no. I am not ready. I am not ready!'

'Please do not be so agitated. Sit down a moment more.' Jemimah waited until Georgie sat again. 'You remember some time back when you and I travelled to Bendigo?'

Georgie frowned at the twist in the conversation. 'Yes. Some years ago now … not long after I arrived. Mr O'Rourke, I think was his name, had just visited.'

Jemimah closed her eyes a moment. 'Yes. Mr O'Rourke.' She studied her hands. 'I had not thought you'd remember that.'

Georgie recalled a great deal, especially the shouting between Tom and Jemimah after the man had left. The next thing she knew, she and Jemimah were on a coach south to Bendigo. A nineteen-year-old Georgie had noted restrained relations between her aunt and uncle. Perhaps Jemimah had needed some sort of respite. Of the man O'Rourke, Georgina's only glimpse of him was memorable. Tall and dark haired, with a serious face and a low, melodious voice. She heard nothing of any conversation.

Jemimah had taken Georgie to her mother's home there, the one she'd left with Papa Rupert as a very young child after her mother had died. 'You remember, when we got to Bendigo, we had the occasion to see a woman in the street, talking to anyone who would listen? Louisa someone, a poor bedraggled-looking person. You listened avidly. So did I.'

Georgie nodded, frowning at the memory. 'She spoke of the plight of women fallen on hard times. But she seemed not an ideal—'

'I want you to remember what she stood for.'

When the newspapers reported on the suffrage movement and the representatives for women in the country, Vida Goldstein and her friend, Annette Bear, Georgie read everything three times over. Even this wretch in Bendigo had her story in the papers. She had been very fierce. Very dirty, and she looked starved, but very fierce.

Georgie nodded again. 'But to what purpose? Her road will never be mine.' She clasped her other hand over her aunt's. 'I am not prepared to live like the woman in Bendigo. She had no family, no work. She was belittled by the police for her beliefs. She was totally independent ... and destitute. That is not a path I will take.' She released her aunt's hands and wiped her palms down her dress. Then horrified, she looked up and tears fell unchecked. 'You are not telling me—'

'No, no, my dear.' Jemimah lifted her shoulders and a sigh escaped her. 'I meant I want you to choose your path wisely as you go on. Your fate is decided by the men in your life no matter what you think—or wish—of this new age coming.' She thumbed away Georgie's tears then put her hands to her hair, smoothing and tucking loose tendrils before clasping Georgie's hands again. 'Choose survival above all else, Georgina, by almost any means. You are so strong and proud, and tenacious ... But choose survival. It will come disguised.' Jemimah pressed her lips together and shook her head. 'Then you can fight for your rights. It is a better way than having your independence.'

Georgie pressed her aunt's hands again, but Jemimah's face was inscrutable. 'I think I understand. I think I do.' She sat erect. 'Am I really to be sent away?' A chill seeped under her skin, shrank her belly.

'We will secure a good position, I'm sure, perhaps even some further education for you.' Jemimah stood up, her eyes bright. 'Who knows, we might even find a family close by who could still support a governess, or a lady's maid ... '

Georgie blinked.

Jemimah spread her hands. 'If only your father had written an explanation.'

Numb, Georgie nodded. *If only.*

———

Georgie fled to her room, pulled off her shoes and threw herself on the bed. Both Dane and Jemimah had now said the family could no longer support her. How was she to make her own way when she wasn't ready yet? Hadn't Dane also said it was thanks to her stepfather's *indulgences*? What on earth could that mean?

She slipped off the bed and groped for the box of Rupert's letters, hidden under the tiny chest of drawers that held her underthings. She found it and lit the two lamps by her bed. She rummaged for his last letter and, re-reading it, found no clue to Dane's inferences, though the letter was dated in August nearly fourteen months before. Rupert spoke of the latest hunt he'd attended, Georgie's cousins' recent marriages and a few new babies, and said he hoped she enjoyed the gifts he'd sent her, which she often wondered about but had never received. He signed it as he always did after wishing her well, as her 'Papa Rupert'.

She conceded her life was hardly as happy as she wanted. She had asked Rupert in an earlier letter to call her back to England, but she hadn't received an answer. He hadn't even mentioned it. So she had resigned herself to the life at Jacaranda, until Conor Foley's promise of a better future eventuated. The thought of the surely impending marriage to him kept her spirits up.

Conor.

Heavy footsteps shook the veranda. She stuffed all the letters back into their box and slid it under the drawers. She held her breath as the footsteps stopped. She dared not look towards the window of her room for fear Dane might just be peering in.

Moments passed. She stayed immobile, breath suspended.

But this would not do! She was *not* afraid.

She clambered to her feet. Her thudding heartbeat shook her hands but she reached the door and pulled it open. And there Dane stood, about to knock. She looked up, astounded, affronted.

He towered over her in the doorway, his blue eyes clear in the low light, his voice calm. 'I'm sorry to intrude—'

'I doubt that.'

His eyes closed, and his chest expanded with a large, silent inhale, then his eyes opened. 'But I believe my mother has informed you of the family's decision. I must tell you it is made with regret, but is unavoidable.'

'I fail to see your regret.' She backed up a few steps to better glare at him.

His dipped his head. 'The decision has been made, nonetheless. There might yet be another solution but for now, there are more pressing matters. I cannot do everything—'

'More *pressing* matters?' Her mouth fell open.

Dane held up both hands. 'You have a roof over your head here at least until I return from urgent business in Melbourne. I hope that will be next week.'

'And then?' Georgie huffed.

He stared at her, his gaze seeming to rove over her face. He clasped his hands behind his back. 'There is discussion that you and a chaperone will accompany me to Sydney to find suitable—'

'I don't want to go anywhere with you. I'd rather be sent back to my father's home before—'

'There isn't one, as far as I'm aware.'

'There is. My father's home in England.'

He shook his head. 'There isn't. He doesn't have one now, it seems.'

'Of course he has a home, Calthorpe Manor in Somerset.' Scorn fired her blood, and her breath came in bursts as she glared at him. 'Just because he hasn't written for a while, nor sent my funds, doesn't mean to say he's deserted—'

'I would say he *has* deserted you. And left this family struggling to survive.' He pursed his lips before he spoke again. 'I can only do so much with what I earn and I will have to support my parents and my sister until the situation eases, if at all. I do regret not being able to offer you the same—'

'Oh, of course! I am sorry I seem to have been such a burden to your family.' She heard the shrillness in her voice and took two deep breaths. 'But I know Rupert sent an allowance for me. I know it! And we all lived high on it here, as I remember. But lately we have seen little but your father's drinking and—'

Dane's hands came to his sides, clenching and unclenching. 'It is a man's business to do what he wishes. I venture *my* father's drinking might be the direct result of *your* father's failure in his responsibilities.'

'How so? Tom takes to the bottle rather than work his way out of the woes of his own making?' Georgie scowled at him and stood taller. 'That is the weakest bloody excuse so far.'

He took a sudden step forward and she scuttled back. 'How so, indeed,' he growled. 'A weak bloody excuse, is it, miss? You sound very much the adventuress.'

Georgie's mouth flew open. She knew enough common talk to know he didn't mean she'd been on a voyage of discovery. In a blind rage, she crashed her open hand against his face.

He staggered under the blow.

She reeled back, aware the pain in her hand must be nothing compared to the pain in his face, and stepped around him and ran out the door, absolute terror pumping in her veins.

Four

Georgie didn't know how far she'd run.

Her heartbeat thudded in her ears, and her right hand was ablaze ... had she broken bones in it?

I hit him. Oh dear God ... I struck him hard on the face. The earth should swallow me up and never spit me forth again.

Barefoot, she pounded over the powdery red dirt of the house paddock, not knowing if he'd followed her, not knowing if he could catch her—

God knows, he could murder me—

The low rumble of his voice echoed in her head. *You sound very much the adventuress.* He thought her a wild woman, or worse, a woman of the night.

The stable loomed in the dark. She steered clear of it. Beyond, she could just make out the paddock fence and ran towards it, clambering up, gulping great draughts of air. A nail on the top rail caught her stupid dress. The fabric rent as she tugged viciously and finally tumbled over, landing on her feet. She kept running, cursing Dane MacHenry as she went, the dust kicking up behind her and stinging the backs of her legs. She tripped and fell, landing arse first on the baked earth, cooler now in the moonlit night. Her body jarred so hard her teeth hurt.

Georgie struggled up again, cursing, and perspiration snaked from her neck down her back.

I should have gone to the stable, I should take MacNamara …

She fell back to her knees, exhausted. *Take MacNamara.* That was the solution. She had her measly few coins saved from Uncle Tom's gambling, her boys' riding outfit … And she would find her love, Conor Foley. She should go back and take MacNamara. She imagined she could even hear MacNamara's thudding hooves carrying her away.

Wobbling to her feet, she dusted herself off and gulped air into sore lungs. Her throat stung with each breath. It was a wonderful idea. Why hadn't she thought of it earlier?

MacNamara's thudding hooves kept coming.

Horse and rider bore down on her as if she were prey under a monstrous eagle's claws. She shrieked, rooted to the spot.

The rider snatched her from the ground and another huge tear appeared in her dress. He wrenched her across the bare back of MacNamara, grabbed her backside by the pants she wore underneath her poor dress, flicked the reins and galloped off.

Dane MacHenry.

She squawked and raged. Her grip on MacNamara's mane was fierce for fear she'd slide right out from Dane's grasp and be bounced on the ground to die under the horse's hooves.

Each mistimed jolt of her body sickened her roiling guts further and her head split with a pounding ache. She clung to the horse, not knowing how much longer she would last.

Then Dane reeled the horse to a halt, slid off and dragged her with him.

Georgie heard MacNamara stomp and huff and dance on the spot as Dane hauled her up the veranda steps by her forearm. Even as she yelled her protests, Dane pushed her inside her room. He swung her around, gripped her other arm as well and shook her. He glared, blue eyes flashing under black brows, his jaw clenching as she tried to tug herself free.

He tossed her from his grip, his breath ragged and unsteady, and she stumbled back, landing on the floor.

'And stay there.' He stabbed a finger at her, swiped a lock of hair from his forehead then leaned over her, a red, angry bruise clearly visible under his left eye.

She stared at it wide-eyed. *I did that … I did that.* Her hand hurt like the devil all over again, and so did her backside. Her stomach churned. She turned her face, expecting an attack, retribution …

He straightened up, arms by his side, fingers curling. He advanced a step.

She scrambled further back and fell hard against the wall. Shaking, she closed the larger of the tears in her dress. She discovered a piece was missing, vaguely attributing it to the fence she'd clambered over. The fabric was dirty, smudged with horse shit and grass stains … What must she look like?

'This is one of my few dresses and you've *ruined* it,' she shouted at him.

Dane MacHenry stood, blinking at her then staring her down, his chest rising and falling, eyes rimmed with red in the dim light. 'Never, *ever*, raise your hand to me again.' He turned and stalked out of the room.

His every movement, his every footfall on the veranda, every squeak of his boots, echoed in her head. Her heart beat so loudly she was sure he would hear it.

When she dared to look up, relief came in too much of a rush. She gulped air again, then crawled to her bed and hauled herself onto it, clutching the pillow, shaking.

It took a few moments, but once she was calm, she sat up and sniffed loudly, swiping a hand over her nose. 'Bugger,' she muttered.

I will get MacNamara, and take myself away. I don't need anyone to send me. Not again. I will find Conor, and I will write to Papa Rupert.

She struck a match and held it to the candle in her room then drew the curtains closed. She plucked the boys' clothes once again from their hiding place under her mattress, shrugged out of the ruined dress and, with clumsy hands, climbed into the breeches and shirt.

Georgie was calm and not calm at the same time. Her plan was flimsy, but her heart determined. She would take control of her future. She wouldn't have any future if she remained at Jacaranda—or worse, if she were dragged to wherever and back with Mr bloody Dane MacHenry.

She tried to plait her hair but could not do it any more than she could fly to the moon. It just would not go. Stuffing it all under the hat, she had to suffice with stabbing pins into it. Using a shawl tied with a knot as a carry bag, she packed some underthings and the remaining blue dress then pressed her face to the window in the least obvious place to peer into the night.

Her hand was on the door latch before she remembered the coins she had scrounged. She squatted on the floor and clawed at the loose board. There in the dirt under her room was a small cache, wrapped in a man's handkerchief. She slipped it carefully into the carry bag and pulled the bag onto her shoulder.

Back to the window, then the door. It sounded enormously loud as she opened it and she held her breath, praying no one had heard. Her heart leapt into her throat as she took a step onto the veranda with her booted foot. The other foot followed, and then she bolted for the stable.

Mid-stride, she remembered her stomach. She made a stealthy, fraught-with-nerves visit to the kitchen pantry, and groped around for bread—stale, but edible. She grabbed some apples, a chunk of Aunt Jem's fruit cake and some cold beef. It would have to do. She stuffed whatever she could into the tied-up shawl, wiped her hands on her breeches and headed back to the stables.

Beloved MacNamara whinnied as she approached. He was warm and dry, and had a blanket over him. He nuzzled her hand and she whispered to him that he must be quiet, else they would be discovered. She let the bag slide from her arm, threw her hat on it and groped for MacNamara's saddle.

She almost tripped over it, not expecting it to be on the ground. Dane must have left it there, for Joe certainly would not. *Poor form, Bloody MacHenry.*

As her eyes adjusted to the night, she reached for the bridle and halter, fumbling as she fitted them to the horse. MacNamara snorted at her rough efforts and she struggled to keep from screaming with frustration. The saddle seemed heavier than she remembered, but she hauled it over his great back, securing the girth. All the time she spoke in whispers, hoping to soothe him. It was clear he knew something was afoot.

She fixed the little bag of clothing and her hat to the saddle. Crooning softly to MacNamara, gently rubbing his nose, Georgie walked him as quietly as she could out of the stable. This was no time for a stallion's shenanigans, as Joe would say.

Douglas shuffled in his stall, but that was the only sound she heard.

Georgie and MacNamara padded past the house and the dilapidated shrubbery and onto the treacherous home track. For every step she took, she expected a tap on her shoulder. Her heart hammered, and sweat popped out on her brow. They plodded carefully around the potholes, dodging what they could. Every sound of the night—a chorus of cicadas, the snap of a twig, leaves rustling in a thin breeze—sent a shudder of terror to her stomach. A wallaby bounced in front of them and nearly brought her undone; her yelp had MacNamara dancing and snorting. She shushed him as best she could and pressed on.

The night was clear, and the stars of the Milky Way bright and twinkling. She only glanced up from time to time, wary of where she stepped. The crisp September night air had Georgie wishing she'd grabbed one of the coats from the stable and perhaps the canvas sleeping mat that hung on the wall.

Too late, she thought. *Can't go back. Won't go back—I'll just keep riding until I find Conor.*

She was nearing the driveway gates, so she stopped MacNamara and hauled herself into the saddle, feeling very comfortable on his back. He wanted to run then, but even if he thought he could see in the dark, she much preferred to see where she was going; she held him back.

Georgie rounded the parched old eucalypt that marked the boundary gate. Here she knew she was well out of ear's reach of the homestead. She turned MacNamara east along the track that would join the main road.

It was familiar ground and her mind wandered.

She was anxious about her Papa Rupert, and the things Dane MacHenry had said about him, things about indulgences and burdens. It was as though Dane was talking of somebody else. She would not believe it. She should have brought Rupert's letters, to re-read them, to study them for any clues she might have missed.

Shaking her head, she determined not to worry about that now; it would sort itself out as time went on. She need never see the

MacHenrys again, and would be spared the fate Dane MacHenry intended for her.

'So there, take *that*, you uncouth lout,' she said aloud. MacNamara lifted his head at her voice. In that moment, Georgie felt as fearless as she had ever been. She was about to make her own life, though when she thought of Jemimah, a stab in her chest kept her honest.

Bloody Dane MacHenry.

How unlike Dane and Elspeth were, so different in looks and personality—surely an unfortunate mistake of Mother Nature? Elspeth was just plain, and very much like her father in looks, with her mother's colouring. And Dane, well, he was strikingly—

She closed down the thought. Not ladylike at all.

But I could be.

Aunt Jem had instilled ladylike behaviour befitting young unmarried women in both Georgie and Elspeth, and as long as they both behaved politely in company, day-to-day misdemeanours were overlooked.

Aunt Jem. She was nothing like her two sisters in England, who'd shunned Georgie when Rupert had first taken her to England after her mother had died. Jem, to whom Georgie had been sent, was more like her brother Rupert. He was so particular about niceties and etiquette and protocol and manners.

She pushed MacNamara on, checking the sky again, dismayed to see clouds threatening to block the moonlight. She tapped the horse lightly and he responded with a canter. She forgot the cold, though the breeze she and the horse made whipped at her cheeks. The road ahead was her salvation—the road to a better life.

At the turn-off, the end of the track to Jacaranda, she'd gone about four miles. Hardly far enough away to get lost. She turned onto the road as it angled back towards the river. Her stomach fluttered. *I've done it. I've run away. I am independent!*

Independent.

But she didn't want to be destitute. That thought sobered her.

For now, she was safe until dawn. Joe would discover MacNamara missing and raise the alarm. No one would think to look in on her until well after breakfast; she was not in the habit of eating early. So she would be long gone and there wouldn't be anyone to imagine which way she was headed. They'd never catch up with her.

Georgie patted MacNamara's neck. Her stomach was still aflutter, more so at the thought of Dane MacHenry and her striking his face than anything else.

I wish I could remember what he looked like when I hit him. She wanted to laugh aloud. So she did.

She looked up into the moonlit sky, watching the clouds waft over it, and thought of Conor Foley. She would find her red-haired man and he would take her away from all her troubles and woes and she would live happily ever after.

Of course he would marry her. Of course he would.

Could she be a married woman and independent? Miss Goldstein had forsworn marriage to that very end, believing she could not fulfil her life's work if she were married. But to be married to Conor Foley was just what Georgie wanted. She would be his wife, a grand, benevolent lady who would grace his society with her wit and her verve. She would be an intelligent conversationalist, a compassionate woman willing and able to help those who had not her privilege. She would have horses and manage the stables, and be quite the accomplished woman.

And when she wasn't riding and managing, and being otherwise grandly accomplished, the river would call and she'd be sailing with Conor on her majestic Murray, in the peace and quiet, the ambient rhythm of its ancient life soothing her.

She would learn about his business and work with him to build it ever grander and more robust. His sister, Kate, would help her adjust to her new married life—

She hauled her thoughts to a stop. She'd barely given any mind to the marriage bed.

Well. It sounded a very tedious duty to be performed—she doubted if Conor indulged—and she thought only of the fine gowns, the stables and the horses he would buy her. Life would be good again. Georgina Calthorpe Foley and her new husband would visit Papa Rupert, and afterwards she would hold a great ball. Then she would go and work with the poor people, teaching the women—

The thud of galloping hooves startled her. She slowed Mac-Namara. She could see nothing behind her, it must be from up ahead. MacNamara surged forward and she let him have his head until they could see the other travellers.

Georgie pulled off the road, deep into the bush, hugging MacNamara's neck to avoid being knocked from the saddle by a low branch. She dismounted, quieting the snorting horse, who stamped and pawed at the ground, still wound up by the ride. She shushed him more firmly and led him back closer to the road, to a place where she could see clearly.

Two riders were coming from the opposite direction and would surely have intercepted her and demanded to know her business. She held MacNamara's head tightly, and listened, horrified, as the riders pulled up not far from her hideout. MacNamara shied, and she whispered to him softly, without urgency.

'I don't see no rider 'ere,' one man said, peering about in the dark, his face lit by the moon. Georgie could see he wore a mask over it.

The other was insistent. 'I saw a rider.'

'He ain't around now. But it looks as good a place as any to camp for the night. Must be nigh on midnight.'

'I don't like it. I saw someone riding around here, and I don't like it. I say we keep going.'

Georgie thought that was a very good idea.

'And I say you're getting pushy. How could you tell where it was—bloody dark as soot around here before the clouds moved. I'm camping here the night.'

'I ain't.'

Good for you, Georgie thought. MacNamara was beginning to fidget again. Any small noise in the dead of night would give her away. She stood stock still, one hand firmly on the horse's head, the other over her heart to still the thudding in her chest.

'Aw, for Gawd's sakes.'

MacNamara threw his head in the air, and Georgie held her breath, giving him a good yank with bridle. He baulked and she began to pray.

'Whassat?'

'Orright, orright, no need to try and spook me—let's just go and—'

The sound of more hooves reached her ears. She waited, almost too afraid to breathe, her hand holding the reins tightly. She squeezed on them, willing MacNamara to remain silent.

'Quick—in the bushes.' They scarpered off the road to the other side.

Thankful, Georgie heard them crashing through the scrub to a point further along the way. She released her stranglehold on the reins and shook her hands to force the blood back into her stiff fingers.

If I had a brain, I would mount and ride away as fast as I could.

'Bail up, mate!' the men yelled in unison at the other person on the road, walking their horses back into view, blocking the approaching rider's access.

MacNamara lost his calm, and wheeled about in the bush. Georgie shushed him again and swung up into the saddle, keeping low to his neck, holding his mane.

'Out of my way, scum,' the new rider growled as his mount danced in a circle, eager to depart.

Georgie's arm jerked as MacNamara's head swung up. She shushed him, low to his ear, sure he'd hear her heart hammering.

'I said to bail up, mate. Stop moving and get off yer 'orse.'

'Out of my way, you fools, I've no time to dally tonight.'

That voice!

'Dally, is it, ya poncey bugger.'

MacNamara strained against her grip. She held him tighter than before, but the men were hedging back her way, their trio of horses dancing and pawing the ground. She wished the wind would spring up and hide the noise her horse was intent on making.

A gun went off with a startling roar.

MacNamara shrieked, reared, then bolted out of the scrub and onto the road right at the men. Georgie flattened herself against his neck, clinging with hands and elbows and knees.

The first two riders wheeled about, and one lost control of his horse. It reared, screaming in terror, and threw its rider, before bucking, pig-rooting and squealing off into the bush. The man landed with a thump and a bounce and lay in a heap.

The other man threw himself upon the newcomer, knocking him off his horse.

MacNamara was now face to face with Douglas. And when Georgie squinted into the melee at the men grappling on the ground, she recognised Dane MacHenry, fighting for his life.

Georgie lurched over MacNamara's neck and grabbed Douglas's reins, kicking MacNamara hard. They leapt around the men, and tore along the road. Though her arm felt like it was tugged out of its socket, she dared not let go of Douglas. They galloped and galloped and galloped, until spent. They slowed and she finally felt able to pull to a complete stop.

Mortified, knowing she was in deep trouble, she dismounted. Her legs wobbled and she sank to the ground at the horses' feet. MacNamara bent his head low and blurted and huffed his breath over her. Both he and Douglas were lathered with sweat, quivering from the run, and she wished she had a rag to wipe them down.

Breathing hard, Georgie framed her head with her hands. *Oh bugger, bugger, bugger.* She covered her mouth with a shaking hand, thinking fast. It was Dane MacHenry back there, perhaps after her. And now probably lying dead on the road. And there were two others out there, too. They could return at any time. She tilted her head, held her breath and listened carefully.

Nothing.

The night air was still. All she could hear was the horses' breathing. She let go of her own breath and slapped her forehead, rocking a little back and forth.

I should do the right thing.

What is the right thing?

I should go back and find Dane MacHenry. But I would walk straight into more trouble, either by finding him and taking the consequences, or by finding the thieves. Which would be worse?

Think, girl. Think. He could be lying there dead—in which case my going back there wouldn't make any difference.

Yes, but he might only be hurt.

But I could fall into the hands of the thieves. Worse—I could be attacked by either party.

Georgie stood up and paced. Nerves drove her legs with such energy the wobbles had disappeared. She rubbed her face, pushing the sticky, sweaty tendrils of her hair aside, wiping her hands on the legs of her pants to dry them. She clasped and unclasped her hands.

What was that?

She stopped, her heartbeat thumping in her throat. She checked the horses. They were undisturbed. She took a couple of deep breaths. *Take control of yourself, fool, you must think properly.* She tied Douglas's reins to the branch of a fallen log, tied MacNamara's around the low limb of a tree. In the moonlight she noticed Douglas had a pack on his back. She stared at it, then listened again for riders.

Nothing.

Douglas stood still as she untied the bundle from behind his saddle. A bed roll, a small bag of personal belongings, and a purse of gold coins, heavy and jingling in her hands.

Had her luck turned? She rummaged some more through the small bag, found some papers, which, in a generous snatch of light, she could see were addressed to a firm of solicitors in Melbourne. There was also a leather wallet. She opened the wallet and held it up to catch more light, but it was impossible to make out its contents.

Georgie replaced everything where she'd found it—everything except the bag of coins. There must have been ten old sovereigns in it, certainly a fortune. She would take one and secrete it with the rest of her cache in her bag on MacNamara. If he ever found her, he would not miss just one, she was sure … She shifted a little with that thought. *I'll only take one … perhaps two …*

She threw herself onto MacNamara and, with a hefty crack on Douglas's hide, sent him back the way they'd just come. Hopefully he would find his way to the homestead or, with any luck, to Dane MacHenry. She couldn't think about that, or him. But at least the riderless horse would be a sure sign someone was in need of help.

She turned MacNamara around and brought him to a canter. She wouldn't go much further tonight, her horse was tired and she was exhausted. She still had a long way to go, but Conor would be at Echuca, and that's where she intended to be.

She moved along, telling herself they would stop here, then there, then just a bit further on until finally, weary and bedraggled, she pulled MacNamara off to the side of the road, dismounted and unsaddled him. She tethered him to a shrub and curled up to sleep, his blanket over her and her head on the saddle.

Five

Dane MacHenry struggled onto his haunches.

'Sweet Christ.' Balancing with one hand on the ground, he fingered a lump the size of a duck's egg on his head, before sliding to his arse.

He craned his head to check the night sky. The moon was bright now, with no cloud drifting over it, no sign of rain. The Milky Way lit a path across the dark cloak of night, but its ethereal stillness meant nothing to him. There was no way to tell how much time had passed.

He'd been riding—firstly, to get to Melbourne as early as he could to speak with the family's solicitors. And secondly, because Elspeth had alerted the family that the troublesome Georgina was nowhere to be seen. A floorboard in her room had been removed and her bed was in disarray.

He'd sprinted to the stables, and a quick glance in MacNamara's empty stall was all the confirmation he'd needed. She'd flown the coop.

He'd cursed and ranted as he saddled Douglas, grabbed his packed kit bags and strapped them on. He took off at a gallop, determined to track her down. When he caught her he'd carry on to Melbourne, as planned. She might be a handful to cope with during the business dealings, but he'd manage.

Then two thieving bastards jumped him. They were nowhere to be seen now, and neither was his horse. What had happened? Another rider had approached ...

It had been MacNamara he saw in the dim light, the horse panicked by his gunshot. It was her.

'I'll be damned.' He stood up, tested his steadiness, dusted himself off. No other lumps, he decided, as his thumping head settled. His sight was clear, no dizziness. Good. He looked skywards again to get his bearings, turned around and headed in the direction he had originally taken.

I'll make for the river and flag down a vessel. Georgina will surely head for Swan Hill, I'd lay gold on it. I'll find her and when I do ...

He trudged on into the dawn, and sat wearily on the river bank in a little clearing. Any vessel going either way would be seen from his vantage point, and even if he fell asleep, he'd hear something coming.

Some hours later, with the sun already high and the air warm, he woke. His mouth tasted sour. Dirt had coated his skin and sweat had dried under his arms, he could smell it. His stomach growled, but there was nothing he could do about it for the moment. He'd gone without food before today, and a couple of hours more wouldn't hurt him. A boat would be able to supply him with some jerky or biscuits. He knew he wouldn't have to wait long, for the river was busy with trade boats.

He stripped and washed in the river, dunking his shirt. He dried off under the morning sun then pulled on the damp shirt and dirty breeches and settled back on the bank.

He watched the water of the mighty river. A fish flopped somewhere in the middle of the wide expanse, and a kookaburra called in the distance. Peaceful.

How life had changed, how the wheels of fortune turned.

I should have returned more often.

Ten years earlier he'd left Jacaranda to find his way in the world. In his first few years he'd earned money on the boats, and sent much of it home when he could. Then he followed more work to Melbourne. There, he literally fell over Reuben Cawley one murky night near a tavern. Reuben had run foul of a group of thugs and Dane had come to his rescue, taking the badly beaten Reuben to his family's home. Dane subsequently found himself with very rich benefactors because of his good deed. And under the guiding hand of Reuben's father, John, and his mother, Angeline, Dane's business acumen grew.

But he was misplaced, he told Reuben. Nonsense, Reuben had bellowed good-naturedly before going out and buying another hotel in Sydney. A brothel, in fact, still operating as such until Dane won it over a game of cards and set himself the task of cleaning it up. He renamed it the Captain's Cabin. And a brothel it was no more.

Dane lived at the Cabin, and his visits to Jacaranda had been delayed, year by year, as the business required extra care. But the recent letter from his father had forced him to return.

And here I am, sitting on the bank of a river, sleeping in the dirt and chasing a piece of baggage on my way to a solicitor's office, hoping to fore-stall a foreclosure. Perhaps this could be another turn in the eventful path to my fortune.

He chuckled. *Perhaps fortune's not likely.*

He waited only another hour before a paddleboat came into view, steaming around the bend upriver.

He clambered aboard, grateful to the crewman who rowed ashore to fetch him. It was Mr King, captain of the fine boat *Gem*, who was gracious enough to take him on board. Captain King knew of the MacHenrys of Jacaranda, and a promissory note as payment for passage was accepted. Dane asked to disembark at Swan Hill, where he would buy passage of some form or other, somehow, to Echuca. From there he would head for Melbourne, with or without his stolen belongings, and with or without the girl, Georgina.

———

She awoke with a start—someone's hairy nose was on her face, blurting hot air and snot.

Bleary-eyed, Georgie focused on MacNamara standing over her, his loosened reins dangling in the dirt. But it was the sight of Douglas that shocked her, his head down, breath creating little puffs of steam in the air.

She groaned. 'Douglas, what are you doing back here?' She reached up to touch his face. 'You naughty horse.' He nodded his big head at her, as if very pleased with himself. She stood and brushed herself down.

What a terribly untidy individual. Her breeches had holes in the knees and grass stains and shit on them. Her usually neatly tied hair was a tangled mess, half out of its ribbon and hanging loosely about her shoulders. She shrugged. She was in no position to run away with her best hairbrush and luggage, meagre as it was, nor could she afford the luxury of time to undertake the necessary ablutions.

Dismayed the other horse had seen fit to follow her and not return to Dane MacHenry, she stood looking at Douglas as he fed on a clump of grass closer to the road. She would just have to take the two horses to Swan Hill and think of something to do with Douglas there. Surely someone would take him back to Jacaranda?

Her stomach growled. She bent and hunted in her little bag for breakfast and chewed on some still tender beef and the thick slices of crisply stale bread. The apples she fed to the horses, and the cake she would keep for later. The meal would still her hunger pangs for a short time, but she would need to find water to slake her thirst.

Overhead, the brilliant sun reminded her that more tardiness would be a mistake. She saddled MacNamara, tied Douglas's reins to the saddle and mounted wearily, not looking forward to another day's ride.

She wasn't far out of Swan Hill. It normally only took Uncle Tom five or so hours to ride there from the homestead, so by her calculations she was almost there. She would be very glad to arrive and, with her new found wealth, she would outfit herself properly. She dimly recalled that perhaps it was against the law for a woman to dress in a man's clothes, however convenient they were. Then she would purchase a coach seat to Echuca.

She remembered the packages in Douglas's saddle. Reaching into the saddlebags, she retrieved the bundle of papers she'd peered at the night before. She untied the soft leather-bound compendium embossed with 'D MacH', and lifted the parcel into the light. It was addressed to a firm of solicitors in Melbourne. She turned it over—

Georgie stopped then. There was some chance Dane would come back into possession of these papers and it would not be proper for her to have deliberately broken into his private business.

The saddlebags also held a small pouch with medicinal ointments and oils in it, a needle and some thread, a tin of pills she didn't recognise, some matches and a bandage. She stuffed it all back.

The small gentleman's wallet, made of the same fine material as the compendium, was beautiful. She let her fingers glide over the leather, cool to her touch. She lifted it to her face and breathed deeply.

Inside, among some pennies, which she added to her stash, and notes referring to a 'Captain's Cabin', she found the most exquisite photograph of a beautiful woman, a small *cartes* wrapped in a protective card, tucked deep into an almost invisible sleeve. It looked worn, but its subject's loveliness did not. For some reason, Georgie's heart skipped a beat.

She stared at the picture for a long time and turned it over. On seeing the handwritten message on the back, her face burned.

To my darling Dane on his birthday, My love forever, Rebecca.

Georgie pushed the picture back into the wallet. Did that horrible creature have a wife?

Remembering what Josephine had told her about the act between husband and wife, she shuddered. She wondered if Dane and this Rebecca had engaged in such a base act. A strange little thrill stabbed her deep within. Hardly attractive behaviour, she decided, though her face grew hot.

I would be well rid of all of this.

Georgie thought of her own intention to marry Conor Foley. Josephine had said this husband-and-wife act was the only thing you could do to get babies. She had scoffed. 'I don't want babies,' she declared.

She remembered Josephine said men hankered after this thing from women, married or not, because it was immensely enjoyable to them. Georgie couldn't imagine Conor 'hankering' after such a sordid act. He had never suggested it to her in any fashion.

It would not be something we would do, she decided.

She kicked MacNamara into a light canter and headed back to the main road. When she finally caught a glimpse of the river through the trees, she turned MacNamara for the water, but he needed no prompting. He'd have been able to smell it for miles.

She dismounted at a cleared spot at the water's edge. She squatted and scooped handfuls of the cool, clean water to her mouth. So intent was she on quenching her thirst and trying to clean her face and neck of grime, she barely registered the chug-chug of a paddle-steamer coming around the bend in the river.

The loud horn sounded so close her heart leapt in her throat. She would have fallen right in if she hadn't still had hold of the horses.

It was a beautiful boat. Georgie waved at the man in the steering cabin, and he waved back. A couple of men had appeared on the deck, one darting back out of view, the other standing to stare at her. He shouted something to her from the deck and she shrugged and spread her arms, indicating she couldn't hear him. The engines dropped away slightly, and the helmsman steered a little towards the bank.

The man on board shouted again, 'Where are you headed?'

She shouted back, 'To Swan Hill—how far is it?'

There was some discussion with another person Georgie couldn't see and then the voice floated over to her: 'About two hours. We'll beat you there.'

Georgie gave him a wave. She could see his and two other faces staring at her from the cabin, but she was sure it was no more than natural curiosity. She wouldn't be far behind the paddle-steamer into Swan Hill, but she wasn't going to push MacNamara to prove a point. As long she could eat and drink something, and freshen him up, she could take her time. Douglas was still reasonably fresh.

The paddle-steamer swung gently back to the middle of the river. She watched as it glided away. She recognised it, read its name on the stern to confirm it was one of the loveliest boats on the river, the *Gem*, its captain and crew very experienced. Just before she mounted, she took another look at the boat and saw a crewman staring at her from within the shadows of the steering cabin. He lingered for a moment, then ducked out of sight. She dismissed him from her thoughts.

Georgie pulled MacNamara and Douglas from the banks of the river, glad she would be safe in Swan Hill in a few short hours.

Six

Dane waited patiently for her to appear in town. A good vantage point meant he could see clearly down the street in the direction she would come. There'd be enough time to duck out of sight.

He would soon have his horses, his money and his belongings. And her. He would certainly make her regret running away from the homestead. For a start, she would write an apology to his parents for all their inconvenience.

A thought struck him—if he was going to Melbourne with Georgina, then perhaps Angeline would take her in and find her a suitable position. Why had he not thought of that before now? Of course! It fit well, he would just have to plead the case to Angeline, considering he wouldn't have time to appraise her of the situation beforehand.

But perhaps it would be too much to ask of his foster family. He shrugged. He would reassess the situation when he got hold of the wayward girl.

He didn't have to wait long. In Georgina rode on his horse MacNamara, with old faithful Douglas in tow. He wondered how she thought she would reach her destination, wherever that was—coach or train or paddle-steamer?

Georgina dismounted at the blacksmith's shop.

He could clearly see her figure, very obviously female in boys' clothing. Her thick, dark hair had been tucked up into a hat, but there was no mistaking the sway of her hips and the swing of her gait. The proud bosom was hidden, but he was aware of it. He had been thinking the same when he'd spotted her on the banks of the river from the paddle-steamer.

She disappeared into the smithy's shop, carrying a light cloth bag. He squinted, and saw his bags were still attached to Douglas's saddle. She remained inside for a good length of time then emerged with the smithy, who directed her to what Dane guessed would be stables for the horses.

He was right. She mounted MacNamara, clearly confident in the saddle. He couldn't help but admire her as a capable horse-woman. Her hat slipped back and sunlight flashed off the shimmer of her hair. How could he possibly miss anything about her? He blinked at the thought, watching her replace the hat.

She turned up the street with Douglas in tow. The smithy watched her as she left. With a slight shake of his head, he retreated into his dark shop.

Dane covered the few hundred yards behind her at an easy pace. Outside the two-stall stable that was just on the edge of town, he overheard Georgina talking to a man.

'I can pay you to keep him here, but I'd pay more if you could find someone to take him back up to Jacaranda,' she was saying.

Dane took no notice of what the man said. Instead, he stepped into the shed. The man had seen him and Georgina turned to look at the newcomer.

Dane moved quickly, rubbing his hand up and down her arm. He flashed a grin at the man before speaking to her. 'There you are, my dear. No need to arrange for Douglas to be returned, we'll carry on with him from here.'

Georgina looked thunderstruck. She couldn't take her eyes off his face and her breath seemed somewhat laboured.

Dane nodded at the stableman. 'Thank you for your time, anyway.'

'Right y'are, then.' The man turned back to a stall and slammed the door shut.

Dane grabbed hold of both horses' reins with one hand and Georgina with the other, then hustled her out of the stables.

She resisted enough to drag her feet, clutching her cloth bag close. 'At least let me explain—'

'In a minute, young lady. Let's make our way along the river before we have a little chat.'

'Would you please let me walk without your assistance?' She tried to free herself, but his grip remained firm. 'I can explain every—'

'And so you will. Until then, my grip neither relaxes on your arm nor on my horses. And if you try any nonsense, I will throw you over the saddle and tie you, face down, to it. Is that clear?'

She nodded.

'Good.'

They walked in silence until she huffed and tried to shake him off again. 'You don't have to hold so hard. Your hand is making me numb. It'll bruise my arm.'

Dane marched on.

He slowed up once on the banks of the River Murray and gave her a little push. Her hat fell off and she scrambled for it, stumbled and landed on her arse. She sat where she'd fallen. He paid little attention while he secured the horses close to the water where they immediately began to eat what they could find, and then to drink.

Looking at her, the downturn of her mouth, the worried frown wrinkling her forehead, her eyes glassy with unshed tears, he couldn't hold his temper. He flung his arms in the air. 'What in God's name made you do it?'

Her features puckered and as suddenly as he had bellowed, the tears popped and fell down her face.

Those tears grabbed his heartstrings. He baulked and momentarily softened. Her nose began to run and she swiped at it with the back of her hand. He glowered, dug into his trouser pocket and thrust a handkerchief at her. 'I don't suppose you thought to steal one of these.'

She took it, unfolded it with a flick of her wrist and trumpeted into it.

He sat on the ground nearby, his arms on his bent knees. 'Tell me.'

She gulped in air, wiped her nose back and forth.

Dane rubbed his face with his hands. 'For God's sake, you bloody fool. You stole one horse, left me for dead on the road, stole my other horse and my possessions, which I note you were about to use for yourself, and here you are snivelling as if I had done *you* some injustice.' He scratched his head, wincing as he found the bump.

He couldn't ignore the movement under her shirt, or the thick hair as it fell about her shoulders. He couldn't ignore the shape of her legs in the pair of his, he now realised, old breeches, nor the feet clad in a shapely pair of boots, laced from ankles to calves.

She snivelled and blew again.

'That crying business is going to get you nowhere. Now, no nonsense. What were you going to do?'

Georgina shook her head.

He stood and stalked over to Douglas and pulled the saddlebags from him. 'Well?' he called over his shoulder.

She swallowed, her face pinching as she did, and remained silent.

Throwing the bags at her feet, he stood beside her again. 'I can play your little game for only so long before I hand you over to the police as a thief.'

She gaped at him. 'What?'

'Finally, she speaks. Cooperation may save you a gaol term. Or worse than gaol. I believe that in some places stealing a horse is a capital offence, and you've stolen two—and my possessions.'

She shook her head, held her hands up as if to ward something off. 'I did not want to be sent away to God knows where, at the mercy of who knows what.' She hiccupped. 'I've been sent away before … '

'So, you took yourself off. Where did you think you were going?'

She blinked swollen and malevolent eyes. 'None of your business.' Her voice jerked in her throat. She rubbed at her arm where he'd held it.

He ignored that. 'For a start, have you any idea what sort of worry your disappearance will cause my mother? Someone who took you in and treated you like a daughter.'

There was no response. She had the good sense to stare at the ground, experiencing some guilt, he hoped.

'They fed and clothed you and are now broke apparently because of your damned drunken stepfather and all his debts.'

'Drunken?' She snapped a glare at him. '*My* father? Did you take a look at your own?'

Dane ploughed on. 'My dear Uncle Rupert in and out of debtor's prison.'

She staggered to her feet, swiping a hand at her dribbling nose and rebellious eyes. She huffed and puffed, and gulped once or twice. She wobbled a little, then shouted, 'What utter bollocks!' Her voice broke. 'He doesn't owe your family a debt. It's exactly the—'

'Bollocks, is it? You have the mouth of a guttersnipe *and* you're calling my father a liar.'

'He is if he's told you that! Where's your proof? Where's *his* proof?'

He stared her down. *Indeed. Where's his proof?* He'd asked to see the books and his father had fobbed him off. He'd fobbed him off about talking to Jemimah too: 'Not a word to your mother.'

He rubbed a hand over his face, thinking hard. *Have I been a gullible bloody idiot? Could this girl be right?* He squinted at her, shaking off the niggling doubt. She could still be fooling him. 'Were you sending Rupert money too?'

Her mouth dropped open again. 'I'd no money to send—Rupert would send *your* father money to support *me* … I have letters he wrote and—and—'

'Where are they?'

'They are at Jacaranda.'

'How convenient.' He stepped closer to her.

She stood her ground. 'You clearly don't have the God-given intelligence—'

'Now, be careful with your tongue.'

'Careful with—?' She pulled herself upright. 'You are so dim-witted,' she said, sniffing, her teeth bared, 'I'll wager you wouldn't know your quims from your strumpets!'

'*What?*' He snaked out an arm, grabbed her shirtfront and hauled her off her feet.

She squawked. 'I said—'

'I heard what you said. Not another word from that gutter mouth.' He gripped her by the collar and half dragged, half carried her down to the river, then grabbed the seat of her pants, lifted her off her feet and dunked her head and shoulders into the water. 'Most unladylike.' His teeth clenched as he hauled her back up.

Georgina sputtered, attempting to draw breath. Muddy water streaked her face and clothes.

He let her drop to the sandy bank and she scrambled back on her arse. He stabbed a finger at her. 'And if there's any more of that language, I'll find some soap and do it again.'

She wiped her mouth with a soggy sleeve and glanced at Mac-Namara then back to Dane.

His mouth twitched. 'You are not really that foolish. Don't even think it.'

She scowled. 'You have it all back now, your horses and your money.' She hiccupped and sniffed noisily. 'Aunt Jemimah told me they had to send me away, that they'd find a place for me. But I'll go my own way, no more trouble to any of you.' Wet hair hung in damp strings on her shoulders.

'And how you'll manage that by yourself, I don't know. We will go to Echuca and from there we will go to Melbourne. Perhaps I'll be able find you a position there instead of dragging you to Sydney. It will be a hard few days' riding, but I can tell you have the seat for it.' He eyed her. 'Did you happen to bring an outfit more suited?'

'This *outfit* makes riding long distances much easier.' She stood and brushed herself off, swiping at her wet hair before stomping towards the horses.

Dane stepped ahead of her. 'You take Douglas. I'll ride MacNamara.'

'They need to rest.' Georgina reached out to stroke a softly pawing Douglas.

'Pity, there's not much to do about that.' He swung onto Mac-Namara. 'Mount up. We will ride until late afternoon and then camp. They'll rest overnight.' He turned away and barked a laugh. 'And so will I.'

———

Georgie thought about running then, could easily have done it, but even though Douglas was the freshest, he would still be no match for MacNamara. *My horse, not his.*

Certainly having male company on the journey to Echuca, a good three days' ride or so, would stave off problems from other travellers along the way. She should make the best of a bad situation. With reluctance, she did as he bade.

They travelled in moody silence.

Georgie knew Dane MacHenry would land her in a situation she'd never find her way out of, and the last thing on earth she wanted was a lifetime of servitude in a big ugly city. At least life on the river was clean and quiet.

I will never go to Melbourne or Sydney with him. Ever.

She was glad they were going to Echuca. Conor Foley would be there and he would certainly give this braggart a going over.

They rode for hours, the heat of the day unnoticed as they made their own breeze. Perspiration dried on her before it ran. The great aromatic eucalyptus gums scented the air as the temperature soared. She caught glimpses of the huge river, and once saw, fleetingly, a paddle-steamer sailing its way downriver. Her heart lurched in anticipation. In Echuca, she would be free again.

Then Dane signalled to pull off the road. She directed Douglas to the place Dane indicated, and slowed the horse to a walk. He examined a couple of areas up and down the bank before deciding on a camping spot. He removed MacNamara's saddle and blanket then led him to the water. Georgie followed suit, aware that Douglas was very pleased to have stopped. He had kept up valiantly with the younger horse, and she wished for his sake she had taken him riding more often.

Talking to him in soft whispers, she removed his saddle and blanket, and heaved them over a low-slung branch. The ride had tested even her endurance, for her knees wobbled and her arms ached. She tried to relax twitching muscles, shaking her arms then her legs one by one. She rubbed dried mud from her face and neck and it was then she noticed the fabric around her chest had loosened. It had clearly wriggled free of the pin that fastened it and was now settling itself uncomfortably about her middle. She would have to adjust the windings of the old bed sheet that bound her breasts flat or remove it, neither of which she would do in front of Dane.

She looked at him and saw he was intent on finishing a sleeping area for himself. When he was done, he began to build a fire.

The sudden cool of the late afternoon breeze on her sweaty skin through her shirt had an undesired effect on her body. She looked at Dane again.

'Well?' He glanced up, oblivious.

'I need to—to—'

'Go. But don't go too far. I don't want to think you've taken off again.'

Georgie reddened and suddenly very much needed to do what she had suggested. She hurriedly took herself off to a clump of scrub entangled around a thick tree trunk. She'd just pulled at the old piece of bed sheet under her shirt when his voice drifted over.

'Give me a shout—else I'll come looking for you.'

She gritted her teeth. 'I'm here.' A low chuckle was the only response. She tugged the piece of fabric, finally pulling it free, and dumped it over the bush in front of her.

'And again.'

His drawl grated on her nerves. 'I'm still here.' She struggled with her breeches but couldn't do anything once she'd come free of them.

'Louder.'

'If you don't stop talking I shall never be finished,' she yelled at him, past any embarrassment, seeking only to relieve the urgency.

'That's better,' he said and she heard another chuckle.

Finally, she pulled up her breeches. 'Act like adults,' she muttered, and grabbed the strip of sheet from the bush.

'What did you say?'

She tried her best to convey a certain indifference as she marched back to him with the strip of bed sheet in hand. She went straight to Douglas and began to wipe him down with it. He deserved a good grooming, but her strength was waning.

'Please clarify certain things you accused my Papa Rupert of.' She stopped to catch her breath. 'All this talk of debtors' prison and the like. If you knew him, you'd know it could not be true.'

Dane looked over from where he squatted. He studied her for a minute, which started her rubbing Douglas more firmly. 'Take off your boots.'

Startled, she stared at him. 'Why? They are all I own from my stepfather now.'

'I'm not stealing them. You might be a princess, but only a fool would run in these parts with no boots. Take them off.'

'I won't run.'

'And I am Queen Victoria.' He turned back to his little fire, the makings smoking cheerfully. 'Your boots.'

'I can still ride without my boots, you know.'

'But you won't get far walking without them. *Your boots.*'

She dropped to the ground and unlaced each boot, taking her time. 'I'm not an imbecile.'

'Don't make me comment on that.'

She flung a boot at him, and then another. He caught each one and tucked them under MacNamara's saddle. He turned to watch her, his arms folded. 'Since your arrival at Jacaranda, the family fortune, such as it was, has been on a slide into non-existence.'

Georgie felt hackles rise. 'That could not be my fault.' She checked herself. It would do no good to enter into an argument again.

'It seems my uncle, your dear Papa Rupert, has been begging for funds to keep himself afloat.' He stood up and stretched. 'So, much of my parents' hard-earned savings, and it seems my payments to them, have gone to him these last years. Combined with the downturn in wool prices and keeping you alive, the family is now no longer able to sustain its own bank notes. So the bank is threatening to foreclose.' He found a fallen tree branch and sat on it.

She turned to finish rubbing Douglas, who began to flinch under her determined hand. He'd said it so calmly. She began to wonder if all her drama was part of some strange delusion conjured by an overworked brain—his or hers, she couldn't decide.

She turned to him and tried to be equally calm. 'It just *cannot* be. If you knew Rupert, you would know it's impossible. He is not a man to gamble, or—or whatever else he is accused of. Your mama knows he is not—they are brother and sister. He married my mother and took me in—that's not the action of a man obsessed with destroying himself. When I left England he was quite—'

'I barely knew my uncle,' Dane said dismissively. He rubbed his forehead. 'When I left Jacaranda the first time over ten years ago, it was a fine run. The stables were full, we had kitchen staff and jackeroos, flocks of sheep.' He spread his hands. 'I returned every year for six years, and all was well. But this time I come back after four years away to find you in situ, and the place less than grand. There is no money. The money I wired has all gone.' He slapped both hands on his thighs. 'Yet, there have been no improvements on the property since then, no fine clothes on anyone's backs, no new stock, no staff to mention. Nothing. My father says he sent most available funds to your stepfather.'

She stood there staring at him. That contrived story wouldn't fool a ten-year-old child, yet Dane MacHenry accepted it without so much as a whistle. She wondered whether she should again ask him to prove it.

'What are you staring at?' he asked.

A fool. A fool who's been away from home too long to know anything about it.

She wanted to ask him if he knew how much Uncle Tom drank. Whether he knew how long Uncle Tom would stay away from the homestead, only to return thanks to free passage on some boat. They'd drop him off at the MacHenry landing on the river.

Her feet wouldn't remain still, they tapped and shifted under her. She wanted to ask him if Uncle Tom's absences had anything to do with his family's demise, not to mention her impoverished state. She wanted to know if the condition of the homestead was indicative of the financial climate, or of poor management under the influence of a bottle.

She wanted to shout at him, 'My Papa Rupert would not have drunk away all his money like your father has!' And realised she had.

She pressed back against the nearest tree, conscious of his icy blue stare. She returned that stare, though the defiance that swept through her had dropped away. She twisted the grimy cloth of the wrapper in her hands, dimly aware it wouldn't serve its original purpose again.

'I just ask for proof of what you've been told.'

Dane remained immobile, his frown deep, his chest slow to rise and fall.

Georgie fidgeted under his scrutiny and a hot itch scurried all over. Her skin prickled, and a rush of heat burst across her back and shoulders, burned. 'How can you blindly believe that?'

'Enough. Please.' He moved towards her and she pressed against the tree, her back now ablaze with fiery stings and intensely fevered pulses. He was squinting at her, scanning her, coming closer. Panic leapt in her throat, and the heat charging her blood made her light-headed, woozy.

He grabbed her by the shirtfront. Before she could utter any noise, he yanked her away from the tree and brushed furiously at her clothes. He started to laugh, holding her by one arm and brushing her pants and shirt with the other.

Georgie slapped his hands away. The itching and burning had become a stinging.

Through his laughter he managed to say, 'Ants. Bull ants.'

'Oh, God! Get them off me,' she cried and started to jump and hop.

He let her go, doubling over as she wrenched away and rushed for the river. 'Can you swim?' His laughter burst again.

Georgie waded only a little way into the river and ducked well under the water. She surfaced, her back to the bank, kicking furiously to keep from drifting into dangerous depths. She found a place to stand and wrenched her shirt over her head and shook it with all her strength. Long-bodied ants floated about her in the water.

She kept her back to the bank while she wrung out her shirt. She slashed at the ants in the water, furious with them, herself and him. There was no semblance of modesty now. She struggled into the sodden shirt, checked it again for the clinging little beasts. She half turned, prepared to haul herself against the shallow undertow back to the bank … *I will come out of the water with my clothes clinging to my body, with not a dry stitch to protect my virtue.* She was entirely dependent on his conduct.

'You can't stay in there forever,' he drawled, laughter still in his voice. He squatted again. He obviously thought it very funny indeed.

Georgie waded towards the bank. 'A gentleman would avert his eyes.' She folded her arms across her chest and carefully felt her way out of the river to a spot in the sunshine. She didn't know whether he had been a gentleman, but she assumed not. Her cheeks were on fire, and so were the bites on the cheeks of her arse.

'You'll need to get something on those bites.'

He didn't sound so amused now. She flicked a glance at him. He'd stood up, no hint of laughter at all.

She was so uncomfortable. She couldn't soothe the number of bites all at once, and her harsh rubbing irritated and inflamed them further. In desperation, she looked at him for help.

'I have some oil in my saddlebags. It's all I can offer.'

She nodded and he fetched it for her.

'You'll need to dab every bite. They'll be merciless unless you do.'

Digging in her pocket for the handkerchief he'd given her earlier, she held out her hand for the oil.

Instead of handing her the bottle, he bent and peered down the back of her shirt. 'They'll need attention.' Still holding her collar, he faced her.

She nodded. His assistance soothing these ant bites would be the least of her worries.

He dropped her collar and pulled MacNamara's blanket from the tree. He spread it on the ground. 'Lay face down and lift up your shirt.'

She knelt, then dropped to her elbows and fell forward, her face resting on the blanket. The stings seared long strips of flesh and her legs moved restlessly. Then the strong scent of eucalyptus oil rent the air, its pungent odour already soothing. A gentle press of the handkerchief he'd taken from her and the stinging reduced a little. His hands slid the oiled cloth over her back, dabbing along her rib cage and down the knots of her spine.

When she sobbed her relief, the cloth immediately lifted. 'No, no—it's too good. Please keep going.'

He pressed the bites once again, this time determined, deliberate. Firm. So gentle, it seemed as if he'd touched her lips with his fingertips.

Shivers sped along her skin and danced under his hand.

'Lift the leg of those pants.'

He touched, daubed, the press of his fingers on her flesh tentative but resolute, the oil warm and soothing on her skin.

'Now the other one.' And his fingers slid along the calf muscles of her other leg. The press of the oiled cloth brought another soft sob to her lips.

She felt his hands leave her while he tipped more oil onto the cloth. She silently begged for the relief to continue, wriggled in agitation until his hand descended once again, pressed and slid.

'There are stings on your … upper … '

She dragged the trousers up over her knees and exposed the backs of her thighs. They burned like blazes until the press of the oiled cloth and the silken brush of his fingers crept over her skin. Her head felt funny, light …

He took the scrunched-up pants from her hands and pulled them down over her legs.

'No.' She needed more relief.

'Hold the waist band down. You'll have to help if you can.' His voice was whisper soft, his breath close to her neck.

She struggled to push the pants down, fumbled with the raw-hide tie at her waist then abandoned it. 'I can't.'

He gripped her pants and tugged an inch, two inches. More. Georgie felt her rump hit the air but the oiled cloth came down and pressed firmly before she could object. He daubed and patted some more, oil descended afresh once again. She felt herself writhe a little, wanting relief here … and there … and—

'Here.' He offered her the oily ball of cloth under her nose. 'Turn over, just a dab or two on each bite—can you do all over?'

'Yes.' She pushed herself up, muddle-headed. 'Thank you.' She wriggled back into her pants, certain her face was as red as her arse.

He turned away and busied himself with MacNamara.

She quickly dabbed at her neck and chest and stomach. With a quick glance over her shoulder to check his activity, she pushed her breeches down further and dabbed at the angry red lumps at the top of her legs. She lightly rubbed the oily cloth over the hair of her private area. The horrible creatures had bitten her absolutely everywhere.

A few more dabs here and there and Georgie could do no more.

A little time later, the stinging dissipated and her nerves calmed. Exhausted, she lay on the horse blanket, hot all over.

His voice drifted across. 'Better now?'

But she couldn't even nod her head. She was just too tired.

———

Dane watched from a distance as the girl dabbed eucalyptus oil on the last of the ant bites. She seemed to fade and then slipped, boneless, onto her back. She'd fallen asleep, worn out. He waited until he was sure her breathing was easy. He reached across for the other blanket and took it to where she lay.

He knelt and placed it over her, brushing a lock of hair from her face. He remembered the sunlight shimmering on her blue-black hair as she rode and he suddenly longed for handfuls of it to bury his face in.

He sat back, alarmed.

A tiny frown twitched above her eyes and he wanted to reach out and smooth it away.

He stared at her a moment and stood up. What in God's name was he thinking? He'd charged off to find her and thrash the living daylights out of her, to take her back to Sydney and have her work off her debts. But now …

He stared at the lovely face again. He must be going off his head.

She'd called his father a drunk. It hadn't unduly surprised him. But he didn't want to press the issue with her—it was none of her business.

Although it *was* her business and should have been his more than anybody else's. He thought on that. She was right. Tom certainly looked like a drunkard.

He went back to his tree branch and sat against it—after he checked for ants. His eyes settled on Georgina but he wasn't seeing her. He went back over the dilapidation of the homestead, the state of the place, the lack of staff, the neglect in the paddocks. It was not just recent. He knew, really.

But he didn't understand any of it. And why would his father choose a defenceless girl as his scapegoat? What happened to send Tom off his head like that—and when did it all start?

He would talk to his mother about it. But she would stand by Tom through the very worst, and act as though the world was all put to rights. Perhaps not so much any more. She looked tired, worn out. And Elspeth seemed to run riot. He couldn't understand that either. Despite whatever had befallen Georgina, she could still behave properly—when she wanted to, he conceded.

Well, almost. She could certainly swear with the best of them. And flounce about the countryside looking like a beggar in the clothes she wore. He pursed his lips as he focused on the sleeping girl.

How could he hold her responsible for what had befallen his family? There was clearly no benefit to her that he could see. Her pride had bothered him, he admitted. He wanted to see that fall ahead of anything else. She was beautiful and courageous. She was intelligent and an excellent horsewoman who loved her animals.

Despite his behaviour, she had kept her pride, even as she was hopping up and down with those damned ants crawling all over her. He laughed again. A rush of warmth for her hit him solidly in the chest. A tight coil began in his belly.

He didn't want *that*. No, no, no. He had his plan set, his life was in Sydney for another year then—

He studied her anew. She had the breeding—that was obvious in spite of the immoral dress habits, the spit and fire. The swearing.

She's brave and quick to temper and utterly feminine. Perhaps—

He pushed at the growing erection in his pants.

What the hell am I thinking? Why am I wasting time on her like this? There are dozens like her where I've just come from. Rebecca for one …

He sighed aloud. *Fooling yourself, MacHenry.*

This slip of a girl already had him by the balls like no one else.

Certainly not Rebecca. Rebecca was as far removed from Georgina Calthorpe as she was from the moon. Rebecca with the gorgeous face and voluptuous body, insatiable appetite for men and money. He laughed at himself for comparing spirited Georgina to the worldly, painted creature who was Rebecca Middleton. He had certainly never entertained ideas about making Rebecca his wife. He pushed her out of his mind. Her presence sullied the new avenue his mind was exploring.

And what of the homestead? Of Jacaranda and his devil of a father?

He'd visit the family solicitors in Melbourne to see what could be done by formalising a partnership with his father, though he doubted it would achieve anything. If his father needed five hundred pounds, he couldn't help him. Five hundred pounds. He couldn't imagine the type of financial trouble Tom had encountered to incur a figure of such debt. But Tom was a drunkard. No point hiding from the truth. Was that where the staggering amount of debt had come from—gambling and drinking?

Georgina Calthorpe knew, and Joe had said anyone within coo-ee of Jacaranda knew. So, how could the debt have escalated? Why hadn't someone stopped Tom or alerted Dane?

He kicked the ground. There was more to this than he understood. And he admitted a measure of guilt, too. All those years working away, sending his money back to abdicate his responsibility, living with Reuben Cawley's exceedingly rich family in Melbourne and Sydney while the homestead went to wrack and ruin. A young man's carefree life …

He shook his head. *I'm not responsible for this.*

Yes, he had chosen to stay away from Jacaranda, working hard elsewhere, building wealth to underpin his next move: the dream that was Jacaranda.

A chill drifted in the air. The light was fading. His stomach was empty, but he wasn't uncomfortable. He took Douglas's saddle and carried it over to where Georgina slept. With the saddle for a pillow he settled beside her, taking some of the top blanket for himself.

Propped up on one elbow, he looked at her in the dim light. He knew her clothes were still wet. He pondered for a moment. If she wasn't feverish, she needed to get out of those wet garments. He might as well do what he had to and take the consequences, he couldn't be in more strife with her at this point anyway. Either that or let her catch her death of cold.

He hesitated at the odd few buttons on the old shirt clinging to her. He didn't want to remove her clothes. He laughed at himself. Since when had removing a woman's clothes bothered him?

He looked at the breeches, crudely tied to her waist with a simply fashioned plait of leather. He touched it and withdrew his hand hastily.

He laughed again. This was the big, bold Dane MacHenry, who'd affronted her in the house garden on the night of his arrival. Big, bold MacHenry who was hesitating to save her from pneumonia by removing her shirt. He knew there was nothing underneath the clothes. He had seen that much when she emerged from the river.

He also knew he should wake her so she could remove her own clothes.

He reached out again and gently nudged her shoulder. 'Georgina.'

She didn't make a sound.

He nudged again. 'Georgina. Wake up.'

She mumbled something and turned her head. He could see angry ant bites on her neck, swollen, merging into one another.

He touched her forehead but couldn't detect a fever. He didn't know what an adverse reaction to ant bites might have been, but he sincerely hoped she didn't have one. 'Georgina.' He dipped closer to her ear and shook her shoulder. 'You have to get out of those clothes.'

She groaned and tried to sit up. He helped her. 'I can't,' she mumbled. 'I'm cold. And I feel strange.'

'You have to remove the wet clothes. I'll fetch another shirt of mine. Can you stay awake?' He stood and watched as she slid over to one side. He left her there and went to rummage in the saddlebags. He pulled out a favourite, a soft, well-worn shirt he wore mainly when riding long distances.

He sat beside her and encouraged her to wake and sit up again.

She took the shirt, fumbled with the buttons and then opened one puffy eye to look at him.

'Can you manage?' he asked.

'I will have to.' Her voice was thick and her fingers clumsy. She became impatient quickly. 'But they wouldn't be wet if you hadn't—'

He scratched his head. 'Then please forgive me.' He moved behind her, pulled up the blanket in front of her. 'Hold this.' His tone was brusque, he knew, but his thoughts were in turmoil. This was not proper, a young girl was in his charge and he harboured notions that ran to long, delightful nights wrapped in her arms—and legs.

He caught his breath, cursed his cock.

She did as she was told and he helped with hands that shook only a little.

There was silence as he slowly undid one button, then the next, fingers working carefully as her back fell against his chest. He slipped first one arm then the other out of her shirt as she clutched the blanket, pulling it up further to cover her chest.

He flung the wet shirt aside. 'I'll help you slip this one over your head.'

She turned and her eyes met his, her distress in the tears that welled.

He silently cursed all things anew.

Georgina held the blanket as Dane slipped the soft old shirt over her head. The blanket dropped and she buttoned.

'And the breeches,' he said.

'I'll be bare arsed,' she cried.

'Aye. And I've never seen one of them before. Shush. Take off the breeches.'

She wrapped the blanket as best she could around herself and worked the breeches down.

He took the clothes and hung them on the bushes to dry, and by the time he had returned she was asleep in a tangle on the ground.

He moved her to straighten the blanket—and caught a glimpse of her slender body as she turned in discomfort. A leg kicked off the blanket and rested by his thigh. He stared at the slim limbs, the calves shapely and lithe.

She muttered and his attention was diverted for only a moment. The red bites were scattered over her thighs, interfering angry little lumps that rose in ugly mounds over otherwise perfectly shaped contours. His eyes roved to the dark patch between her legs and the black curls took his breath away. In the fading light he could see the tiny bumps of shivers on her flesh and he quickly, gently, wrapped her up again.

He backed away as if she were a heat that would scald him. Quelling the desire curling in his gut, he pushed again at the heaviness in his trousers. Slipping off his coat, he threw it around his shoulders, grabbed MacNamara's blanket, laid it beside her, and settled himself on it.

His head went down on the saddle and he took too long to drift into a troubled sleep.

Seven

'Is it night or near morning?' Georgie tried to sit up and away from him.

He murmured, turned towards her. 'It's late, perhaps nearly midnight, but there's a bright moon. Go back to sleep.'

She listened to his voice. It was soothing and sleepy, too. It was a nice voice when he wasn't yelling. It was melodious, calming. She wasn't accustomed to hearing the gentle resonance. She was conscious of his body warmth and a feeling of—

'Where are my clothes?' She grasped the blanket around her more tightly.

'They'll be dry by the morning, there won't be a frost. Nothing untoward has happened.' The dreamy voice pacified her panic and when she realised he was sleeping, she settled back and drifted off again.

Georgie woke when his stretching interrupted a dream soon forgotten. She tried to protect herself by clutching at the blanket as he drew away. She needn't have bothered, he seemed uninterested. He wandered a little way off into the bush and she stood as quickly as she could, wrapped herself in the blanket and hopped over to her clothes strung out, as he'd said, on a tree.

The urgency in her bladder was alarming but she managed to climb into the nearly dry breeches before she made a dash in the opposite direction for the safety of a large tree.

She checked for ants before shucking off her trousers.

When she returned, the dampness in her clothes had nearly disappeared, and the cool fabric was soothing to the bites on her body. She threw her old shirt over his newer, cleaner one and sat in the dust to pull on her boots he'd tossed there, lacing them only loosely as her feet throbbed.

'Good morning.' He was saddling MacNamara.

'Morning,' she returned briskly, but her tongue was thick and her voice sounded muted. She went to Douglas with blanket and saddle. She seriously doubted if he was going to leave and let her go anywhere by herself.

'Feeling better?'

She glanced over, watching his hands as they worked the leather. When she grew hot, she looked away. Each time she took a furtive glance, it was as if there was some spell upon her, heating her up. Which was worse—the discomfort from the ant bites or from him?

'Yes, thank you.' She didn't want conversation. Things were not as they should've been and she couldn't possibly pretend she was happy about the situation when she was not. She rubbed the back of her neck, the pulpy lumps of flesh alien and squishy under her fingers. She felt squeamish.

'Still troubling you?' he asked. 'I'll help you with some more oil in a minute.'

There seemed a strangeness about him this morning and Georgie was immediately suspicious. 'No, thank you.'

He stopped his work and looked at her. 'Suit yourself.' An eyebrow lifted, and so did a shoulder.

Georgie tried not to rub the throbbing, irritating burn all over her body. Too proud to admit she was being foolish, she would just have to suffer with it. Her head ached dully as well. Her stomach rumbled. 'I'm hungry.' She rummaged in Douglas's empty bags for food. Nothing.

'You'll survive.' He finished with MacNamara's saddle and flicked Georgie a glance. 'There's nothing except what you had in my saddlebags.'

Everything would be too stale by now. Hungry, hurting and dishevelled, she eyed Dane then threw the blanket over Douglas, saddled him up and climbed wearily onto his back. The simple moves stretched her swollen skin and the irritation flared anew. Her involuntary gasp as she settled in the saddle fell on deaf ears. There was misery in ant bites.

'Ready?' He nudged MacNamara on without a backwards glance.

The pace he set was a canter. Thank God he wasn't in the mood to gallop. It was obvious that he fully expected Georgie to traipse along behind him without a murmur of protest. She followed on Douglas, not having to instruct the horse as he fell in alongside MacNamara, his old stablemate.

Georgie's misery deepened. Her backside chafed on the saddle. Her head ached and her stomach was a hollow pit. She glanced at Dane, his strong body at one with her other lovely horse as he drove him steadily. Georgie struggled to stay with him. She clung to her horse, fearful of falling off.

This was all quite strange. She was not in control, and felt very unwell. She hung on, praying he would stop soon and give her some peace.

Sometime down the track, he shouted above the noise of the horses' hooves that they would take the next turn right off the road. Georgie held a hand up to indicate she understood him, and nearly came out of the saddle. Her hands had cramped around the reins and Douglas's mane from having hung on so tightly.

Not long after, she saw with great relief there was a gate ahead and they would be entering a property. Perhaps he intended to get something to eat there.

They reined in at a house hidden behind two great pepper-corn trees and a vine growing along a well-kept trellis. Its wide veranda, shading the porch swings from the sun, looked cool and inviting. Tranquil.

She could feel her grip on the reins loosening as she began to slide sideways—

Cool hands held her head up to the cup to drink.

'What on earth happened?' Georgie asked as she stared into the kind face of an older woman, who simply smiled and encouraged her to drink before anything else. It was broth, strong and tasty, and she managed a slurp or two before her head dropped back to the pillow.

'There,' the woman said happily. 'That's much better than before.' Her face creased into a smile and Georgie smiled back, basking in the kindness. 'Now, I bathed you, dear, and dressed those nastier ant bites. I don't think we need call the doctor out, you seem to be coming along nicely. Nothing a good meal and some pampering won't fix.' She patted Georgie's hand. 'How do you feel?'

'Better, thank you.' Georgie glanced around the room, large and homely. The bed was huge after her rickety old one at Jaca-randa, and comfortable, and the crisp sheets were indeed cool on her skin. The burning of the bites had dissipated and she closed her eyes, marvelling at the soothing comfort. 'Where am I?'

The lady stood up and plumped the pillows. 'I'm May, dear, Mrs Rossmoyne. You're at our place a few miles out of Echuca.' She smoothed her hands over her hair, soft blonde dusted with silvery sparkles, caught back into a bun that sat at the nape of her neck.

'My husband, Charlie, is out a few nights mending fences. Now, take your time, and you'll be up and out of here tomorrow or the next day.' She smiled at Georgie again, and Georgie smiled back. She swallowed all the broth and May seemed very pleased with her.

There was a tap at the door. May called, 'Come in,' and Dane poked his head inside. 'Ah, Mr MacHenry.' May beamed at him.

Georgie's face dropped. Not for a minute would Aunt Jem allow a gentleman—or any man for that matter—into a lady's room, whether she was sick or not. She tried to give Dane her best stony look, but he grinned widely at May. He carelessly dropped his hat onto the dresser and removed his jacket.

'Our patient is much better, now, Mr MacHenry. Perhaps you would like to look after her for a little while.'

'Delighted.' Dane's brows arched and the grin remained.

'No. No, I—' Georgie protested.

May obviously misunderstood. 'There, there, dear. I'm sure your husband can do more for you than I can.' She left the room.

Georgie was aghast.

Dane stood leaning against the closed door. He screwed up his nose. 'How fares my lovely wife?'

'*Wife?*' Georgie raged at him in a whisper. 'Is that what you told the kind woman—that I was your *wife?*'

'What else was I going to say to the "kind woman"?' he whispered in return. 'That you are my runaway urchin, who I am accompanying to Melbourne? Or perhaps a lone young woman thief? What would you have me say? I thought you'd be grateful I considered your, ah … virtue.' His voice had risen.

Georgie ignored his goading. 'What happened to me—did I faint?'

'Spectacularly. Threw yourself off Douglas and landed at the veranda steps. I had thought to leave you there in that crumpled little heap but—'

'Oh, stop. It's not funny.' She folded her arms. 'I was simply without food for too long. Hardly a dramatic turn of events.'

'My, my, the bravado returns. So, how are those nasty ant bites?' He moved away from the door and sat on the bed. He took her hand in his and turned it over, inspecting the stings. 'Hmm, you'll have them for some time to come.' He ran his fingers over the less affected skin of her arm, and studied her. 'It's a very good thing they didn't get to your face.'

Her eyes met his and her cheeks burned. 'Please don't ridicule me. I know you think you have cause to hate me, but I cannot abide this—this—'

'This what?' He turned her hand over, palm up, and raised it to his lips. 'It's not ridicule. I certainly don't hate you.'

Georgie pulled away. He mocked her regardless of his words. The strange flutter in her belly started again and she lay her hand there to still it. He stood up, towering over her, and she closed her eyes to block him from her sight.

'We will be sharing this bedroom for at least tonight, Georgie. Perhaps the antagonism will entirely disappear after that.'

'I won't have you sleeping in—'

'Keep your voice down. I'll sleep in here at the foot of the bed. And you'll just have to put up with it.' He turned and left her alone in their room.

Eight

Conor Foley reached up and gripped the architrave of the boat's cabin. He stretched, easing his big frame, his loosening joints protesting long nights at the helm.

He stood on the deck of the *Lady Mitchell* and watched as the crew got her under way from the dock at Renmark. With the chug of the boiler beating rhythmically, he looked skywards, checking the weather. Bright blue skies, high wisps of clouds in the distance and nary a breath of wind. There'd be nearly a full moon tonight. If it remained a largely cloudless sky, the river would be a ribbon of milky light leading him serenely through the evening. He stared upriver while his mate guided the steamer through the channel. He barely noticed the tall gums lining the banks of the Murray as he squinted into the morning sun.

As was his habit, he looked towards the west and found himself thinking of Jacaranda and the girl there, Georgina Calthorpe. He smiled to himself. He'd be there in a few days if all went well and he looked forward to seeing her. He would claim the homestead as his own, rightfully his thanks to Tom MacHenry's drunken challenge at cards and his own exceedingly good luck. He was not a man to let opportunity slip through his fingers. And he would claim the girl. He was winning whichever way he turned.

He hardly expected a warm welcome from Tom and Jemimah MacHenry. He didn't have to be there long, certainly Georgina would leave with him especially if there was a promise of marriage to encourage her. She had caught his attention eighteen months ago—she was a beauty—and MacHenry, in his decline, had opened the door to good fortune.

Georgina, the perfect wife. Beautiful. Intelligent. Virginal.

Conor Foley would have his young and beautiful wife, untouched by society and unused to the ways of life. A woman who wouldn't know what to expect of her husband, a woman who needed what he could offer and only that. And he had found her living at Jacaranda, almost buried under Tom MacHenry's sodden habit and debt-ridden life.

With Georgina he was certain to regain what he had lost over the years, the thing that defied all the voodoo and magic and useless potions and lotions he tried, and all the whores and ladies he'd had. The Boers. The Transvaal. Wounded at the Battle of Majuba Hill in 1881. Shot in the cock, the fucking thing mangled and stunned for all time into flaccidity. He even pissed crooked. The medicine men all said there was nothing to be done.

But with Georgina, he would become whole again. He could feel a stirring he'd barely felt since his injury. To once again feel the deep pull in his lower belly, the swelling and the weight of his cock as it filled, the powerful thrusting ... the anticipation of having her legs and her tight little cunny around him ...

Only her. She would make it work for him again. He could almost feel how good it would be.

He would not whisk her away to his riverboat as he could have done—and wanted to do—on each visit. Her conversation, intelligent and inquisitive, had passion. Her manner told him Georgina was untouched, and that was why he wanted her. He would bide his time.

Of course there would be some things he would have to curb about her. Far too independent. Far too capable of thinking for herself and not toeing his line. Those traits did not suit him. Neither did her horse riding, though she was a natural. Her riding days were numbered. He'd rather be driven in a carriage. It wouldn't do to have his lady wife riding on the back of a horse— and better at it than he was.

She would do nicely with that little edge smoothed off. Just perfect, in fact. Once more he thought he felt a stirring in his loins. As usual, it slipped away before it began.

We will have to elope, he mused with some satisfaction. MacHenry would never consent to a marriage now, not after the card game. Had it been the plump and untidy Elspeth he wished to marry, MacHenry wouldn't hesitate—his problems would be over. But Georgie could do naught to save him.

It had happened at that rough, rowdy table when Tom MacHenry lost Jacaranda only those few weeks ago.

'Tom, there's too much rum at this table,' Charlie Rossmoyne had growled.

'Don't worry about that.' MacHenry's speech was already slurred. 'Just deal me another hand.'

'You're already out of the game, Tom,' Charlie whispered furiously at him.

'Oh.'

Foley had glanced at Rossmoyne and the other five players. There was Ted Davis, Will Cumber, Cyril Smith and Andy Morton, all local boys and well known to the river man. His river run often took him onto most of their properties, delivering merchandise or picking up stock and wool bales for sale at market. The games started out in a friendly fashion, but they

were never without stakes. The men bet what they could and
debts were paid.

At this particular game, MacHenry had already consumed a
great deal of rum and boasted about the money he was able to
raise, with which he could do whatever he liked.

Foley refrained from asking where this money came from, for
to visit the unkempt homestead, with its sagging fences and lack of
workers, it was obvious the money he gambled was coming from
somewhere else. He doubted MacHenry had the wherewithal to
generate extra funds. Perhaps the absent son had made a fortune
somewhere, but Foley doubted it.

'Come on, boys.' MacHenry glared around the table. 'Ready
to deal me in again?' The drunker he got the louder he bragged.
And now he offered the homestead as stakes.

Foley remembered the shock on the faces of the other men.

'Don't be a fool, man,' Charlie Rossmoyne had snarled at him.
'You're too drunk—the stakes are too high. Take back what you
said—withdraw the offer, you fool.'

'I'll not,' MacHenry bellowed into Charlie's face. 'The red-
haired devil can't take me.'

Charlie shook his head. 'You're more the fool than I thought.'

'Think of the missus,' Cyril Smith added quietly, and the others nodded in agreement.

'I'll stake Jacaranda.' MacHenry slammed his remaining cards
on the table, challenging Foley to a private game.

The others threw their cards down in disgust. Foley asked
them to stay as witnesses, and acknowledged they weren't happy
about the twist in the game. His mind worked fast. He'd need
witnesses if he won Jacaranda, witnesses who would attest to the
legality of the game. He would win not only a home on the river,
but a halfway port for his vessels. Foley's River Carriers could
be docked here, close to Swan Hill and Echuca, and halfway to

Wentworth, where the Murray met the Darling. He could see enormous benefits, even though the trade was weakening. He could squeeze more from his stake than he imagined. There might still be twenty good years in it.

He needed MacHenry sober.

'Mr Foley,' Andy Morton cautioned. 'Ye're not takin' the mad fool serious, are ye?'

All eyes were on Tom.

'Sober him up, Mr Foley. It's not right to be takin' his challenge up now,' Morton continued.

'I'll sign a paper,' MacHenry bellowed.

Charlie urged Foley to drop the game and walk away until next time. But Foley saw he had something within his grasp, certainly if luck went his way. He had nothing to lose.

MacHenry banged the playing table belligerently. The others shook their heads.

'Tom, I'll play. Charlie, Andy, if I lose, I'll pay out Tom's banknotes.' Foley sat, the fingers of his left hand drumming quietly on the table. He wanted Jacaranda. He could wait. He would wait.

MacHenry's reddened eyes lit up.

Charlie wrote it down, reciting as he did, and Foley nodded in agreement.

Foley wanted to play, but he wanted a fair game with a capable opponent. No one was sure that MacHenry would have offered Jacaranda had he been sober. The conundrum was laid bare on the table, and after a few moments of silence, MacHenry asked for a paper, quill and ink. Charlie wrote what MacHenry dictated and all five signed the paper. The unease remained.

Andy Morton insisted MacHenry sleep first.

'If I sleep I'll have to play with a hangover and that would be worse,' he grumbled.

Morton removed the bottle of rum and shook it in MacHenry's face. 'Ye'll have no more,' he cried angrily. He turned and sent a baleful glare at Foley.

The poker game began and was played best of five. Foley won three to two on a pair of fives. Foley capped his glee. He sat, head bowed, fingers laced on the table.

Tom MacHenry crumpled before them all. Jacaranda had slipped from his grasp.

He was helped from his seat in silence. Andy brought him back the rum bottle. There was no begging to play again, no pathetic pleading to renege on the deal, no appeal to begin a fresh game. He pushed the paper at Foley. 'I need three months to tidy up my affairs, then we will move off the homestead.'

The silence around the table was deafening.

Conor Foley was at first doubtful about the easy compliance. 'I'll wait till morning. You cool off, sober up, man.'

MacHenry lurched to his feet. Charlie Rossmoyne had to hold him up. 'Take the paper now. Endorse the handover and be done with it.'

Foley accepted. Three months it was. The men left with MacHenry, broken and pitiful in his drunkenness. Foley was unaffected, but acknowledged a small concern for his family.

He wondered if he could be challenged by law.

Since then, he had not been welcomed at Jacaranda. Hardly a surprise. MacHenry was surly, Jemimah cold and Elspeth her usual self, which he could ignore. Georgina was Georgina. It was obvious to him neither of the girls had any idea of what had passed; that Foley held their lives in his hands because he'd won a game of cards.

Only three weeks to go before MacHenry and the family were due off the property, and as observed on his last trip, not much had been done to expedite their moving out. He wanted to speak to Jemimah in private but she remained unapproachable.

He knew from Georgina that the prodigal son had been called home and would surely have arrived by now. Little the lad could do, if anything—perhaps he could persuade his father to see some sense. But perhaps he would be just like his father, and be no help at all. In any case, he could not invalidate the agreement; it had been made fair and square and legal, albeit under unusual circumstances.

Foley wondered again if it could be challenged. He shrugged. A challenge might never be made.

And Georgina. He had an affection for her, that was true, and in her was his salvation. But he didn't intend to give up his roving on the wide river simply because he had a young, beautiful and useful wife in Melbourne. Nor did he intend to give up visiting his one or two favourites en route. After all, Georgina was a young woman, unsure of the duties of a spouse. He would have to school her carefully.

He would teach her, and gladly, but these things took time. He knew his young bride would eagerly await his return from each trip and, under the watchful eye of his loyal sister, Kate, she would reside as his lovely wife and hostess of the Foley home. And only that.

He turned towards the wheelhouse, intending to retreat to his cabin, when he heard his name being shouted from the banks of the river. He looked up.

A tall, straggly man with a sack on his back was sliding down the bank not far from a landing. He stood at the water's edge. 'It's me, Mr Foley,' he shouted in a heavy brogue. 'It's Seamus Reilly and I'm back for me job.'

Foley scarcely recognised the Irishman beneath the filthy rags. He folded his arms across his broad chest. 'For your job, Reilly? And what job does a drunk have on one of my boats?'

'He's trouble, Mr Foley.' Ned Strike, the mate, had come up from the boiler room to check the charts. 'But we could use him.'

Foley shouted to the man, 'Reilly, if you want your job, empty out the grog now.'

'No grog, Mr Foley,' Reilly shouted back, hastening into the river until it was up to his waist. He was holding the sack above his head.

'He's a shit-eating liar, Mr Foley.'

'I know. But some help is better than nothing if you need it. Have someone row out and get him,' Foley said. Ned ordered the deckhand to oblige.

Once Reilly was on board, Foley snatched the sack from him and emptied its contents. Two bottles of rum crashed to the deck. 'You know how I feel about grog on board, Reilly.' He uncorked both bottles, poured the dark liquid over the side while Reilly watched, aghast. 'Get below to the fireman and don't come up until I send for you.'

Reilly's eyes glittered for an instant. 'Miz Hodge says to say hello. Sir.'

Foley stilled for a second. Annie Hodge knew his secret. 'Is that so?' was all he said. If Annie Hodge was entertaining the likes of Reilly, Foley would no longer be visiting.

'Get below and sober up, or I'll throw you off myself.' Foley turned to Ned. 'This is the last job for him. If he falls overboard, leave him to it. In fact, if he even gets close, shove him in.'

Ned Strike glanced at his captain. 'That I will, Mr Foley.'

'Gun her up again, Jim,' Foley called to the helmsman and the big paddle-steamer sailed gracefully down the river. 'All's safe,' a voice bellowed from below in the boiler room and a familiar ease crept through him. The low chug was as regular a tattoo as his own heartbeat, which took its rhythm from the river itself. The river was the blood in his veins. He took a deep breath of air, warmed by the sun.

And as the *Lady Mitchell* crept forward, Foley's heartbeat quickened. He never left a dock without that excitement, another journey. The unfortunate docking at Renmark for repairs had cost him a large consignment, but with two working steamers, the *Lady Mitchell* and the *Lady Goodnight,* his loss would be recovered in quick time.

Of course with Jacaranda under his belt, things would be more promising than before, so losing the Ross contract was a small wound healing fast. He knew his captain Finn and crew would be at the Echuca cranes by now on the *Goodnight,* so he would afford himself the luxury of easing the old *Lady Mitchell* downriver to Jacaranda, where he would bask in the sunshine of his lady love. He snorted a laugh.

He went to the wheelhouse, where Ned had taken over the steering. 'Wake me at four, Ned. I'll take her through the night.' Ned had lost his nerve for the night steering a long time ago. He'd lost good mates as the *River's Best* lay wallowing and groaning as she sank.

Foley himself revelled in the challenge of night steering. With the bright lamps on board illuminating the water and his intricate knowledge of the channels and shifting sandbars, he would deftly guide his boats safely, without incident. He'd spent most of his life on the rivers, knew the Darling and its treachery almost as well as he knew his much-loved Murray.

He was aware he was despised for his financial success. It couldn't be said he was always a gentleman in business. He also knew the time fast approached when riverboats as trade vehicles would be obsolete. There was talk of damming the river with locks and weirs, but he knew that was a long way off. He needed an income that wouldn't be so heavily reliant on the weather, and the flow of the water. He wanted to be well ahead of his competitors when the end came.

He foresaw passenger boats carrying holidaymakers and had signed a contract to pick up a new boat he intended to run as another luxury passenger vessel. It would be bigger and better than the *Goodnight*; the *Lady Georgina*, named for his future wife. He would sign the final papers soon and was confident he could begin to outfit the boat within the next couple of months.

His eyes were scratchy and burned with fatigue. He'd had an uneventful night, which was how he preferred the watch to pass. Ned Strike appeared on deck, bleary-eyed himself, and handed Foley a mug of strong tea.

'River's up, Ned.'

'Glad of that, skipper.' Ned yawned. 'They say we're in for a long summer—won't be much rise in her then.'

Foley stretched. 'Time I was gone. Dusk tomorrow night at Jacaranda?'

'I reckon, Mr Foley.'

'Call me by noon, would you?'

He left the wheelhouse, finished his tea and then threw himself into his bunk for some sleep.

———

'What do you mean, she disappeared?' Conor Foley roared in Tom MacHenry's face.

'I mean just that. She disappeared days ago, without a trace. Took one of our horses with her.' Tom's tone was sour. The hangover was one of his worst.

And Jemimah had been berating him for days now over Georgina's disappearance. 'We've driven her to running away, but my boy will find her before something happens. He'll bring her home. I know my son.'

Tom had only shaken his head at her naivety. Their son was no boy.

'Disappeared,' Foley repeated. 'Why would she do that?'

Tom shrugged, hoping to Christ this towering bastard bellowing his head off would disappear as Georgina had. He didn't have the strength to fight Foley, nor did he wish to. He had hoped never to see him again.

'Did you mount a search, man?' Foley asked, running his hands through his thick red hair.

'Oh, it's all right, Mr Foley. My brother has gone after her,' Elspeth piped up. 'He'll bring her home, in his own good time, Pa says.'

Tom closed his eyes. 'Elspeth.'

Foley glowered at her.

She shrank against the wall but it didn't stop her prattle. 'Well, everyone knows what Georgina's done ... anyone who rides a horse in the same fashion as a man can only be—'

'Elspeth, come with me, now.' Jemimah held out her arm, waving Elspeth to her.

'In all my visits to this station, Miss Georgina has not said one word of pettiness!' Foley thundered. 'But you, Miss Elspeth, if you had half the good nature and spirit about you as she has, you would be far better off.'

Elspeth fled the room, slamming doors as she went down the small hallway.

'Mr Foley.' Jemimah shifted her glare to her husband then smartly left the room after her daughter.

'I demand an apology and an explanation.'

'An apology?' Tom shouted. 'An apology?' He went to stand, leaning on the table for support.

'I might remind you, this is no longer your house.'

'Good God, you bastard, you may think—'

'And what's this about your son looking for her, MacHenry?'

'—that you own this homestead, but you don't have any right to question the comings and goings of my family.'

'Question your family?' Foley was incredulous. 'It seems to me you've let one of your family stray, Tom. Someone in whom I am very much interested. When I catch up to them, that son of yours had better have behaved like a gentleman or else I'll make you both wish you'd never been born.'

Tom shrugged off the threat. He slumped into his chair and reached for the rum decanter.

'There's your downfall, mate. In the bottle. Does your wife know about the settlement?'

Tom nodded.

'And your daughter?'

Tom shook his head.

'You have dug a very deep hole for yourself, Tom.'

Another shrug.

'The deal is signed and legal. I intend to be installed here in less than a month and I am prepared to talk about reparation.'

'If you mean charity, I don't want it. We'll be off your hands by month's end.'

'I was thinking of Jemimah.'

'We're none of your business, Foley.' Tom took another swig from the decanter. 'And why would you be so worried about young Georgie in the first place, eh? I know you're not the gentleman on the river you make yourself out to be.'

Foley snorted a laugh. 'Do you now? I thought it was obvious, man. I'm going to marry her.'

Tom spluttered and wiped the rum from his chin. 'Marry her?' He eyed the big man. 'You don't think I'd consent to that, now, do you?'

Conor Foley leaned on the table. 'I wasn't going to bother informing you.'

'She'll never be accepted if it were known she married without our consent.'

'And you care why?' Foley straightened up. 'I buy acceptance, if needs be.'

'You're a cold bastard.'

'At least I'm not a fool. You once had the respect of your peers around here. What ever happened to that?'

Tom glowered at him but remained silent. The glass in his hand began to shake, and rum slopped onto his shirtsleeve.

Foley stabbed a finger at Tom's chest. 'You better hope I don't come across your son.'

Tom met Foley's eyes momentarily. 'If you do come across him, you might well meet your match. He's no slip of a lad.'

'You have only to make up your mind whether you stay on here as caretaker until I establish my own men, or if you leave.' Foley dismissed Tom's threat as yet more drunken drivel. 'It's up to you. If you decide to leave, make sure you're off here by the time I return. Your personal possessions are yours to take as you will, but try to destroy any part of the buildings, or what's left of the fences—'

'I'm not a fool, Foley.'

Conor Foley merely raised an eyebrow.

Tom watched as he left, slamming the door behind him.

Nine

Georgie sat for a long time in the big bed, propped up by thick pillows. She couldn't help luxuriating in the richness and warmth around her one minute, and dreading a new encounter with Dane MacHenry in the next. He made her unsure and skittish and she hoped he would at least behave in a gentlemanly fashion while they were here with the kind Rossmoynes.

She must have dozed a little for when she next glanced about the room, May Rossmoyne was hanging dresses on the back of the door.

'Oh, you're awake, I hope I didn't disturb you.' Her cheeks dimpled in a smile. 'Is there anything I can get you?'

'No, thank you, Mrs Rossmoyne. You have been kind enough already.'

'We could hardly let you continue your journey in the state you were in. And besides, I couldn't let a young lady go riding around the countryside in the get-up you were wearing. Really, whatever was he thinking?' She shook her head. 'I hope you don't mind, dear, but I've brought in these dresses. They belonged to my daughter, but she's gone off to Melbourne, to a convent no less, bless her. She won't have any need of them.' She held up the plain but well-made dresses.

Georgie was humbled by the simple generosity. 'Thank you so very much. I am grateful, you've thought of everything. I haven't known such kindness for—' She had to stop talking, for her lip quivered.

May sat on Georgie's bed. She had a face that seemed to smile all the time. She took Georgie's hand. 'There, there. You're obviously feeling lowly, right now. All those dreadful ant bites can't be doing you one bit of good, but it's the fainting I was worried about.' She looked at Georgie closely. 'You're not feeling poorly for any *good* reason, are you, dear?'

Georgie looked at her blankly. 'I just hadn't eaten … '

'That's all right, dear, but if there is to be a baby, we'll have to take extra special care,' May said plainly as she rose from the bed.

Georgie's mouth dropped open, but May didn't see, she was busy pulling and tucking the bed covers. 'No, no baby,' Georgie said, stupefied. What on earth had he told this woman?

'Now, I'll be back in a couple of hours with some tea for you. I think your husband would like a word, dear, so I'll send him in. He is very worried about you.' She bustled out of the room.

My husband *is very worried about me.* Georgie absently scratched an ant bite on her arse. *I should get out of bed and pull on one of the nun's dresses, march out of here and hit my husband on the head with a big branch of a large tree.*

It seemed like a ridiculous nightmare, and she couldn't wake up. As she swung her legs out of bed, in he strode.

'Where do you think you're going?' Dane made himself comfortable on the end of the bed.

A feathery shiver danced over Georgie's spine. She tucked herself back under the covers, aware of her feet and ankles and a man in her room. But he hadn't taken his eyes off her face.

'I was going to dress. Mrs Rossmoyne has loaned me some clothes,' she said, pointing.

He glanced at the clothes on the back of the door. 'Far better than before.'

Georgie stared at the floor, away from his gaze. 'Don't let this farce get too out of hand. It's embarrassing.'

'Ah, but more so if you suddenly become a single lady. I suggest you behave like a married lady and you'll find nothing embarrassing about the situation at all.'

'You're gleeful about this!'

'Interested, not gleeful. I love exploring possibilities.'

He rested contentedly near her feet, watching her. The heat of his body warmed her through the bedclothes. She had to scratch another bite, and then another. 'When will we leave here?'

'When you are feeling better.'

'I feel much better now.' She didn't look at him. His weight shifted imperceptibly, and she moved her feet further away.

'I don't think so. A day more won't hurt.'

Her head came up. 'I thought your business in Melbourne was urgent.'

'It is, but I don't want to be carrying a half-dead woman with me. I'd prefer she was in good health and spirits.' He tapped the bites on her swollen hands gently.

'Would you not leave me in Echuca? I—I have friends there.'

'Of course you do. No, I don't think so. Echuca will be a stop for the horses, I want to stable them until we return. We'll take the train to Melbourne.'

'I don't want to go with you.'

'I know. But there's not a lot you can do about it. If you run again, I'll simply track you down. You have to see the sense of it—it just doesn't do to have a young woman roaming the countryside on her own. God only knows what scoundrels are out there.' He looked at her from under raised brows.

Georgie huffed and moved further away from him. 'I really don't want company now.' Her stomach was doing rebellious little leaps and her heart had suddenly decided to leap with it. *What is the matter with me? I'm all a-squirm.*

'Well, you've got company. For all intents and purposes, I'm your husband. And I feel like having a little sleep.'

He began to take off his boots. Georgie stared at him and gathered the bedclothes around her as if they would protect her. He loosened the buttons at his waist, undid the couple at his throat and laid down beside her. He snatched a pillow from her bundle, made himself comfortable and closed his eyes.

She sat rigid on the bed, unable to move. Surely he was only pretending to sleep and any minute he would leap over her and— and what? She didn't know what he would do. Perhaps he would try to touch her breast or—or something else. What about that *thing* Josephine used to speak of?

Never.

She shook her head and glanced at him. It looked as if he was sleeping.

She began to edge off the bed, one eye on him, but she wasn't quick enough. His hand snaked out to grab her wrist. Her hands tingled and her stomach fluttered.

'Don't,' he said sleepily. 'Just stay where you are. You should lie down, too.' He tugged her back into the bed.

Arrogance. Effrontery. The *gall*. His grip on her wrist didn't slacken for a minute and she began to despair of the blood reaching her fingers ever again. She tried to pull away but he held steadfast. In desperation, she wrenched her arm.

He leapt up and hovered over her. 'Lay down,' he ordered gruffly. 'If you know what's good for you, you'll lay quietly while I sleep. You are alone with me—again. I would find it very difficult indeed to remain a gentleman now, *wife*.'

The heat burning in her face travelled to her toes. He settled down to sleep again, the grip on her wrist now looser. The press of his fingers hummed on her flesh.

She stared at the ceiling, trying to relax. Truly amazing how all those pieces of wood joined together. They must have been specially made. Then she turned her head ever so slowly to gaze at him.

His face in repose was a handsome one and her belly fluttered. A fine face, beautiful in that strange masculine way not unlike some Greek gods whose pictures she'd seen when at school in England all those years ago. A strong shadow of blue-black beard stubble coated his cheeks, chin and jaw, yet his eyebrows were fine and dark, not overly thick. She wondered what it would feel like to smooth a finger across them, or perhaps along the edge of his jaw. Would it scratch and send tingles to her toes?

His eyelashes were long and dark … there was a small bump and bend in what would have been an otherwise regal nose—when he wasn't yelling, which was when the nostrils flared and went white. And his mouth …

Her own opened a little.

His bottom lip was fuller than his top, and she wanted to feel those against her skin as well …

Her face grew hot.

The blue-black shadow crept down over his neck. His Adam's apple bobbed as he swallowed. She froze. A moment or two after, when no more movement occurred, she continued her scrutiny.

Georgie inclined her head just a little to peer under the opening of his shirt. His skin there was paler than that exposed at his collar. The hair on his chest was black and wiry, and there was plenty of it. As his torso rose and fell, a delicious peculiar feeling in her stomach darted pleasure to the juncture of her thighs.

Those feelings—Josephine had called them her lusts. *I am having lusts, and have no idea what to do with them.*

Georgie still stared at him. Absently, she scratched an ant bite and then all the itches in the world begin to crawl over her flesh. With one hand in his grip, she fidgeted, trying to reach more of the bites, until she saw his deep blue eyes on her. She yelped and decided to remain still.

Finally, she dozed, and when she woke, found herself eye to eye with him once more, though his were closed. She'd rolled onto her side, facing him, and had settled into the hollow his weight created between them. She would have had to touch him to move away, she would have to lay her hand on his chest, which would be warm and hard and ... So she lay there, quietly, hoping he would move instead.

He smelled of leather and soap and musky man. Up so very close, she could see every pore through which the rough stubble of beard poked. She could count the dark freckles high on his cheeks, and trace the contours of his crooked nose. Long eyelashes formed the perfect curve across his eyelid. And again, her gaze lingered on his mouth—

She was staring at his mouth when it moved.

'Close enough, do you think? You sorely test my good manners, Georgina.'

She jerked back.

Awake now, he said, 'It wasn't enough you had to fidget for an hour—now you've taken to ogling me from two inches away. It makes a person very ... uncomfortable.' He propped himself up on one elbow.

His gaze on her deepened her blush. With his free hand he reached out and touched her face, so gently she almost didn't believe it had happened.

His hand slid behind her neck and pulled her closer to him. Awkward, unsure and shaky, she stared again at his mouth. Then with both hands he drew her to him, and her heart stood still.

He kissed her chin and her nose, her cheeks, her throat. The unexpected, exquisite touch left each place tingly and hot. Dane pressed his mouth along her neck, his lips slid into the soft, velvety hollow at the base of her throat. He groaned quietly and slipped an arm behind her, drawing her body closer.

Her heart thudded so loudly she was sure he could hear it.

He pressed his lips to her forehead and broke away. A long sigh escaped him as if he struggled with something. Georgie laid a hand on his chest to balance herself and he covered it with one of his own. He murmured something and turned his face away from her. He had not kissed her mouth and every part of her cried out for his lips on hers.

'What is it?' she whispered into his neck.

He groaned. 'I will not do it.'

She barely heard him. 'What did you say?'

He turned back to her, his features pained. 'For the love of God—' he grated, '—for the foreseeable future I am responsible for your well-being.' He pushed her hand away and sat up abruptly. 'It is not seemly to be—' He stopped himself, wiped a hand over his mouth. 'Get up, and get ready to leave. I will tell the Rossmoynes we cannot delay any further.'

'But—'

He pushed off the bed, buttoned his pants, cursing and shoving at his clothes as he did, and pulled on his boots. He strode to the door, yanked it open and was gone.

Georgie sat for a moment, the strangest feeling of disappointment paralysing her.

The door flew open and he marched back in to the room.

'Hurry.' He grabbed a dress for her from behind the door—certainly not the one she would have chosen—and threw it on the bed. 'Fifteen minutes.' And out he marched again.

What is the matter with him? He was back to the boor she knew him to be. She harrumphed as she left the bed, chose another of the dresses and struggled into it. She dragged fingers through her hair to arrange it into some order and managed a reasonable plait. She pushed her feet carefully into her boots, laced them, and paced the room, desperately trying to button the dress properly behind her, muttering under her breath. Ready to wrench the dress apart, she started at a soft tap at the door.

'Come in.'

May Rossmoyne entered and Georgie nearly burst into tears.

May took one look at Georgie's face and gave her a quick hug, then turned her around, deftly threaded each button through its hole then neatened the collar. She turned Georgie around again and took her by the shoulders. 'There, there now.' She raised her eyebrows sympathetically. 'Men are truly funny creatures at times, and they seem to think they know best. However, I must be sure you are fit to ride, dear. I have informed your husband if you are not, you are to stay with me.'

Georgie hesitated. If she could stay here, she could get word to Conor Foley. *He could come and rescue me and—No. May Rossmoyne has been told I am Dane's wife. I would not be able to call for a man other than my 'husband'.*

She could, she supposed, run away again.

But Dane left no option. He stood in the doorway. 'You see, Mrs Rossmoyne, she's as good as she says she is. You are ready, aren't you, my dear? Believe me, if she were not well, I would not be taking her with me.'

Georgie glared at him then turned to Mrs Rossmoyne. 'Thank you so much for your kindness. And for the dresses. When I get to where I'm going, I'll have them sent back to you.' Georgie smiled and retrieved her bag from under the bed. 'Goodbye, Mrs Rossmoyne.'

'Goodbye, dear.' May kissed her cheek. 'I'm sorry Charlie wasn't back in time to meet you.'

Dane held out his hand for Georgie's but she pushed past him. She could feel his frown, but wasn't worrying about his reaction.

She hoped he had at least offered Mrs Rossmoyne some sort of payment.

She stood on the wide veranda in front of where the horses were tied, and tilted her head up to meet the sun. It was quite lovely here with the vine along the trellis swaying gently in the breeze. She was reminded of something long ago, but the memory drifted past her.

Mrs Rossmoyne followed Georgie out, and stood alongside her.

Dane untied the horses. 'I wish we'd been able to stay longer, but as Georgina is well rested, I think it best to continue.' He held out his hand for Georgie, but this time she dared not take it.

Georgie shot a look at Dane, who merely raised a shoulder. Then he gave her a leg-up into her seat.

Dane turned to May. 'Thank you once again, Mrs Rossmoyne, and I do assure you I will look after my wife.' He mounted and turned MacNamara's head for the road.

Georgie waved at May. She followed Dane out the gate, feeling very peculiar.

Ten

Dane pushed on to Echuca.

He cursed himself silently all the way for being a fool over this girl, allowing her to slot under his skin and niggle at his heart-strings. The harder he fought it, the greater his interest grew, and the greater his desire became. He believed without a shadow of a doubt she was virginal and unexposed to rough life, in spite of her sometimes surprising language.

He hadn't been able to shake the acute desire he'd experienced at the Rossmoynes' homestead. He cursed, then praised himself many times over for denying himself. He'd never experienced such an overwhelming hunger for a woman before in his life. The episode at the river bank had whet his appetite, and at the Ross-moynes' she was there for the taking. Yet still he held back. He was a fool and a gentleman simultaneously, but could not promise he would be the gentleman at any time in the future should the opportunity present itself again.

He shook his head. She clouded his thinking—she was a hot-blooded woman waiting for a man to show her the real world. He wanted whole-heartedly to be that man. He wanted no other man to have her, not if he could help it. The thought of marriage entered his head—

What?

Rebecca had hinted at marriage over the years and the thought of it left him cold. Yet here was a snippet of a girl—hardly a snippet, a full woman—he'd known not a week, the cause of a great deal of trouble for his family, and he was thinking of *marrying* her?

He'd spent too much time in the goddamn sun.

Reuben would laugh himself silly. Dane MacHenry, so enamoured of a young girl he had to marry her before he could get into her bed.

He glanced over his shoulder at Georgina. Her determined face made his heart thud and he turned back to the road ahead. Echuca dotted the horizon along the sweeping plain.

He could approach her in two ways. One, he could take her and offer marriage later, or two, he could court her.

Court her—she'd most probably laugh at him. He'd transgressed against her person in the house garden, pushed and shoved her, threatened her verbally and given her a dunking in the river—treated her at best as a tomboy used to roughhousing. What hope did he have of courting her?

What? Throwing in the towel, MacHenry? Work harder, man.

What if she didn't want to be married to him regardless of the pressure he'd place on her? And would he want to pressure her? No, no. He wanted her to want him. She'd come around, he thought. He'd work harder.

And the family. His parents would have to be told. Then she would be his responsibility, not theirs. And her damnable stepfather would have no hand on him.

He shook his head. Irrational thoughts. If only he could have just had her that afternoon and got it out of his system—that's all that was wrong with him, a sudden itch that hadn't been scratched.

Echuca, the river port town, was bustling as usual, the dock alive with gliding riverboats, the cranes busy unloading freight. Dane noticed Georgie's straining in the saddle to catch a glimpse of the boats, but thought nothing of it, and rode on into the town centre.

He slowed MacNamara and Georgie followed suit on Douglas. They tied up at the post office. He glanced at her. 'I must send a telegram to Sydney. Then I'll find a place for us to stay for the night and we'll leave for Melbourne tomorrow morning.'

'You'll undoubtedly look for two rooms.'

He smiled. 'Undoubtedly.' He left her to wait with the horses and went inside to advise Reuben of his protracted stay away.

He waited as the telegram was tapped out, and handed over the fee.

The postmaster's assistant, a little fellow, slowly scoured the parcels at the back of his counter. 'MacHenry, MacHenry, MacHenry. You're not the Swan Hill MacHenrys, are you? I think there's a parcel here for you.'

Dane shook his head. 'We are from out of Swan Hill, but I wouldn't think it'd be ours, coming here to Echuca.'

'Sometimes parcels are sent to us to be picked up by the Swan Hill MacHenrys,' the clerk insisted. He looked back at Dane. 'Yes, yes, for another Mr MacHenry. A Mr Tom. Are you a relative?'

Dane frowned. 'His son.' Why on earth would his father's mail come here?

'Perhaps you'd like to take your father's as well, then. He always picks up parcels for this lady.'

Dane was about to protest when the clerk heaved a large package onto the counter. It was addressed to Georgina.

'Mr MacHenry—senior, that is—often rides down here, yes, yes, perhaps once a month or more on some occasions. I'm surprised we haven't seen him lately.'

Dane lost interest in the conversation as he eyed the package. It had come from England.

He signed for it, and picked it off the counter.

'He usually takes the packages from England over to Mary at the Pastoral Hotel,' the clerk said, jerking his head a little in the direction of the pub.

Dane met his stare. 'And that is your business, somehow, is it?'

'Small town.' The clerk shrugged. 'Thought you might want to do the same with it.'

'*I* mind my own business.'

He left the post office and at the hitching rail, eyed the parcel again. He glanced up at Georgina. 'This is for you.'

Her eyes grew wide. 'For me?' She studied the postmark. 'From England,' she cried and hurriedly tore the package open. She took the half-opened bundle to the veranda and deposited herself on a bench with it. She rummaged through the thick paper and hauled out a dress, rich burgundy with lace at the collar and cuffs. 'Oh,' was all she could say before she delved into the package again. She withdrew another gown of some pale copper colour and it rustled softly as she held it, like a breeze high in the trees.

She exclaimed again with delight.

There was yet another garment—a fine piece which appeared to him to be night attire, flimsy and looking cool to the touch. She attempted to hide it from his gaze and set about packing them all away again.

In her haste, she missed a letter that had fluttered to the ground as she pulled the clothes from the brown paper parcel.

Dane picked up the letter, skimmed the lines quickly then folded it. He lifted his eyes to the brilliant sky and rubbed a hand over his mouth. He handed it to her. 'I'm sorry—I've read a little … it fell out as you were otherwise—'

She snatched it from his hand. 'From Papa Rupert.' As she read, hungry for news from her father, joy swiftly fell from her features and bewilderment slowly took its place. She looked at Dane. 'Did you say you read a little?' She held the pages at arm's length. 'What does it mean?'

Dane scuffed the dirt at his feet. His temper had risen. 'I don't know.'

'What does it *mean*?' she repeated. Her voice trembled.

He untied the horses' reins. 'Come with me. We must put our heads together on it.'

She gathered up the dresses in the wrapping paper, the letter still clutched in her hand, and tottered after him.

———

She waited mutely, clutching the untidy bundle, as he paid for two rooms at the Pastoral Hotel, one pair of saddlebags slung over his shoulder. He signed them in as sister and brother. He requested care for the horses, paid extra for the stabling, and then he took her elbow, room keys in hand. He marched up the stairs, Georgina on his heels. She didn't protest as he deposited her in a room with a door adjoining his room and told her not to move. He needed time to think. He needed time to absorb Rupert's letter and what it meant.

He ran downstairs to the desk, asking for directions to the stable. He needed to get the other pair of saddlebags for his own security. Directed out the back, he found a lad unsaddling Douglas. Dane strode to where MacNamara waited in the next stall.

He went to take the whole pack up to the room with him, then he thought better of it. He grabbed the letter for the solicitor, and was packing Georgina's discarded boys' breeches back into the bag when he realised the lad was talking to him.

' … so just beware,' the stablehand said, hands on his hips and his mouth pursed as if waiting for an answer.

'What?' Dane glanced distractedly at the boy.

'I said, I heard tell Hayes Baldwin is out there again. That's what I said.'

'Who's that?'

'He's only the most wanted man since Captain Moonlight.'

'Bushranger?'

'Bushranger and more. Wanted for stagecoach robberies and he's done some cattle duffin' as well. They reckon he's got a hide-out here somewhere.' The boy was rocking backwards and forward on his heels, arms crossed over his chest. 'Talk is he comes to town quite regular, but as nobody knows who he really is, no one can shop him to the troopers.'

'Good luck to him,' Dane muttered to end the conversation. He patted his horse's neck and left the stable, the envelope in his hand.

When he returned to the room, he knocked first on her door, then opened it after he heard her assent and walked in. He flipped the correspondence for the solicitor onto a small dresser that had a little mirror and a washbowl on it. Georgina still sat on the end of the bed, clutching the bundle her uncle had sent tightly against her chest. Dane slumped into the only chair available.

He rubbed his hands over his face. 'I'm shocked,' was all he finally said.

'I am very confused.' Her face was white, her mouth pinched in an emotion he could only guess at. A few remaining red splotches from ant bites stood out on her neck. Her beautiful face was hollow with the shock of what she'd seen in Rupert's letter. He wanted to hold her, to smooth the problem from her brow.

His heart lurched, and a stone lodged in his throat. *What has my father been doing all these years?*

She twisted around on the bed and carefully laid out the dresses and the nightgown, caressing the fabric of the coppery coloured gown. She looked over at him, distractedly, before her glance returned to her hands. 'He says in his letter that—that he hopes I have liked his previous choices in dresses and gowns, and asks if the sizes have all been correct.'

Dane nodded. She hadn't really begun on the letter and its contents yet. He remembered the postal clerk had mentioned Tom taking the packages over to someone here, in this hotel. He steepled his fingers in front of his face, musing. What had his father been doing?

'He says that—' she swallowed painfully and Dane realised she was fighting back tears, '—that he is considering enlarging my allowance and wants to organise some finishing for me.'

Dane closed his eyes.

She read from the letter.

'Would you write back to me, my darling girl. You have been so lax with letters lately, I haven't received a one in two years. Tell me that I have chosen well for you. Don't let me hear it from Jemimah ... though I haven't heard from her in such a long time either. It must be those hot Australian summers ... '

Her voice faded to silence.

She looked up at Dane again. 'I write every month,' she cried suddenly. 'Even though this is the first letter I have received in nearly two years, I have written every month. Uncle Tom takes them to the post—Oh.' She stared into the distance. 'I have told Rupert things hoping he would have me taken away from Jacaranda. Here he writes as if he's nary received a one. And of the "previous choices", of the other dresses—I have never seen even one. Not one. And an allowance? I haven't seen that much in more than two years.' She looked back at the letter again. 'I thought he had abandoned me, and left me to wither just like my poor Aunt Jem.'

Dane baulked. 'What do you mean?'

Georgina sniffed. 'You mother has been very kind to me. She is a kind person. Your father … ' She waved a hand and let it drop back to her stepfather's letter.

Dane pressed fingers to his temples. 'How long has my father been drinking?'

'I don't know.' She sighed. 'Three or four years, getting progressively worse, I suppose. Your mother begs him time and time again to stop, asks him where the money comes from, asks him when the new grain stock will arrive, where are the stores she ordered, why does Elspeth need to wear second-hand clothes, when would they visit—Oh, I could go on.' She stared at the letter. 'All this time he was taking my money, wasn't he? All this time he was squandering my allowance and blaming Rupert for his decline.' She shook her head. 'And what of my letters to Rupert? Was he not even sending them?'

Dane had sat forward in his chair, studying his hands. He was sick to his stomach. His father had lied to him. And there was the pressing problem of the bank's foreclosure on Jacaranda to consider. What lies were behind that story, he wondered.

He reached over to the dresser for the wad of paperwork he was to have taken to the solicitors in Melbourne. Why would his father send him on a wild goose chase—this business with Jacaranda must be the truth. As he broke the seal, he looked at Georgina. She glanced away so he skimmed over the papers. There was nothing in them to hint at any impropriety.

'How much was your allowance to begin with?'

'I can't remember … if I ever knew.' Her face was downcast, and her hands twisted in the folds of her skirt. Her frown had deepened, her mouth was pressed into a thin line. Her chin puckered and relaxed, puckered and relaxed.

He didn't like to see it. He felt sad for her, and guilty about his rough treatment of her. His heartstrings tugged once more. But there was no friendship between them yet, and he didn't want to jeopardise what little progress he'd made ... progress he thought he'd made.

'I would give the letters I'd written to Uncle Tom to post when he would go on his travels—'

Dane looked up. 'Travels?'

'—and he would promise me he'd sent each one. I thought my Papa Rupert had forsaken me and I was doomed to stay at Jacaranda.'

An enormous weight settled upon him as he watched her.

Doomed ... at Jacaranda. His father had stolen her allowance, had sold her dresses—of that he was sure—and had lied and cheated and drunk his way into large amounts of debt at her and his family's expense.

A rock sat in his gut, heavy, cumbersome.

Dane reached across and pressed her hands. 'I'm sorry. I don't know what to make of this. Of any of it.' She bent her head lower, her shoulders shaking. He had an overwhelming urge to take her in his arms and soothe away the hurt.

He sat back. He needed a solution.

His father was coercing him into his debt-ridden life, intending to burden Dane with huge notes to pay out. When he got to Melbourne, he would seek advice of his own, but he had to save Jacaranda—at any cost. What else did his mother and his sister have? And what to do about his father?

What the hell had happened?

Fury ate him up, sudden and terrible. And as swiftly, a sadness descended, the anger and frustration whipped away as if on a gust of wind. His family had inflicted a terrible hurt on this girl, who had had the gumption to fight then flee. He needed to protect her. He needed it like he needed to quench his thirst with a jug of cool water after a day in the saddle. He would make things right—the most important thing to do. Yet how?

Dane sat beside her and leaned in a little, but she stiffened.

His guts churned.

He stood up and held his hands in the air as if in surrender. He paced the room, then came back to her and bent down to meet her gaze. 'You need sleep. I'll come back for you at tea time. Is that all right?'

She nodded mutely then turned, curled up on the bed and closed her eyes, her stepfather's letter tucked under her chin.

Dane closed the door gently behind him. He turned the key in the lock, as much as a safeguard against the unknown types staying in the tavern as for his peace of mind. And because Georgina could take flight at any time; he hoped to at least delay that.

Downstairs, he returned to the reception.

A sun-wizened man of indeterminate age met him there, drawing a heavy curtain behind him, hiding the bar from view. 'What can I do fer yer?'

Dane leaned an elbow on the bench. 'I'm looking for a woman. Mary. I believe she works here.'

The man's eyes hooded. 'Yah, there's a Mary here. Appointment only.' He turned away to tidy loose papers from one side of the counter to another.

Dane frowned. His father had stooped to lower levels than he'd previous considered. A curl of heat turned in his gut. 'I don't want her services, man,' Dane snapped. 'I want to talk to her.'

'Don't make much difference to me what you want to *do* with her, she gets paid by the hour.' The man turned his mouth down. 'And she's available right now—if the matter is urgent. Sir,' he added.

Dane thrust a hand into his pocket to retrieve the soft wallet. 'How much?'

He was directed back up the stairs and to a door down the hallway not far from his own room. He knocked, and heard a languid, 'Come in.' He entered and closed the door behind him. Cloying perfume drifted around him. His nostrils twitched. A spice, perhaps, or a pungent herb.

'Hello.' The woman was dressed in the finest gown, a deep blue fabric with a raised design, and overlays of silk. He knew as much because Rebecca often paraded for him, extolling the virtues of this fabric or that. She looked older than he, but not, he thought, any older than his mother.

She smiled at Dane and held out her hand. 'I was not expecting a guest.'

Dane took the proffered hand. 'I'm sorry I am unexpected, madam, but my business is not your usual kind.'

'Is that so?' A pencilled brow rose. Her face was not unpleasant but the layers of paint did nothing to enhance it.

He side-stepped to a seat by the large bed that dominated the room. 'Would you kindly sit, madam?' He indicated a chair opposite and she settled back graciously, clasping her hands in her lap.

He sized her up against Georgina. This woman could not have worn the clothes if she had purchased them from his father.

She still smiled at him. 'Why don't you tell me your name first, before we get down to your "not usual kind of business"?'

'I am Dane MacHenry.' He noticed a flicker in her eyes. 'I believe you know my father, Tom McHenry.'

The smile never left her face. 'Yes, I do know Tom MacHenry,' she said. 'I didn't know he had such a strapping lad for a son. Tom and I have been—business partners of sorts for many years. He has not fallen into some trouble, I hope?'

'Not of a physical nature, madam.'

'Mary,' she corrected. 'How can I help you? I doubt Tom would have sent his son to me for a night's relaxation.' Her brows rose again.

I don't know what my father would send me to do. 'I believe he sells you items of clothing when he is here in Echuca.'

'He does, indeed. Young ladies' dresses.' She did not elaborate.

'May I ask, for how long this ... arrangement has been in hand?'

She frowned slightly, but the pleasant smile never left her face. 'May I ask why you need to know?' Her flawless grace irked him. She seemed most unsuited for her business.

"Tis of a personal nature.'

She inclined her head. 'Perhaps for three or four years, now,' she answered evenly. 'I have a daughter in Ballarat and the clothes are sent on to her. I pay a good price, he is not cheated.' The smile was gentle. 'Does that satisfy your curiosity?'

Dane flinched. 'A daughter?'

Mary held up both hands in protest. 'Mr MacHenry. She's *my* daughter, not your father's daughter,' and the laughter that followed mocked him. 'This business is between your father and me. And it is only the business of the dresses, nothing else.' The smile still didn't waver but her gaze was direct and steely.

Dane thought better of delving any deeper. He stood up.

She stood with him. 'You still have a good deal of time on your credit, Mr MacHenry.' Her hands were barely inches from his chest as if she would stop him leaving the room.

He shook his head. 'Thank you, no. I ... find my time is indeed far too short.'

She smiled. 'Polite.' She tucked her arm through his and walked him to the door. Stepping into the hallway, she leaned against the doorjamb, appraising him. 'You must take after your mother's side of the family, Dane. I wouldn't have thought Tom to have a son such as you. Your dark hair, your features. You are a much bigger man ... ' She reached out and laid her palm on his chest.

He lifted it away from him. 'His own daughter has the look of him, madam,' he said. He bent a little over her hand and let it drop.

'His own daughter?' She looked surprised to hear of a sibling. 'Oh, I see. I understand your concern about the dresses. Yes, I do see. I am sorry. I was not aware he also had a daughter.' She shook her head a little. 'I wonder why he would sell—'

'No matter. It's not your concern.' A door opened somewhere down the hall, and it reminded him Georgina was waiting inside a locked room. He gave Mary another slight bow, ready to depart.

She tiptoed up to him and pressed her cheek to his. 'Goodbye, then.'

The door slammed with a thunderous crash.

He turned abruptly and strode down the hall, his hand passing over his cheek to wipe off her touch.

By the time he'd taken the stairs two at a time back to the ground floor, he needed a drink and the noisy bar would do him well. He'd gained a little information from the confident, perfumed business woman in the room upstairs and needed to think on it.

His father had stooped low, there was no question about that. It wasn't just the matter of a few dresses, but the total lack of regard for Jemimah and Elspeth.

And Georgina.

This wouldn't be—couldn't be—something Dane would ever confide to his mother. It was one thing to whore around and carouse with single men and pub workers, wharfies and the like. Quite another when a man was married and supposed to be providing for a family.

He shook his head. Since when had he become judge and jury? He was no saint, either. Then again, he wasn't a married man.

He ordered a rum, and paid the exorbitant asking price for what was, by its taste, well watered down. He swallowed it in two gulps, winced, then rested the empty glass on the counter. He looked around.

The room was starkly furnished and thick with tobacco smoke and wood smoke from a fire somewhere out the back; mostly full of card-playing, drunken revellers spending their coin on the cheap liquor and the cheap women, and losing whatever they'd worked for.

He noted money changing hands, how far more went over the bar and into the pockets of the card dealers than went away with the customers. His shrewd gaze caught the barman throwing the slops back into a tray then pouring its contents into a large jug under the counter. He saw the women he presumed were employed at the hotel sift through the pockets of the drunks carefully and transfer the booty to a bucket under the bar.

How not to operate my new premises.

Dane ordered another rum, threw it back in one gulp and left.

He walked towards the wharf thinking he could do much with a pub such as the Pastoral if it were his. He would make enquiries to see if it was available to purchase.

His thoughts turned to the homestead. His homestead … his *inheritance*. Once full of promise, the land still rich even though drought had been and was coming again; all the old men talked of it. It would curtail growth for a few years. *But if only I can—*

He couldn't imagine what sort of problems had led his father to stoop to selling a young girl's dresses for grog money. In hard times, Dane would have condoned the action if the money led to improving the family's situation, and directly benefiting Georgina. But it hadn't. And to sneak around in another town and tamper with the mail was far from moral.

And all that aside from the business with Mary.

It was hard to accept.

Rupert's letter indicated bank drafts had been made in favour of Georgina. Therefore, Tom as her guardian would have access to her money. How much money had been misappropriated over the years? Could Rupert have sent a small fortune? Perhaps he did. Tom had said five hundred was the amount he needed.

Enormous amount of money. I should take it upon myself and write to Rupert. But to what end? More trouble, no doubt. Maybe even prison for Tom.

Dane wandered to the wharf, stood and stared at the cranes as they lifted the swaying wool bales and crates of cargo from the paddle-steamers and the barges below to the holding squares. The boats lined up, first come, first served, and he could see six or seven vessels waiting to be unloaded. The place was alive, humming with the thrum of commerce and hard work, men shouting back and forth, cursing and praising as the cargo warranted. All boats crews were on hand, but the job on the dock was left to the workers there.

He turned back towards the hotel, surprised to note that the afternoon sun was setting rapidly.

Georgina! She could not be trusted to stay put for long and God knows what sort of tricks her mind would be playing now. His pace quickened.

Eleven

Georgie had read and re-read Papa Rupert's letter, trying to understand all that had befallen her. It was too much to take in. He *had* been sending an allowance—which she had never lately received, not even indirectly. He *had* sent more dresses, which she had never seen. Where on earth had they gone?

Sick and tired of the confusion, she threw the letter away from her and paced the small room, her hands clasping and unclasping. There seemed to be no answers, and the added complication of Dane MacHenry being too close only weighed on her further.

She stopped in front of the door adjoining her room to Dane's.

She would not wait patiently for Dane to return. She was not about to be kept like an excess piece of baggage awaiting allocation to some dowdy corner of this part of the world. She turned her back on the door, grabbed her few belongings and marched to the main door. She pulled at the door knob but it stuck fast. Locked in! She marched back to the other door, and tested the knob before she yanked at it. The flimsy lock gave way and the door popped open.

The other room was identical to the one she was in. Georgie strode over to the outer door, and with some trepidation this time, tested the lock. It clicked open and she poked her head outside.

The squeaky hinges and groaning as the door scraped on the floorboards interrupted a couple at the end of the corridor—

She gasped. That despicable, arrogant Dane MacHenry was at the end of the hallway, a woman all over him.

Georgie pulled herself back inside the room and slammed the door as hard as she could. It cleared the bow in the floor without so much as a whisper, and the noise of it banging reverberated in her ears.

He's a useless, overgrown, gormless excuse for a horse's arse! A cocksure show-off with his hands on that frumpish baggage's fat backside.

He thought to take himself off to dally with that thing at the end of the hall, did he? He must think her a naïve fool and easy prey. Perhaps he'd planned it that way all along, locking her in her room.

Her stomach fluttered. Perhaps that woman was one of *those* women Josephine had talked about.

Georgie had left Josephine behind in England years ago but her education was indeed enduring.

She threw herself on the bed again, plopped back onto the meagre pillow, and closed her eyes before the ready tears threatened to spill.

The things he would have done with that woman—she couldn't imagine.

For goodness' sake, would he have had time to do whatever men do?

She turned on her side and stared out the window at the sun on its afternoon descent. Her eyelids were heavy. Perhaps just a small nap to tide her over before she made any big decisions …

———

Only a few minutes had passed, she was sure, but Georgie had a sense she should wake. Opening her eyes to weak sunlight in her room, she sat up quickly, but her head was foggy with the temptation to return to sleep.

She swung her legs to the floor. Standing, stretching and needing water, she took a mug from the dresser and poured a drink. Then she took stock of her situation.

She could not stay here.

She eyed the crumpled dresses on the foot of the bed. They were her only possessions now. She wrapped them back into the sturdy parcel so they could be easily transported. She would head for the stables and take one of the horses. She would ride to her river. Sooner or later she would meet up with Conor Foley and life would be returned to an even keel.

The bundle under her arm, she poked her head out the door and checked up and down the hall again. She stepped outside, closed the door quietly behind her and headed for the top of the stairs.

Dane cut her off at the landing. 'Where do you think you're going?'

Georgie made to sidestep him, but he blocked her and herded her back to their rooms. She was firmly ushered back inside, still clutching her new dresses.

'Sit down a minute, Georgina.' His face was grim. Georgie sat where he indicated, her parcel of dresses across her lap. 'And please don't speak until I ask you to.' She opened her mouth to protest, but he held his hand up. 'I should think you know enough not to wander about on your own. That's one thing young ladies do not do—under any circumstances.'

She opened her mouth again and this time he nodded at her to speak. 'I could not possibly wait here one more minute for you to come back after seeing you with that—that—'

'With that what?'

Heat flamed her face. 'That type of woman.'

He looked bewildered. 'What woman?'

'At the end of the hall. Earlier.'

He raised his brows. 'And you know what type of woman she is.'

'Not nearly as well as you, obviously,' she snapped.

He bent down and looked at her, digging his hands deep into his coat pockets. 'What did you say?'

'You heard perfectly well.'

He brought his hands up to rub his face, and sighed. 'Georgina, your imagination is vivid, but your education is lacking.' He straightened and pulled a chair over, turning it around to sit astride it.

She took several deep breaths but the intensity of his gaze stopped a tirade. Instead, she gritted her teeth. 'It's not your business to educate me.' The itchy heat crawled over her again and she scratched absentmindedly.

'A whore is someone who sells her body for money.'

'I know that!' Georgie was aghast. 'Oh my God—did you pay her?'

'Sweet Jesus.' He ran his hands through his thick, black hair. 'What on earth do you think you saw?'

'You—she—in the hallway, your hand on her ... arse,' she finished lamely, and stared at him accusingly.

'I did not have my hands on her arse. You saw nothing.'

Heat bloomed over her face. Of course it was nothing.

He folded his arms on the back of the chair and leaned towards her. 'When men go to women like her—'

'How disgusting.' She covered her ears. 'I don't want to know what you did.'

'Not me, you fool. Others who might visit here might mistake ladies on their own in an establishment like this as having easy virtue.'

Her head came up and her eyes connected with his. 'I'm aware of that.'

'Are you just? It didn't seem like it. You were about to la-de-dah down the stairs on your own. You'd be easy pickings for some unscrupulous—'

'Stop!' Georgie cried, shaking her head.

'So, would you please—please—refrain from trying to traipse all over the countryside?'

'You think I'm a naïve fool who needs a chaperone.'

He nodded solemnly. 'At present, yes, I do, and for the moment the chaperone job has fallen to me.'

'I was not going to traipse all over the countryside.' She was just going to charge down to the wharf and find Conor Foley. But she couldn't tell Dane that—couldn't tell him of Conor Foley.

Her shoulders sagged. There was no way out. She glanced at him, glanced again as he straightened. He seemed to relax just a little.

'Would you care to have some dinner if I can find a decent eating place somewhere?'

Food. Yes, she needed food. She nodded. 'I think I would.'

He stood up and returned the chair to its place by the wall. 'Come on, then. Let's go. But you'll have to put your parcel down, there's no need to walk around town with it tucked under your arm.'

He waited patiently until she sorted the dresses on a hook on the back of the door, until she checked the little mirror for any hair that had strayed out of her plait, and pinched her cheeks. Then she allowed him to open the door and lead her out.

They ate in relative silence in a small restaurant close to the hotel. She was hungry, but the meal was chewy stew with unappetising vegetables. She glanced at Dane only to catch him doing the same to her. She burned anew, heat curling up from her toes and stopping—curiously—in her belly. There it churned and fluttered, and seemed to have a will of its own. She longed to be on her own, sorting out her unruly emotions.

Georgie stared at his hands on the knife and fork, the broad fingernails, the strong fingers with a smattering of dark hair on each knuckle, the way the veins on the backs of his hands were raised. She watched his fingers grab a piece of bread and swipe some gravy with it. His hands were tanned, they would be warm ...

They returned to the hotel before the cool of night descended. He walked her to the room they occupied and opened the door. He bade Georgie enter before him, said goodnight and left her standing in the middle of the room, in the fading light. He locked her door from the outside.

A moment later and she heard the door to his room open. His footfalls stopped and then squeaking bed springs sounded. She imagined the next two thuds were his boots coming off, and then there was silence.

Georgie sighed and sat heavily on her bed, unnerved, frustrated and lonely. She thought she was worldly. She thought she knew the things she had to know to keep her alive in this world. But the world around her was a good deal harsher than she had been aware.

She threw herself back on the bed fully clothed, exhausted.

———

Dane wearied of the day and was ready for sleep. He pulled off his boots, stripped down to nothing and climbed between the musty sheets. His thoughts once again turned to Georgina, who slept in the room next to his.

He was not equipped to deal with a beautiful young girl who had little understanding of the wider world. Her confidence and natural grace belied her lack of experience. The threat to which she'd almost been exposed as she'd attempted once again to run had sobered him.

He would have to become equipped to deal with her. She was in his charge now whether she—or he—liked it or not. And not only that—he wanted her for himself. He wanted her spark and her fire in his life, he wanted her lively mind and her courage. How would he protect her, then, from what he wanted?

He closed his eyes a moment and pictured her slim body under his. He stirred uncomfortably. He wouldn't visit her again tonight. She would be his, though, of that he was certain, perhaps when she was more accustomed to living in the world he knew. Until then, he would have to find her a female companion, someone he could trust.

His thoughts turned to Angeline, Reuben's mother. She would take to Georgina like a hen over her chicks. Or there was Reuben's wife, Amelia … perhaps not, with youngsters of her own to take her time and attention. No, he would approach Angeline. If he sent her to Melbourne to live with Angeline and John, there would be no impropriety. He would visit her in his foster parents' home and there he would woo her.

He stretched his naked body. A loud sigh from the room next door reached his ears. He smiled and slept as comfortably as he could.

Twelve

The bright light of early morning woke him. He pulled on breeches and a shirt and left the room to ask for hot water to be sent up, thinking once again about the luxury of an indoors bathing room. He would definitely look into it for his tavern, as soon as he reached Sydney again. *If ever I do reach Sydney again.*

A young boy brought a bowl of steaming water. He took it, set it on the small dresser and began to soap his face for shaving.

Fifteen minutes later, clean and refreshed, he knocked on the adjoining door. When Georgina's muffled reply reached him, he said loudly, 'I've ordered some hot water for you. We'll go down and find some breakfast in thirty minutes.' He waited for her answer, a sleepy muttering, and finished dressing.

He'd woken with a clear thought that it would be better if they rode to Melbourne, after all, as opposed to taking the train. He reasoned that, although the horses would tire, they could stop and start as they pleased. He wondered idly if she'd be up to it, then checked himself. There was no doubt she would, she'd proven her excellent horsemanship.

Minutes later he heard a knock at her door and a woman calling, 'Miss?' Georgina answered and thanked the woman.

He waited a little time, impatiently checking his bags and pacing the room then, fed up, knocked again on the adjoining door.

When she answered, her freshly washed face, neatly combed and tied hair—fragranced with a light scent of roses that lingered in the air around him—took his breath.

'Morning,' he rasped, gazing at her.

'Good morning.' She briefly met his eyes.

'Ready?'

She nodded, gathered her bundle of clothes, neatly back in their package, and her bag, and followed him closely downstairs. She was dressed in the clothes she'd worn the day before.

He bought some freshly baked bread from the hotel kitchen, apples and a lump of beef jerky. It would have to do until he could find something more appetising, but it was early morning and the chances of any stores being open were slim. They trekked outside and around the back to the stables. The stablehand greeted them as if they were his long-lost friends.

Georgina eyed him warily. 'You said train.'

He shrugged. 'Now it's the horses.'

She asked for her saddle rather than the sidesaddle he ordered on Douglas for her. He took one look at her dress and shook his head. 'You never know who's going to be out in this country.' He finished saddling MacNamara and attached all her belongings to him. Georgina glumly eyed the sidesaddle.

Strapping the girth in place, Dane opened the saddlebags and rummaged for his map. He sat on a sawn-off lump of tree trunk outside MacNamara's stall and concentrated on the route south, calculating how many hours between stops, where to stop and where to buy food and drink.

He asked where he could fill his water flasks and the stable lad pointed a finger at a well.

As Dane pumped water, the boy helped Georgina into her saddle. 'You better be careful,' he warned, frowning as though to give depth to his advice.

He finished with the bottles, and turned to see the look of concern on Georgina's face. He gazed at her, trying to convey calm—the stable boy's warning caused him no concern—then tied the water bottles to MacNamara's saddle, mounted and left the stable. He nodded his thanks at the boy and tossed him a coin.

After they rode a little way out of town, Georgina following him, Dane indicated they should pull off the road.

'What is it?' she asked as he beckoned her to dismount. He pulled clothes from the bag tied to his saddle.

'Here.' He threw them over to her. 'I've changed my mind. It might be a good idea if you wore these after all.' As she grabbed the garments out of the air, he began to remove the sidesaddle from Douglas.

It was her old shirt and breeches, cleaned and patched. Mrs Rossmoyne must have fixed them. She gaped delightedly at him then glanced around, spotted a dense clump of bush and darted behind it. She emerged from the bush and packed her dress into the saddlebags on Douglas, who now bore her usual saddle. She grinned widely at him.

Dane had already remounted, eager to continue the ride. He'd removed his waistcoat and handed it to her. 'Wear this, too,' he ordered.

'I don't need it.' She swung onto Douglas's back.

'I say you do,' he replied. 'And do it up, all the way to your neck.'

She complied and then he turned MacNamara back to the road and galloped off.

Not two miles gone, they saw the riders in the distance. Dane slowed them up, their pace dropping to a canter.

He wheeled MacNamara around. 'If they're who I think they are, you'd better make a run for it back to Echuca.'

'What are you talking about?' she said, Douglas dancing under her.

'Dismount,' he directed as he slipped off MacNamara. 'That stable boy said there might be bushrangers out here and I think he was right.'

Georgina dismounted and held Douglas's reins tightly in her hands. MacNamara danced on the spot, and Douglas shied at him, bumping his hind quarters. Georgina shushed them both.

The riders slowed their approach and Dane felt Georgina step closer to him.

'Take MacNamara's reins and mount up.' He handed her the reins. 'If I yell, bolt out of here and back to town. Do you understand?' He pressed her hands in his, a brief squeeze of encouragement.

'Yes.' She swung into MacNamara's saddle. She edged the horse as close to Dane as possible, but he was feigning concern at Douglas's fetlock.

'Try to look like a boy, would you?' he muttered between his teeth and handed her up his hat. She crammed it onto her head.

The horsemen, eight or so, were only a couple of hundred yards away. As they pulled kerchiefs up over their faces they bent low on their mounts and, as one, rushed forward in a gallop.

'Get going. Run for it,' Dane barked.

'Dane—' Her eyes met his.

'I'll head away, then turn back to Echuca. Go.'

Still she hesitated but he cracked MacNamara hard on the rump. The horse darted forward. She turned him sharply and took off but not before Dane swung onto Douglas's back. He galloped in the other direction.

———

Georgie flew across the open country, Dane's hat lost in the first couple of leaps. MacNamara pulled harder with every stride, and with her encouragement he unleashed a surge of power. She hugged his neck as they raced back to Echuca. She didn't even turn to look behind her—the gang of riders would not chase her into town, and if they attempted to, she would easily outrun them.

It was too late to do anything for Dane even if she could have helped. She would notify the police at Echuca and let them handle it.

He will be all right ... he will be all right ...

The township came up quickly and her only thought was to get to the police, then to the wharf as soon as possible. She'd won her reprieve—her next stop would be Conor Foley.

She galloped hard into the main street, shouting for directions to the police station. Pedestrians jumped out of her way, waving their arms in alarm, others pointed her further north. She hauled up at the little police station, dismounted, threw the reins around a veranda pole and burst into the office. She stood taking in great gulps of air.

Two men, seated on either side of a sturdy desk, stared at her. One wore a uniform and the other, a blond-haired man, was in shirtsleeves and trousers.

'You must—'

'Speak when you're spoken to, boy.' The uniformed trooper's pinched face soured at her.

'I don't think it's a boy, sergeant,' the blond-haired man said. 'Miss, Sergeant Love here will help—'

Georgie waved her arms. 'I don't have time to be polite— I—
we were riding just out of town. Bushrangers—'

'Bushrangers?' Sergeant Love shot out of his seat.

The other man frowned. 'Close to town? Which direction?'

'South.' She was still breathless. 'And they're after my—my
brother.'

The blond man strode out the door, across the narrow veranda
and onto the dusty main road.

The sergeant followed, grabbing his hat on the way out. 'Now,
Harry, wait for a couple of us troop—'

'Get moving, man,' Harry shouted over his shoulder. 'We may
be able to catch them up.'

Georgie ran outside and watched as the two men shouted orders
into the street. The blond man leapt onto a waiting horse tied
up out the front, and galloped down the street, shouting names.
Men, uniformed and otherwise, poured out of a few shops and
the hotel, mounted horses and followed him at a gallop out of
town.

It happened so fast she didn't realise she was free.

Yet she was. They were gone.

But wait—she glimpsed the blond man ride back into town via
the back street behind the hotel. That couldn't be right ... he'd
been very keen to get out on the road. She must have mistaken—

No matter. Get going. Conor awaits.

She took up MacNamara's reins, and stood for some moments
rubbing his face and crooning softly to him. MacNamara stamped
and snorted his frustration at the run being cut short. He'd need
a rub down before anything else. She reached into the bags tied
to the saddle and groped around for her money bag, pulling it out
and tucking it against her body under Dane's heavy waistcoat.

She headed for the stables behind the Pastoral Hotel, leading
MacNamara at a steady pace. As she coaxed the big horse the final

few steps inside the main doorway, voices reached her from the stalls.

'Who was it they bailed up, Eddie?' a gruff voice demanded.

'I don't know his name, but he stayed at the hotel here last night. Shouldn't be difficult to find out.' The stable boy's voice.

'Would they have got anything from him?'

Georgie began to move MacNamara towards the stall from where the voices came, but the lad's answer stopped her short.

'Think they must've, Mr B. He had a coupla heavy bags with him, and even came back to check on them last night. Reckon he was good for it. Hope the boys grabbed some for me.' He chuckled. 'Though I 'druther have his big black horse.'

Georgie hardly breathed.

'An' there was a girl wi' him.'

'I know that. She was the one to raise the alarm. Jesus Christ, I hope the boys haven't done anything stupid. I told them to stay clear of town.'

Georgie began ever so slowly to turn MacNamara around. She lifted one foot to the stirrup ...

The stable lad let out a yell at her and she faltered, her foot slipping to the ground. She steadied, flicked the reins smartly at MacNamara, who shied, backed up and pushed his weight around to bump the stall door shut, trapping the two men. She took off on foot and ran as fast as she could.

She ran through town, rounded the bend at the end of the shops, and charged along the grassy hill to where the river and the paddle-steamers came into view. She kept on, heard shouts behind her, and dared not slow even to catch her breath.

Sliding down the dirt slope then taking one great stride after another, she stumbled onto the wharf, going down on all fours. She stopped for a moment, dragging in air, gulping it down, and steadied. She glanced over the edge of the wharf, the water some yards down, and could just make out a familiar-looking boat tied up much further away. She thudded along the boardwalk, eliciting much amusement from the workers, one or two of whom tried to stop her.

'Conor Foley, Conor Foley,' she muttered as she pushed her way past. She imagined she could hear the two men from the stables close behind her. Near panic, she gulped painfully, glancing wildly here and there, hoping to see—

Ranald Finn's *Lady Goodnight* was almost at the cranes. She dragged her legs into a run again, began to shout for Finn as she bore down on the boat. Then the majestic line of the *Lady Mitchell* chugged into the port area and took her breath away altogether. Tears blurred her vision.

And because she kept running towards the *Goodnight*, and heard Ranald Finn yell up to her, 'Miss Georgina—be careful,' she didn't see the thick bow rope coiled across her path.

She tripped, landing face first on the wharf above Mr Finn's paddle-steamer.

Thirteen

Douglas tried valiantly to answer Dane's commands for more speed. He thundered through the bush, weaving where he could to avoid the thick entanglements of Wimmera scrub. Dane hugged his neck and urged him harder.

The gang of men behind him shouted curses as they plunged into the dense vegetation. Dane knew that had they been on a plain, they would have overtaken him by now. The shouts sounded for some distance, then after a while he could hear nothing. He hauled Douglas to a stop, allowing the horse to dance as he cooled down. They made another circle or two and stopped. Dane couldn't hear any noise except his own and the horse's heaving breaths. Douglas was blowing hard and his muscles twitched after the exertion. Dane reassured him with a couple of hard pats to his flank and started back to the road.

He moved as quietly as he could through the bush, knowing the men had not given him up totally. He rode across and back over the dense scrub until he was satisfied they were not lying in wait for him. He dismounted close to the main road and allowed Douglas to feed.

He reached into the saddlebags and his hand settled on the dress Georgina had swapped earlier in the day in favour of the breeches. It would have to do. He gave a silent apology to May Rossmoyne as he tore great strips from it and began to dry Douglas.

He thought hard as he worked. Georgina would have made it back to Echuca. He wouldn't leave her.

Besides, all the papers he needed for the solicitors were with her on MacNamara. He needed them to try to square this unpleasant business of his father's, but that would have to wait until he found her, until he knew she was safe. And he could be no more than half an hour or so from Echuca. There wouldn't be much time lost … providing he could find her.

He wiped the sweat from the saddle and waited a few minutes while it dried off completely in the noonday sun. Douglas had found a patch of grass and still nipped at it, so Dane waited another few minutes before he saddled up again, mounted and rode cautiously back to Echuca.

He tied Douglas at the front of shops at one end of town. He stopped a couple of pedestrians to ask if she'd been seen—a girl in boys' clothes. They waved towards the police station, clearly not impressed.

He headed for the station and when he entered the office, came upon two troopers hurling abuse at each other. The argument continued even as he walked between the two men, one hefty and hairy, the other tall and slight.

He shouted them down: 'I need some information.'

Hefty turned on him. 'What is it, mate? We're in the middle of a police matter here.'

Dane watched the other man retreat, red-faced, behind a desk. He addressed both of them. 'I'm looking for a young woman who may have been seeking assistance from you earlier today.'

Hefty shook his head, glanced at the red-faced man. 'Description?'

'A dark-haired young woman in boys' clothing, about yea tall.' Dane indicated his shoulder.

'No, mate. Didn't see her in here. Check with the boss. He's across the road at the pub.'

Dane ran to the Bridge Hotel. The first person he spotted inside was a blond-haired man who was surrounded by three or four men all talking at once, all agitated. When the man saw Dane enter, he held up his hand and the conversation died away.

The men looked at Dane and for an instant it was quiet inside. The blond man issued a curt command, 'Get lost,' and the group dispersed. He turned away from Dane and settled back into a chair, papers scattered on a small table in front of him.

Dane continued to the bar, towards a trooper. 'Your men at the station directed me here,' he said. 'I'm looking for a young woman who may have needed some assistance earlier today.'

Dane went through Georgina's description again. The trooper shook his head. Dane added she was wearing boys' clothes.

'And riding a magnificent black horse. Yes,' the trooper said. 'She was here—Harry? Harry, that girl dressed in boys' clothes—where did she go?' he called across to the blond man seated at his little table. And to Dane he said, 'And you are her brother?'

Dane hesitated before nodding. 'Yes.'

'She came into the station to alert us. You did very well to beat those bushrangers, my man, but we couldn't find hide nor hair of them.' He clapped Dane on the back with a hand as big as a shovel. 'Harry,' he called to the blond man again as he walked Dane over to him. 'This here's the fellow who beat those damned bushies. Here, meet Harry Bolton—and your name, sir?'

Harry Bolton stood up, extended his hand.

'MacHenry, of Jacaranda, out from Swan Hill. I'm grateful for any light you can shed ... '

Harry Bolton sized him up a moment. 'Can't tell you much, Mr MacHenry. She ran like a mad thing in the direction of the wharf the moment she'd stabled the horse and we've not been able to find her either.'

'The wharf?'

'Aye.' Bolton glanced at the trooper then rubbed a hand over his mouth. 'Your horse, however, is well looked after and can be retrieved from the stables behind the Pastoral. Perhaps you were thinking to sell him?'

'Thank you. And no, my horse is not for sale. I'll head for the wharf now, and be back later for my horse.' He nodded at both men and took his leave, realising with a jolt that if he didn't find Georgina, he would be taking two horses to Melbourne on his own.

When he reached the wharf he strode out on the boardwalk, looking over the side at the boats below, weighing up the possibility Georgina might well be on one of them. Most were clearly trade boats, some loaded high with wool bales and timber crates, pulling barges, hardly the sort of vessel a young girl would head towards. Then why on earth would she come to the wharf? Something niggled at the back of his mind, something to do with the paddle-steamers, but he couldn't remember what. He paced, thinking, trying to sort his thoughts.

A smooth gliding vessel caught his eye. He could see her name on the wheelhouse and stared a moment at the beautiful *Lady Mitchell* slowly making her way out of the port area.

It struck him then, that niggle. Elspeth had rattled on about a riverboat captain. Was that his boat—the *Lady Mitchell*? How it connected to his present task he didn't know, but it kept at him. He couldn't reach the thought, and shrugged again, confounded.

He stood for a moment on the wharf, the busyness of the men and the cranes working proving no distraction.

I've lost her.

His chest pained with a peculiar heaviness.

He didn't know what else to do to find her. If nobody had seen her, how could he hope to track her? With his head down, he watched his feet scuff at bits of debris. He turned towards the town.

I've lost her.

Nothing prepared him for the loss. He'd had her under his wing, and as quick as a blink, she was gone. His heart hurt, and his breath was jagged in his throat. A girl, a headstrong, wilful, intelligent girl ... and he was besotted. Worse than besotted—he was bereft.

He stopped as he noticed another small carrier, its name written over the stern: *Lady Goodnight*. Two men worked the tie ropes, then began clearing empty cargo crates out of their way onto the foredeck. They reached for the ropes and untied bales of wool stacked high on the deck.

'G'day,' the shorter one called up to Dane and tipped his cap. The other nodded. They continued to toil as he looked down on them.

'Looks to me like yer got the world on yer shoulders, mate,' Shorty ventured, shoving a bale towards the other man.

Dane gave a short laugh. 'I have at that.' He pushed a hand through his hair. 'You haven't by chance sighted a young woman along here, have you?'

The shorter man straightened and looked up. 'Plenty of them wandering past,' he said. The other man jumped below deck. 'Yer in the wrong place though, if it's a bit of puss yer after.'

'Not that. She's a young woman from my family.'

Another man, weather-beaten, wiry and tall, stepped onto the deck. 'And which young woman would that be, sir?' he called.

'Lost perhaps. She was wearing boys' clothes, had been riding hard before she got lost.'

The tall man folded his arms. 'I'm Ranald Finn, the captain of this vessel.' He waved his arm behind him. 'Your name, sir?'

'I am Dane MacHenry and she was in my charge—'

'MacHenry, is it?' Finn interrupted. 'Well, Mr MacHenry, Miss Georgina is being well looked after.'

'What do you say?'

'She was in a state of fright, sir, when she arrived here. She is known to us from our stops at Jacaranda. I believe you've been away for some years.' Finn squinted as he looked Dane up and down.

'That's right, but that's naught to do with it. Where is she?' Dane's heart rate escalated. She was close by, he knew it. He could feel it.

'Well, sir, as I said, she is well looked after. You have my word for it.'

'Mr Finn, where is she?' Dane demanded. 'How do I know she is well looked after?'

'You don't know, except for what I'm telling you.' Captain Finn waited a heavy second or two. 'As we do not know what might have transpired while Miss Georgina was in your—ah, charge.'

Dane's hands clenched at his side. 'That is an unwarranted accusation—'

Ranald Finn eyed him for a moment, then waved his hand towards the *Lady Mitchell*, almost gone around the bend and out of sight. 'We settled Miss Georgina on the *Lady Mitchell* to return her to your father's homestead. The journey will take a few days, as you well know, but I can assure you she is in the best of hands. You can go about your business.' Captain Finn dismissed him, leaving the deck with a curt nod.

Dane stared for a moment after the captain and shook his head. He rubbed his face, then clenched and unclenched his fists.

The other men stood by watching, waiting.

There was no reason for him to challenge the river man. The captain seemed no ruffian. The fact he'd spoken of Dane's family lent integrity to his story. That and the fact the captain had known of Georgina's time spent with Dane.

He watched the *Lady Mitchell* slip around the bend. Even if he charged off after it, he'd be a mad fool ... chances were Captain Finn had issued orders not to stop for anyone along the way. Dane had no way of reaching Georgina.

He turned abruptly and stalked back to the hotel stables. He would let events take their course. He would collect MacNamara, head down the street to retrieve Douglas and be on his way. Georgina couldn't get off the paddle-steamer until it docked at Jacaranda—or she wouldn't, if she knew what was good for her.

She would be safe at the homestead, albeit at the mercy of his mother's wrath.

He would be back from Melbourne soon after if he rode hard and finished his business with the solicitor quickly. And after that he would return to Jacaranda and deal with her.

Fourteen

'*What?*' Dane shot forward in his seat and stared at the solicitor.

'That's correct, Mr MacHenry. Jacaranda was signed over some time ago to a, ah—a Mr Conor Foley.' Mortimer P Tawse peered at Dane over his spectacles. 'Obviously, you didn't know.'

Dane slumped back into his chair. 'Obviously.'

Mr Tawse stood up, his lanky frame unwinding from the chair. 'Here,' he said, offering a splash of pale green liquid in a glass to Dane, before pouring himself an equally generous shot. 'A fine absinthe. Brought it back with me on my last visit to the old country.' He glided back into his chair and took a sip from his glass. 'Guaranteed to fix almost everything.'

Absinthe. Dear God. All he needed. Dane sat his drink on Mr Tawse's desk, his arms resting on his knees. 'Why? Why did my father lie to me—what good would that do?'

'I can see you're clearly shaken by the, uh, turn of events.'

'I am. I've ridden long and hard to get here hoping I could turn things around, only to find it was a useless waste of time.' Dane wiped his palms over his dusty trousers. 'I apologise again for my untidiness. I've had no time for bathing.'

'No matter. As for your father, it is pride, I suspect, Mr MacHenry. Nevertheless, I'm afraid he has sent you on a wild goose chase. Perhaps he had hoped by sending you here with a document stipulating another interested party he might stave off the inevitable. However, I assure you, everything is in order with the paperwork and the contract of sale.' He leaned over the desk to tap the bound papers and continued, 'I received notice from Mr Foley's solicitors some time ago regarding the situation and although the whole affair was conducted in, shall we say, an eccentric manner, it nevertheless holds as a legal document. By and large, your father, in effect, sold his property to Mr Foley and there are signed witnesses to that.'

Dane changed his mind and took a mouthful of absinthe. 'My father sent me here with this—this—' he shook the wad of papers, '—useless rubbish, hoping I could contest what's-his-name becoming the owner of the property.'

Mr Tawse spread his long, bony hands. 'It would seem so, but to no avail, as I'm sure you now understand. The property legally belongs to somebody else. All the necessary financial commitments were also met by the purchaser. Your father knows he has no comeback, regrettably for him. It is far too late in the day for him to be hoping to regain his ownership.'

Dane scowled. 'These papers state I am a partner in the family business. It was sold without my consultation.'

Mr Tawse cleared his throat. 'I'm very sorry, Mr MacHenry, but those papers are dated incorrectly, for a start.'

'Well, fix them.'

Mr Tawse's sympathetic look hardened visibly. His long fingers drummed the desk. 'That I cannot do, sir. Perhaps another solicitor would assist, but neither I nor any of my partners would. In any case, it would do you no good. The fraud would be uncovered immediately. There were witnesses to the game who have signed sworn declarations—'

'What *game*?'

'Oh, come now, young fellow. You must know of the game.' Mr Tawse sighed loudly. He left his glass on the desk and smoothed his pate. He sniffed. 'Am I now to believe you don't know the circumstances of this peculiar sale was via a game of cards? Poker, to be exact.'

Dane sat stunned for another second or two. He simply shook his head.

'Mr MacHenry. This is very awkward.' Mr Tawse steepled his fingers and rested them on his nose. He sighed again. 'But I venture I could handle your father's vengeance if he chose to exact it. Tell me first what you have been led to believe.'

Dane spread his hands. 'That my uncle in England was squandering money, given to him by my parents, getting himself in debt. My father blamed him and his problems. I have since learned the opposite is the truth. And now this.' He swallowed the remainder of his drink in one gulp. 'A game of cards, you say?' He remembered his own game of cards.

Tawse nodded. 'Well. At this point it seems your father was, er, inebriated, and challenged Mr Foley to a sort of duel with poker instead of swords, or pistols, thankfully. The practice was once the paddle-steamer—the *Lady Mitchell*, I believe—docked at Jacaranda, a card game would be organised. Mr Foley was quite a regular visitor.'

Dane frowned. 'You know a lot about the business at Jacaranda.'

'It was my business until the contract of sale settled. Yours also, Mr MacHenry.'

Dane swallowed the rebuke. He had gone his merry way with his life. He had sent money for Jacaranda and the family and expected it was well looked after with his father at the helm. And why should he have thought otherwise? There was no indication in these last four years things were not well. There had been only that last letter.

'Surely this Foley could be approached—?'

'He must have wanted the property very much, Mr MacHenry. And no—' Tawse held up his hand as Dane started forward. 'There was no impropriety at the game, if that's what you're thinking. But where material wealth is concerned there are always more businessmen than gentlemen, Mr MacHenry.'

Dane waited as Mr Tawse refilled his own glass. 'Is that all?' he asked.

'It is all I know.'

'So this Conor Foley owns Jacaranda?'

'Yes.'

Dane stood abruptly and extended his hand. 'Thank you, Mr Tawse, for your hospitality and your honesty. I apologise for my manners.'

'I understand. But there really is nothing I can do. Nor can you, for that matter.' He stood and shook Dane's hand.

Dane headed for the door then turned back to Mr Tawse. 'Do I owe your office, Mr Tawse?'

'For today, no. I am happy to have spoken with you. And as for the previously unpaid debts, they have all been cleared by Mr Foley.'

Dane's jaw clenched. 'I see. I'm grateful to you. Thank you.' He left the Collins Street office quietly seething, the alcohol burning in his belly.

Astride MacNamara and tugging Douglas along behind, he made a weary journey over the Punt Road Bridge to the Cawley residence in South Yarra.

By the time he arrived, the fire in his belly had cooled. The imposing white stucco house, with pillars at the front portal, a second storey and a tower room, stood in timeless welcome to him. The gardens were lush with lawn and shrubbery clearly thriving in the early Melbourne spring.

One of the groundsmen, Ben, greeted him and as Dane dismounted, took the reins of the horses. He shouted for Mr Johnson, the butler, who appeared at the front door of the house to usher Dane inside and deliver him to the Cawleys' drawing room.

Amid the flurry of activity surrounding him and the look of horror on Angeline's face at his appearance, he managed a weak grin. 'I apologise, Angeline. I am in a filthy state, one to match my mood.'

He vigorously shook John Cawley's hand then bowed over Angeline's, though she protested again at his dirty garb.

'You will get to a bath this instant, Dane MacHenry. Do not sit on any of my chairs before you smell sweeter and look more like the man I know.' Angeline raised her arm to point him in the right direction.

John Cawley spoke up. 'My dear, Johnson will already be preparing a bath for Dane.' He clapped Dane on each shoulder. 'So happy to see you, my boy. Two years is too long.'

Dane nodded at John and then at Angeline then wearily took the stairs to his room.

When he got there, staff had laid out fresh clothes and a deep bath was being prepared, already half full with hot water. He wasted no time stripping down and stepping in. Johnson came through the door with two men lugging more tubs. They poured the water in, just hot enough to bear.

Johnson hovered. 'A back brush, Mr Dane,' he said and handed over the long-handled brush. 'The soap is here, and the towel's on the chair.'

'Thank you, Mr Johnson.' Dane always addressed the butler the same way.

'Just Johnson, sir.' Johnson always corrected him.

They nodded at each other, and Johnson left the room.

Dane sank into the heat and thought of nothing but the luxury of being back in this elegant home. He scrubbed the dirt of travel from his body.

He couldn't think straight on the loss of Jacaranda. He would put it from his mind until he could speak to John.

Georgina. He couldn't think straight on her either and found his bathing harder to achieve. He wanted to sink under the water and languish there in the guilt of leaving her. His physical reaction to the memory of her legs under the horse blanket and the brush of her breast as he changed her shirt didn't help. He banished her from his mind and then easily finished his ablutions.

Dressed in a fine white cotton shirt and dark breeches and waistband, he returned to the elegant morning room where tea was being served on silver service. He smiled to himself. His troubles never seemed heavy in this house. He wished his mother had been brought to these magnificent heights, but it was not to be. And now, never to be. Certainly not by his father.

'I can see by those dark circles under your eyes, and the fact that you have lost weight, not to mention a slight sprinkle of silver at your temples, that you have had a hard time of it these last couple of years.' Angeline Cawley waited until he sat. 'Now, tell us everything.'

So he told his story. He wasn't after pity or assistance, just an understanding ear and the friendship he knew would be there.

'That is just a terrible thing about your old home. We will think on that later.' Angeline's dark eyes flicked to her husband then back to the young man. 'We have never questioned your family life, Dane, although we would have enjoyed meeting your parents and to have them visit.' She straightened her skirts and took a refill for her cup of tea.

Dane stared at the level of tea in his own cup.

'Angeline,' John Cawley said, 'leave the boy be.'

'I have despaired of ever meeting your mother, and often wonder if she knows anything of us. I doubt it.'

'My dear Angeline,' Dane said quietly. 'If you glare at me any harder I will turn inside out. My mother does know of you. But her circumstances—'

'Your youth has disappeared behind a handsome mature face.' She studied him. 'I like the age on you. Are you being straight as a die, Dane MacHenry?'

'Ange, what sort of question is that?' John Cawley asked.

'Methinks there's more to this story, Dane.'

Dane smiled. 'How on earth can you divine anything else from this unfortunate tale, Angeline?'

'Call it a mother's intuition.'

John looked at his wife. 'I fear one of your revelations coming on.'

'I did detect the presence of a young woman somewhere in this terrible story, didn't I?'

'Of course you detect a young woman, just look at the lad. He's probably got more than one young woman on a string.'

Dane remained silent. He had told the entire story, only leaving out his very ungallant treatment of Georgina; that was expressly to save himself from Angeline's chiding. He didn't think he'd given Georgina any more attention in his story than was necessary.

'This girl,' Angeline prompted.

'Woman, is nothing of the man's business sacred?'

'Not in my house, John Cawley. And I know enough about this young man to have the right to ask. Now,' she addressed Dane again, 'is this girl a terrible burden on your conscience, or is she merely a thorn in your side? I am of the sudden belief—aided by your silence on the matter—that she is somewhat more important to you than you would have us believe.'

Dane knew, as did Reuben, that very little escaped Angeline's notice. 'She is unmarried, and very, very attractive. And I was alone with her on many an occasion.' He looked at his cup again, then drained its contents.

'Dane,' Angeline cried.

'My dear. Do not pry so.'

'John, please, no exasperation. He is like my own son to me and I treat him accordingly.'

'Angeline, I behaved in a most gentlemanly way towards her. Mostly. How could I not?' He spread his hands innocently.

'Mostly?' She eyed him again. 'Now tell me the truth, young man.'

John harrumphed into his tea.

Angeline straightened in her chair. 'All of it.'

Georgina Calthorpe. He related everything, but neglected to mention he'd entertained ideas of marriage; Angeline would have made immediate wedding plans for him, with or without a bride present. And there was the unhappy situation of Georgina being returned to Jacaranda.

By telling the tale to Angeline, his heart had begun to lighten again. He wanted to see Georgina before too much time had lapsed.

'And what was her name again, dear?' Angeline asked.

'Georgina Calthorpe,' Dane replied, and his thoughts drifted.

John spoke up. 'My dear, now we've heard the gossip, we need to hear about the Captain's Cabin and how to sort something out to help his family. The man needs an injection of funds.'

Fifteen

Conor Foley watched as Georgina sighed in her sleep. She shook her head feebly and he placed his hand on her forehead.

'Truly, Mr Foley. She'll be all right now,' the nurse said kindly to him. She was a slender woman, plain but pleasant in her demeanour. She smiled.

Foley looked up at the nurse. 'It's been nearly a week, Mrs Jenkins.'

'Mr Foley. Those bad bruises and bumps would have sent a weaker lass off for a month or more. We administered the drops early enough to keep her comfortable and now we have to wait and see. Your fiancée, sir, she's—'

'Yes, yes, but when will she wake up?'

'It's a wonder that sort of fall didn't kill her. Now, you must leave the room, sir. You are entirely too agitated. Come along.' She held her hand out for him to rise from his bedside vigil and leave the room.

Foley muttered and growled all the way downstairs.

His Melbourne home in Hawthorn, a two-storey, five-bedroom mansion, had been occupied by his widowed sister Kate Hannaford for these past six or seven years and she had kept it beautifully, refitting the place to her taste. The gardens were especially beautiful as Kate had worked in them herself, overseeing the caretakers and his small band of gardeners. She favoured natives for the climate so the gum trees were not removed, and saplings were planted. Small exotic shrubs dotted the planter beds and rows of herbs ordered the stately elegance of roses. So it was Kate who had met him at the door when he'd burst into the place with the bedraggled body of a sick girl in his arms.

The shock of seeing Georgina carefully tucked up in a bunk on his boat, Ranald Finn's *Lady Goodnight*, had taken its toll. She held much for his future.

He'd hired a nurse, widowed Mrs Jenkins, to travel with him, and as he'd been too impatient to wait for the next morning's train, he hired a coach and driver.

Mrs Jenkins had loudly protested his plan.

'Mr Foley! I assure you your charge is well enough under the circumstances for train travel, but she doesn't need any nonsense bouncing about in a rackety old cart that calls itself a carriage.'

Foley had raged until he booked passage on the train to Melbourne that afternoon.

On their arrival at his house in Melbourne close to midnight, Kate had taken over with a tired but efficient Mrs Jenkins in tow. Foley had stormed around to his own doctor's rooms to drag the man out of his bed. The doctor had been less than impressed and insisted he would visit at first light on the morrow.

In the morning, Kate had thought it wise that the nurse working with Conor's doctor examine the girl for any injury that may not be apparent. She was relieved, for her brother's sake, that the examination cleared any lingering doubts about the girl's health. Georgie had not been assaulted in any way.

The doctor declared there was nothing more to do. 'Perhaps you have been a little heavy handed with the laudanum drops, but she seems comfortable enough. She'll wake soon. And no more of that drug, if you please, Mr Foley. And for yourself, keep calm.'

Foley was banished from the sick room and Kate took to monitoring the bathing of the young woman, dressing her hair and clothing her. At first he had raged around the house, his anger directed at the MacHenrys, blaming them for whatever had befallen Georgina.

'For heaven's sake, Conor, you're ranting and raving like a mad thing over these MacHenry people. You're sending me into a nervous state and could most likely hasten your own demise,' Kate complained. 'Be still.'

''Twas not only for Georgina, Kate. Ensuring her safety meant I had to forgo the purchase of my new boat in Echuca. The builder required payment on the day agreed and I had to let the deal fall through. It'll be some months before I can secure another good boat.'

Kate looked her brawny brother up and down. 'I see that love for her has not changed your love for your money and your boats.'

'The boat was important, but more so is Georgina.'

'As it should be, Conor. I am pleased to see you are at least shame-faced.'

Foley looked away.

With each passing day, his temper grew worse as Georgina's health grew stronger. 'What on earth is keeping her from waking up?' he shouted.

'Really, Conor,' Kate admonished. 'Anyone would think the poor girl was sleeping just to aggravate you. For heaven's sake, the doctor said it could take quite a long time—be patient, please.' She dropped her needlepoint to her lap in exasperation. 'I have heard the drug is not as innocent as we have been led to believe. She could sleep for a while longer yet.'

Foley, who stood by the mantelpiece, a rum in his hand, shook his big head. 'I know, I know.'

'She's very beautiful, Conor.' Kate retrieved her work and pretended to concentrate on it. 'And young,' she commented, softly.

'She's twenty-two. Don't you talk to me about "young", Katie Hannaford. You weren't even seventeen years old when you married Peter, God rest his soul,' he reminded her, rising to the bait.

'Oh ho, big brother,' Kate mocked. 'And tell me, has she consented to being your wife?'

'Don't take on so. And no, not yet.' He sipped his drink.

Kate's brows arched. 'You chased her all over the countryside and you don't even know if she'll say yes?'

Foley gave his sister a look but remained silent.

'So, if you're to be married then, I shall no longer be mistress of your household.'

'That's right, sister, I'll put you out on the street,' he said. 'Don't be ridiculous, Katie. You know this is your home forever.'

'Oh, but I must go, Conor.' She rested her needlepoint again and folded one hand over the other. 'You see, you've been so taken up with your lady love you've not noticed my newest acquisition.' She waved her left hand at him slowly, and he caught a glimpse of white fire. She laughed gaily as his brows shot up.

'What—you and Angus Forrestor?'

'The very same.'

Foley set his drink on the mantelpiece and hugged his sister tightly. 'I am more than pleased, my dear Katie. This is wonderful news. You've been alone far too long now,' he said, gripping her until she winced. 'And Peter would have approved, too. Good for you.' He released her, took his rum and raised it in salute.

Mrs Jenkins knocked and entered smartly, the soft swish of her plain dress a whisper in the room.

'What is it—what's the matter?' Foley demanded, rum slopping over his hand in his agitation.

'Our patient is awake, Mr Foley. Would you like a couple of minutes?'

But Foley threw back the last of his drink and thrust the glass at Kate. He bounded out of the room and up the stairs before the nurse could finish speaking.

Georgina sat propped up by numerous pillows and she smiled weakly as Foley burst into the room. 'Good morning,' she offered.

'Good afternoon,' he answered gruffly and then dropped to the floor by her side. He took one of her hands in his and kissed it. He studied her face. It was pale, but her eyes were clear, if sleepy. She smelled of freshly applied scent, her hair had been brushed and her nightgown changed. He suspected she'd been awake for some time and that Mrs Jenkins had helped her pretty up. She had lost weight, but as those gorgeous eyes regarded him evenly, he knew she was well on the road to recovery.

'That silly woman wanted me to sleep some more. I feel like I've been asleep for a month,' she complained. 'My head is foggy.'

'You've been asleep for a week, by and large too long. I can now let Jemimah know—'

'Oh no, Conor, don't let them know where I am.' She groped for his other hand and held it as tightly as she could. 'They don't want me there. I don't want to go—I came looking for you … '

'Shush, shush, shush.' He touched a finger to her lips. 'You're miles from them. You're here at my house in Melbourne and you'll stay as long as you wish.'

'In Melbourne.' Her eyes grew wide.

He reached into his coat pocket. 'Perhaps this will convince you how I feel,' he said as he withdrew the small box. 'I hope this means you'll stay as long as we both wish.'

Her eyes left his and focused on the glowing ruby. It was as big as her little fingernail, and set in a delicate band of gold.

Foley took it from the box and slipped it on her wedding finger. 'It hardly does you justice, my dear Georgie.'

'Oh,' she whispered and sank back on the pillows, closing her eyes momentarily. Then she looked up at him, a frown on her face. She shook her head just a little and looked back at her hand.

He waited for her to speak. He couldn't read what was in her eyes. It occurred to him then that she was not as excited about her engagement as she could have been. He chided himself. *Even I can see she's still not quite recovered. Of course she's excited—she's still not well enough ... what a fool I am ... what a damn fool—*

'Will you marry me, Georgina?' he asked, clarifying his intentions.

He became alarmed as her eyes filled with tears. He was just about to jump up and call the nurse when Kate joined them.

'May I come in?' she enquired, already well and truly inside the room, Mrs Jenkins on her heels.

'Of course,' Foley cried, suddenly distracted from his purpose, ill at ease, as if caught at something he should not have been doing. 'Georgina—my sister, Mrs Hannaford—'

Kate brushed Foley aside and sat on the edge of the big bed. 'I am Katie, my dear.'

'She needs to rest some more, Mrs Hannaford,' Mrs Jenkins interrupted.

'Are you all right, my dear?' Kate asked and placed the palm of her hand on Georgina's forehead. The nurse fluttered over to the two of them, Foley immediately on the outer.

'Yes, thank you,' Georgina said. 'But my head is starting to ache.'

'Perhaps it is the breath of rum all over you.' She glanced at Foley over her shoulder and waved a hand under her nose. He scowled. 'A powder, please, Mrs Jenkins, no more of the drops,' Kate ordered. Her gaze dropped to the ring on Georgina's finger as she held her hands. 'Oh,' she cried, giving Mrs Jenkins a start. 'Oh, how absolutely exquisite.' Katie held Georgina's hand up to the light for the nurse to admire the ring.

Nurse Jenkins moved. 'Please, everyone. This is quite enough for one day. Now, out you go, yes, even you, Mrs Hannaford. This is too much at the moment. We need some more rest.'

———

Georgie's head ached, her arm ached where Kate had held it aloft to gaze at her engagement ring, her heart ached and she wanted to cry. She bit her lip.

Once Mrs Jenkins had delivered the required powder and cleared the room, Georgie fell asleep almost immediately. In her dreams, the enormous weight of the ring on her finger felt like a yoke on her neck.

Her groaning had brought the nurse to her side, shaking her awake, fearful of a fever. Her medical enquiries satisfied, the nurse allowed Georgie some more sleep, tucking her in.

'I'll be right in there if you need me,' Mrs Jenkins said, indicating the small servant's room.

Georgie watched her go, her eyelids dropping with fatigue.

Engaged to Conor Foley. Everything I wanted …

Before Dane MacHenry.

———

Georgina's convalescence took little time. She and Kate took long walks in the extensive gardens, enveloped in the early season's scent of eucalyptus from the towering gums. Wafts of delicate perfume from the Alba roses Kate had been instrumental in planting accompanied their mornings.

Kate found the girl to be quiet and withdrawn, far from Foley's description of her. At first Kate put it down to Georgina's ordeal, but as September withdrew and October gloried in the full onset of spring flowers, and still there was no change, Kate realised something was amiss.

She decided, one afternoon, to draw the girl out. Someone needed to do it, especially as the girl had no family to assist her in times of uncertainty. She would have to inform Conor if the problem did not have an easy solution.

On a garden bench, Kate began the conversation with some news of her own. 'I want you to be the first to know, Georgina, but you mustn't tell a soul.'

'You have a date?' Georgina cried.

'Yes, sometime in December, a summer wedding and hopefully in this garden.'

'How very wonderful.' Georgina clasped Kate's hands joyfully. 'Oh, how lovely, and in this beautiful garden.'

'Why don't you and Conor plan to marry with us? Don't you think that's a grand idea?' She squeezed Georgina's hands.

Georgina stiffened. 'Oh, but—'

'You haven't named the date already, have you, dear, and not told me?' Kate asked.

'Oh, no—we haven't ... '

Kate sat back. 'You've gone a shade of white, Georgina. What on earth is the matter?'

Georgina removed her hands from Kate's. 'Oh, it's my fault, Katie. I'm sure Conor would marry me tomorrow if he could. But I can't quite seem to settle down to it just yet. I thought I could ... all this time and before, but I can't seem to.' She closed her eyes, the heels of her hands on her brows.

Kate straightened. So, Georgina was unsure about marrying. And why would that be? She patted the girl's arm. Conor had told her Georgina had accepted his offer unconditionally, yet this did not seem to be the case.

'Oh, my dear Georgina,' Kate began. 'Forgive me, but is it because your heart lies with another?'

Georgina's eyes flew open. 'Oh no, not my heart. No, no, no. Just my thoughts ... and only sometimes—'

'My dear girl,' Kate cried and took her by the shoulders. 'You must realise Conor loves you heartily. You mustn't make him wait too long for an answer. I can see you love him.'

'It's just that ... all of a sudden having someone to blurt it out to seems to make things more ... real. I wanted to be with Conor, that's why I ran in the first place. And now I am, and beautifully dressed, and well looked after, and loved and with a beautiful engagement ring ... ' She cast her gaze about the gardens, wringing her hands.

Kate still had her by the shoulders. She squeezed her arms. 'Is there something you want to tell me, Georgina?'

The girl shook her head.

'Well, then, do you need to know anything ... about ... being married?'

Georgina shook her head again, but with less certainty.

Perhaps that was it, Kate mused. No one to ask about marital duties and that sort of thing. 'My dear, you are aware, are you not, that Conor is a big and—well, healthy man.'

Georgina nodded, blushed bright red.

'It would not be right to ask a man to wait for his bride when she lives under his very roof and has not yet consented to name the date of their wedding.'

Georgina straightened herself, brushing her skirt and pulling at her hair. 'I shouldn't burden you with my silly problems. I promise I will make a decision with Conor as soon as I can. I will order my thoughts appropriately.' She looked to the arbour at the far end of the garden. 'It would certainly be lovely to be married here.'

Now Kate was sure Georgina's heart was with another. She silently despaired for her brother.

Sixteen

It had been difficult to order her thoughts appropriately. For one thing because there was nothing appropriate about Dane MacHenry. She had tried repeatedly to forget him, but it was proving useless. His face kept coming back to haunt her.

She didn't understand her growing obsession with him.

By now Dane would know she was with Conor Foley in Melbourne, and engaged to be married. Conor had told her he'd telegraphed Jemimah with the news, to be courteous.

There was no escaping her reality.

And so what of it? Dane would hardly be bothered seeking her out after their short time together, especially as she'd run as fast as she could to be clear of him.

A distraction was what she needed. She needed to ride again, to feel the blast of the wind on her cheeks and the power of a horse beneath her.

She couldn't have chosen a more contentious subject if she tried.

Now Georgie sat stiff-backed opposite Conor in his office. 'Conor, you have known all along I had horses on Jacaranda.'

He was bent over a ledger and didn't look up. 'That was before you took a terrible tumble and had to be carried unconscious to my house.' A strand of ruddy hair dropped onto his forehead and he flicked it back.

'I was not unconscious. I was administered a drug to aid my transportation after my fall on the wharf.' She felt a frisson of triumph when he blinked at his numbers without raising his head. 'I mean to have my own horses, Conor,' she stated. 'And I mean to have at least one horse to ride, and soon.' She edged her seat closer to the desk. 'I am quite well, I have recovered—'

'No.'

'No?' she asked, bewildered.

'There will be no horses for you to ride. There is a carriage at your disposal. I don't want you to go to the stables, I don't want you to be seen anywhere in the yards, or to be asking to work the horses.' He turned a page back and forth, studying something closely.

Her cheeks burned. Someone had reported to him that she'd been to the stables.

'Why not? The stables are on the grounds—hardly out of bounds. Why on earth would you demand such a thing?' She spread her hands, hoping to catch at least a glance from him. 'Horses have been my life for years now.'

He did glance up, gazing at her for a minute before returning to his books. 'You have a carriage at your disposal, and Buttons will drive you anywhere you choose. Within reason,' he added. He picked up a pen and dipped it in the ink well, made a note and underlined it.

'Conor. I have had my fill of sitting here in this house. I need to be out in the fresh air, riding. I will purchase my own mount if I have to.' Her voice shook a little and her hands had gripped the arms of the chair. Why did it feel as if she was always fighting? The weight in her chest was heavy.

A gleam from her finger caught her eye and she glanced at the ruby ring. Her heart thudded unhappily.

Trapped.

He dropped the quill onto the blotter, clasped his hands on the desk and looked at her. 'My dear girl, you will do nothing of the sort ... even if you had money. No horses. Get out in the fresh air. Walk.'

Heat rushed to her cheeks again. She sat forward. 'I insist on my own horse.'

'Your insisting is not becoming. A carriage or nothing. I will not be providing you with a horse. And that is that.'

This was not the genial man she knew from those days on the river, the attentive caller courting her, looking after her every whim. The man who seemed to agree with her bid for freedom, her vocal opinions on emerging women's rights—such as she knew them. She had to try again.

'I did not hurt myself riding—'

'There is no discussion to be had. You have seen the last of your riding days.' He looked down at his papers again, picked up his quill and continued to makes notes.

'You will not dictate to me what I will and will not do. I am not some servant to be ordered around by the master of the house.' She leaned over his desk and poked a finger at the neat stack on invoices. 'I would rather go back to Jacaranda and what little freedom I had there, than sit here cooped up like some prize monkey.'

He placed his pen on the desk and patiently neatened the skewed stack of invoices and bills. He looked at her, his steady gaze icy. 'Is that so?'

Her stomach dropped. Heat beaded through her veins as if she'd placed her hand on a hot iron. Georgie willed her temper to cool, willed herself to show no more emotion. Her thoughts raced in time with her heartbeat. If she could not be free here, she was well and truly trapped. If she walked away from the engagement and subsequent marriage, she would be destitute and on the street. No woman survived well without family or a husband.

Choose your path wisely.

'Georgina,' he said, a whisper on cold breath. 'Had I known you felt so strongly I would have responded differently. Humour me a little longer while you convalesce.' His hands once again clasped on the desk in front of him. 'It's been just over three weeks, and I'm only thinking of your welfare. Let me find something suitable, a manageable mare. But in the meantime,' he continued, 'get yourself well and calm. You have a lot of excitement ahead with our forthcoming marriage.'

She stared back at him. *How to escape …*

'At least agree to wait until after we are married. Then I can concentrate properly and source some good stock from which to choose a horse. You have only to name the date of our wedding and your every wish is my command.'

She calculated quickly. If she could bide her time, she could try again. She would not make herself destitute over a mistimed battle. She would have her horses and her home—here, with Conor.

But now her picture of the future looked very different than it had before.

'Are we agreed?' he asked. His hazel eyes had returned to the warm colour she knew.

Her lips were dry. She lifted her hands from the arms of the chair, and nodded.

He returned to his papers.

Georgie stood. 'Good afternoon,' she said and left his office. In the hallway, she leaned against the wall to steady herself as she dragged in deep breaths. She must think.

The newspaper. In the morning room there were the newspapers brought to the house by the help. If she was lucky, they wouldn't have removed them yet—she could still find the article she remembered reading a day or two earlier.

———

A cool atmosphere prevailed over the evening dinner table and at breakfast the following day.

Georgie laced her fingers and rested her hands on the table. 'Conor, I would like to take a carriage ride, today.' It grated to hear her voice echo a pleading she'd heard others use with their husbands.

But Conor gave her a sudden smile. 'Of course, my dear. Delightful idea. Shop for your trousseau to your heart's content. Buttons knows where my accounts are in Spring Street or Collins or wherever might take your fancy.'

She blinked a little in surprise. *Trousseau ... Or wherever might take your fancy.*

He set his tea cup down, leaned over the table and pressed her hands. 'You might think me overprotective but for the most part, my dear, I would do anything for you.' He poured himself a refill from the silver pot.

Once Buttons cleared the carriage from the gates, Georgie gave a loud sigh and fell back on her seat. Free at last. She was certainly not going to purchase anything on Conor's accounts—although she would hide some of the coins he'd given her, because she had no clue what had happened to her own purse—even though her instructions from him were to buy whatever she wished. She thought it might have been his way of apologising for being so overbearing the day before, but she doubted it.

No, she would just revel in the freedom of being out of that house.

Once they'd crossed the Punt Road Bridge, Georgie tapped on the ceiling of the coach.

Buttons pulled aside and leaned down. 'Yes, miss?'

'There's a presentation of sorts in the south end of the park in the city, Buttons. Please take me there.'

'Very good, miss. A presentation. Where would that be?'

She leaned out a little. 'Just drop me at the gates and find a place to stop. I might be an hour.'

Mrs Isabella Goldstein and her daughter, Vida, were addressing the ladies of Melbourne in the streets and in the parks. They wanted signatures for the Women's Suffrage Petition. Georgie was eager to sign, and to hear from the ladies Goldstein for herself.

She could see a little group of women milling about, some with intent and purpose, others looking around furtively, only to move away. She stood and watched her heroine, Vida, a tall young woman about her own age—she recognised her from the newspaper picture—approach and chat to a lady, then stand unhappily as her target walked away.

Georgie hesitated only a moment before approaching the group, careful she didn't slip on the damp grass. She stood before Miss Goldstein, who smiled at her and held out a clipboard, a paper secured to it, already half full of signatures and addresses.

'Are you here to sign for us, miss?'

'Yes, Miss Goldstein. We must have women's suffrage. We have new property laws but—'

'Yes, we do, but so much more work to undertake. Thank you so much for coming. Will you please sign here and give your address ... here.' Miss Goldstein smiled again, handing Georgie a quill dipped a moment before. She was intent on her next signatory but looked back at Georgie. 'We have a long way to go, but with your help ... ' She was distracted again and as she removed the board and quill from Georgie's hands, she nodded and smiled.

'Do not forget there is so much more work for us women to do to enfranchise ourselves.'

Georgie watched as she moved further into a tight knot of women whose hats bobbed and skirts swished. Their subdued voices carried, low key but determined. Miss Goldstein moved along and Georgie's gaze swept around until she found Mrs Goldstein, who stood with someone who could be no other but Miss Annette Bear.

I am part of history, Georgie thought. She smiled at the throng of women as if she herself were moving the Victorian Parliament to a glorious decision. She was positive Miss Goldstein would bring about change. Perhaps the vote for women in Victoria would come soon if Miss Goldstein and company had their way.

There was no more for her to do at the moment. She didn't know anybody here, could not just fall into a casual conversation with a group of women without an introduction, as she had no formal society, so she refrained. That in itself annoyed her. This was the reason women needed a vote: to be independent of constrictions and outdated customs. Yet, with no money of her own ...

Be sensible. You are not married, have no family standing, and do not know a soul. Yet.

It was time to go back to Buttons and the carriage. When he helped her inside, she said to him, 'Let's drive down the city and back up again, Buttons. But tomorrow, I will need to go out again.'

'Certainly, miss. To where?'

'To wherever the best horses are for sale.'

Buttons did not bat an eyelid.

Spending Conor's money was not the purpose of her drive but she thought she should at least glide past the shops, as he expected her to do. She let the pretty gardens of Melbourne soothe her as the carriage trotted into town. Federation was not far off and Melbourne looked as if it would revel in it. Such a growing cultural centre. The gardens, the wide roads, the bobbing carriages. The road works and the new buildings.

The slums, the depression, the angry men.

The sights of Melbourne really did nothing to distract her from thoughts of the certain confines of her approaching marriage. She would have to make her own way as best she could. Oh, she was certain Conor loved her—in his own way—but she wasn't sure what she felt for him was love at all. Not at present.

Now, when she was all but living her dream, things didn't seem to be quite as she'd expected when she lived at Jacaranda. At Jacaranda, the aroma of the eucalypts was not lost as it was in the busyness of the city. At Jacaranda, you could hear the birds trill and caw, ride to the banks of a mighty river and sit in the dirt, throwing stones, or doze off under a tree.

It was true she had the most beautiful dresses, a house full of servants, and a friend in her future sister-in-law. She twisted the large engagement ring on her finger.

A terrible financial depression gripped the country and men in every colony were begging for work. Now she was among the privileged, she would not rock the boat. There were many stories of destitute women, fallen by the wayside, pushed out by angry or unhappy husbands, and she did not want to be one of them. She would toe the line with Conor.

Why would I want for anything else? I will have more freedoms and the finances to underpin them than most.

She would marry and—

Dane MacHenry popped into her head. She shook him away. It was quite ridiculous of her to think of him at all—he was such a know-it-all, so arrogant—and yet, for all those things, there had been a touch of gentleness, an amused glance, compassion when she needed a shoulder to cry on. She thought of the time spent with him riding from Jacaranda to Echuca …

She knew perfectly well her feelings for him were very different from her feelings for Conor.

She shook her head again to clear it of Dane. She would never see him again, she was sure.

Georgie rested her head against the window frame, her face bobbing with the rhythm of the carriage. And as she glanced at the passing throng, there, a tall, striking figure marching up Spring Street.

She bolted upright.

There was no missing that easy, swinging gait, or the unruly head of black hair. She simply couldn't believe her eyes. Had she conjured him up by simply thinking of him?

She leaned out of the window, squinting as her carriage went past him, her mouth open in disbelief.

It *was* him. She gasped as he swung around to check his bearings.

'Oh, my dear Lord,' she whispered when she looked straight into his eyes. Her breathing stopped and her heart rate soared. A constriction around her forehead squeezed her head and she pressed her hands to her face.

She watched through them as Dane bolted across the road to the carriage, where a startled Buttons had begun to raise his quirt to fend off an attacker. Dane uttered a few urgent words to him and the quirt was lowered.

'Buttons, the gentleman is known to me,' Georgie cried and although it was obvious Buttons was unsure, he pulled the carriage around and stopped at a length of gardens.

Dane followed in a few bounds, and helped her alight.

'I'll wait and watch out for you, miss,' Buttons told her. 'We don't have much time before we need to be back.'

Of course Conor would have limited her time away from the house. Georgie walked in agitated silence as Dane gripped her arm, steadying her and steering her into the park. He found an unoccupied bench far enough away from other people to offer some privacy. He waited until she was comfortable then sat beside her. His nearness was like the pull of a magnet.

Her heart was making such a loud noise she half expected him to shout over its din. He stared at her, and the colour rose in her cheeks. She lowered her head, sure he could see the confusion in her eyes.

'I can hardly believe you're sitting here.' She looked up again, composed.

'Indeed, unexpected. But I hoped our paths would cross again.'

The silence that followed was awkward. There seemed so much to say to him, but what, and how? Her heart still clamoured.

'And you?' he continued. 'How did you fare after Echuca? I was told you were on a steamer back to Jacaranda—'

'—Mr Finn shouted at me and that's when I tripped on the dock—'

'I saw the steamer go around the bend in the river. I thought you were safely returned to Jacaranda—'

'I was on Mr Finn's boat.'

'You weren't hurt?' His brows furrowed.

She waved a hand. 'Bump and gash on my head. Quite a few days not myself. Still not completely steady on my feet.' She spoke about Ranald Finn's delivering her to Conor Foley, who was in Echuca hoping to buy a boat, and of her convalescence at Conor's house.

Dane nodded, his lips drawn tightly across his mouth. 'You still don't look well, Georgina.' His gaze swept over her and a different kind of heart-thumping sped through her as he leaned in a little. Georgie wondered if she'd willed him to be on the street and then, there he was.

'I don't know what to say to you. It was an unusual time.'

'That's Foley's carriage?' he asked. She nodded. He took her hand and studied her engagement ring. It sat loose on her finger, heavy with the richness of the stone and the gold. 'So, not married yet, but very nearly.'

She pulled her hands from his as much to hide the ring as to still their shaking at his touch. 'Dane, I—'

'I apologise to you,' he said.

Georgie didn't want his apology. It seemed to her the ring caused him some misery. She shook her head. 'No. No.' She held up her hand. 'Let's be clear. It was my intention to meet with Conor after leaving the homestead.'

The atmosphere became strained. Georgie thought she would have done anything then, had he reached for her. But he didn't.

Instead he asked, 'So, when are you to be married?' His dark eyes searched her face.

'Soon.' She did not want to speak of that. She hadn't expected to see Dane again, and the feelings he evoked were confusing. 'No date yet.'

He looked at her, cool, distant. 'I've been in Melbourne since we parted. The visit to my father's solicitor was an interesting one, after all.'

'I had forgotten you were to visit a solicitor.' She shifted slightly in her seat.

'I was wrong about you and about your stepfather, Georgina.' He looked away. 'Our solicitor told me everything. I don't like to think my father has been a mean-minded, cowardly drunk, and a liar, but there it is.' He studied his fingers, turned his hands over. 'He took advantage of the responsibility placed on him. He took advantage of your allowance and, as a consequence of his greed, he lost Jacaranda.' He looked back at her intently.

Her mouth dropped open. 'What?'

He moved his shoulders as if he needed to stretch then stared hard at her. 'I suspect he gambled with your allowance, and most likely with the money he got from selling the things Rupert sent you. God knows my mother and Jacaranda have certainly not benefited. And it seems your last lot of dresses disappeared from the stables before I got back to MacNamara. Stolen, I expect, sold off.' He shook his head. 'It seems my father also wasted the funds I'd sent every three months, for years. I presume the problem with drink set in when he realised no matter what he did, he couldn't pay his way out of his growing debts. Whatever money he could get, by any means, was not nearly enough.' He was studying his hands. 'The only thing he had left was the homestead. He got himself roaring drunk, gambled with Jacaranda at cards, and lost.'

Buttons loped down the slope, waving his arms. 'Miss! Miss Georgina!'

'How terrible! Oh no, poor Aunt Jemimah. I will write to her. I must. Is there anything I can—?' She stared at him as he said some-thing so quietly she had to lean towards him. Something about the person who had cheated his father. 'What did you say?'

'Miss Georgina! We must get along—'

Dane frowned. 'You don't know who ended up with Jacaranda?'

'Well—no.' She shook her head.

'Miss Georgina! It's time we—'

'This is the first I've heard of it.' Georgina waved a hand at Buttons, stalling him as he approached. 'I rarely saw the people Uncle Tom met for those occasions. The games were often at Jacaranda, or turn about at different farms, or even on the boats.'

He looked at her hands, taking the bejewelled one in his. 'You have absolutely no idea?' He touched a finger to the large stone.

Buttons stood in front of them. 'Miss. We *must* go.'

'None.' She withdrew her hand from Dane's. 'I could not pos-sibly know such an immoral person.'

'Is that so?'

Georgina didn't like Dane's tone. She stood abruptly and paced on the damp grass in front of the bench. Buttons followed. 'How ridiculous you think I would know. This is awful. Poor Aunt Jem. What will they do? Where will they go?' Unsettled by his stare, she walked towards the duck pond and spoke over her shoulder. 'Is there nothing to be done? Something I can do?'

'Perhaps.' Dane fell into step with her.

Buttons hovered close by. 'Please, Miss Georgina. Please. We have to—'

Dane bent to her ear. 'I imagine there are no secrets between you and Foley. You live under the same roof.'

She turned to him, uneasy and angry at the same time. 'I don't understand what you—' Her foot slid out from under her. As she dropped, the back of her head hit the ground with a crack and the breath left her in a rush.

Dane grabbed for her. 'Dear God.' He scooped her up and strode back to the carriage. Buttons ran alongside, spluttering his agitation, panic on his features.

Her head throbbed and her tongue felt like she'd bitten it in half. She clutched Dane's shirt front and an arm, and held on tight.

'For pity's sake, Buttons, try to be useful. Help me get her on her feet.' Dane steadied her. She heaved, trying to catch her breath.

Buttons held out his arm. 'My God, miss, are you—?'

'She fell, man, she's winded. Take her straight home, and mind your manners when you get there—her fiancé need not know she had a friend nearby.' Dane helped her inside and onto the seat. He kissed her hand. 'Georgie.'

She glanced in his direction, her breath still caught in her chest. But he'd turned and gone.

Buttons threw the carriage into a frenzied drive home and Georgie couldn't tell if it was the lump on her head, her lungs screaming for air, the ride back to the house or the encounter with Dane that had her hands shaking uncontrollably.

The dull thud of her aching skull was beginning to subside and her breathing had eased, but her heart was heavy. The terrible news of Jacaranda, and the accidental meeting—

What had Dane been trying to say to her about secrets?

———

Conor was clearly concerned. 'And I thought it was safe to let you go out in the carriage,' he said. 'Katie assures me you're all right, but Buttons should have walked nearby, not left you on your own.'

Georgie breathed a sigh of relief. Thank heavens Buttons hadn't said anything to him about Dane, or about the meeting in the park. A discreet manservant was surely a blessing. She would repay Buttons with an extra shilling from her savings.

'It wasn't Buttons' fault, Conor.' Propped up on far too many pillows in the morning room, she felt fussed over, as though she were a sick infant. The bump on the back of her head only hurt when she touched it.

It was my own stupid fault letting Dane MacHenry upset me like he did.

But with that thought came an uncontrollable lump in her throat.

It wasn't as if she could confide the terrible news about Jacaranda to Conor without admitting that she had met with Dane MacHenry, albeit accidentally. Not to mention the implication for Buttons. He had not confided in his employer about either the meeting or the presentation to which he had taken her.

Georgie would tell Conor she wanted to visit with Miss Goldstein, though she suspected her interest in suffrage would not impress her fiancé, just as her interest in riding and having her own horse did not impress him. If he didn't agree, she would have to choose a more reckless path and hope she would survive it. She would not be stifled for the rest of her life.

She inhaled as her heart banged under her ribs. The roads ahead were shrouded in fog, and she felt the clamp of doom at her heels.

It would not do to be paralysed by her fears, and yet, which road was the one to take?

Conor sat beside her and held a damp sponge. 'My dear, my dear,' he said soothingly and placed the sponge on her forehead.

'Oh, Conor,' she snapped and pulled her face away. She worked at the ruby ring on her finger.

He glanced at her hands and, sat back, wary. 'What is it?' He watched as she drew the ring along the length of her finger and gripped her hand firmly. 'No.'

'I cannot, in all conscience allow you to—'

'I was an overbearing lout. I was arrogant, and unfeeling. I am known to be ... quick-tempered. I'm sorry.' He stopped the ring leaving her finger. 'I should know how much a horse of your own means to you—God knows I saw you riding often enough at Jacaranda. It was your delight and skill that attracted me in the first place.'

Her gaze steadied on his face.

'At least allow me the time to choose a fine animal for you.' He still pressed his hands over her ring. 'Do not be hasty. I do want you for my wife.'

He thought she meant to break the engagement! She had begun to say she did not want to hide her interests from him, and would argue for her rights, always, as she saw them. She shook her head a little, aware she could press an advantage. She fervently hoped she was right to do so. 'There are many things I wish to do with my life and if I marry you without—'

'My promise is that you will have what you wish, my dear Georgie. I can well afford whatever you want.' He rubbed her fingers between his, and his eyes never left her face.

'This seems to me to be a change of heart, Conor.'

'I am contrite.' His eyebrows moved under a flop of red hair as it fell over his face. He bent to kiss her hands. 'Name the things you want.'

She pressed against the settee, thinking. How would she know what they were? There were too many unforeseen things in the future. She would not restrict herself by naming only the few which sprang to mind. 'I would want to follow the things which take my interest, at any time. And to have your support.'

He hesitated only a second. 'Of course.'

'I would like to work for you, within your business in some capacity. I would require payment in exchange for my work. A weekly purse.'

'An allowance from housekeeping. But that goes without saying.' He smoothed the back of her hand.

She tried to remove it from his grip, but he pressed her. She let it rest, aware of the calluses on his palms. 'Not an allowance, Conor. A wage.'

'You want your husband to pay you a wage as if you were a common worker?'

'For work undertaken in his business.'

'And would this wage extend to your own purchases of fine gowns, and pretty shoes?'

She lifted an eyebrow. 'That would depend on the negotiations.'

He barked a laugh. 'My dear, I could use someone of your tenacity. I will explore the opportunities for such an employee.'

He was laughing at her, she knew. She kept going. 'And I would need to be provided for should something happen to you. There are new laws allowing a woman to be protected by her husband's will, should he—'

Conor's eyes widened. 'There are new laws, though somewhat untried.'

'Nevertheless.'

'You are bargaining with me.'

'No. I mean to be protected in order to survive if the unthinkable were to happen.' She tried to remove her hands from his grip again. 'I am aware of too much misery for a woman if she cannot protect or support herself. However if you cannot see your way clear ... '

He looked at her. 'If they are your conditions, I will have a new will drawn up to sign the day we are married—'

Georgie's heart skipped. 'They are not conditions, they are—'

'—so let us be married as soon as possible—before Katie and Angus marry. I don't want to wait any longer, wonderful, darling girl,' he said and continued to massage her hands despite her discomfort. He planted a kiss on her mouth, the first he had ever given her.

And she recoiled a little.

He took her face in his hands and kissed her again, then pressed his face into her neck. His arm had slipped behind her back and his breath fanned her chest. 'Within the week. I can get the licence. I know I can buy someone for that.' He smiled. 'We will marry in an office and then have a grand reception later when there is time to plan.'

It was now or never. She squeezed her eyes shut, put aside Dane MacHenry's face as it popped into her head. 'Yes.'

And when Conor lifted his head in surprise and saw her expression, he bellowed for the housemaid to bring a sleeping draught.

Seventeen

The two elegant ladies sat in the well-lit morning room, sipping tea from delicate china cups. A tray of dainty sandwiches, one bite each, was placed on a small table between the women, and linen napkins were draped over their laps.

Angeline Cawley dismissed the girl preparing to pour tea. 'You don't mind, my dear Kate, if we have a lovely chat without all the fuss? It's been far too long.'

'Actually, I long to put my feet up and simply drift away with the clouds,' Kate said.

'Delightful, dear, but a bit on the naughty side. In any case, I could hardly allow you to drift away without providing me with all the titbits of your brother's wedding.'

Kate Hannaford laughed and poured tea for both of them. 'All quite proper, Angeline, despite the hurried arrangements. It seems my dear brother has been chasing this girl for some time, unbeknownst to me until quite recently.'

'I see,' said Angeline, accepting the delicate cup and saucer. 'Quite exciting. A wedding—and soon. Next month, isn't it?' she asked as she sipped. 'We received our invitation last week.'

'To the reception, yes, next month. I do hope you and John can attend. However, they are to be married in Mr Arthur's office tomorrow.'

'Tomorrow?' Angeline started, her tea cup rattling on the saucer.

Kate settled back into her chair. 'It would appear neither wants to wait any longer.'

'I see.' Angeline paused. 'I'm not sure at this stage if John will be able to accompany me, but I shall attend the reception with an escort if that is acceptable, my dear.'

'Of course.'

'I shall formally reply this afternoon.' Angeline smiled at her friend. 'But in the meantime, tell me all about the romance.'

Kate sipped, took a small sandwich then sat back. 'It's quite a romance at that. You know my brother spent years building up his business on and around the paddle-steamers, and I know him to be quite the shrewd businessman. Well, certainly as he tells it.' She laughed a little. 'And certainly by the look of it, more to the point. He has a number of companies and it was through one of these he met Georgina, the girl he's about to marry.' Kate popped the tiny sandwich into her mouth and chewed. 'Apparently, she's originally from Bendigo but returned to live for some time with her stepfather in England.'

Angeline sat forward to take a sandwich for herself. 'And then somehow she's been returned to Australia?'

'Yes, to live on a homestead in the north of the state, of all places. Near some outback town on the river. Her stepfather has a married sister there, so she was sent back to live with that family.'

'How interesting.' Angeline knew it was no coincidence the name of the girl Kate's brother was to marry and the name of the girl Dane was so artfully trying to forget were one and the same.

With little prompting, Kate talked about her sister-in-law to-be at length. That she liked the girl, Georgina, was obvious, but Angeline could hear uncertainty in her voice. 'My dear, she is about to be married. What on earth could be amiss?'

'It's just a moment's hesitation here and there. Sometimes I get the impression her heart is not with Conor at all.' Kate refilled both tea cups. 'She's really quite lovely, very bright, but there's something missing, like—like … '

'Like love?' Angeline prompted.

'Well, yes. I think that's it. Not that love is everything, of course,' she qualified and lifted her eyes to the heavens, 'but I see trouble looming.'

'Perhaps love will grow.' Angeline sipped her tea and reached for a bite to eat. 'Or perhaps she loves another, or thinks she does.'

'Perhaps. Who knows? But whatever her feelings, she consented so I suppose she must have finally come to terms. And of course, there is her youth to consider.'

'But she is over twenty-one, I believe? All young women should be well married by that age,' Angeline said.

'Perhaps I should have said "her innocence", then.'

'Tell me more.' Angeline leaned back, her cup and saucer in her hands.

'You are very interested, Angeline,' Kate commented, smiling.

'Oh yes, weddings always interest me.' Angeline eased further back in her chair. *Especially this one.*

Kate smiled. 'Me, too. And this marriage will have my brother on his toes for once. Georgina seems somewhat headstrong.'

'Not such a bad thing if she plans her battles.'

Kate agreed with an incline of her head. 'True. She is certainly smart enough. She is well read, pores over the newspapers, and mentions with monotonous regularity the new laws regarding—of all things—married women's property rights. And the suffrage, of course.' Kate picked up a little sandwich and took a bite. 'There's not really much more I can tell you of her upbringing, except to say her stepfather is quite wealthy, landed gentry apparently, back in the home country.' She took a sip of tea. 'I wished we could have introduced her long before now, and had some more time to learn about her. Never mind, we will simply have to rely on our friends to accept her at the reception.'

Angeline's thought wandered a moment. According to Kate, the girl was perhaps preoccupied with someone. She shook her head.

'Is something wrong, Angeline?' Kate asked.

'Oh, my thoughts drifted. I was thinking of the difficulties society sometimes places on our young people. Do go on, I'm quite intrigued.'

'Yes, I suppose it is intriguing. Though my brother is quite unaware she is distracted.' Kate reached for another little sandwich. 'The poor man is totally enamoured with her.'

'Is that so? And are you quite sure you like her, my dear?'

'Oh, yes, yes.' Kate waved away Angeline's comment. 'But I am worried about their life together. I shouldn't, I know. Conor is much older and quite used to handling his own affairs. There does however seem to be a story to her.'

'Do tell.'

'From what little I've been able to drag from Conor,' Kate began, 'it seems she was actually a runaway at some stage. Thrilling, really, but not the done thing. I can tell she has some steel in her, but what he told me is really very unusual. Apparently, she quarrelled with the son of the homesteader on the Murray and left the home, dressed in boys' clothes, stole a horse and some of the

son's possessions and made for the hills, so to speak.' She raised her
eyebrows.

'Really?' Angeline smiled. Definitely one and the same girl.

———

Mrs John Cawley sat alone in her morning room, deciding what
she would do. It was true her husband would not be able to attend
the reception. He had business in the Western Districts, something to do with a whisky still, he'd told her. He would be away
from home for several days.

She knew she would not go to the event alone. She would ask
Dane to escort her to the reception. Very simple.

She also knew she was playing with fire. It would hurt Dane.
It could make a mockery of the girl's marriage. It could embar-
rass Kate and Angus. She pursed her lips as she thought about the
ramifications.

Angeline wondered again about her handsome foster son's
childhood and about the parents she had never met. She wondered
that, in all the years she had known Dane, there had never been a
hint of romance, or dallying. Not that she had expected to learn
of the latter, she chided herself, but of romance, she was sure she
would have known. And now, with the merest hint from him of
his feelings for this young woman he'd known only a couple of
months, her motherly instincts sharpened.

There was something about this girl that set him afire; she
could see the emotion smouldering beneath that cool facade Dane
tried to hide behind. It didn't fool her for an instant.

Yet he'd let the girl slip through his fingers. He'd probably
never in his life come up against something he couldn't have,
something that defied him completely. This girl had caught him
hard, and it seemed the emotions were as bewildering to her as
they were to Dane.

Her heart ached. There was nothing Dane could do to make this girl his own. She was to be married in a lawyer's office tomorrow. Angeline scoffed at herself. It was one thing to glean information from one's friend, but quite another to burden oneself with the problems in another's life.

Even if Dane was like a son to her, it was none of her business. But what a dreadful problem for him, and what a terrible start to a marriage for the girl. Angeline felt for Dane, this powerful young man whose zest for life and uncanny knack for survival had carried him through some very dangerous times. Should she ask him to escort her to the reception—or would it be inflicting too much pain on him?

She stood up and hurried to the window, her thoughts tumbling over.

Perhaps if he were to attend the reception, his pain might lessen quickly, knowing she was wed. He would be able to get on with his own life and leave the past behind.

She shivered a little. What a delicious story, even if it meant people were hurting. It was high romance, and high excitement.

Perhaps I'm just trying to meddle, she chided herself again.

Perhaps she would leave the decision to him. She would tell him of the invitation, tell him she didn't have an escort and leave the rest up to him.

Eighteen

The morning of the wedding, Kate came to Georgie's room especially to bring her something that had belonged to Conor and Kate's mother. The pearl drop, on a single delicate chain of gold, gleamed dully against Georgie's skin. When Kate clasped it around Georgie's neck, the heavy bead fell between her breasts.

Kate gave her a quick hug. 'Conor will recognise it, too.'

'Thank you, it's lovely.' Georgie touched the pearl and glanced at her reflection. Her wedding dress fitted like a glove and she wondered fleetingly if that were acceptable. She smoothed the fabric over her hips. As she moved, the pearl caught her attention. It gleamed in the light of mid-morning. A gift from a mother …

Her own mother should be here today, but she'd died long ago. Georgie barely remembered her, but often wished for her presence. Or at least Jemimah, the only woman she'd ever known as a mother figure, should be here.

On her wedding day …

Georgie glanced at Kate, an unguarded flicker.

'Oh, Georgie, Georgie, Georgie. Do cheer up, dear—one would think you felt dreadfully unhappy. This is such a happy day. Listen to Conor booming downstairs, frightening the staff.'

Georgie smiled brightly, or hoped she had.

Kate's face broke into a quick smile too. 'No more jitters?'

Georgie shook her head firmly. 'I'm just a little bit overwhelmed. I'm glad there's only a few witnesses today, and it has come awfully quick. And then I'm not sure of the dress ... Why am I wearing this to an office ceremony?'

Kate straightened the gown. 'Whatever can you mean? It's beautiful. Just beautiful. It is your wedding day and you should wear what you wish.' She took Georgie's shoulders and spun her around gently, appraising every angle.

'It seems daring for a registry wedding, it's not the fashion. Queen Victoria would disapprove.' Georgie tried to make light of the weight in her chest.

'Queen Victoria.' Kate repeated. 'I'm sure she's a wonderful woman, but she's not my queen, nor Conor's, and her own dress sense leaves a lot to be desired.' Kate turned Georgie again and adjusted a seam over her hip. 'Besides, Her Majesty will not be attending. I will send Deborah up to do your hair.' She squeezed Georgie's shoulders and left.

The dress, made of fine silk, had cost Conor a small fortune. Lace overlays and tight sleeves added to the richness of the underlying fabric. The dress hugged Georgie's hips and it was a good thing for modesty that Kate had purchased a specially fitted undergarment for her to wear because Georgie had asserted she would not wear cotton bloomers on her wedding day.

Georgie's ample bust was well and truly shown off and she fleetingly wondered if she looked the opposite of a virginal bride. Her chest seemed ready to pop out of the dress. Perhaps her living in the country for those years had kept her behind the times, because Kate thought the dress quite proper and hers was the only opinion Georgie had to go on. Kate certainly knew more about these affairs than she did. She kept saying Conor would like this or that and it brought home to Georgie the enormity of the commitment she was about to undertake. She was filled with a certain dread.

Had I not wanted it—and with all my heart? Had I not prayed aloud he would marry me and I would live happily ever after? And now I have what I wanted.

Even on the dawn of her wedding day she found it hard to reconcile. There was no thrill at Conor's touch, no flutters of anticipation in her belly of his arrival, no longing thoughts of seeing him, not like there had been with Dane. She wondered if she did indeed love Dane MacHenry, for she knew now she didn't love Conor Foley.

Perhaps it would come … she would just have to make the best of it. She had laid this path.

And, she reasoned, by marrying Conor Foley she was securing her future. She could begin her new life with the confidence that she would never want for anything again. Conor had spoken of changing his will, so she would be protected should anything untoward happen. As soon as the wedding ceremony was over, Conor would sign his new will in Mr Arthur's offices, with Angus Forrestor as his witness.

Her stepfather Rupert had sent his love and congratulatory wishes. She wondered if he had breathed a quiet sigh of relief upon hearing of her marriage. He had expressed his great shock about Tom MacHenry but only mentioned he would contact Jemimah and offer her assistance.

They would visit Papa Rupert as soon as Conor could organise his affairs to allow for the long trip to England. But that would be after the reception, in a month or so's time. She remembered wistfully that she'd hoped her papa would walk her to her new husband, but that was not to be.

Deborah, a long-time and trusted downstairs employee of Conor's, had been assigned to Georgie to help her dress. Now with only her hair to fix, Deborah chatted as she approached her task.

'We will fashion your hair up,' she said as she gathered Georgie's heavy plait and loosened it. She used both hands to caress the dark mass as it fell free across Georgie's shoulders.

For some reason the statement made Georgie remember Ruth from Jacaranda and she pulled her head away. But Deborah gently guided her back to keep working with the thick and unruly hair. Georgie eyed her reflection again. The image staring back was pensive. 'Perhaps he will think me beautiful.'

'But you are truly beautiful, miss, has not Mr Conor said so?' Deborah paused her brushing. 'Just watch him, miss, Mr Conor will hardly be able to wait to show you off to all his friends.'

But it was not of Conor Foley that Georgina was thinking.

She drifted to when she was sitting in that old room of hers, fighting with Ruth for the hairbrush. She wanted to lash out at something but when Deborah gently and firmly smoothed the scowl from her brow, she resigned herself to the inevitable again. However, the unsettled feeling didn't leave, a heat building inside her.

Deborah stood back to admire her work. At the back, she'd wound the black, shimmering locks into thick braids and held them loosely at the back with pins. She'd used another section swept back from Georgie's forehead to create soft, voluminous waves piled high. 'It's the newest fashion, miss.'

Georgie stood and waved her away impatiently. 'Just tell them I'm ready before my nerves are the undoing of me. I'm heartily sick of all this fuss.'

Deborah stood back. Her mouth pressed into a line before she said, 'I will let Mrs Kate know.' She left the room.

A few minutes later, Kate arrived. Deborah followed her in, hovering with a tray holding a cup of water and a small glass bottle.

Georgie was pacing the small room, clasping and unclasping her hands. 'I don't feel as if I can—'

'My dear, I definitely think it's a good idea to take a restorative before the ceremony. Your nerves seem quite unstable.'

Deborah tapped a little of the contents of the bottle into the cup, stirred it with a silver spoon and bade Georgie drink.

'What is it?'

'For your nerves.'

'I don't need that.'

Kate lifted the cup from Deborah and pressed it into Georgie's hand. 'Yes, you do.' Kate folded her hands over her stomach. 'It will help. Of course you feel nervous, it's only natural. But there's nothing to be worried about. Go on, drink.' Kate watched the mixture disappear as Georgie swallowed. 'That should steady you,' she said and patted her arm. 'No need for hysterics now. You will want to enjoy yourself, my dear. Remember that,' Kate said, and with a glance at Deborah and a nod of her head, she left Georgie to the maid's care.

Deborah made a small fuss about Georgie's dress, and patted her hair needlessly. 'We can go now, miss. Buttons is waiting to drive us to Mr Arthur's office.'

Georgina didn't acknowledge her. She took the small bouquet of tightly budded roses in pink and white and let Deborah guide her to the stairs.

From there her memory blurred. She barely recalled the drive to Conor's lawyer's rooms, where she was to be married. She could have slept for a week instead.

The ceremony seemed short and Georgie didn't remember the details.

She did remember seeing the registrar, a funny little man whose hat and coat looked too big for him, and that he spoke to Conor just before they began the ceremony.

'Miss Calthorpe looks a wee bit unwell, Mr Foley.'

'Not at all. She is perfectly fine, aren't you, my dear?' Conor squeezed her elbow.

'I am a bit—'

'Ten extra pounds for your wonderful service, Mr Abernathy.'

Mr Abernathy proceeded smoothly with the ceremony, a new note tucked into his coat pocket.

The weight of the wedding band as it slipped over her knuckle to sit gleaming and smug on her finger was foreign, out of place. The ruby engagement ring sat beside it and as Georgie looked at her hand, it seemed as if it were not hers.

What have I done?

Stricken, she looked about for help, but in that instant, Conor pressed a kiss on her hand and squeezed it. That ended any more thoughts she had.

I am married. I am now Mrs Conor Foley.

She did indeed feel strange.

Foley led Georgie up to their floor and led her inside her room. 'You may wish for some time to prepare, Georgie,' he said.

Georgie shook her head vehemently but remained silent. She wanted to yell, but couldn't. She didn't even know what she wanted to yell about, and besides, that would be so completely unacceptable it would be embarrassing. She simply stood inside the doorway and looked at him.

Her throat was parched and her lips dry. 'I would like a cool glass of water.'

He touched her face tenderly and said, 'I'll send Deborah for you.'

He left. She turned to see a bath had been placed near the window, a little waft of steam rising from it. It distracted her for a second or two, then Deborah entered carrying towels, a large bar of soap, and a sponge.

Another downstairs woman followed behind with a pitcher. 'Water, miss,' she said without making eye contact and left it on the dresser before departing.

'Mr Foley requested a nice hot bath for you, miss,' Deborah said and then placed her hands on Georgie and turned her around. Georgie smarted, realising she was about to be undressed. 'Mr Foley thought you would feel much better after a good bath.' Deborah's skilled hands unbuttoned the dress as deftly as she had buttoned Georgie into it.

'He sent you in to help me bathe?' Her head was woolly, her thoughts slow.

Deborah smiled and nodded. 'You're a married lady, now, and your husband requires, ah … '

Georgie stepped out of the dress as Deborah guided it from her body. The pearl was left dangling on her bare chest. She stood in her stockings, which Deborah carefully removed by rolling each one down her leg while Georgie, a little light-headed, leaned on her shoulder.

She swayed, and reached out for Deborah as she stepped into the bath. She looked about for the soap, but Deborah was already lathering silky bubbles, and began to run them over her back.

Georgie sighed despite herself, the exquisite satiny touch thrilling her. 'I can bathe myself.' Her voice sounded unlike her own, dreamy and inattentive.

'Mr Foley requested I help you.'

Deborah led her to the bed and sat her in the towels. Moving swiftly to the bureau, she withdrew a nightgown, almost a replica in satin of Georgie's wedding dress. The nightgown sheathed Georgie's body, her breasts straining at the low-cut bodice held together by a little tie. The hem was shorter over the ankle than she was used to, but to Georgie the gown looked grown-up and elegant.

With her body perfumed and clothed, her hair brushed out of the pins and hanging long at her back, Deborah left her side without a word. On her way out, she gathered up the wet towels and the discarded wedding gown.

Georgie's head reeled and she fell back on the bed. Although Deborah's ministrations had been gentle and careful, she was still unprepared for what she had been told to expect. She stood up to pace as her door opened.

Conor stepped inside her room and closed the door behind him. He had bathed, his hair was wet and slicked back behind his ears. He was in breeches and a shirt open at the collar, his feet in soft leather brogues. Staring at the expanse of his broad chest and the ginger-coloured hair sprinkled across it, Georgie gave a tenuous smile.

Kate had explained what to anticipate, and some time before, so had Josephine, but Georgie had no idea of how one reacted to proceedings. It was the man who dominated and demanded, she'd been told, but she couldn't even imagine anything else.

Perhaps it would be as she'd always believed ... Conor would not be interested in doing that ... thing.

'You look absolutely beautiful, Georgina.' He reached out gently and took the pearl droplet in his hand. With it, he tenderly drew her towards him and kissed her fully and softly on the mouth. He bent his head and kissed her bosom, rising and falling above the opening of her dress.

'Should I undress?' She stood rigid as he kissed her on the mouth.

He opened his shirt, the hair on his chest glistening in the low glow of the lamplight. She reached up to touch him, trembling, but he took her hand.

'Turn around,' he said and guided her back towards him to stand between his legs. He pressed his hands about her waist and slipped them down over the nightdress to hold her hips. He drew her body closer and as she moved against him, both his hands came up from behind to cup her full breasts and tease her nipples.

Then his fingers found the shoulders of her gown. He traced the lace to the front and slowly pulled the tie at her bodice. The satin fell from her shoulders and her arms slipped out. The night-gown slid to her waist and she clutched at it, fearful of her nudity before him.

Shivers sped over her bare flesh but the moment she sought the warmth of his body, turning to him to hide, his hands were on her. He kissed her neck and shoulders. His mouth lowered to her breasts. She cried aloud at the exquisite pull in her belly as he suckled the nipple thrusting forward for him. The urgent thrill tripped through her body.

His rough, whiskered face buried in her breasts sent tingles between her legs. His broad powerful hands held her body firmly as he nuzzled and suckled. Every inch of her skin his face and tongue and mouth touched was aflame with a hunger she never knew existed. Her breath became ragged and shallow.

He picked her up and placed her on the bed.

Conor allowed the flimsy fabric of the nightdress to remain covering her lower body. He pressed his face over the junction of her legs through the gown and Georgie burned with the heat of his breath on her private place. She gasped aloud and he pressed harder.

He came up to kiss her, full mouthed and languid. When she slid her hands tentatively down his back, he pulled away.

'Not yet,' he whispered, and ran a finger along the line of her hip. Confused, she pulled the nightgown back up to cover her breasts but he brushed it away. His hand fell over her lower belly and he grazed the plump mound between her legs, watching her face as she pressed into his hand.

He kissed her mouth, and sucked her lips. She pushed up to meet his fingers, but he teased her and persisted with the gentle stroking, just out of her reach.

Georgie thought she would go mad with need. Her head shifted from side to side, her nightgown bunched around her waist as she squirmed, and she pressed her body closer to his. His warm hand slid over her bare thigh, stopping before the joining of her legs. She opened thighs and he touched her privacy, a slick finger sliding a little way in ...

Her breath caught.

Then, with a grunt, he rolled off the bed.

Startled, she stared at him. He pulled the gown from her body, stared at the sight before him: firm rounded breasts, a triangle of dark hair covering her sex, slim waist and slightly rounded belly. He dropped to his knees beside the bed, slid his hands under her buttocks, dragged her down the bed and pushed his face between her legs, his hot mouth open and wet on her.

Pleasure rolled through her ...

She purred, gasped and tried to push him away but he came up powerfully and smothered her face and neck with hot, sucking kisses. He nuzzled and licked her breasts, nibbled the nipples until they hurt. He plunged lower until she could feel his hot demanding tongue inside her most female area.

He had one large hand under her buttocks and had pressed a finger between the cheeks, forcing her to stay close to him.

She writhed.

He sucked high up on her sex and her hips bucked beneath him, a pulse driving her ...

He flicked that pulse with his tongue. She cried as a new wave of pleasure crashed through her. His fingers slid up to her breasts, rolling the hard nipples. She cried again and he buried his face into her, squeezing her buttocks, kissing and sucking and licking the soft flesh of her inner thighs. Then he parted her and licked and licked until she soared out of her mind as wave after wave of ecstasy engulfed her.

Exhausted, mindless, boneless, she sank.

He ran his tongue along her legs. He planted a wet kiss on the tuft of dark, damp, curling hair, and when she cried out that she could stand it no more, he threw off his shirt and came to lie on the bed beside her.

She rested, her tongue touching her parted lips. He pulled her to him. His big, powerful arms gathered her close to him and they lay together quietly.

'Perhaps next time,' he murmured.

Georgie barely heard him. Revelling in the physical, she hoped he would bring her to such heights again, and soon. She waited quietly, totally absorbed in the fever rolling through her body. She listened to his heart beat under the broad chest and rubbed her face in the coarse hair there. How replete, how fulfilled, how ... released.

Never in her wildest, most private thoughts had she ever believed she could feel like that, and by those means. She wondered sleepily why the only parts of him that touched her private places were his tongue and his fingers. Josephine had told her of more. Much more.

She shivered a little, remembering the total lack of modesty, and looked to see whether he was pleased.

He was watching her, his face sombre. 'Next time, my love,' he whispered.

He had not removed his breeches.

She wondered if perhaps she hadn't pleased him.

———

Georgina nestled closer, her strong, young body beside him, relaxed and content. Conor knew how inexperienced she was, and how there was a possibility she wouldn't know enough of sexual relations to question him. He was a little pleased. There would be no difficult explanations as long as he could keep her happy and satisfied. He could mould her into the wife he wanted.

It hadn't been very difficult to give her pleasure.

His poor shot-up, decrepit appendage, his excuse for a penis, would do him no good, no matter how he wished—*willed*—it to be different. The fucking Boer's bullet that sliced a meaningful chunk of cock clean through be damned, and the field surgeons who clumsily stitched him up and give him a bent and useless tool.

Be thankful, he was told. He'd wished for death.

When that didn't happen, he healed and, later, distracted himself with pleasuring women in other ways. There'd not been too many complaints. To the contrary, the majority of his partners had become clingy and grasping of his attentions. It interested him greatly to know other men were not as adept as he at relieving a woman of her tensions. He'd laughed at that. They didn't know what they were missing. He had perfected his art, hoping one day someone would ignite the fire in him once more.

But his body would not respond. Did not respond, not even to Georgina.

He closed his eyes yet again to feel the tease of urgency only to have it recede beyond his grasp, a tantalising promise of what once had been. He licked his lips and tasted bitter disappointment.

He had been ready to take a wife.

Georgina had, in ignorance, long ago told him she had no desire to have children, and he took it at face value. He could never have children, and the doctors had assured him there was no cure for his condition. But he'd hoped with Georgina he would feel something. Something more than the elusive twinge which was, they told him, only in his mind. Georgina would be utterly loyal to him and never betray him, he was sure. He would keep her happy at home and satisfied in the bedroom. He had chosen well after a long wait to find someone suitable.

He had changed his will—Angus and Mr Wardle had witnessed it—as she had requested. Not without reservations. A woman was not ready to handle all her husband's affairs, no matter what the law said.

However, he had not lodged it and wouldn't. He would write another will, have it witnessed by another office of solicitors and lodge that.

He moved her under the covers, blew out the lamp, stripped naked and slipped in beside her. She reached for him and he held her close, drifting into a light sleep.

In his heart, he knew she was not enough.

———

Georgie lay beside him, bewildered.

The light was out, which was what she had been told would happen, but Conor Foley was going to sleep. She didn't know what to do. It wasn't happening like Josephine had said, nor as Kate had explained.

Perhaps they hadn't known everything, after all. Perhaps she had been right all along about Conor and he wouldn't want to indulge in the things they said every man would. She smiled to herself. She was right. Nothing Conor had done to her was anything to be frightened of. She gasped as little delicious thrills began again in her belly. It was most enjoyable. All those feelings she had experienced before were definitely her 'lusts', as Josephine had said, and now there was no need to feel bewildered about them again.

What perfect things to have experienced.

When she drifted off to sleep with a contented smile on her face, she dreamed. Even though it was her husband's hands on her body awakening the fire in her again as she slept, it was of Dane MacHenry she dreamed.

———

When Georgie woke one morning later that week, the sunlight streamed in to her room and warmed her face. Oh, today would be a lovely day for a ride.

She dressed with care, then disappeared after her breakfast to meet with Buttons in his sheds. She came back to the house light of step and went looking for her husband. She found him in his study.

'Conor, it's the most marvellous day. I'm ready to choose a horse. I have instructed Buttons to take me to the Domain Street stables later this afternoon. I hope you're free to come with me,' she said, standing at his desk.

His expression took only a moment to change from pleasant to ugly. 'Buttons will not take you.'

'Why ever not?'

He shot to his feet, his chair crashing into the heavily laden bookshelves behind him, and charged around the desk. 'Because I will instruct him otherwise. And if you persist with Buttons, I will dismiss him.'

Georgie's delight crumbled as fear iced through her. 'You wouldn't do that to the poor man! All I want is to have my own horse. You agreed—'

He grabbed her by the arms and shook her roughly. 'Did you not hear me at the time, woman?' His hot breath, already stinking of cigars and rum, flew in her face. 'I said *I* will choose a horse for you. Until then no riding for you, *no horses. No* visits to the stables.' His hands on her arms were biting and his shouts rang in her ears.

He gave her another cruel shake and thrust her away.

Georgie's head snapped back, and her hair fell out of its pins. Bone-deep pain flared as the blood returned to her arms. Heat prickled her neck and her jaw ached as she clenched her teeth.

Manning, the butler, burst into the room. 'Sir, I heard a terrible crash and—'

'Get out.' Foley's face was ruddy, his eyes narrow.

Manning stepped out the door, and closed it swiftly.

Georgie stood shaking in front of Conor. She watched stonily as his shoulders squared and he stamped back to his seat, pulling it upright and back on its feet. He tugged at his sleeves then sat. After a deep breath, he pushed a hand through his hair, picked up his quill and continued at his bookkeeping.

Her chin quivered with a mix of rage and fear, but this was not a fight she would take on now, fully aware of the brutal power in the man. She held her tongue, raised shaking hands to her hair and began to re-pin it, then dropped to the floor to retrieve those pins that had fallen out.

'We will lunch in thirty minutes,' he said, his tone soft and his eyes clear. 'My dear, your frown spoils such a pretty face.'

Stabbing the final pins into her hair, she turned and left the office, slamming the door behind her. She did not appear for lunch with him, but ate on her own, an hour later.

He took his time with her in their bedroom that night. She was wary of the man in her bed, his mouth on her body, his total possession of her. He still coaxed his desired response, her body defying her, but his power and his size, which had been once her protection and delight, were now her jailers.

She was sullied—unclean, spoiled. For her husband, she felt only loathing.

She pushed that down. All would be well if she did not defy him again.

All would be well if she was clever and careful.

Nineteen

They mingled among the guests and although Kate hovered nearby, she need not have worried: Georgie began to enjoy being the centre of attention. Acknowledging the admiring glances and the compliments, she started to believe perhaps this life would be good after all.

Conor had introduced her to a number of his friends, some of whom were politicians and business people. There were friends of Kate's and her fiancé's too, most of whom were bankers and lawyers. Governor Hopetoun and Lady Hopetoun were in attendance and their presence elevated Georgie's wedding to that of a high point in the season. Lady Hopetoun had been delighted by the introduction to Georgie until she was made aware that in fact Georgie was colonial born, and not English, as she sounded. Georgie consoled herself with a glass of sherry and toasted the haughty woman from afar with an expletive she'd almost forgotten.

Through the whirlwind of other introductions and conversation, she noticed Kate and Angus talking to a very attractive woman dressed in deep blue velvet. There was refinement in the lady's demeanour. When she approached, Georgie could hear the culture in her voice and a slight accent, which she couldn't identify.

Kate hooked her arm through Georgie's and took her away from Conor with a smile. 'Georgina, let me introduce you to a dear friend of mine, Angeline, Mrs John Cawley.'

She was quite the most beautiful older woman Georgie had ever seen.

Angeline smiled at her. 'My heartiest congratulations, Mrs Foley. And might I say how gorgeous you are in your wedding gown. It's quite unusual these days, but very, very fetching.'

Georgie reddened to her chest. Mrs Cawley's scrutiny unnerved her, and the previous forlorn mood she had tried so hard to shift descended again. She needed to rush upstairs and throw on some old blouse to cover up.

Desperate to shake off the uneasy sensation, she almost missed Mrs Cawley address her again.

'And I do apologise.' The older woman smiled at her. 'It seems my escort has been delayed, but I hope he'll be along shortly.'

'Oh, no apology necessary.' Georgie hoped for a distraction from the woman's inspection.

And there it was in the wedding waltz. As the music cut through her fog, Conor guided her to the dance floor and Georgie heard the crowd whisper and sigh as they began to dance.

'My beautiful, beautiful wife.' Conor's voice shook as he pulled her closer.

Georgie stiffened, but smiled as she danced.

They'd had a peaceful few weeks after the violence of the first few days of their marriage. Conor had been most attentive, and had coaxed her delicious responses most nights. She had not wished to touch on the subject of her riding. She would wait to see what he decided to do.

Conor promised a short honeymoon—he had not said where. But that didn't matter to her. Georgie had begun her reign as Mrs Conor Foley.

She danced into the evening. She was her old self, laughing and happy, light-headed as guests swirled about them. Conor had trouble partnering her for many dances as she was much in demand. But he didn't mind, she was sure.

Georgie was about to accept a dance from another friend of Conor's when she caught sight of the curly-haired head of Dane MacHenry approaching. She stilled, her heart missing a beat or two then beginning to hammer. In an instant, it seemed, Angeline Cawley was at her side.

'My dear Georgina.' Mrs Cawley's eyes were steady on Georgina's face. 'This is my escort, Mr Dane MacHenry. Dane, the new Mrs Conor Foley. Mr MacHenry is like a son to me and he graciously agreed to accompany me today in the absence of my husband.'

A pause greeted the introduction, then Dane bowed over Georgina's hand and pressed it to his lips. 'Mrs Foley,' he said, formally. 'My congratulations.'

Colour had drained from her face the instant she saw him, and now it surged back in a fierce blush. 'Mr MacHenry,' she acknowledged with a slight tilt of her head. 'I do apologise. My husband is not here at the moment to receive—'

'No. He is there, madam, speaking with the Governor. Looks likely to be in conversation for some time.' Dane's intense gaze did not follow his hand as it gestured in Conor's direction.

Georgie didn't turn away from Dane to check for her husband.

Why is he at my reception? She was numbed to her feet, rooted to the spot.

Mrs Cawley was by her side. 'You look surprised at something, my dear.'

Dane's fierce blue eyes stared Georgie down, his body stiff and formal. 'I should be honoured if you would take this dance with me,' he said and held out his arm.

Georgie could not refuse, it would cause too much consternation. She told herself it was just another dance, after all. Her arm looped through his.

'Smile,' he urged as they swept around the room, 'and keep smiling.'

She saw Conor wave at them, but it was distracted. Dane acknowledged it with a polite nod but her husband had already turned away.

'No doubt the Governor holds a riveting conversation.'

Georgie was swept around the dance floor by the very man who sent her heart beating wildly, but who was not—and now never could be—anything to her but a memory.

She opened her mouth to say something but Dane stopped her.

'Before you speak, Mrs Foley,' he began, 'before we spar on the rights and wrongs of my being here, let me just tell you that you are the most beautiful woman I have ever seen. I should have married you myself.'

He was obviously mocking her. 'Is that so?' She tried to pull away, intending to leave the dance floor. 'I should be eternally grateful, then, that you didn't show up for the actual ceremony.'

'Had I known about it, I just might have, believe me. But I would have done something truly unforgivable and that would have served neither of us.' Dane tightened his hold a little and smiled as they glided around the floor. 'Do smile and chat, Mrs Foley. I don't want your husband to suspect anything amiss or improper between us.'

'But it is improper.' Her voice shook. 'When he finds out who you are—'

'And who am I? No one here knows me except Angeline. And besides, it seems to me the Governor holds more interest for your husband than his new wife's dance partner.' He turned her smoothly to place his back to Conor Foley. 'So by the time he asks, if he does, I'll be long gone.' He smiled, a small curve of his lips. 'You are truly beautiful, Georgina.'

Her teeth clenched. 'You mock me.'

Dane whirled them about the floor. 'On the contrary.'

'Why did you come—?'

'I needed to see for myself that you are lost to me.'

His words ricocheted in her chest. 'Then what is it you want?'

'Only my chance to dance with the bride and, I admit, perhaps my last chance to see you.' He pulled her a little closer. 'It's clear you've found your riches.' He indicated the finery around them, the splendour of her guests.

His words stung her. Bah! He was toying with her again. He'd never had any intention of marrying her, of that she was certain.

'Ah, the innocence again,' he began and this time pulled her closer than propriety allowed. 'I've been told that treachery often disguises itself in the form of exquisite beauty, but until I saw you tonight, I never really believed it.'

The soft barb was cruel. The quick gleam of triumph in his eyes crushed her even further. She stiffened, only too aware of the warmth of his body, though his words were languidly cold. The solid wall of his chest, his warm breath on her shoulder …

'Georgie, I truly desired you. You know yourself what began between us.'

Breath hissed out of her. 'Whatever it was, it didn't last,' she snapped. 'It could never, with a man as shallow as you.'

'Shallow?' He drew back. 'Oh, I disagree. There is deep feeling on my part. And where that pearl lies on your breast is where I once laid my hand.' His eyes looked fevered and Georgie thought for an instant he was drunk, or had gone mad. 'Tell me you don't feel it burning still. You were mine.'

'Your possessiveness is misplaced. Nothing occurred between you and me. I am now a married woman and your presence here is unwelcome. Your behaviour is not gentlemanly.'

'Oh, I agree with you there,' he countered easily. His grip on her tightened. 'Don't try to leave the floor, Mrs Foley. You would only have to explain yourself.'

'Leave me alone, Dane.' Alarmed, she searched her mind, desperate for an excuse to escape. 'My choice was already made before I met you, I told you that day at the park. And you made it clear to me that you—'

He lowered his voice. 'I would give you love, which is not what you are getting now.'

'What would you know of—? You talk of love,' she scoffed. 'I won't dignify this conversation a second longer.' She tried to pull her hand from his, but his grip remained firm.

'Oh, do not give me the opportunity to create a scene here—I wouldn't hesitate to answer his challenge, despite Angeline being in attendance.' His arm on her back pulled her body to his. His low voice whispered against her ear, 'I shall never forget how you look tonight, Mrs Foley, how beautiful you are.'

It pierced her heart. *Is he truly mad? Am I?*

'And my dear Georgina, when you are abed tonight with your husband, I dare you to wipe me from your thoughts.'

'Your arrogance is worse than before,' she hissed. Why was he not as breathless as she? 'Never attempt to see me, ever again. Conor has a terrible temper, and—'

'And so do I.' He swept her around the floor once more, the heat between them a living thing that burned her cheeks and flamed in her belly. 'You should be mine. Do not think that your marrying him will save you from me.' Dane held her away from him now, the pearl he had mentioned earlier, or rather its placement, a focus for his attention. He looked back at her eyes. 'I will bring ruin to him. I attempted to tell you as much that afternoon in the park. Your husband took advantage of a drunk, my father, and played my family out of their home. I will get it back, Georgina.'

Shock and anger streaked across Georgie's face. 'What are you talking about?'

The music stopped, the dance ended and Dane led a shaken Georgie to her husband. 'My congratulations, Mr Foley,' he began politely, the steely glint in his eye recognised only by Georgie. 'You have chosen an exquisite partner. Thank you for your hospitality. Good night.' And with that, he turned on his heel and, offering his arm to Mrs Cawley, promptly left their company.

Conor raised his eyebrows and stared after him. Then he turned his gaze to Georgie. 'Who was that accompanying Mrs Cawley? It seems he forgot to introduce himself.'

'I have forgotten the names of those I've danced with tonight, there were so many,' she said, a little breathlessly, waving a hand in the air.

Conor stared at her. 'My dear, are you quite all right?'

'Perhaps I've danced too much.' Georgina touched a finger to each of her temples. 'I have a pounding headache and need some fresh air,' she said and made her way out to the gardens.

Looking back, she saw Dane and Mrs Cawley speaking heatedly on the other side of the room. She ducked out of sight as they glanced in her direction. She took great gulps of the cool night air into her lungs and placed a shaking hand to her head to steady the throbbing there.

What had he said? That Conor had *played* his family out of their home—Jacaranda? Did he mean—was it *Conor* who played at cards for Jacaranda? When had she learned of the game? Yes, yes, the day in the park, when she'd slipped on the grass, Dane had tried to tell her something, had asked her—

It was conceivable.

It was *not*!

It was possible, but Conor had said nothing to her about it. Nothing.

Her hand covered her mouth, and appalled, she breathed deeply until her stomach settled. She dropped to sit on the cold stone of a garden bench, holding herself upright, her spine rigid.

Conor was leaving for the river the day after tomorrow. She would ask him tomorrow. No, no, perhaps not tomorrow. Perhaps afterwards, when she'd had time to digest …

Had everyone known the truth but her? Aunt Jem? Elspeth? Uncle Tom, certainly, if it were true. Was this why no one had answered her letters? Was this why no one had made any attempt to contact her … because they felt betrayed by her?

'There you are, sitting outside all alone in the night air,' came a lilting voice behind her. Kate had breezed into the garden before Georgie had time to compose herself. She was silently glad the dark night hid her agitation.

'You have made quite an impression, my dear.' Kate took Georgie's hands, a smile in her voice. 'You look delightful in your gown—as certainly one gentleman was no doubt aware.'

Georgie felt the reproach.

'And that last dance simply took our breath away,' Kate continued. 'The two of you floated around the room like you had danced together forever. My, he is a handsome man, that Dane. Angeline is so full of surprises. If I hadn't known how close she was to her husband, I would swear—' She stopped and sat beside Georgie. 'Oh, my dear. It was a joke, an awful one by the looks of things. Angeline is the epitome of good breeding and manners. Is something else the matter?'

'Oh, dear God,' Georgina muttered and put her head in her hands.

Twenty

Dane journeyed back to Sydney with a heavy heart and a tired body.

He'd made a decided error attending Georgie's wedding reception. The display of immature churlishness towards her was not lost on Angeline, who had soundly admonished him as they drove home in the carriage.

He trudged into the Captain's Cabin after leaving MacNamara in the stables behind the building. The greeting to his employees was weary. He collared young Jock and ordered a large bath and a bottle of rum, silently reminding himself again to look into an indoors bathroom. He climbed the stairs to his private chambers. Catching up with Reuben would come later. There would be much to discuss.

He had stripped to his waist when a knock on the door interrupted him. It was the bath, a huge tub hauled into the room by two women. Their grins were familiar as they welcomed him home. Sarah and Sally had been with him from the start. He enjoyed a joke with them and waited patiently as they brought in the hot water.

As soon as it was deep enough, he stripped off the rest of his clothes and sank into the bath. He gave neither of the women a second glance, and waved them away good-naturedly.

'We can scrub yer back, Mr Dane,' Sal said, leaning on the door frame.

Sarah snorted and flicked her on the arm as she stalked past to the small closet. 'She's a rude girl, Mr Dane.'

He smiled. The hired help didn't interest him.

Sarah brought out a fresh shirt and breeches and laid them on the bed. Sal gathered up his travelling clothes and took them with her.

They paused at the door while he left final instructions that he was not to be disturbed until nightfall.

He had just settled into the hot water when another discreet knock interrupted him. 'Yes?'

'It's me, sir, Jamieson. I've ye rum.'

'Come in, man. And pour me a large one.'

Jamieson, skinny, weathered, bald-headed and only about as tall as Dane's shoulder, was the head man at the Captain's Cabin. He swung the door wider with his foot, a tray with a bottle and large tumbler balancing on it in his thick wharfie's hands. 'Welcome home, sir.' He set the tray by the bath and poured Dane a large tot. 'You look all done in, Mr MacHenry. I'll leave you to it and we'll talk another time.'

Dane nodded his thanks and Jamieson left.

He sank as far as he could, the water humming heat through to his bones. The only other heat like it was on a clear summer's day with the sun beating down on his back at Jacaranda.

Jacaranda.

The last thing he'd wanted was to lose Jacaranda, yet as quick as a wink it was gone. It had always seemed safe, beyond any danger of leaving the MacHenry name. He had never thought it would. It would have been his when Tom was ready to hand over the reins. He needed to have it back in the family name. That was the first thing he would try to do. A business proposition to Georgina's husband.

It would mean contact with her. He knew he was clinging to it, but it was all the excuse he needed. To have her in his arms, to bury his face in those lustrous tresses of shimmering black hair …

He laid his head back on the bath's rim and thought of Georgina Calthorpe Foley for the thousandth time. They were alike, fired with a passion for life, for adventure. Visions of her floated through his mind and he squeezed his eyes shut. It must just be simple lust after all. Just lust. He hadn't had time to feel anything else, had he? Love? What of it?

His mouth soured. By now she would be a very satisfied young matron, probably with a brat in her belly. He winced. *Bitter, MacHenry.* No amount of cheap barbs and cruel taunts—at himself—would change anything.

Get on with it, man. There's nothing you can do about the woman. Just get on with it.

A plan took shape. Reuben Cawley and his family. If they would extend him a loan—

A statuesque woman burst into his room, frightening the life out of him. 'Jesus!' Rum splashed into the bath water.

'Dane! Darling!'

He twisted in the bath and saw gloved arms flung wide in greeting and a smile on the cleverly made up face of Rebecca Middleton. She bent towards him, her low-cut gown hiding very little of the ample, wobbling bosom.

He slammed his glass down on the little stool beside the bath. Fuck's sake, was nothing sacred from this woman? 'Hello, Rebecca.'

'Hello? Is that all? No jumping up ardently to meet me and carry me off to bed?' She stood at the edge of the tub.

He sighed. 'I'm in my bath.'

'Never stopped you before, Dane MacHenry. Come on, over here.' She sailed past the tub and sat on his huge bed.

'Do you think you could shut the door, Rebecca?'

'My, my.' She pouted as she returned and slammed the door. 'Not in good humour after your little holiday, are you?'

'No, I'm not. If you insist on being here, rub my shoulders, would you?'

'Of course, my darling man.' She knelt behind the bath, stripped off her gloves and threw them into the water. Leaning over him to lick a kiss on his mouth, she kneaded his shoulders. He fished the gloves from the water, squeezed them and dropped them on the floor. He took his glass once again and sipped.

She nuzzled his neck, nipped his earlobes, whispered, 'I hope that lovely cock of yours is ready for me.'

He splashed an imaginary bug from the water.

She traced a fingernail down his chest, over his nipples and belly to disappear under the surface, following the wiry black trail of hair.

'Oh, Dane. You have missed me. We are standing to attention so very powerfully under the water.' Her hand gave a couple of smooth strokes as she watched his face.

After a quick little grasp of his balls, she let him go and moved into his line of sight, lifting her skirts and untying her knickers. She pushed them to the floor. She unbuttoned her skirts and they fell away.

The bath water moved a little.

He watched her, the rum dangling in his hand over the side of the bath.

Then, only in her corset, her full breasts straining against the underclothing, Rebecca peeled her stockings away. She turned her back on him, bending over to remove her feet from the silken hose.

He leapt out of the bath, a great wave of soapy water following him. She laughed delightedly as they crashed onto his bed, the remainder of her clothing strewn about their bodies, entangling them.

She was a big strong woman, a hearty lover. He entered her hard. She scratched at him, pulled his hair, sucked at his neck, pushed him up so he could see her large breasts spilled out of the corsetry, swinging and driving him mad, all the while urging him deeper and harder into her.

She pushed him out of her and crawled under his body to pleasure him, and he greedily fell on her open legs and moist sex. She reached her peak quickly, wildly and he wasted no time. He drew her back, sliding her up the bed and drove into her, pounding, and she cried out, a delighted gasp as he ground inside her.

Then, his fingers digging into her flesh as he gripped her, he gave one violent shudder and collapsed on her ample breasts. He breathed deeply for a minute, the last of him pulsing into her before he slid away and onto his back, eyes closed.

She barely waited the moment to catch a breath. 'Oh dear. A decided lack of stamina, Dane.'

He only lifted a brow.

She plucked gently at the dark hair on his belly, and swirled her finger lower. 'You've never come to me like that before.' She raised herself up on one elbow. 'Perhaps you missed me.'

'Of course.'

She pushed off the bed. 'Not even an enthusiastic lie. It's only gentlemanly.' She picked her clothes up from the floor.

He, too, left the bed and went back to his bath. 'On the way out, let Jamieson know I need more hot water, would you?' He climbed into the tub, refilled his glass of rum, closed his eyes and sank as far as he could.

'I'll come back when milord feels more like my company.'

He opened one eye and looked at her. Her tall body was proud and still firm even though she was a few years older than him. 'I've told you time and again, Rebecca. We have an understanding, nothing more.'

Hands firmly on her bare hips, she stood facing him. 'You have some scheming little bitch to service, have you? Well, I'll just wait here until she arrives and we'll see who stays and who goes.'

'You'll be waiting a while,' he muttered, pulling his ear.

'Or is it perhaps your tastes have reversed and you wait for a boy? Is that why you didn't last diddly—'

Dane sat bolt upright in his bath. 'Jamieson!' he roared. 'Jamieson!'

Jamieson hurried into the room. He stopped dead and stared goggle-eyed at the statuesque, nude and shaking Rebecca.

'Get her out of here—and don't let her back again,' Dane ordered.

It was a sight to see skinny, brown-faced and wizened Jamieson scuttling Rebecca, a naked Amazon, out of the room, her bottom wobbling and her shrill protests echoing down the hallway.

It should have been funny.

He heard loud slamming of doors and suspected Jamieson had shoved her into a room to dress.

He slumped back in the water. 'A boy, for Christ's sakes,' he said through his teeth. Not a boy—a girl in boys' clothing.

After his bath, he slept well into the afternoon, awaking to Jamieson's knock, telling him the evening meal was ready in the bar below. Dane dressed and left his room, noticing the bath had been removed. He had clearly slept heavily.

'My, my, old fellow, you do look well rested.' Reuben Cawley surprised him at his table. They shook hands as friends, and embraced as family. 'Good to see you.' He sat down. 'Thought you could do with a few of these to catch up on things.' Reuben dumped a number of copies of *The Bulletin* on the table in front of him.

'Reub, you are a sight for sore eyes. I'll need to catch up, that's certain, but for now ... ' A meal of mutton and vegetables in gravy was delivered, served up in bowls for them, hot and steaming and fragrant.

He had a good deal to tell his friend, much to discuss, a few urgent problems to solve, but now, first, they would eat.

Dane didn't wait too long. He ran through the last few months' turmoil as quickly as he could between mouthfuls; the discovery of Jacaranda's demise, its loss to Foley, his father's duplicity ...

Reuben picked up his spoon to scrape the bowl. 'There seems to be something else. What's all this leading to?' His dark gaze was fixed on Dane's face.

'I'm unsettled by it. Not happy that I let it go on for so long. I want to go back home to Victoria.' Dane's statement was flat.

Reuben showed his surprise. 'Whatever for? You said yourself Jacaranda has gone. Why on earth would you want to go back there? What about here?' He waved his hands around, gesturing to the filled tables and the noisy bar area.

Dane forked the last of the stew into his mouth, chewed and swallowed before answering. 'There was only another year in it for me, you knew that. A hotel in Echuca caught my eye, I was fairly taken with it. Thought I could offer its owner good money, perhaps relocate.'

'I'm bewildered. What on earth brought this on? You never do anything in business without great caution.' He spread his hands, palms up. 'Is that all? You want to be closer to your family?'

Dane shrugged. 'Perhaps, but that's not the only reason.' He lowered his voice. 'I need to exact a revenge, Reub.' He wiped his mouth with a cloth, and pushed his plate away.

Reuben stared at him. 'Not worth the effort, mate,' he stated flatly. 'We both know that. Is it this fellow who got Jacaranda?'

Dane nodded.

'Why bother? It's your old home, yes, but find your parents a new home. Obviously your father's lost interest in it.'

Dane nodded. 'It's only the thing I've worked all my life for,' he said. 'I just need to do something to give the thieving bastard something to come up against. Somebody who can deal straight with him. He just walked away with the homestead, Reub. Just walked away without so much as a kick in the arse.'

'You're out to ruin him.' Reuben narrowed his eyes and finished off the last of his meal, then took a slurp of rum.

Dane snorted. 'I'd need a lot more free money than I have to do that.'

'Do we need to talk of finances now?'

'I thought I would ask the company for another loan and buy the hotel—The Pastoral—but on second thoughts, I can perhaps cover it with notes over this place … if your father approved, of course.' He pushed his chair away from the table and stretched out his legs.

Reuben shrugged. 'There isn't much my father won't approve of where you're concerned. This business is showing very handsome growth and profits. It would even make sense to expand. And,' Reuben leaned forward, 'speaking of my parents, my dear mother has written to me.'

'Is that so?'

'About you in Melbourne. It seems perhaps you have not told your oldest and dearest friend everything.' Reuben's eye glinted as he lifted his rum. 'And perhaps that's why poor old Rebecca got her marching orders this afternoon.'

Dane snorted again. Word travelled fast. His behaviour towards Rebecca had not been kind, and he regretted it. It didn't alter things. He'd found what he wanted and though it was beyond his grasp, a substitute was not going to do.

Reuben ignored the derision. 'Looks like this little Melbourne lady has you badly, old boy, by the bollocks. And a real beauty, according to Mother.'

'Not for discussion.'

His friend once again showed surprise. 'You should try. It's not like you to suffer in silence.'

The jibe brought a wry smile to Dane's face, but also a shake of his head.

Reuben leaned over the table. 'She's married now. And she married this fellow with the cards, is that right?'

Dane nodded.

'Then forget her and get on with it. Leave them to Jacaranda.'

Dane inhaled deeply. 'I cannot.' He didn't want to talk about it, even to Reuben. But he knew that wasn't going to stop his friend.

'Better yet, you could always be totally dishonourable and chase the lady outright. That way, you could exact your horrible revenge doubly.'

'If that's your solution, it's pathetic.' Dane's heart dipped. Nothing would get Georgina back.

Reuben tapped his fingers on the table. 'Perhaps we should go into direct competition with this fellow on the river and run freight and passengers, just like he does. That would surely plant you back in the scene. Tell me,' he said, warming to his theory, 'what sort of money is in this paddleboat stuff?'

He told Reuben his story, his early days on the river, and what the trade had become.

'Interesting. Think of it, Dane. A company of steamships in direct competition with your man. I like it. I really like it. I like the idea that we could create absolute havoc for the bastard.'

'You're serious.'

'Of course!' Reuben cried. 'Think, man. Let's look at the administration of it in the morning and I'll wire my father and have him look further into the situation. To be perfectly honest, I wouldn't mind being back in Melbourne myself, although Amelia—'

'Reub, forgive me.' Dane tapped his forehead. 'I haven't asked about your wife and your children.'

'All's well.' Reuben waved his hand, dismissing Dane's over-sight. 'I'll telegraph Papa tomorrow morning.' He yawned. 'Look, I promised Am I'd be home before dawn even though you have just arrived back. I'll head off now and see you tomorrow. Say ten in the morn?'

———

The next day they ate a late breakfast in Dane's rooms to discuss their next business ventures.

Reuben told Dane his father had replied by telegraph ahead of their ten o'clock appointment. 'John is not overly enthused about the paddle-steamers,' he stated, and Dane raised an eyebrow. 'Says the railway to Swan Hill's nearly finished and that will undo carrying freight as we know it. He's also begun pressing us to sell this place. Says we need to realise cash and buy land. The coming depression, apparently. And the poor publican in Echuca might not even want to sell, Dane.' He dumped a sheaf of papers on the side table. 'Besides, buying the hotel won't get you on the river much. If you must, research the paddle-steamers—see where the market lies.' He tapped the table with a forefinger. 'Let the river answer, boyo. We can always ditch a boat quickly if we have to. Wait until John mails me the information we've asked for. I might tell you, too, that Amelia has agreed to go back to Melbourne for a season or two—sort of a compromise, I suppose—so I can be in the thick of it as well.'

'Who looks after this place?' Dane swilled a mug of hot tea, and bit into a thick slice of bread and beef.

'Jamieson, of course.'

Dane agreed it could be done. Jamieson was up to it, trained thoroughly by him and Reuben. 'Will he do it, though?'

Reuben nodded. 'Champing at the bit. He almost said as much to me some time back, hoping we weren't going to sell the place.'

'We still might if John has his way.' Dane rubbed his forehead. 'I'm not getting my hopes up, Reub. I'm more clear-headed than I was last night.'

'MacHenry, it's not like you to get cold feet.'

'I've been on a slippery slope for three or four months now. Cold or otherwise, I just want my feet to touch solid ground again.'

Reuben nodded. 'Your family's life has certainly been turned upside-down. Even I can see how your girl's marriage to this Foley fellow has knocked you.' He reached over and thumped Dane on the shoulder. 'Easy as it goes, my friend. You know we Cawleys won't let you make a wrong turn. Should have gone off with you into the sunset four months ago, but you were gone so fast, I didn't have time to pack.'

'Yes, easy as it goes.' Dane's spirits lifted. 'Would you really have come with me?'

Reuben gave him a grin and shook his head. 'Amelia would've skinned my balls and showcased them on the mantelpiece. Now let me tell you of the plans I've made for the Captain's Cabin. Even if John says we have to sell, we have to have something decent to attract a buyer.'

———

Dane distanced himself from attachment, but not from a discreet dalliance here and there. He thought himself extremely lucky no angry father or brother had come knocking his door down.

None of it was enough.

'Dane, Dane, Dane,' Reuben grumbled over lunch at the Cabin. 'I see a change in you. You've mellowed, you're not forever chasing skirts as you have in the past.' He cut a lump of mutton and stabbed it with his fork. 'You're milder. More tolerant. Amelia says you've a warmer side emerging. I'm surprised by it. Worried, in fact.'

Dane shrugged. 'Perhaps I'm just tired.'

Reuben scoffed. 'My wife thinks it's the brooding. She is sure you'll eventually catch up with this young woman of yours, and things will be resolved one way or the other.' Reuben laughed at Dane's expression. 'Though it's totally scandalous, old friend, I don't disagree with her.'

'Impossible.' Dane scowled at his own plate of mutton stew, then pushed it away. 'Now where's this packet of papers from John?'

Reuben reached under the table and dragged up a leather satchel. John Cawley had mailed extensive written material for them to pore over, figures and graphs and river fluctuations over the last ten years. Enclosed were sketches and photographs of riverboats from the dirtiest-looking tubs to the grandest paddle-steamers, from freight vessels to passenger boats, including one or two sketches of Conor Foley's most prized vessels. Dane traced each detail of his adversary's boats, and studied every piece of information he could find on the industry. How else would he compete with Foley?

John had advised strongly it would not be a good time to invest in the river trade for freight. Wait until prices had plummeted, he advocated. It wouldn't be long and they'd pick up boats for next to nothing.

Dane wondered if buying anything at all now was wise. Another economic depression was underway; the river was crowded and highly competitive; railways were cutting time and costs and though completion of the line from Ballarat to Swan Hill was a little way off, it bode poorly for the industry. He understood John's advice.

But he'd seen a beautiful vessel for sale in one of the missives John had sent. She sat idle at Echuca, her previous owner having lost her to the banks. Sale after sale had fallen through.

Dane sent a telegram to John. The vessel was much reduced, within his means. He'd outfit her for passengers, not freight ...

John reluctantly agreed.

The boat would go a long way to soothing him. His ache for Jacaranda, however, would not leave, and his thoughts of Georgina were constant.

Twenty-One

After their reception, Conor's first trip away immediately gave Georgie the distance she needed and the time to steel herself, to prepare.

She'd carefully craft questions he would not be able to avoid answering. She would confront him about Jacaranda.

But upon his return a week later, he announced he would only have a few days before he'd be leaving again. She would have to act swiftly. Now.

He was in his bedchamber, overseeing the packing. Clothes were folded and satchels of papers were stacked about the room. Manning, his man, nodded at Georgie as she entered, then took his leave.

Conor glanced in her direction. 'What is it, my love?'

'You now seem to have no time, once again, to advise me of the extent of your business. To start to apprentice me.' She stood with her hands on the back of a leather chair, her fingers clutching the firm padding.

'There is time for that when I return after this trip. I will have a clerk—Mr Bailey, I think—seek some filing, some figures to add, which would accommodate your wishes.' He looked at her again, this time attentive.

She smoothed the chair's antimacassar, and huffed out her frustration. 'Filing would not accommodate my wishes.'

Conor pressed the folded shirts Manning had stacked on his bed into a bag. 'One must start with simpler tasks and master them before taking on the more complex. Why the hurry now? We have discussed this.'

'Because I would prefer you were honest with me sooner rather than later.' The antimacassar scrunched in her grip.

He narrowed his eyes at her and became still.

Georgie positioned herself on the arm of the chair, her body rigid. 'I have heard it said you now own Jacaranda, and have done for some time. That my Aunt Jemimah is to be removed from her home.' Her voice, she thought, sounded calm. Placid, in fact.

'Have you indeed heard that? And you are upset by it.' He hesitated before reaching to the floor and throwing a pair of riding boots into another bag. 'Well, it is true. I go there in two weeks after business on the river at Swan Hill.'

'You didn't think to tell me yourself?' She stood up and moved in front of him as he packed.

He stepped around her. 'Clearly you already know.' He shot her a look. 'What does this discussion hope to achieve? I own it. It is part of Foley's River Carriers, now. A landing along the river to safely tie up.'

To calm herself, she looked around the room at his big bed, at the masculine accoutrements of leather and timber, and inhaled scents of tobacco and rum.

'And you did not *buy* it.'

He grunted. 'I acquired it legally.' He stalked past her to grab a hat.

'Why would you even want it?' Her voice was beginning to sound shrill.

'It was an opportunity, and I took it. That's what I do. As I said, it's a safe place to tie up.' He flicked her a glance.

Georgie felt the feathery slide of goose bumps on her arms. 'Where are they to go?'

'That is not my concern.' He stopped in front of her. 'Nor yours.'

She squared her shoulders. 'But it is, Conor.'

He pointed at her. 'I am being patient, Georgina. I want no repeat of the episode before we were married.'

Episode? Georgie barely blinked as he reminded her of his vitriolic, violent outburst.

'So I will tell you this,' he continued. 'I offered MacHenry reparation, which he refused, and yet I paid his outstanding debts. I could do no more.' He turned his back.

'You could have paid him out instead of just beating him at cards.' Her voice rose, and her hands prickled as she stepped carefully, gauging his mood.

'That's not how gambling with cards works. He got what the place was worth. Almost nothing, after his neglect.' He stood over her. 'And who told you of this? Jemimah? I think not.' He turned back to his packing.

Georgie followed. 'But you won this game before we were married.'

He straightened. 'There are many things you don't know about, before and after our wedding. They are not necessary for you to know.'

'I might not have made the decision to marry you had I known that.' She shook with contained rage, her voice tight, her jaw clenched.

His eyes narrowed again and Georgie felt a cold brush of air glide over her neck.

His gaze locked on hers. 'We will never know, will we, my dear Georgie, for you are married to me now. And unless you'd prefer to be destitute and degraded, living in the streets, begging for your next meal, you will remain so.' He tilted his head a little. 'I don't believe for a moment you would want otherwise,' he said softly. 'Those new laws you so love to speak of would not save you. You brought nothing to this marriage to take away.'

Georgie bit her cheeks at the thinly veiled threat. She held his gaze, though her heartbeat thudded in her temples. She exhaled quietly. 'How will I know that you'll *ever* tell me the truth now?'

'Whatever you ask me I will tell you the answer truly.' Conor's face had flushed. His scowl deepened.

'That supposes I know which questions to ask.'

'Precisely. Do not presume that your conditions to marriage entitle you to more than I am prepared to give.'

The cold slide of air wisped over her throat again. She sucked in a breath. 'You deliberately concealed from me information which deeply embarrasses me—'

'You could not wait to be rid of the place, Georgina. Especially as MacHenry saw fit to squander your father's allowance to you. Why should you care?'

'I care because Jemimah was very kind to me. She deserves better. She deserves more for her time and effort. It was her home!' Georgie breathed out the anger before it overpowered her. 'You should be open and honest with me, not omitting things and believing you haven't told a lie. How much more deceit and manipulation is in store for me?'

'Oh, none from me.' He didn't look at her. Instead, he pointed to a purse on his bedside dresser. 'And there, that is filled with coin for you to do with as you see fit while I'm away this time. You see how comfortable you are here, my dear.' He gave a little smile, and a flop of red hair fell over his forehead. 'Anything else, you have authority to purchase on my accounts.'

She stared at him. 'That just fobs me off. There is more to discuss about this.'

'There is not. I have done much of what you asked of me, but my business dealings are my own.' He went to the back of the door and pulled a coat from the hook. 'I had just a moment ago thought I'd stay another night before leaving, but perhaps it is better I leave today.'

She willed herself to be still. 'Conor, I'm asking you to sign the deed to Jacaranda back to Uncle Tom. See the solicitor before you leave.'

'I will be seeing my solicitor—I already have an appointment. That is a truth for you. But I will not sign Jacaranda back to MacHenry, even if he would take it.'

She met his gaze squarely.

'Enough!' Conor took a step closer to her. He spoke softly, eerily calm. 'Now, I am to be gone for some time, Georgie. Let's kiss and make up before I go. Perhaps, if we did, I would stay that extra night after all.' He dropped his coat on the bed, held out a hand and took one of hers.

She hesitated. 'You keep secrets from me.'

'Aye.' He lifted her hand. 'And who told you of Jacaranda?'

She maintained her gaze but shook her head.

He pressed her hand to his lips, caressed her neck with his other hand then brushed her mouth with his. 'So it seems, my dear Georgie, you also keep secrets from me.'

Twenty-Two

Georgie let the newspaper fall into her lap as she looked out at the garden. She had been Mrs Conor Foley for only a couple of months, and in that time she and her husband had barely had more than a few weeks together.

She leaned back in her seat and shuddered a little, recalling the argument that spilled the day before he left this time. She'd brushed away thoughts of leaving and instead had turned her mind to the positive things she could do.

This morning she'd been reading of the 'Monster Petition' she'd signed in the city gardens all that time ago. The right for women to vote had been defeated in the Legislative Council. Miss Goldstein would be bitterly disappointed, but Georgie was sure the parliament had not seen the last of the fight for women's franchise, for the suffrage movement.

Her brother-in-law, Angus, would tease her mercilessly when he learnt of the defeat. Kate and Angus Forrestor had married and moved to their new home in Hawthorn, so Georgie was finally sole mistress of Conor's great house. Now that Kate was not looking over her shoulder every minute of the day, Georgie started to make plans.

The first thing she did the day Conor left was to write to Jemimah once again. Georgie had gleaned from him that the family still lived on Jacaranda as they hadn't as yet secured other lodgings. She begged Jemimah to answer, swearing she had no knowledge of the card game that saw Jacaranda lost.

In the meantime, she would purchase her own horse. She missed MacNamara keenly. Missed the daily ritual of his grooming. Missed how that habit had kept her thoughts ordered and her heart calm. There were stables on the property. Though Conor had relented from his stoic insistence she forget about her horses and leave finding a horse to him, no purchase had yet been made, so she would do that herself. Buttons knew exactly where to take her.

The closed door to Conor's office beckoned on more than one occasion. He had not yet begun to teach her any part of the business. She found advertisements in the newspapers for courses in bookkeeping and would enrol herself into whatever was available. Angus, although he hadn't offered to assist in any such thing, had inadvertently pointed out two or three colleges that would offer her education.

She poured the last of the tea into her cup. Life with Conor would be comfortable—they were financially secure—but it might also be peaceful and whole if she herself was at least gainfully occupied, and not just a showpiece.

One other area of their lives together worried her. There was something very much missing from the physical side of their relationship. According to Josephine, there was the extra act of penetration yet to be performed, when the gentleman would insert the stiff, hard part of his private anatomy—which grew on contact with a female, a most extraordinary phenomenon—into the secret warmth of his wife's body.

Georgie knew how horses did it—she could *not* imagine that was how humans did it, with all that shrieking and screaming—and how other farm animals mated. As much as it had seemed unsavoury to Georgie, she was now curious as to why the particular part of Conor's body that should have been stiff and hard had never been so when they were together. He'd explained it was the result of an injury, and that he was hopeful of a full recovery, given he now had a beautiful wife to comfort him. And as he didn't know how much time would be needed, it was a good thing they didn't want children.

Nevertheless, the attention Conor lavished on her body when they fell together in bed was certainly satisfying.

The other perplexing thing was that he would take leave of her soon after their lovemaking, gruff and dismissive, and disappear into his own bedchamber. Next she would often hear what she thought was an anguished grunt. When questioned, Conor would only say he'd had to attend his injury.

Georgie needed someone like Josephine around with whom to discuss these matters.

Wonderful gifts of English crystal and china had arrived from Papa Rupert. Beautiful clothes, including a most handsome riding suit complete with a split skirt, delighted her, and spoke volumes of Rupert's delight as well. The day his parcel arrived, Georgie admired herself in her new riding outfit in front of the mirror. She was more determined than ever to have her own horse again. It turned her thoughts to the lazy days at Jacaranda that had come to an abrupt halt just before she married Conor.

How had she not realised she loved the mallee country, and the river that gave it life? Now she missed it sorely.

Memories of Jacaranda always led her to thinking about the other MacHenry, the one who sent her heart a-skittering, and she tried to push him away.

Dane's last bruising words to her at her wedding reception were the ones she found hardest to dismiss. When she and Conor were in each others' arms, his face pressed to her breast, she would blush hotly and struggle against the warmth that curled in her belly for Dane MacHenry.

She shook herself out of her reverie, immediately dismissing the turmoil that followed whenever she thought of Dane. It would do her no good to continue to think of another man now that she was married. No good. No benefit to her whatsoever.

So why, oh why, do thoughts of him continue to quicken my heart?

Impatient with herself, she stood up and dropped the newspaper beside her chair. Pacing in front of the window, movement outside caught her eye: Kate and Angus's sulky driving up to the house. Delightful! Her sister-in-law and her husband were very welcome company. She hadn't seen Kate for weeks it seemed, and when Conor left for his business trips, there were very few people Georgie ever got to see outside of the staff.

Rushing to the door, she kissed each of them in greeting. She ordered more tea to be served in the morning room, which overlooked the garden Kate had once so lovingly tended. The bright and sunny, yet cool Melbourne morning bathed the grounds with a pale golden glow.

'My dear, we've had another invitation from Angeline. She wants us to take tea with her tomorrow at her home.' Kate sipped from her delicate china cup.

One did not refuse an invitation to tea from Mrs John Cawley, but Georgie was hesitant. 'Yes, of course, how lovely.'

Mrs Cawley had unnerved her at the reception by bringing Dane as her escort, and ever since, she was always uncomfortable in the older woman's presence. At every invitation, Georgie became increasingly uneasy, and there had been quite a few in the weeks since her wedding. She absently twisted the heavy band on her finger, then reached for her cup of tea.

Angus groaned.

Georgie wanted to groan, too.

'Another invitation, Katie? I can't keep up with all the social-ising you ladies do,' he said. 'What on earth do you find to talk about?' He was standing by the mantelpiece over the fire, sipping tea, into which he'd sloshed a tot of rum from the bottle on the sideboard. 'Georgina, before we get lost in such riveting conversa-tion, when is your husband due to return?'

'Some weeks away, now, Angus.'

'I have to catch up with him on some legal matters.'

'I could consult his diary ... ' Georgie placed her cup and sau-cer on her side table, ready to go to Conor's study, ' ... but in the meantime, perhaps I could help you if you simply needed—'

'No, no. Thank you all the same. I'm sure half of these mat-ters Conor keeps in his head, anyway. We'll attend to it ourselves. Right—I'm going over to Domain Road to check the stables with O'Brien.'

Georgie turned to Kate. 'I would so love to visit the stables. Let's go, too.'

'Oh, no, my dear.' Her sister-in-law looked alarmed.

'No, Georgina,' Angus hurriedly said, backing his wife. 'Now, I'll be back in an hour or so.' He swallowed the last of his tea, excused himself and left a peck on his wife's cheek.

Georgie watched him leave. Perhaps it was not wise to bring her in-laws into her plans.

Kate took her hand. 'Perhaps we'll go out somewhere. We could take the sulky and make an afternoon of it, visiting all sorts of places.'

Georgie nodded absently. Perhaps Conor had not informed his sister about his change of heart regarding a horse for her. And why would he? She and Buttons would find a suitable horse.

'The sulky. Hardly an exhilarating ride.'

Kate brushed her aside. 'Georgina, I fear you're becoming like those new types of women I've read about recently—the kind who want to do more than sit at home and have babies.'

Georgie hid a grimace. 'Of course I am.' And as there wasn't a baby in sight and she knew there wouldn't be, fending off the hints and the prodding was becoming more than tedious. She stuck to her subject. 'I already am one of those types. Lots of women ride, they do at least that much, and many women work outside the home.'

Kate went on as if she hadn't spoken. 'And Angeline always shows immense interest in your welfare, which is wonderful, so afternoon tea there tomorrow will be delightful for you. You have the best introduction to society here.'

The conversation at Mrs Cawley's afternoon teas could sometimes be quite lively, especially when Georgie began to talk of suffrage. Interesting conversation would range from politics in England and at home—which surprised and delighted Georgie—to babies, children and husbands. Inevitably, Mrs Cawley would talk of her grown-up family, of Reuben and his wife and children, and of course Reuben's best friend, Dane MacHenry.

Georgie would try hard not to squirm.

There was no excuse she could muster to avoid going to afternoon tea at Mrs Cawley's home. So she would sit stoically as she had done before and hope her discomfort would not be obvious.

Kate reached for another tiny piece of cake. 'So, tea on Wednesday. And when Conor returns, you might be able to take a short holiday.' She smiled.

'Yes, perhaps.' Georgie laced her fingers. 'Apparently he has bought a small house in Port Fairy. We might visit once the purchase has settled. I think he's also buying some transport there, bullocks and drays—the Western Districts are very lucrative, and he wants to be a part of the trade.'

'What—finish with the river?'

'Oh, I don't know about that. Add to his companies, I should think. Broadening his horizons, finger in every pie, that sort of thing.' Georgie laughed, and noted Kate had a keen eye on her. It was rare she laughed aloud. *Probably too much time on my own*, she mused.

Kate reached across and squeezed Georgie's hand. 'My dear, are you all right?'

'Yes, of course.'

Leaning back, Kate said, 'I thought you might be feeling a little bit lonely with Conor away so often.'

'I know I'd be more useful if he let me learn about his businesses. I know I could do quite a lot to help him—'

Kate cut her short. 'Georgina, we women don't need to work like the men.'

'But they have such exciting lives, Kate. They do what they like. I haven't been out for a ride in … oh, I don't know how long. There's no fresh air in the house, someone else tends the gardens … It's very exasperating.'

'You must do something about that. Take up a charity.'

Georgie shook her head, felt her loosely pinned hair threatening to tumble down over her shoulders. She put a hand up to steady it, poking pins back in here and there. 'I am going to purchase my own horse in the next few days. That will help.'

'I thought Conor—'

She threw her hands up. 'He knows I have been riding all my life. I will find myself a horse. I'm certainly not interested in pressing flowers. Perhaps I will find an interesting subject to study, particularly pertinent to Conor's business.'

Kate suggested a string of avenues to follow up, mostly volunteer work in charities. Each was met with a fervent shake of the head.

'I wonder if Conor would mind if you worked for Angus for a while?' she said finally. 'Would that help things a little? Though, now I think of it, I'm not sure what Angus would make of it.'

Angus Forrestor was a solicitor. Georgie could just imagine filing in some stuffy little office in the city for her brother-in-law. She shook her head. 'I don't think either of them expect me to be other than wife and hostess.'

'That's your role now, wife and soon perhaps, a mother,' Kate said. 'But he can't expect to leave you all on your own for weeks on end without something you love to do. We shall tackle the issue tomorrow at Angeline's. I'm sure she'll have a few ideas.' Kate patted her sister-in-law's hand.

Georgie just shook her head and stared at her hands.

Twenty-Three

Conor Foley moored the *Lady Mitchell* in a channel away from the dock at Echuca after she'd unloaded. It cleared the way for other boats at the cranes. He'd sailed her from Echuca to Renmark and back again, helping to shift the extra load of the Ross merchandise, a contract he'd recently won back despite previous difficulties with breakdowns. She'd wait there until ready for reloading.

On his way through, he'd left a number of men to work at Jacaranda while he was away: Barnes, his foreman, was stocky, weathered, tough; Reilly, the drunk, still bothered Foley by his very presence; the McCormack boys were lanky and hardworking roustabouts; Smith, Dawson and young Billy, the shearers, were all wiry and lean. Barnes would oversee old man MacHenry, who was still on Jacaranda with his wife and daughter. Barnes was under orders to report by mail on a regular basis.

In Echuca now for nearly a week, Foley finalised some business matters. He'd taken a night or two over a personal matter in a discreet townhouse then lodged at the Pastoral. He was most at peace with the world. He didn't stop in at Jacaranda on the way back to Echuca. He hadn't wanted to undermine Barnes's confidence, but would return there in two months after time at home in Melbourne.

Now, he waited for Ranald Finn to finish unloading the *Lady Goodnight* then he would catch up with his captain in the pub. He was in the middle of organising a ticket at the railway office for passage to Melbourne when one of the postal clerks found him there.

'Saw you crossing the street, Mr Foley. Thought you'd like to know there's some mail for you and also a telegram.'

Foley thanked the man and finalised his rail booking. He'd be home by Thursday lunchtime. Striding across the busy main street to the post office, he wondered who would have sent a telegram.

The letters were Barnes's reports, dated weeks ago, painful to read, for, as the man had said, his writing was poor. Barnes informed Foley that all was well, that there'd been little trouble with Reilly, although he still drank more than was acceptable, and no bother out of Mr MacHenry, though Barnes described him as 'merows'. Morose was right. Foley wasn't surprised by that description at all. Jemimah was cooking for the men and by all accounts it was edible and adequate. Elspeth was making a nuisance of herself, trying to treat the working men as servants. Foley grunted. *Spoiled brat.*

The telegram, however, was dire news. Dated just days ago, it read: *Mr Foley sir, there's trouble here. A life is lost. Mr Finn has word. Please advise writer. Barnes.*

Foley stared at the paper. *A life is lost.* Good God, whose? He stared absently from the telegram to the postal clerk, who stared back, startled. Then Foley barged outside and rushed for the wharf. He had seen the *Lady Goodnight* dock. Finn would still be there.

But then he reckoned if Finn had news that bad, he would have gone to the Pastoral Hotel to seek Foley.

He bounded back towards the township and hurried into the bar. Ranald Finn was waiting patiently, two glasses of liquor on the bench in front of him. He sighted Foley the moment he entered the room and signalled to the corner table.

They seated themselves and exchanged greetings.

'Ran, what's this terrible news Barnes has?'

Finn tossed back his rum. 'Where to start, Mr Foley? Seems some time ago there was a terrible dust storm at Jacaranda, and the old cook-house roof blew off. Story is, Mr MacHenry was in there and got himself fairly knocked on the head when one of the wooden beams fell in.' He signalled the bartender for refills.

Conor swallowed his rum and held his glass up for another as the jug was brought to their table. 'Is that it?'

Finn waited until the waiter left with his payment. 'That's what the McCormack boys will say if asked. But it's just a story.'

Foley watched his captain hesitate. 'Yes, and? I don't have patience.'

Finn spread his hands. 'The real story goes that Reilly had fingered the old man's daughter and when MacHenry went berserk, he got himself done in, sir. By Reilly.' He took his refilled glass and downed the rum in a swallow.

'Murder?' Foley stared at him in shock, then shook his head. 'Tom MacHenry is dead—and Reilly killed him? I need more information, here, Ran.'

'I don't have much more, Mr Foley. Barnes wanted you there first, before the police. We haven't notified them yet.' Ranald Finn rubbed his weathered face, the sound of it like sand on paper. 'The missus and the girl have locked themselves inside the big house and Reilly is locked in the cool room. Barnes threw him in a few bottles of rum hoping he'd kill himself, but it hadn't happened by the time I arrived there.'

Foley shook his head again, and groaned. 'What a godawful mess. We'll get the Swan Hill police out there quickly.'

'There's something else I think you should know, Mr Foley.' Ranald Finn's mouth flattened.

'Jesus. What?' Foley's elbows were on the table, his hands clasping, unclasping.

'A new boat pulled in at the dock today. A passenger boat, sir. Beautiful, she is.' Ranald Finn cocked his head. 'I reckon you might recognise her if you saw her. I believe you were about to purchase her when Mrs Foley disappeared a while ago.' Finn sat back, rolling his glass in his hands.

Foley stilled. 'The *Lady Georgina* is here? Who bought her?'

'A company, Melbourne Lands and Holdings. Partners are well-to-do, I believe.'

Foley grunted. 'I don't know the name.' He blew out a breath. 'Another operator on an already tired river. Don't much like the idea of it, we're just ahead in the passenger game.' He was curious all the same. 'I'll make myself known to them. Ran, I need passage back to Jacaranda.'

Finn shrugged his shoulders. 'Might be faster by horse, sir.'

'No use battering a poor horse over a dead body. Barnes will have Reilly well in hand—I'll ask around for passage to Jacaranda. Someone will be going past there down to Renmark. So, where did they bury MacHenry?'

'About a hundred yards from the house.'

Foley nodded. He threw down his last rum, clapped Finn on the shoulder and instructed him to telegram Barnes, alerting him to his arrival within the next few days.

He strode back to the dock, the rum warming his stomach, but the news deadening his heart.

Of all the bloody things … And Reilly, that good-for-nothing piece of shit. The bastard. I hope I get to him before the police do.

The *Lady Goodnight* was still unloading; the *Mitchell* was awaiting her turn to take more freight, and as contracts were back-
logged he didn't want to commandeer her for his one-way trip
up to Jacaranda. Foley passed the *Gem* and asked Captain King if
he was going back towards Swan Hill. A shake of the head. Foley
waved and stalked on.

He was about to ask Captain Spears of the *Maiden* when he spotted
the gleaming white hull of the river's newest boat not fifty yards from
where he stood. He whistled softly through his teeth. He'd forgotten
the splendour of the vessel he would have named the *Lady Georgina*.

Foley bounded towards it and smiled to himself as he read its
name. Now she was the *Sweet Georgie*. If his fleet hadn't had names
prefixed with 'Lady', he might have chosen the same name. The
Lady Mitchell ran a poor second to this boat. He whistled again in
admiration. The vessel was slim-lined, sleek as he remembered, a
dainty elegant river lady built for cruising. His interest in his rival
grew. He would meet with the owners, formulate business dealings involving the boat. He would—

A voice addressed him from the deck below. 'Afternoon.'

'Afternoon.' Foley smiled affably. 'Just admiring this magnificent craft. Are you its owner?'

'Yes.' The black-haired man straightened up, made it obvious
he was sizing up his visitor.

'Beautiful. Nearly bought her myself.' Foley was still smiling
at the man on the boat. Was he familiar—had he met him somewhere before? 'I was wondering if you might be taking her down
river at all in the next few days. I need passage.'

'We are at that. Passage shouldn't be a problem, that's what
we're here for.'

The reply was friendly enough, but the man's tone sent warning bells tolling in Foley's head. 'Good. I want to be landed at
Jacaranda.'

The momentary silence puzzled him.

Then the man said, 'I thought you might.'

Foley shaded his eyes against the early afternoon sun and squinted down at the man on the boat. 'Have we met?'

'Mr Foley, I escorted Mrs Cawley to your wedding reception. I am Dane MacHenry.'

Foley stepped closer to the edge of the wharf, staring at the man. This was the 'pimply-faced youth' he had thought Tom MacHenry's son to be. Of course, that explained the animosity—they were adversaries. And where on earth could MacHenry's son have found himself such good fortune and wealth to be able to purchase such a fine vessel? 'Ah, yes. I remember. I'm sorry I don't recall we'd actually met.' He also did not recall Georgina explaining to him who Dane MacHenry was. She *had* known his name after all. She had danced with him. The man she had purportedly run from, and been caught by—but that could wait.

What was MacHenry doing here? Would he already know of his father's demise?

He found his voice again. 'May I come aboard?' At Dane's delayed but curt nod, he found the closest manhole in the board-walk and got to the lower tier on a level with the boat. He took the gang plank onto the vessel and offered his hand. 'Conor Foley. I am pleased to meet you, though not under these circum—'

'So, passage to Jacaranda. I suppose I should ask your permission to pull up at the landing there.' Dane MacHenry barely gripped Foley's hand before he let it drop.

'No, no, of course not. Certainly not under these circumstances.'

Dane MacHenry looked at odds, and scowled. 'I'm about to visit my parents. I trust there'll be no embarrassment.'

Foley frowned. 'You've received no word from Jacaranda lately?'

'No. I've had my hands full these past months. This visit is part of the maiden journey.'

'Look, I—may I presume upon you for a drink? Perhaps we could go below.'

Dane snorted. 'I'm well aware of the situation at Jacaranda with you and my parents. It's not necessary to—'

Foley interjected. 'Very well. This is neither the appropriate time nor place, nor perhaps am I the best person to deliver this message.' He straightened. 'I certainly don't know how else to tell you. My foreman has reported that your father is dead.'

Twenty-Four

The *Sweet Georgie*'s maiden voyage was subdued, hardly the type of journey Reuben Cawley had planned. He consoled himself with thoughts of the full and paying passenger list from Echuca to Goolwa, and of how the profits would come rolling in. Thank God this maiden run carried a little freight to cover wages.

He considered both Conor Foley and Dane MacHenry. He admired their restraint with each other, although Reuben was sure Conor Foley knew nothing of Dane's story with the lovely Georgina. Reuben was also sure Dane would break before too long.

The mate Dane had employed allowed Reuben a turn at the wheel and he spent most of his time in the wheelhouse being carefully watched. Foley offered to take the wheel by night.

'I'm glad of it, Dane.' Reuben leaned over the stern rail just after Foley had entered the wheelhouse. He'd heard on the dock that the man's navigation skills on the mighty, moody river were legendary. 'It also means that by day, neither Foley nor you are very much in each other's company.'

Dane, who rested his back against the rail, grunted and grudgingly agreed. 'True. But do you see him? He can't keep his hands off the boat. He can't refrain from loudly wishing he'd been quicker to purchase her.' Dane stared at the banks of the river receding in the dusk light. 'Is he looking for a response as he repeats the tale of his wife's disappearance from Jacaranda to Melbourne? My blood boils at every mention. And here I have to watch him enjoy our hospitality.'

'You're doing well, my friend.'

'If Foley mentions one more time he was once going to name this boat the *Lady Georgina,* I'll knock him to the ground.'

'I don't doubt you'd try,' Reuben responded.

Dane was brooding and miserable, naturally, at the news of his father's death, and in a quandary regarding Foley. Common sense told both of them Foley was not to blame for this terrible tragedy, but the black mood descended heavily day by day. There was little consolation for Dane MacHenry in his growing animosity towards Foley, who was obviously well known and well liked along the river, and by as many women as men.

The boat pulled in at one of the landings. The few crates of freight were unloaded, and more taken aboard. River business had to be acquitted for the new boat's reputation despite the urgency of its sad maiden journey.

Foley winked at Dane and Reuben and disembarked, saying he would be back in a few hours. It was obvious the man had women all along the river and, married or not, it seemed he led the life of a single man.

'I'm tempted to ask Foley if his wife knows of these jaunts.' Dane watched as the big man strode up the banks and disappeared over the hill.

'And that would be so beneath you, old friend, not to mention childish, churlish and certainly none of your business. The man can do as he wishes.'

'Ever my conscience, Reuben.'

Reuben snorted, then slapped his friend on the back.

———

Landing at Jacaranda weighed on all of them. Reuben opted to stay on the boat.

When Dane and Foley arrived at the homestead, the situation became painfully clear. Jemimah and Elspeth, having seen Dane arrive from their vantage point inside the house, began screaming for his help.

Dane burst inside the house.

'Dear God, Dane. Thank God.' Jemimah clung to him.

He held out his other arm and Elspeth rushed in. Unusually quiet, his sister hugged him tightly.

'You're both all right?' he asked over the top of his mother's head.

'Unwashed, a little hungry, but we are all right.' Jemimah nodded her head against his chest. 'The men have been kind, but bewildered for us. For themselves, too, I think.'

'Damn the men. Ma … ?'

'I'm all right, Dane. And Elspeth.' She separated herself from him and tugged her daughter away. She straightened her clothes, and stood a little taller. 'You look very fine.'

'I don't feel very fine.' He felt his eyes water as he stared at his mother.

She gripped his hands. 'You must see to … it, along with Mr Foley. Then, you must visit Tom's—your father's grave is over in the next paddock.' Jemimah let him go and turned to the cupboard in which Tom had kept his rum.

She slid a rifle from on top. 'While we have been locked in here, I have cleaned and oiled it. It's loaded.'

Dane strode from the house, Tom MacHenry's Martini-Henry rifle by his side. Behind him, Jemimah was dry-eyed but Elspeth clutched at her mother, dishevelled and tearful.

'Foley,' he called. 'My mother and sister can't stay here now. I'd like to get them into Swan Hill as soon as possible.'

'Of course.' Foley looked at the two women, and approached them. 'I am so sorry this has happened.' He looked at Jemimah, who brought herself to her full height to face him.

'I want to talk to the man who reported this to you.' Dane's interruption was brusque.

Foley nodded. 'Barnes. He's up by the cool room, where they've got Reilly.'

Dane stalked ahead of Foley.

Barnes came up quickly to greet them. He nodded at Dane, expressed his condolences, but addressed Foley. 'Mr Foley, I dunno what to do. We need the coppers here. The Mac boys will talk in Swan Hill, that's for sure.'

'That'll be all right, Barnes. We can say we reported it when we could.' Foley flicked his hand at the trapdoor near their feet. 'Is he tied up?'

'No, sir. Was all we could do to throw him down there. I was hoping the rum woulda killed him by now, or us shoving him in the hole. Seems like he's got some other agitation.' Barnes tapped his head.

'Let him up.' Dane pulled the rifle onto his arm.

Foley nodded at Barnes who, with the help of two of the other men, hauled open the trapdoor. The bellowing, belligerent Irishman made his way up the shallow steps of the cellar. He squinted in the daylight and howled as the sun stung his eyes, then fell over the top of the opening and lay prone for a moment or two. Barnes and his men took a couple of steps back.

'Reilly,' Foley uttered in disgust. Reilly lifted his head, still squinting against the light. 'You'll hang for this, man.'

Reilly growled and spat into the dust. He turned his head towards the sound of the cock of the rifle's loading mechanism. 'I can't see yer, but I can hear yer, Foley. So, you weak-as-piss excuse for a man, yer brung the troopers.' He spat again and rubbed his eyes, swiping at the tears that flowed from them.

'You're still drunk, Reilly.'

'That I am, Mr Foley. I reckon ol' Barnes thought I'd kill meself down there with the gallons of the stuff they threw at me. Not likely. Not likely on rum. An' where's that girl—'

Dane took a step closer, shouldered the rifle and took aim at Reilly's head. 'You filthy bastard.'

Reilly swung his head around, blinking fiercely. 'Whosat?'

Foley stepped closer. 'Get up, you imbecile. You'll be going to gaol in Swan Hill.'

'Not fuckin' likely, Mr High an' Mighty. But come and get me anyway.' He struggled to his feet, oblivious to the rifle aimed at his head. 'Course, p'raps yer couldn't come get me—Mrs Hodge sez yer not got the block 'n' tackle to take a trick on her—'

Foley roared and lunged at the drunk. Reilly swung an arm and took a fist of Foley's hair and they both crashed to the ground on the other side of the cellar's opening. Reilly beat Foley mercilessly, as if his brain had snapped.

Foley's head, held by hair still clutched in Reilly's fist, was crunched down onto Reilly's knee, the *thwack thwack* of bone against bone sickening. Reilly bellowed, spittle leaping from his mouth as he battered Foley bloody. Foley's voice had gone, his throat crushed under the first brutal assault.

Dane aimed the rifle back and forth as the two men grappled close to the edge. He couldn't get a clear shot at Reilly and instead fired into the air, hoping to stop the fight. Then he aimed at

Reilly's feet and the rifle reported again. Somewhere in the distance, a woman screamed.

Reilly bellowed again, bursting with rage, his face mottled and purple veins swelling over his forehead. He swung Foley down the steps of the cellar as if the other man were a rag doll. With both hands now in Foley's hair, he lunged the man's head at the closest step.

The crunch was gut-churning, the explosion of blood and bone and brain hideously final; the loud splat of it landing on the ground was loud and would echo in Dane's nightmares.

The rifle roared again, and Reilly's own head burst like an overripe melon.

Twenty-Five

Georgie had, as always when Conor was away, amused herself. She had persuaded Buttons to take her to the stables on Domain Road.

'I dare not, Mrs Foley. It'd mean me job. Mr Foley has forbidden—'

'There's a gold sovereign and a month's supply of quality rum in it for you.'

Buttons looked despondent.

'What is it, now?'

'I'd never be able to spend a sovereign, Mrs Foley. They'd think I'd stolen it.'

Georgie reddened. She hadn't thought of that, and immediately found shilling pieces to impart.

At the stables, she'd had a great deal more trouble convincing the stable boy to allow her any horse to ride. The man was staunch in his refusal, and no amount of cajoling could budge him. On one occasion when he was trying to politely ignore her pestering, Georgie's temper rose and she let fly with a tirade only Joseph O'Grady, the stableman on Jacaranda, had heard.

That, too, had cost her a sovereign's worth in small pieces and a month's rum, to keep the boy quiet about her visit to the stables and to ensure poor Buttons wasn't punished for bringing her. Conor Foley's temper and fondness for retribution were well known. Buttons had even suggested there was a violence to his master. Her insides fluttered and her arms ran with goose bumps with her own memory of it.

Her next outing would be to the horse sales. Buttons would certainly drive her, and she would choose a mount.

Removing herself from afternoon teas with Mrs Cawley and the other ladies would be the next item on her list of things to do. Her plan was to plead illness to Kate if she had to attend another such afternoon. She wondered how her sister-in-law managed to enjoy herself as much as she did. Heartily sick of tea, Georgie found the Madeira from New South Wales that so many others seemed to enjoy did strange things to her eyesight. She would decline that type of refreshment as well.

Kate was coming to lunch today and she would certainly be armed with invitations to more tedious daytime parties, all of which Georgie would try to turn down.

Conor had been gone longer than expected this time. He'd always told her he would arrive as close to the day he had originally said, but not to expect him until he actually arrived. She had let this Thursday pass without a thought of his being late. She used the time instead to sit in his great study, a room normally off limits to her.

At first, she just sat in his big chair behind the ornate timber desk inlaid with a fine burgundy leather. His scent, faint but still present, pervaded the room. She was smiling, as much for the unexpected pleasure it gave her to sit in the room, as for the knowledge that he would have frowned upon her being there. She clapped her hands on his desk and leaned forward over it, grumbling wordlessly at an imaginary employee.

Spying his cigar box, she flipped it open and removed one. She hesitated before putting it in her mouth and when she did, she promptly withdrew it and threw it back in its box, a grimace on her lips.

She ran her hands along the numerous volumes of diaries and adventure biographies. Nothing really captured her interest until she spied a large pile of books stacked neatly under the desk. When she reached for the top one, she noticed it was the main book Conor's accountant normally carried with him.

Bending down to lift it with both hands, she laid it on the desk. It fell open to where a marker had been placed.

It only took a couple of minutes for her to realise she didn't have a clue as to its contents. A lot of figures in columns, notations, the names of various companies. Really, nothing she could decipher.

Sitting back in the deep leather chair, her feet swinging off the floor, she stared at the globe across the room, and focused on England. Loneliness surged through her. It wasn't that she longed for England, or even to see her stepfather, but seeing that tiny island so far away from Australia made her feel suddenly small and inconsequential.

She shook her head quickly. *I must be going soft. It's the lack of activity—I should be riding every day and educating myself.* She made a mental note again to tackle Conor on his return about being a part of his business.

She envied Kate and Angus for their loving relationship. She knew her relationship with Conor was not the same as the Forrestors's. Kate loved Angus. Georgina and Conor's marriage didn't contain the type of love she'd previously thought it would. It wasn't the type of love she'd *hoped* it would be. In fact, it was as far from it as she could have imagined.

As Conor never let her know anything of his business, she had become, so she thought, just an addition to the porcelain and crystal—a possession to be petted. When she tried to argue with him or press a point, he would merely laugh at her, and pat her hand absently. In time, he said. In time. It had been her frustration with him that had led to the last insidious scene. Georgie had witnessed Kate, on the other hand, argue a point politely with Angus—something she had once yearned to do, but now she no longer dared to offer Conor so much as a differing opinion.

But she was an intelligent woman. She would do what she wanted and not ask for it. Perhaps, like Conor, she would only answer when questioned.

At least babies were not on her agenda. She had no maternal instincts at all. Thankfully, Kate had only broached the subject once, and Georgie had shrugged and that had been the end of it. She knew enough to know that a certain act would have to have occurred between her and her husband for there to be a chance of babies. And she was glad it had not. Foley knew she was not interested in children so perhaps that was why. And she was heartily glad of that. Especially now, when she looked forward to his absences more than she did to his return.

She glanced at the desk under her hands. She should write a letter. The only people she had ever written to were Rupert and, more recently, Jemimah.

As she found some clean paper, Manning bobbed his head inside the doorway.

'Oh, Mrs Foley. This is the last place I would have looked.' He stepped inside, giving the open drawer and the papers in her hands a swift glance. 'I'm sorry to interrupt you. There is a gentleman to see you.'

'A gentleman.' Georgie looked at the clock on the mantelpiece. It was nearly midday. 'Has Mrs Forrestor also arrived?'

'Yes, madam. Mrs Forrestor is in the Garden Room. She's ordered your lunch be served there.'

'Oh good. Now, a gentleman, you say. Who is it?'

'A Mr MacHenry, madam.'

Georgie's stomach lurched.

She instructed Manning to have the gentleman wait in the drawing room for her. She hurried into the Garden Room and Kate smiled as she entered.

'Oh, there you are. Are we ready for lunch? I'm absolutely famished. Sandwiches in here, is that all right?'

Georgie nodded, then found her voice. 'He's here,' she blurted, wringing her hands on her skirts.

'Who's here?' Kate, unperturbed, rearranged cushions on the settee.

'I wondered how long it would take him to come here. He must know Conor is away.'

'Who, dear?' Kate asked, this time attentive.

'Dane MacHenry. The man at the wedding reception. The man who—'

'Oh, *that* man. What on earth can he be here for, I wonder?' She watched Georgie as she blushed furiously. 'Well, for heaven's sake, go and see what he wants.'

'Come with me, Kate,' Georgie pleaded. 'You must.'

'Off you go, you're a big girl now and a married woman. I doubt there's anything to worry about. Perhaps he has word of his mother for you.'

Georgie stared at her for a second or two, and decided not to compound her problem by arguing. She marched out of the room, her heart thumping madly.

What on earth could he want? It's been months—what possible piece of news could be so important he would have to come to my own home? It would be about Jemimah, or Tom … In that case he could have written me a note.

Manning was waiting outside the drawing room. He seemed in a hurry as he hastily opened the door for Georgie to swish through, her temper rising. As he closed the door Dane MacHenry had his back to her, infuriating her further.

'Why have you come?'

Dane turned and faced her, a glass in his hand. 'I have—'

'I see you've helped yourself to my husband's rum. As he is not here to receive you, please state your business quickly and leave.' She stood not two paces inside the door, her hand on the back of a chair to steady her shaking limbs.

He stared at her.

She began to tap her foot.

'Sit down,' he said softly.

Georgie thought his eyes looked red-rimmed with fatigue. 'Why?'

'Sit down, for God's sake. Don't make this harder for me.' He waved her into a chair.

She sat, swallowing any retort. His tone of voice ... Dread coiled in her belly.

He handed her the rum. 'This is not for me, it's for you.'

She looked at the glass, bewildered, and then at him.

'I've come from the homestead, Georgie, from Jacaranda. I met Foley on the way up there.' He sat down on a chair opposite her, steepling his hands and concentrating on them. 'It's about Foley, Georgie.' He looked at her then. 'I'm sorry to have to tell you. Foley's dead. He was murdered in front of my eyes.'

She placed the glass carefully on the table in front of her. *Foley is dead, he tells me. Murdered.* She folded her hands in her lap and sat upright, eyes unblinking as they focused on him. 'What a dreadful thing to say to anyone.'

He shook his head. 'Georgina, I have his death certificate with me if my word will not suffice.' He removed an envelope from his pocket and laid it beside the glass of rum. 'I made a decision to come and tell you myself, rather than having a policeman deliver the news.'

Georgie stared at the envelope, her eyes still unblinking. She picked it up, turned it over, tore the seal and retrieved the paper.

She recoiled as she realised he was telling the truth. She folded the paper and looked back at him. 'Murdered.'

Dane nodded. 'Shall I call someone in for you?' he asked quietly. 'I have sent Manning for Forrestor.'

'Who killed him?' She held a hand to her head. Her face was hot, damp.

Dane said little of the turn of events except to tell of the murderer and the reason for both men visiting the homestead at the same time.

Georgie broke at that. 'Uncle Tom as well?' She reached out to Dane and clasped his hand.

It was then Kate walked in and stood at the door. 'Mr MacHenry?'

Dane went to her, and took her to a seat close to Georgie. He related again the events that had unfolded and found himself with two bereaved women, one in silence, the other weeping softly into her handkerchief.

Upon Forrestor's arrival, Dane retold his story once more as quickly as he could. Angus rushed to comfort his wife. Dane called Manning to order a doctor.

Deborah was brought upstairs and informed of the news. She fell to weeping, struggled a moment to regain composure then came to stand by Georgie. 'Let us go upstairs, Mrs Foley,' she said.

Georgie hesitated at the door and looked over her shoulder at Dane. 'Thank you for coming to tell me. I know it would not have been easy.'

He inclined his head.

Angus helped Kate to the guest room, not before inviting Dane to meet with him in the drawing room.

The men sat and nursed glasses of rum by the fire.

'I cannot believe what you told me. Murdered—both of them. You do have my most heartfelt condolences, Mr MacHenry.'

Dane nodded. 'Thank you. Mr Foley had the unfortunate chore of telling me of my father's death only days before, but to witness his death in turn—it was an atrocity I will never forget.'

'And the murderer?'

Dane bent his head, then raised it. 'Dead, at the scene.'

'Terrible business. Terrible.' Angus rubbed his face tiredly. 'You must be exhausted.'

Dane took a swallow of rum. 'I got to Melbourne in the early hours yesterday and at my place of abode took advantage of a bath, a good night's sleep, clean clothes. One day more was not going to change the news.'

'Of course not. My wife is taking it very badly, as you would imagine. However, according to Deborah, Georgina has shed few tears. It will be a long road for her.' He stared into the crystal tumbler. 'At least Foley's affairs are in order. He had a will, legal and witnessed—by me—and he named his wife his legal heir.'

Dane hesitated. 'He named his wife his heir?'

Angus raised the glass and downed its contents in one gulp. 'Oh, yes. God only knows why, but he did. As his widow, she inherits everything anyway, but due to a little known law passed some time back, she also gets to administer it all.' He tut-tutted. 'Conor presumed he would live a long life, as we all do. I don't believe there will be any children to inherit, so truthfully, she's now a very rich young woman. Quite frankly, she has absolutely no idea of the enormity of it.'

Dane stared at him a moment. The family was, of course, unaware of his feelings for Georgina. He reasoned it should stay that way, at least for the present.

'I would like to help in any way I can, certainly with any advice I could impart. I have considerable holdings myself, though not as lucrative a portfolio as Mr Foley.'

'Yes, yes, thank you. Georgina may have need of a family member in the very near future.'

Dane nodded and shifted in his seat. He wouldn't exactly be offering brotherly support. His true intentions would have to wait a while, but at least he had her brother-in-law's approval to stay close.

'As his executor,' Angus Forrestor continued, 'I will be reading the will tomorrow. By the way, Conor's burial place?'

'He was taken to Swan Hill, interred there. After the inquiry, the magistrate suggested because of the state he was in, it was deemed wise to leave him there.'

'Yes. Quite agree. The heat and dust and flies … you did the right thing. We will check with authorities there to finalise the bill, organise a headstone.' He extended his hand and Dane shook it. 'On behalf of the family, I do thank you for all your trouble. Of course, you'll stay to hear the will read?'

'I wouldn't intrude, but I will be close by. I have rooms at the Cawley home. However, I would like your permission to call every day, if I may.'

'Of course. Absolutely. I must also arrange for a chaperone to stay with Georgina. I don't want to leave Kate here for too long, although this week we must certainly stay. But do stay here, Dane, at least until we leave. There's plenty of room.'

The door to the drawing room opened as Dane began to answer. Georgina stood there, startled.

Both men stood.

'Georgina.' Angus stretched his arms out to her. 'Are you sure you should not be resting?'

Georgie hesitated, then her chin came up. 'No, thank you, Angus. I'm really all right.' She eased away from her brother-in-law's arm and looked at Dane. 'Thank you once more, for coming to tell us of—it's not easy to be the harbinger of bad news.'

'The very least I could do.' *We are being so polite to each other—it irks me.* Everything had happened so fast Dane hadn't had time to process his own feelings. He'd had to re-settle his mother and his sister, and organise to clear Jacaranda of their remaining property. He'd also had to face a magistrate over Reilly's death, but thankfully it was decided there was no case to answer.

But days later on his ride south, the dull and heavy weight in his heart could no longer be swept away. He had wept for his father: tears of grief, and tears of guilt. He was a prodigal son, returned too late to be a cautious one.

He watched Georgina, attempting to gauge her grief. It pained him to think she might be stricken by the death of her husband, but to his eyes she did not appear so.

Angus steered her towards a chair, as if she might be frail or tired. 'Did you want to see me about something, Georgina?' he asked as she was seated by the window.

'No. Actually, I was sitting in Conor's office earlier when Mr MacHenry arrived. I felt I had left something unfinished. And then I heard your voices.'

Angus frowned.

Dane spoke. 'Yes, I believe I might know how you feel. Though in my circumstance, not a spouse gone, but a father. This house still has a presence.'

'Yes. Yes, that is it.' Georgina was dry-eyed, and although she was pale, there was no sign of hysterics or the faints. She looked around the room calmly and her gaze rested on Angus. 'I will have a lot to do in the next few days, I expect, Angus.'

'You don't have to worry about those things right now, Georgina. There'll be time enough.'

She nodded. 'What should I do?'

'Why, nothing at all, my dear. We will finalise the formalities of course, and from then, we can appoint a manager or caretaker for the companies until we sell—'

'I see.' She raised her brows.

'Is something the matter, my dear? Other than the obvious, I mean.'

'Perhaps this is not the right time, Angus.'

Dane stepped forward. 'It is time I took my leave. You have much to discuss.'

'Do forgive this talk of *family* business in your presence, Mr MacHenry, but I fear if I don't say something now, my wishes might be overlooked.' Georgina sat with her hands folded in her lap, but her gaze was steady on her brother-in-law.

'There is nothing you can do,' Angus said.

'Why not? They are my companies, now, are they not?'

'Well, yes, but—'

'I am of age, I am widowed and they are mine by right. I believe Conor had a lawful will.' She sat very still, upright and calm.

'You have absolutely no knowledge of the business or of the affairs of men and—' Angus blustered at her then threw his hands in the air. 'Georgina. This is a very trying time for you, but the businesses were completely run by Conor, and his accountant, Mr Wardle. We should perhaps leave the running of things to him for a little while longer.'

Georgina nodded. 'You will, then, please read his will this afternoon. I don't wish to drag this out any longer.'

Angus's mouth opened, shut, then opened again. 'Of course,' he said, quietly. 'As you wish.' He excused himself and closed the door behind him.

'And if you don't mind, I'd like to be alone in here,' Georgina said to Dane.

'I came primarily to see for myself that you are all right, Georgie.'

'That is too familiar, Mr MacHenry.'

When she looked up, Dane saw her eyes were clear, and there had not been many tears at all, if any. It surprised and heartened him at the same time. To see her saddened would have distressed him.

He took a step towards her. 'I could assist if you—'

She held up her hands. 'Though none of your concern, my reasons for independence in these matters are well founded. They would have me ensnared here unless I speak up for myself. I have begged to become part of it all and nobody has listened. In fact, if anything, life has been more stifling and restricted.' She squared her shoulders and looked at him. 'Now I am free to learn everything I need to know about it.'

'You don't sound like a grieving widow.'

She stared at him coldly. 'You know nothing about my feelings.'

He inclined his head, then poured himself a drink. 'As you believe, they won't let you run any of it.'

She nodded. 'They will try to stop me.' She laughed shortly. 'Why am I telling you this? You said you would ruin him. Or us. Had it not been for the death certificate you brought from Swan Hill, I might have suspected your hand in his death.'

Dane flinched. 'I beg your pardon?'

'I know you bought a paddle-steamer. Was that the first step in your plan to ruin him, as you said you would? Or perhaps instead you would have engaged him in a card game.' Her brow furrowed.

'You believe none of your ridiculous assertions.'

She reddened.

He took a swallow of rum. 'Are you aware Angus has asked me to stay on as long as he and Kate do?'

Georgina's lips thinned. 'Angus has asked? You see? *My own home* is out of my control.' Her voice rose. 'It leaves me breathless. Guests telling me when they stay and when they go.' She stood up. 'I was used to wide open spaces and a certain freedom ... certainly not the—the forced—' She huffed out a breath and steadied. 'I should perhaps look for someplace else to live.'

'Running away again?'

'I would need my own horse first.' The words flashed from her mouth. 'Which I will soon acquire.'

'I hear more self-pity than the grief of a widow.'

'Perhaps you hear neither,' she shot back.

Dane's retort stopped as Kate and Angus came into the room. Angus carried a long, narrow packet. Kate's face was ravaged, eyes puffy and her nose red and scratchy. She had done her hair simply and wore a plain, dark gown. She acknowledged Dane, then addressed her sister-in-law. 'Angus says we should read the will now, dear, if that's all right with you.'

Georgina looked at her brother-in-law, and he met her gaze squarely. 'Of course, it's all right. Will you excuse us, Mr MacHenry?' she asked.

'No need, Dane,' Angus parried. 'Please take a seat.'

Georgina rolled her eyes.

Angus looked at her, glanced at Kate, at Dane, and back at Georgina. 'This is not the will I witnessed. The date on it is a month later.'

Dane heard Kate inhale but his eyes were on Georgina. She sat forward, and her hands slowly clenched in her lap.

Angus shook his head. 'I was not aware he wrote another will. But it seems so. This is his solicitor, Mr Hodgkin's, crest.' He turned the envelope to them as if to prove it. 'It is legally lodged.'

Kate turned to stare at Georgina. She reached out for her hand, but Georgina ignored it.

'Please open it and read it, Angus.' Her voice was low.

He glanced at Dane, who lifted a shoulder. 'She must hear it sooner or later, Mr Forrestor.'

Angus sat in an armchair, cracking the seal with a fingernail. He withdrew the thick lawyer's parchment, opened it and spread it on his lap. 'Properly witnessed … ' he read briefly, opened and close

his mouth, then tried again. '*I, Conor Dalton Foley … and so on …
do bequeath the main of my real estate to my sister Katherine Mary Forrestor being the house in Main Street, Hawthorn, the residence in High Street,
Malvern, and the commercial property at Swanson Street, City, the allotments
of land at … so on, so on … These properties have no encumbrances over
them … and so on … *' He paused to look at Kate, then at Georgina.

Dane had his eye on Georgina, but she sat unblinking, silent
and inscrutable.

'*… The cottage at Port Fairy in the Western Districts of Victoria I
bequeath to my wife, Georgina Foley, and also to her the property known
as Jacaranda in the Mallee District of northwestern Victoria … *'

Dane jolted at that. Georgina blinked.

'*… that the company known as the Carriers comprising paddle-
steamers* Lady Goodnight *and* Lady Mitchell *be administrated for my
said wife by my brother-in-law, Angus Forrestor, until sold whereby the
proceeds shall revert to her … *' Angus paused then, his shoulders
drooping. '*… That my personal estate be divided as follows: that my
funds in account marked Foley Holdings I bequeath to my said wife and
that she also be given an annuity from my remaining personal estate of two
thousand pounds a year until she remarries. That the rest of my personal
estate be administered by my said brother-in-law for my said sister … * and
so on.' Angus sat back. 'It goes on, but that is the main of it.'

Kate dropped her face in her hands and sobbed silently.

Dane made eye contact with a hollow-eyed Angus and both
men looked at Georgina.

Angus placed his hands on the will. 'Of course, Georgina, it
has to be approved through probate—'

She held her hands up and Angus fell silent.

'I have been well taken care of, I see. Yet, what a strange thing
Conor had in store for us.'

She was far too calm for Dane's liking. 'Georgina, should you
wish to speak with Angus about—'

She glanced at him but turned her attention to her brother-in-law. 'There is nothing to discuss other than the finer points, and then probate will determine the final outcome. Isn't that right, Angus?'

He nodded, then left his seat and went to his wife. He dropped to her side, an arm around her shoulders. 'I had no idea he'd changed his will, Georgina.'

Georgina only raised an eyebrow. 'Will you and Kate contest it?'

Kate raised her tear ravaged face. 'Good heavens, no, my dear. If anything we will talk between us regarding a—a fairer distribution. I know Angus would be with me on that—'

'If you will not contest it, then neither will I.'

Dane started from his seat. 'Georgina—'

'If there will be no contest, I am content.' She stood abruptly. 'I ask permission to stay here until I can remove myself to Port Fairy.'

'As long as you like, my dear,' Kate cried. 'As long as you like. This is still your home.'

'Do not be hasty over this, Georgina,' Angus warned.

Georgina nodded. 'Please excuse me.' She turned and left the room, her back rigid, eyes straight ahead.

It seemed to Dane she could not speak more even if she wanted to.

Georgie steadied herself at the foot of the stairs. Words that seemed to come from long ago grew loud in her head.

How much more deceit and manipulation is in store for me?

None from me.

There had been many secrets between them, and no time to unlock any of them.

Jacaranda was hers. Good God, what had possessed him to do that? And the Carriers? A business in a dying industry. She knew because the newspapers were full of it. She wouldn't know where to begin.

Climbing the stairs, her hand dragged on the banister. Conor had provided for her, at least he remained true to that. She was well situated with the cash in his Holdings account. Now she would have to use her wits to ensure she could indeed administer her own affairs. Perhaps that was the best legacy he had left, because she didn't for a moment believe he intended any part of his greater wealth would ever reach her.

———

Dane returned to John Cawley's residence unable to think clearly about Foley's will and its ramifications.

Distracting himself, he sifted through his mail, and found a letter from his mother. Her script was flowing and confident and he felt a familiar pang for home.

He had neglected them for too long. He would rectify that situation later. First he needed to reconfigure his plan.

As he tucked the letter into his pocket, John Cawley poked his head into the hallway.

'Thought it was you, my boy. How did it go?'

'I need to hear myself think, John. I have a plan, but it needs some work.'

'Well, you've come to the right place. Join me for a drink and tell me everything.' John clapped a hand on his shoulder. 'I feel sure we can come up with some solid solutions.'

Twenty-Six

Ranald Finn came to the Foleys' house, where he was ushered in to wait. Deborah went to ask Angus, who was overseeing Georgina's affairs, to receive him.

Angus rose from the desk, tidying the small stack of papers that included Dane MacHenry's letter and offer. He waited for Deborah to return with the riverboat captain. What an odd coincidence that Finn should arrive at the same time as MacHenry's mail.

'I beg your pardon for arriving unannounced, Mr Forrestor, but your man at your house directed me here, said that you'd be with Mrs Foley. I've come with news of the men and the boats, and I felt you needed to hear it.' Finn folded and unfolded his cap in his hands, his forehead partly tanned where the hat had not shaded his face.

'Quite all right, Mr Finn. I've asked Deborah to call Mrs Foley down. She will be along in a moment. She will want to hear any news you have.' Angus waved Finn into a chair and passed him a tot of rum. 'But by all means, tell me what brings you here before she graces us with her presence.'

Ranald Finn placed his rum on a small table beside his chair and sat on the edge of his seat. 'Well, sir, since Mr Foley's passing, I took it upon myself to look after a few things, as you know.'

Angus nodded.

'But the boats are too much for me, now. The freight, the river itself, the men. Times are changing, Mr Forrestor. They're not good times and I'm not Mr Foley, sir. I can't be doing the whole lot by myself.'

Angus thought Mr Finn was getting himself into a state. 'Mr Finn, you're not thinking of leaving us, are you?' Angus couldn't imagine this weatherbeaten river man doing anything else but being a river man. He was leathery skinned after long years on the boats, lean and perhaps fifty years of age; the river would be all he knew.

Ranald Finn, still on the edge of his seat, picked up his glass, his hands steady. 'Well—there's been some talk on the river. It appears common knowledge the Carriers is up for sale. Of course, I don't want to be leaving, but I don't want to be thinking that I might get left, either.'

'It's not true, Mr Finn. The Carriers is not up for sale.'

'That and this bloody depression is harder, Mr Foley, on a man my age.'

'I understand all too well, Mr Finn.'

Mr Finn nodded. 'Also I hear that Mrs Foley will be running things until it's sold.'

'No, Mr Finn.'

Ranald Finn was dogged. 'I hear that Mrs Foley wants a position in the running of the business.'

'No, Mr Finn,' Angus repeated firmly. He hoped he wouldn't be caught out on that score.

'I know the men wouldn't work under a woman, Mr Forrestor.'

'It's not even conceivable.' *God almighty, how did this even get around?* 'Mrs Foley does own the company, but she has me and Mr Wardle to manage for her. And you, of course.'

Mr Finn nodded, this time apparently satisfied. 'Then there's that Mr MacHenry, sir.'

Angus Forrestor held his breath. Perhaps Finn knew of MacHenry's offer somehow, and that was the actual reason for his visit.

'What about Mr MacHenry?' Georgina asked from the doorway. She entered the room and extended her hand. Both men stood. 'It is such a pleasure to see you, Mr Finn. It's been many a long month since you saved my life on the Echuca wharf.'

Ranald Finn quickly clasped her outstretched hand then let it drop. 'Well, Mrs Foley, it's a pleasure to see you safe and sound. Believe me, I am awful sorry about Mr Foley.'

For the first time in weeks, Angus saw her smile.

'Thank you, Mr Finn. And I am very well. But what of Mr MacHenry?'

Angus looked at Ranald Finn, whose eyes were fixed on Georgina's face. 'He's got himself a lovely boat, Mrs Foley. Better than our *Lady Goodnight* or the *Lady Mitchell*.'

'Has he?'

Angus frowned. And that was exactly it—the reason Ranald Finn had come to Melbourne to see him. He worried a rival would drive Foley's River Carriers under. Or … was he talking up MacHenry rather than warning Angus? Clever man if that were so. The men would look up to MacHenry. He was a river man, too. But surely he needed no assistance from Mr Finn?

Mr Finn seemed increasingly uncomfortable. Angus made a mental note to chase the fellow up, if Georgina let him out alive.

'Is that all, Mr Finn, that he has a lovely boat?'

'Yes, ma'am.'

'I understand you came to the house to see Mr Forrestor. Surely not to tell him about a lovely boat.'

Angus glanced at the ceiling. Deborah and her information sharing.

Mr Finn sat opposite her, his hands on his knees. 'Well, Mrs Foley—'

'Tea for anyone?' Georgina asked as Deborah knocked and brought in a tray. She set it on the table to Georgina's right and departed as quietly as she'd entered.

'Mrs Foley, I was in Melbourne to visit some family. Of course, I would not miss the opportunity to visit you, to meet with both of you. As I was saying to Mr Forrestor, I am finding the workload just a wee bit too heavy for me, at my age and all. Perhaps I might ask for an assistant, or an office in Echuca, or some such thing.'

He is a clever man. Angus glanced at his sister-in-law's face. He couldn't read her expression.

'An assistant, Mr Finn.' She glanced at Angus. 'And what would this position entail? Who would be suited?'

'Well, a—a man, or a grown lad. Someone who can read and write and—and put his back to it when required. Someone who knows the rivers backwards.'

'Oh.' She poured two cups of tea and handed one to each man. Mr Finn didn't seem to know what to do with his. He placed it by his rum.

Angus marvelled at the old boy. He'd cut her out of this proposed position as neatly as he could without ruffling her feathers. She didn't have any knowledge of the rivers, and it was an absolute prerequisite. She wouldn't be able to lift a bale of wool—who could? She wouldn't be able to grumble about that, even if she did grumble about jobs for men only. She was taking this suffragist business too far.

'Then you must find someone, Mr Finn. A local person perhaps,' she said.

'Yes, there's always people on the river looking for work, Mrs Foley, this day and age, the depression and all.'

'Tell me, are we faring well at this awful time?'

Mr Finn leaned forward, his earnest face glowing in his appraisal. 'Well, now, considering how Mr Foley had won himself quite a few contracts before … I have to say we're as well as he expected us to be. We're on time, and a day or two back, we were even ahead, so the *Lady Goodnight* got herself a good mooring, first on the wharf, first at the cranes.' He shifted in his seat. 'Mr Foley was my friend, Mrs Foley. He taught me more than I taught him. He was a fine man to work for.' He licked his lips, glanced at Angus then back at Georgina. 'And now we need another man such as him to take the wheel, Mrs Foley, to carry on where he left off.' He wiped his large hands on the knees of his pants. 'The other carriers are moving in on contracts we would normally tender for—it's getting cutthroat—so we need a new man to head us up. I believe I know of such a man—'

Angus didn't like where Mr Finn was taking the conversation. 'Thank you, Mr Finn. We can assure you—'

'Yes, Mr Finn. Mr Forrestor is taking care of that for the carriers. But please tell me who it is you have in mind to head us up. I am very interested in your opinion.' She turned her head to stare a moment at Angus.

'Well, Mrs Foley. I've mentioned him—it's that Mr MacHenry.'

Angus knew then that he would have a battle on his hands. He sighed to himself.

'I see. Thank you for bringing him to Mr Forrestor's attention. I'm sure he will give it due consideration.'

Angus suspected Mr Finn had finally realised that Mrs Foley was not exactly as happy with the advice as he'd hoped.

'So,' the river man said and stood. 'Thank you, Mrs Foley for the refreshment. I'll make my way back to my lodgings, if you don't mind.'

'Of course not. Good day, Mr Finn.'

Angus saw him out.

He went back into the room and found her standing by the window. He would have to take the bull by the horns.

'Georgina, I have some news.'

She turned to him and he was suddenly struck by the maturity in her face. He hadn't noticed it before; she'd never appeared to him to be calm or serene, but there it was. He was also struck by her loveliness. Her glossy blue-black hair framed her face; her chestnut-coloured eyes, her proud and straight nose, the smattering of freckles that was not the blemish her gender believed it to be. She was slim of build, a little tall for a woman, but not overly much. She would have to get herself out of those dull clothes soon, mourning or not. A young life should not be wasted on grieving.

'What is it?' she asked.

'An offer for the Carriers.'

Her face set. 'An offer.'

'Now, hear me out. There's a lot of talk on the river about what's happening to the company, as Mr Finn has told us. The men are nervous for their jobs, and rumours are thick about the place.' He spread his hands in exasperation. 'It's natural someone would speculate—'

'And just who made this offer, Angus?'

He should have stopped, fabricated the name of some individual, but he didn't. He dropped his arms. 'Dane MacHenry. It's a reasonable offer, all things considered. We'll take a loss, but better to shift—'

'I don't care.' She clenched her fists. 'I haven't had time to think at all. Nothing is for sale yet, not a thing. And you can tell the men we will find them an overseer if that will keep them happy, but I'm not ready to sell.'

'Georgina.' Angus heard the cajoling tone in his voice.

'I see very clearly I won't be running the company, so I must hire people who can. At this point, Angus, there is absolutely no question of my selling Foley's River Carriers, and so help me, I am getting sick and tired of being manipulated. If you would like to wash your hands of it all, please, don't feel obliged to stay on.'

Angus fell back in a chair. 'I won't let you down, but I want you to see reason. Sell now. His offer is solid. We might not be able to sell *anything* in six months' time.'

'You don't know that.'

This slip of a girl, silly, stubborn and wilful, was pretending she knew about business. How had he seen maturity a moment ago? 'What on earth, what possible *rational* reason have you got not to sell to MacHenry—or anyone, for that matter? I strongly advise you to accept. It might be more than prudent in the light of the economy and the turn of business now the railway goes to Swan Hill. River trade will slow, if not stop.' Would any man in his right mind in these times refuse an offer to sell?

Still, he wasn't dealing with a man.

'It's not for sale *yet*. I have not thought all this through.'

'Oh, come now. I know you're not going to hang on to the Carriers for sentimental reasons. This is business, this is what you wanted to learn. This is how things work.'

'I want to learn the business.'

'This particular part of the business will not stay afloat, so to speak, until you're able to take the wheel.'

She waved her hand. 'But there's you and Mr Wardle.'

'Mr Wardle has strongly indicated he wants to retire soon.' Angus tapped the arm of his chair. 'MacHenry has made a better offer than you're ever likely to see again.'

'And why has he done so?'

Angus, exasperated, huffed. 'Clearly because he wants to. What possible reason, tell me—'

'You know as well as I do, I can't explain it. He wants to take everything that was Foley's ... everything that is *mine*. Do you understand?'

For a moment, Angus couldn't make sense of what she was saying. Then, 'You mean as revenge, Georgina? What utter bosh. He's a businessman.' Angus slapped the table with the palm of his hand. 'Are you prepared to tell him you're not interested?' He watched surprise register on her features. 'You want to head up the company—*you* tell him. No? Well then, are you prepared to have the men strike because they don't want a woman to answer to?'

'What do you mean? On whose authority do they strike?' He'd stunned her.

'They make their own decisions. And as Ranald Finn is speaking for them, I'd suggest you listen closely. You lose the support of your workers and you'll ruin the business. Wake up, Georgina.' He tapped his forehead. 'Do you really think Ranald Finn doesn't know of MacHenry's offer? Dane MacHenry has probably personally approached every man on your boats. I am not the one manipulating you—I'm trying to keep your head above water.' Angus huffed again. He couldn't remember the last time he'd lost his temper.

'It never occurred to me that being a woman would have some bearing on whether or not employees kept working. What a ridiculous reason to strike.' She stood up. 'I am paying them. I'm not about to do any harm to these men—they still have their jobs. Am I supposed to be weaker in decision making or some such thing?'

'It's exactly that. It's unheard of for a start—'

'Do they object to being paid by a woman? I know I am the boss in name only,' she mimicked Conor's accent, 'and that you and Mr Wardle keep the business profitable, but it is still *my* business.'

'You won't have a business if you have no employees to work it for you,' Angus all but shouted. 'And no one likely to want to take their places.'

'The country is in a depression, Angus. Mr Finn just said there were always people on the river looking for work.'

Angus had had enough. 'Georgina. I can tell you, Conor never spoke to me about administering for you. Has it occurred to you that I might not want to run it, either?'

She looked up at him, startled. Her shoulders sagged. 'No. It hadn't occurred to me.' She studied her hands, folded in her lap, for some time. Then said, 'I'm sorry, Angus. It's obviously a burden to you. I promise to revisit selling.'

He sighed in relief.

'But not to Dane MacHenry.'

Angus threw his hands in the air and left her in the office. He would speak to Mr Finn tomorrow. He would even contact Dane MacHenry. He would sweeten the deal and make it irresistible for both parties.

He certainly didn't need the added burden of his sister-in-law's childish notions.

Twenty-Seven

Georgie heard Manning and her new chaperone and companion, Mrs Dawson, at the front door conversing with a third individual.

Odd. A visitor at such an hour. She'd only just had her evening meal.

The voices came closer to the parlour. She sat in the lamplight, her stockinged feet on a stool in front of the fire, a newspaper dangling from her hand. As the voices approached, she clutched her dressing gown over the loose linen shift she wore before bed.

Manning burst into the room with a noisy Deborah, a tall, imposing man following. Mrs Dawson brought up the rear. Georgie's heart leapt to her throat as she stared into the blue eyes of Dane MacHenry.

'Dismiss these good people,' he ordered quietly.

Both Deborah and Manning looked at her. She rose, and rested a hand on the back of a chair. Deborah rushed to her side.

'Miss, he just kept coming. We—'

'Mrs Foley, I will go for the police.' Manning stood in the doorway.

'For God's sake, Manning, you know who I am,' Dane growled. 'I'm not some bloody bushranger.'

Mrs Dawson gasped at the profanity.

Georgina waved them all away. 'It's all right, it's quite all right.'

'I will be in the kitchen, madam, if you need me.' Manning followed Deborah out after one last glance at Dane MacHenry.

Mrs Dawson wrung her hands, hovering.

'I shall be perfectly safe, Mrs Dawson.' Georgie waited for the woman to retreat before she turned to Dane. 'It has barely been six weeks since I became a widow. Your visit is not seemly at all.'

He scoffed, shot her a look, then wrapped the length of his scarf around his hand, slipped it off and left it in a tidy bundle on a side table. He removed his cravat and placed it on top of the scarf, shrugged out of his jacket and waistcoat, and hung them on the back of a chair. He loosened his shirt and sat down in a chair opposite her, stretching out his legs. 'I've come to buy the business, Georgie. And I'm not leaving until you at least discuss that and other things with me.'

Georgie looked at him. 'It is hardly an appropriate time of the day for business discussions.'

'And pour me a drink, would you?'

She scowled. 'You are not welcome—'

'Nevertheless.' His gaze hadn't left her. 'If you please, a drink. Then let's clear the air.'

For a moment she considered standing by the door and demanding he leave. But what would a shrewd businessperson with a potential rival on her doorstep do?

A shrewd businessperson would hear him out.

She poured him a drink of what first came to hand: rum. She left it on his side table, careful not to touch him, then sat opposite, her hands clamped over the arms of the chair.

He sipped appreciatively, and glanced at her once or twice. Georgie didn't miss the rake over her attire, but it was nothing out of the ordinary for ladies to wear this type of gown in their own home for day or night wear. He was only trying to unsettle her.

The impatient tap-tap of her foot was the only sound in the room.

Dane smiled at her, creasing his darkly shadowed but cleanshaven face in a way that caught her off guard. His eyes lit up and her heart did a stupid pitter-patter and wouldn't stop.

She found her voice. 'Unless you have a ridiculously high offer, which I can't imagine you do, it is not for sale.' Heat threaded across her chest. Strangely, perspiration dampened her throat and a chill followed the heat.

'That's not what I want to hear.' The smile lost some of its brilliance as he shifted in his seat.

'You come brawling into my house like some thug—'

'Hardly. It's been a long time since I've seen you alone, Georgie.'

'Your visit is not proper.'

'Nothing between us was proper, even from the beginning.' A frown gathered on his brow. 'I would like things to be proper, but you're clearly not comfortable.'

'For good reason. I am a woman alone in this house, in mourning, and you are—are … '

He waited as her voice trailed off. 'I'm surprised you can't find a suitable descriptive profanity.' He scratched his ear. 'And you are hardly alone, with three others here.'

Her fingers tingled and she fidgeted, shifting in her seat. He poured another drink and handed it to her. She shook her head.

'Come now, one drink. It's not my way to loosen a lady with alcohol. You are quite safe in that respect.' He placed the glass in her hand. It was only half filled with rum, certainly not as much as she had poured for him. She brought it to her nose and breathed in. He chuckled. 'That's possibly the safest way to approach it.' He watched as she sipped and grimaced. 'Acquired taste,' he said.

She set the glass aside. 'Ranald Finn has been here, and Angus is constantly at me to sell. My affairs are being manipulated.'

'Your affairs have been manipulated since—'

'Angus has been *over* and *over* this with me. Neither you, nor Angus Forrestor, nor Ranald Finn will push me. I am not stupid. If I don't wish to sell the Carriers yet, then I will not.'

'Correct. You're not stupid.' He crossed his legs at the ankles. His booted feet nearly touched hers.

'I have no need to sell.'

'I beg to differ. If you do not sell now, the Carriers will fold.' His voice was low and clear.

She slapped her palms on the arms of her chair. 'How do you know that?'

'I read the market to know the business.' He leaned forward. 'You'll have to sell the Carriers, and soon, if you're going to see anything for them. The men believe you want to stay as head of the company and they are fearful for their jobs.' He sat back and took a swallow of rum. 'You have a very good offer from me and you should not refuse it.' He downed the last of his rum, then reached over to add a couple of logs to the fire.

His familiarity was not lost on her. She stared at him, the tingles burning along her hands and over her arms. 'You won't bully me. I am a woman of means—'

'A woman of means. Of course you are, thanks to your husband's early demise, without which you wouldn't even have your freedom.'

'Oh, I'm aware of that. I was to be shipped from Jacaranda by your parents but then you—' She stopped, mindful it was a subject he hadn't yet mentioned.

'Ah yes. Jacaranda.' He watched her silently for a moment. 'We will also talk of that. But one thing at a time.'

Her mouth worked with unspoken words. Then, clamping her lips together, she poured her rum into the teapot and shoved the empty glass across the table. It slid and clattered onto the floor, landing at his feet.

He reached out, righted it, and partly refilled it. He was very calm, and very close. 'You will continue to be very comfortable financially if you sell now. If you don't, you will lose the Carriers. The river freight trade is dying.'

A fevered chill feathered down her spine. 'Then why do you want the Carriers?'

'As a means of transport still, clearly. But for my own business's use at this point, not as a commercial enterprise. If my plans come to fruition ... '

'There would be other boats to buy.'

'There are, but none in as good condition for freight and for travelling comfort.' He set his glass down, and considered her as he rested his elbows on his knees. 'You know Angus does not wish to continue to administer the business. Mr Wardle is about to retire, and it seems Mr Finn and the working men are restless, not wishing to work for a woman.'

'Why do they think anything of it if they're all still being well paid?' she snapped.

'Well paid for how long? Can you go to the market and bid for the contracts? Can you stand on the docks and bargain with the old river men and the pastoralists and the merchants from the city? Can you negotiate and bargain and verbally grapple with old men smoking cigars, trading wool and cattle and sheep?' He held his chin in his hand, eyes on her face.

'I will learn. There's many a woman can do those things.'

'Name anyone who'll teach you, name anyone who'll stand by you in this. You think you'll be able to learn simply by turning up at the docks?' He shook his head. 'You'd be lucky to leave there safely. Or at the sale yards? These are dangerous times, and men who've families to look after won't be too happy with a woman taking their job.' He took a long swallow of rum. 'Will you be able to read the turn in the trade once the impact of this depression fully hits? It's coming, if it's not already here.'

'Will *anyone* be able to read it?' she shot back.

He ignored that. 'I have made an offer. Sell while you still have something to sell. If you lose the business, you will have nothing to sell.'

'You have already said.'

'It would allow you to have more financial investments, or property, if you like.' His eyes lit up. 'Horses. Perhaps a stud farm. God knows, Melbourne loves its horse racing. Realise some cash before the crash hits.'

'It's too soon to sell.' Her voice drifted as she thought. 'Horses.' She sat up quickly. 'Where is MacNamara?'

'He is stabled at the Cawleys's. Why?'

'I miss him. I've missed him for nearly a year. How is he?'

Dane smiled. 'He is the same big old soft-heart he always was. He is in fine condition. Perhaps you would like to see him?'

Georgie met his gaze, her heart tripping merrily. 'I would.'

'Then we will arrange to see him together.' He gave her a small salute with his glass.

She remained silent.

'The time is always right if you have a buyer, and especially now.' He moved to the edge of his seat. 'Think on it swiftly. You're right, you are not stupid. And you need to be shrewd to protect yourself, not to mention the men whose lives you hold in the balance.'

'That presumes I will fail—'

'If you are not shrewd.'

She wavered; she knew he knew it. The sense of it was clear. She knew it despite all her protests. Conor had left her the Carriers but she had no skills to keep it going. Why on earth did he do that if he knew she couldn't?

Read the market to know the business.

Dane was right. She had no expertise whatsoever. None. Her will alone would not carry it. She had decided so long ago she would pick her battles to win, but for this battle, she was not well enough equipped to succeed.

Her shoulders dropped. 'I will think more about it,' she said quietly and stood.

He stood with her but didn't reach for his cravat or scarf. Instead, he reached across and tucked a wayward tendril of dark hair back behind her ear.

Her eyes did not meet his. If they had, she would have burned in bright flames.

'Georgina, we have not been friends.'

'I agree. We have not.' Her voice dried in her throat and a pulse beat heavily at her temple. The room seemed to close in, and her hands clutched at the front of her gown.

He took a step closer. 'It would mean a great deal to me to court you, and—'

She looked up, a sharp toss of her head. 'To secure a business deal?'

Dane laughed. 'A cynic, as well. No. I would like very much to pursue what I know there is between us. You can't deny there are very strong feelings.'

She inclined her head. 'Perhaps. But there is a proper way to deal with those feelings.' She sighed then, and dropped her chin. 'I just don't know what it is.'

'I do.' He touched her hair again. 'I have thought of this shimmering black silk often since the night by the river. I've thought of it, wrapped, just so, in my hands.' His voice, husky, broke with a ragged breath. 'It's beautiful.'

He pulled a pin from her hair, and as she stood not moving, not speaking, he pulled another pin and another, until the dark mass cascaded over her shoulders. He wound a lock of her hair around the fingers of one hand, and buried his other hand deep in the heavy length at the back of her head. At that moment he exhaled long and deeply.

'Just so.'

There is nothing in this room but Dane MacHenry ... No breath of air, no light or dark, no sound, no scents, just him and everything he is. No right or wrong. Just Dane MacHenry.

But there was mourning to serve. And she was alone with him in this room, unchaperoned. She might not resist, and her reputation—

What were these thoughts? A jumble of immature anxieties or adult sensibilities? She'd tried to build a good life with a husband and a home and—

Georgie's breath left her in a rush. She grasped his wrists. 'You must go. Should Manning—'

'He won't be back and you know it.' He picked up a tress of her hair.

'But Deborah—Mrs Dawson ... ' She dropped her hold on him and stepped away. The lock of hair drifted out of his fingers.

'Neither will they, if they know their place.' Dane came closer again, but made no move to touch her. 'Don't fight this.'

'I should do nothing but that.' She looked to the carpet at her feet. He was so close, the warm thrills of his pulse rushed to her belly. She held her hands out, low, for reason, for time. 'I have tried to live as best I can ... I am in mourning, I must abide by these rules of society, at least.' He would hear her heart thudding. She would lose this game she knew nothing about.

'Yes,' he agreed in a whisper and touched his forehead to hers. 'You are a woman in mourning. A woman, nonetheless. And I am here, and I am alive. We are of the same pod, Georgie. We live our lives. People like us go beyond society's norms.'

His breath on her face, the scent of his body as it floated up to her from under his shirt, the way his hair fell against her face, and the rasp of his beard stubble against her cheek ... She stilled, and every part of her being longed for him. Every part of him belonged to her.

'It is too soon ... '

'It is not soon enough.'

She closed her eyes, tried to breathe slowly, waiting for her heartbeat to calm. 'There must be a proper way.'

'There is.' He enclosed her within the circle of his arms, carefully, tenderly. 'Come to me willingly, Georgie. That would be proper, for us.' He kissed her forehead, a press of warm lips, firm and reassuring.

'There will be unkind talk.' She leaned in a little, his solid chest seductive, inviting under her hands; the soft thud of his heartbeat against her palms.

'We are not unused to that, but there is no need to suffer it.' His chin rested on her head.

Longing curled in her belly. Then his lips pressed softly, softly on her face and on her throat and became languid as he tilted her chin. She caught her breath. His hand slid to cup her breast, unfettered in her linen shift.

Give in to it ...

Her hand slipped inside his shirt and she felt the shivery fever of her effect on him. His skin was warm, and dark chest hair caressed her hand. Her heart turned over as the beat of his life thudded against her palm.

Then he bent to her, holding her hands there against him, and kissed her mouth, lips gliding over hers. The prickle of his stubble left a trail of tingles.

She would take him as hers. She would take him to her room, she would not deny this any longer. She would lay with him, grasp his body to her, lay his head on her breast, take his hand and ...

Georgie smiled a little, leaned into his kiss and then broke away. 'Not here.'

He scowled. 'Then to your room, or it will be here, servants or no. I'm not made of stone.' His voice grew jagged in his throat, but his gaze on hers never wavered.

'I know. I'll not make us wait.' She smiled again and lifted his hands, brought them to her face and kissed his fingertips, took his forefinger to linger on her mouth. 'It is this way,' she said softly. 'Up the stairs.'

She leaned against him, braced by his arm around her as they climbed the stairs. He wouldn't let her go, afraid she would change her mind. He held her fast under his arm, against his chest, murmured to her that she would be his, that he would look after her.

At the top of the landing, she eased away and pointed to a door some small distance to the right. 'Would you like to use that room first?'

'And what room is that?'

She lifted a shoulder. 'A gentleman's room.'

He shook his head. 'The only room I want is yours. Why would I need to use another?'

She pointed to the first door on the left and glanced back at him.

He gathered her to him again, his cheek in her hair. 'Then, my beautiful Georgina, please invite me in.'

She clasped and unclasped her hands. 'I have brought you up the stairs, I know,' she began. 'And I know my intent, I do, but … '

'Good, because whispering all night in the hallway is not *my* intent.'

He looked so fierce she gave a little laugh, fell against him and slid her hands down his arms to his wrists. Her fingers entwined his. 'Then we must get out of the hallway.'

The door was opened and she entered ahead of him, then Dane closed the door firmly behind him.

Georgina faced the bed for a few seconds, then turned to him.

He pulled at his shirt, removed it from his trousers and threw it over a wooden chest at the foot of the bed. He took her by the shoulders and kissed her again, slowly. He kissed her neck, found a curious little spot that, when brushed by his prickly chin, sent shivers down her body.

He bent to kiss her again, his fingers undoing the buttons on her flimsy nightdress. Georgina wrapped her arms around his neck, but he refused to be drawn from his task. He pulled the shift over her head and she wriggled out of it.

Off came his boots.

As her cool hands moved over his chest, he scooped her up and laid her on the bed. His breeches came off, her chemise slid away at his touch and he pressed his body closer, aware his arousal was great and he would not be much of a lover tonight.

She tensed and he looked at her face. 'What is it?' His rigid penis was pressed to her thigh and it was there her gaze travelled, and back to his face. 'What?' he asked again and kissed her neck.

'Nothing,' she whispered back. 'But I am a little afraid, that's all.'

'You, afraid?' He kissed her slowly then touched her lips with his tongue. She sighed and pushed up to him. He bent his head, his mouth taking a nipple and tugging gently, insistently, until she cried out.

He lifted her off the bed to sit in his lap, and she gasped, trying to cover herself. He laughed and kissed her nose, lowered her and pulled her towards him. His hands caressed her full breasts and the hard, thrusting nipples. Then he lapped with his tongue, and she arched. Still she resisted, trying to draw back.

A little game of tease, he thought, and as he firmly drew her closer, he slipped himself just inside her. She made a noise in her throat and he struggled to hold on, to hold back.

He kissed her face and neck, suckled her breast and when he thrust again, found resistance.

'What—what is this?' His voice sounded hoarse to his ears. She shook her head. He couldn't wait, explanations would have to come later—now, he just had to—

He pushed tentatively and the tight warmth of her body took his breath away. She gave a little cry and pushed down. He suckled at the heavy breasts rising and falling, encouraged her to move against him and when he could no longer resist, pushed further into her, holding her hips, driving into her.

The grip of her body on his, the throb inside her and the warm, wet pulsing as she rose and sank on him, her scent, the smattering of freckles on her face, her grip on his arms … holding on, encouraging him …

He'd waited long enough. He thrust up once, hard. She cried out and sent him crashing recklessly into a powerful climax, crushing her to him as he came inside her.

Spent, he pulled her down on the bed with him and they lay entangled until he was able to slip from her. He brushed the hair from her face and looked into the lovely liquid eyes as they widened in wonder.

'What's the matter?' he asked, suddenly tired beyond measure.

Georgina shook her head and hesitantly touched her body where they had joined only a moment ago.

He propped up on one elbow over her and kissed her lightly on the forehead. He frowned. 'Forgive me, but—'

'Please don't say anything. I am—I am very ... '

He kissed her again. 'Your life was not as it seemed, Georgie.' He brushed her face with fingertips.

She shook her head, not speaking.

His heart burst. No other man had been where—he wondered at the strange physical relationship this woman had had with her husband.

She looked up at him as if trying to read his thoughts. 'Does it matter?'

'Yes—no. But I would have been more—'

'Don't,' she cried. 'I don't understand these things.' She went to climb off the bed, embarrassed, but he snaked an arm around her and drew her to him.

He buried his face in her hair, and nestled his chin where her neck met her shoulder. 'Georgie, I should have taken you for my own before you had a chance to run off and be married to him. Here,' he said and pulled the covers back. 'In you get. It's warmer.' She snuggled under and looked at him, laughed when he suddenly growled and jumped under the covers with her.

He was quick to recover, her nearness irresistible. He was uneasy about his treatment of her virginity but then she guided his hand shyly to her most private part. When her pleasure drew to its height, he lost all thought and moved himself inside her. She seized him with a powerful fervour, and he was swept away.

They lay back, Georgie's body tucked alongside his.

He knew he'd found what he'd been looking for all his life.

Twenty-Eight

Georgie woke with a start.

'Is there a fire?' His eyes were still closed, his voice drowsy. His hand draped possessively over her hip as she lay with her back to him.

'It must be nearly dawn.' She made to get out of bed.

'Don't be in such a hurry, Georgie. Plenty of time.' He held her wrist tightly.

'I'm not playing. Please, Dane, it's nearly morning. You must go before the sun comes up.' She had sat up despite his hold on her.

The thrust of her bosom in the early morning light, the nipples puckering as cool air hit them, tempted him too much. His other hand reached around to caress her.

'No,' she cried. 'You must go.'

He dropped her wrist and swung his legs off the bed. 'The coming of daylight will not stop the tongues wagging.' He stood over the bed and saw she averted her eyes from him. 'Is that what you mean?'

'Manning—and the two women. The whole street will soon be talking.'

He came to her side of the bed. 'It doesn't end here with your telling me to go home. I thought you'd have realised that.' Then he cupped her face gently and sat beside her on the bed. 'This is the real beginning for you and me. It won't stop now.'

'I cannot see you here again.'

He laughed. 'I think you will. And soon. Not the time for girlish vapours, now, Georgie. You're mine, and we both know it.'

'It is the same as before, and with nothing more between us but—'

'You're wrong.' He stood and pulled on his breeches. 'I will be back. Besides, there's still business to discuss.'

She clutched the bedclothes to her as much for modesty as for warmth, puzzled at his mention of business. 'No, no business. What was between us last night doesn't change anything.'

He looked surprised. 'I'm disappointed you think that. It changes everything. We will marry.'

Her mind raced. Marry? 'Don't be ridiculous. How can I marry? I am in still in mourning.'

'Georgie, Georgie. Our little tryst is hardly a secret. And I am an honourable man. Of course I will marry you. I want to marry you.' He leaned over and touched her nose with a finger. 'Mourning be damned. I didn't see a mourning widow last night.'

She stared at him as he stood dressing himself in front of her. *Of course he would say he'd marry me—that's why he mentioned business.* 'Honourable. You think if you marry me you'll get not only the Carriers, but Jacaranda as well. You have not mentioned that since. Then you can think again. I know the law.'

'Shush. Those very gossipy servants are probably well awake and fully aware I'm in your room. My scarf and cravat are still in the parlour.' He pulled on his boots. 'I won't be marrying you to get anything you own, but we will be talking about Jacaranda.' He stood up, shrugged into his shirt and tucked it in. 'You'll marry me sooner or later, it's just a matter of nature taking its course.'

'What?'

'I said I was honourable.' He kissed her mouth tenderly before she tried to pull away. 'I will be back.' He tapped her nose with his forefinger again and was gone.

She lay under the covers, angry with herself, then strangely pleased. *Which is it*, she demanded of herself, *angry or pleased?* But as she closed her eyes to think of his body in hers and the smell of him, and the look of him, all she remembered was the intense and utter pleasure she experienced with him beside her.

She drifted back to an uneasy sleep, conflicting thoughts and fears swirling inside her head. There would be a solution. She would find it, she was sure. But as her dreams claimed her, she knew deep down there was really only one way.

———

'Georgina. Georgina.' Kate Forrestor had her by the shoulder, shaking gently.

'What—what's happened?' Georgie tried to sit up in her bed, still groggy from a deep sleep. The covers had slipped to reveal a bare shoulder, and she automatically drew them up over her body. 'What is it?'

'It's so late, my dear. When we called in, Deborah said she was worried about you.'

Georgie knew well why Deborah hadn't come up herself. 'Well, I did have a good long sleep, then.' She laughed breathlessly. 'As you can see, I'm quite safe.'

'Whatever are we to do with you?' Kate asked, and tsked gently.

'What do you mean?' Mindful of her nudity and the delicious warmth that spread through her body as she recalled the night's events, the covers came up even further. She knew it was a waste of time trying to fool Kate. 'I feel bad enough, I don't need you to—'

'Bad enough? Oh yes. I know those widow's weeds are supposed to say it all, but I doubted right from the very beginning that your Mr MacHenry would let you hide behind them.'

'He's not *my* Mr MacHenry.'

'Bosh,' Kate said. 'When a man comes calling in the middle of the night and stays until the small hours, I'd say he was definitely yours.'

'Deborah.' Georgie looked up, defiant, but the smile on Kate's face meant she wasn't being rebuked.

'Manning, actually.'

Georgie huffed. 'It was hardly the middle of the night and I don't know what you—I don't know what I—'

'Conor saw that passionate spirit, that's why he married you.' Kate patted her hand. 'And I'm no hypocrite either.'

Tears pricked her eyes. 'I don't know what I felt for Conor, Katie. He's your brother, I know, but he was not what he seemed. He was a very—'

Kate held up her hands. 'All I know is you were a good and faithful wife, I'm quite sure of that. Yet all the while I knew your heart lay with another. Don't deny it. Anyhow,' she continued, crossing the room to Georgie's wardrobe. She pulled out a fresh dressing gown. 'Your meeting with him seems to have cleared up a few problems.' She returned and held it out to Georgie.

Georgie struggled into the gown, and threw off the bed covers. 'Cleared up what problems?'

'Now with a wedding on its way—leaving the correct amount of time, of course—you won't have to worry about the business.'

'I would not think of marrying so soon after—'

'Perhaps you should have thought of that before you allowed Mr MacHenry into that bed last night.' Kate indicated the rumpled bedclothes. 'Regardless of the mourning period, you need to be married again, and as soon as convention sanctions. A scandal would do your standing in society no good at all. Not to mention the damage to the Foley name.'

A furious rush of blood burned Georgie's face. 'Scandal?'

'Come now, Georgie. Better to stop the tongues wagging before they start. Besides which, I have known Dane MacHenry was your man ever since the night of your wedding reception— and most probably before that.'

'He most certainly was *not*,' Georgie cried. 'Don't say anything more, Kate. And Conor himself—he—we—' She could not bring herself to tell Kate of her brother's condition in the marriage bed, to tell her that their marriage was one based on convenience for both of them.

'I don't see any bodices torn.' Kate glanced at the discarded nightdress. 'Nor bodily harm done to you. You are certainly not screaming your head off.'

Georgie felt her face flame beet-red again.

'Perhaps you should admit it to yourself, Georgie,' Kate continued serenely. 'I do not hold it against you that you have very strong feelings for this man. I suggest you sort them out.'

A knock on the door forestalled Georgie's protest. Deborah struggled in with an empty bath, and Mrs Dawson followed with two large buckets of hot water. Both women were silent, keeping their eyes averted as they dumped water into the tub.

Georgie and Kate watched. 'That's all I need, Deborah,' Georgie said, an imperious tilt to her chin. 'I won't need you for my bath.'

'Mrs Foley, your hair … '

'I'll call for you if I need help.'

Mrs Dawson glanced at Georgie sympathetically, then she looked at Kate Forrestor as though about to speak.

'It's all right, Bess. There's no need for you to worry. There was nothing amiss,' Kate said, kindly.

'I'm sorry if I let you down, Mrs Foley. He is such a forbidding sort of man.'

Georgie snorted in frustration and Kate stepped in again. 'Nothing dreadful happened to Mrs Foley. It's really quite all right.'

Mrs Dawson nodded and left the room.

'You see, Georgie? No amount of denial will erase what's in their minds. But one word out of line from them and you dismiss them—is that clear? Into your bath,' she ordered.

Georgie climbed into the shallow hot water and soaped her body quickly. Kate sat with her. 'There is an acceptable way out of this predicament, and one that needs careful thought so that as little scandal as possible will be involved.'

Georgie soaped some more, her lips pressed together.

'So, what do you intend to do?' Kate prodded.

'Nothing. I won't be here when he returns—if he returns.'

Kate laughed. 'Of course he'll return—no doubt about it.'

'I shall go away. Today. This morning.' Her decision made, Georgina climbed out of the bath. Between her legs she felt tender and a little swollen, and her body tingled in memory of the event.

'And just where will you go?' Kate asked, holding out a large fluffy towel.

'The closest place I own, Kate. Port Fairy. But I don't want him to know that, and find me.' Georgie wrapped herself in the towel and patted herself down.

'My dear.' Kate frowned. 'It should be obvious he won't need me to find you.' She watched as the younger woman dropped the towel, donned the robe and began to pace. Georgie stopped in front of the open wardrobe.

'Oh, he won't come anyway. He's—he's had his way. Men like him don't come back for—'

'Don't say anything unsavoury, dear. And if he won't come back, then why should you leave?'

Georgie was pulling clothes from the wardrobe in handfuls and tossing them onto the unmade bed.

'Take stock, Georgina. You simply can't run away. You have responsibilities. The Carriers—you know you wanted to learn about them and take some control—'

'And you know as well as I do, Katie Forrestor, that Angus and Mr Wardle will have none of that, much less the men, whom I have never met, who work for me.' She stood with hands on her hips as she faced her sister-in-law. 'I'm not so stupid that I should just go ahead and beat myself against a stone wall.'

'Then for heaven's sakes, marry the man. I'm sure he was honourable enough to offer marriage.'

'Him? Honourable?'

'Georgina. I have *no doubt* he offered marriage.'

Georgie huffed. 'An honourable man would not connive into my bed and expect to own my company and property by default.' She grabbed a linen shift and wriggled into it then checked the drawers for a pair of bloomers. 'There is the law.'

'Connive.' Kate raised an eyebrow. 'You know by law he can't own anything already yours before your marriage. I'm sure he knows that, too.'

Georgie drew on the pants and tied the drawstring at her waist. 'And yes, he offered to marry me—or rather, *told* me we would marry. There is no way he will force me into this—'

'My dear girl. It is our belief—Angus and I—that this would be an excellent opportunity.'

'Opportunity?' Georgie smoothed the shift over her underwear. 'I want to make my own decisions. I have the means now to take—'

'Yes, you have the means, now,' Kate interrupted, coming to her feet, and wagging her finger. 'And it is only because my brother decided to lift you out of the mire of that dirty little homestead on that muddy river.' Her voice had hardened. 'If it were not for my brother, you would be still there.'

'I would never,' Georgie cried. 'I had already left there.'

'Yes, with Dane MacHenry after you.'

'No, no, no. You're wrong—he was going to Melbourne. Oh Katie,' Georgie cried, and slumped onto the bed. 'I never meant to hurt you and Angus, or Conor's memory. Things were not as they seemed for us—'

'I don't need to hear. The possibility of Dane MacHenry asking for your hand in marriage has been discussed. It will solve the problems of the Carriers. He might not own them if he marries you, but he will be able to run them, perhaps save them from ruin.' Kate patted a hand to her hair and straightened. 'You already know the business is not a responsibility Angus wishes to take on, regardless of the fact that Conor was my brother. I simply am not interested in it, and Angus has our own business to look after.' She folded her arms. 'If you don't sell—and quickly—as trustees of the company, we will recommend a sale to the highest bidder.'

Georgie's mouth dropped open. 'Are you saying that—even now—as Conor's widow, I have no control?'

'Precisely. You have a majority but there will be no support.'

'I don't understand.'

'No, you don't understand. Dane MacHenry's offer for the Carriers is unexpected but welcome. Agree to sell. Or marry Dane MacHenry, especially after last night. You might just have to.' Kate swept out of the room, saying over her shoulder, 'I will be downstairs in the parlour with Angus.'

Georgie sat on the little stool in front of her dresser.

You might just have to.

That could not happen. She pushed Kate's words aside and gazed at her reflection. She didn't look any different after the heady night, but then again, she wasn't sure she should. If the night's events had changed her life forever, would there be evidence of it in her face … a knowing, or—?

Whatever luxurious feeling she had woken with was now gone, dissipated in the heated words of her argument with Kate. How could Kate, Conor's sister, think she should marry again, and so soon after Conor's death? Just who was the hypocrite now?

She had the grace to lower her eyes so her own embarrassed reflection was not staring at her.

Dane's words echoed in her head. *It's not only the Carriers I'm after.*

Jacaranda. He wanted the homestead back. Of course he did.

What would be so bad about that? Dane had told her Conor had won the place at a game of cards. Certainly, she could right that wrong and give it back to Dane. However one did that.

Angus would know. But would Angus help her if she refused to sell the Carriers?

She tapped her fingers on the dresser and glanced at her reflection again.

Georgie would tell Angus she'd agree to sell the Carriers to Dane MacHenry. However, she would also sign Jacaranda back to Dane, just as she'd asked Conor to do. She would return his home to its rightful owner, whichever way that could be done. That would do it—of course it would! Then Conor's businesses would be free of his dishonourable actions.

Then she would sell the house at Port Fairy. She would leave this colony forever and go into New South Wales. She would start another life, never speak to these people again. She would buy a small holding, build stables, begin a stud program, breed the finest horses in the districts.

That's what she would do. That's *exactly* what she would do. She would finally be free to be her own woman—independent, with money.

She chose a gown she could fasten in the front. She raced down the stairs to call Deborah. And as she dashed into the parlour looking for her, she found Kate and Angus talking together over tea.

Angus rose to his feet, his best stern look on his face. 'Georgina, I believe Katie has—'

'No need, Angus,' Georgie said and held up her hands in defeat. 'No need to say anything, please.'

Angus shook his head tiredly. 'Georgina.'

'I will sell the Carriers to him. For whatever he offers. But not the homestead. I want to sign Jacaranda back to him and the family. I don't want that on my conscience. It was not appropriated morally and I'm not comfortable about that.' She did not look at Kate.

'Well, we would have to look—'

'I will only ask this one thing of you—of you both.'

Kate and Angus exchanged meaningful glances and both began to speak.

Georgie held up her hands again. 'You can force me to sell, so I will not fight it. Just let me deed him the homestead. I believe I have some rights.'

Angus looked at her. 'You've upset yourself, my dear Georgina, you're quite flushed.' He sighed heavily. 'I can't begin to say I understand this troubled relationship between you and MacHenry, but if that's what will satisfy you, we will need you to sign the relevant documents. You will not be able to leave in that case until—'

'I'll not be manipulated any longer, Angus.' She stood to her full height. 'I will not *sell* Jacaranda to Dane MacHenry, I will *deed* it back to him, even if I have to find another solicitor to ensure that happens.'

Kate gasped. It was Angus's turn to hold his hands up in defeat. 'All right, Georgina. I had no idea you felt this strongly about it. And we apologise—' he nodded towards his wife, '—for any discomfort we may have caused you. We believed it only in your best interests.'

'Do you know, Angus,' Georgie said, flicking a heavy lock of her loose hair over her shoulder, 'that for the whole of my life, I have apparently been the cause of, and the target of, much discomfort? From my mother's early death, to Papa Rupert's taking me back to England and then returning me to the colony and placing me at the MacHenrys' home, to my marriage to Conor to—to this.' She paused. 'Never once have I been allowed the luxury of making my own decisions.'

After a moment's silence, Angus said quietly, 'Perhaps you lack the forethought required.'

Georgie threw her hands in the air. 'Forethought? I have not had the courtesy of being asked my wishes from any of you. I have been told I must go, must stay, must marry, must sell, must marry again, stay, sign ... Forethought? I have no need of forethought.'

'Don't get yourself upset, dear,' Kate said, glancing between her sister-in-law and her husband.

Georgie rounded on her. 'Too late. You are Conor's sister.' She swept past Kate to stand at the mantle and faced them both, hands on hips. 'You were the one who insisted I go to all your bloody tea parties. What did you think I was going to do? Call in a brigade of men to entertain me?'

Kate's hand flew to her mouth.

'Georgina,' Angus snapped.

'Not a brigade, dear. Just one man. It was very clear to me.'

'I married Conor to be a part of his life, not a part of his mantelpiece.' She tapped out a staccato beat on the shelf over the fireplace. 'You cannot say I have done anything wrong by him.'

'Until last night,' Angus said, accusation loud in his voice.

'You have no right to comment.' She watched Angus bluster at that. 'Please. Please let us not argue any longer. As of today, the conversation is closed.'

Georgie turned on her heel and left the room. The look of thunder on Angus's face and the frown on Kate's were clear in her mind. She only vaguely heard the Forrestors leaving the house, the sound of their carriage departing drifting through her bedroom window.

She would go to Port Fairy and live there until her chattels were disposed of. It was one decision she could make that no one could deny her. She would rest there, away from Melbourne, away from the Forrestors and the reach of Dane MacHenry. She would regroup, become calm and focus on her new path.

Manning was summonsed to visit the bank on her behalf, with a scribbled letter requesting funds be placed at her disposal in the Western Districts. She sent Mrs Dawson on her way with a generous amount in cash. Manning was also to arrange for Buttons to buy horses on her behalf and have them delivered and stabled close by her new house in Port Fairy.

Deborah would accompany her and pack everything she was told to.

It would all take time to eventuate, but things were in motion. Her way, her will. With her belongings attended to, and Manning's assurance of the bank's support, she settled down for her last night in Conor's house. As she lay down to sleep, she remembered her first night here. It seemed a long time ago, somewhere in the distant past. Time had sped by.

Dane MacHenry had been pushed from her mind during the hectic activity of the day, but that night, with his scent still on her bedclothes, she wept, desperately wanting to see him again.

In the morning, with renewed vigour and self-recriminations for her girlish weakness, she stood on the polished steps of the great house that had been hers for such a short time. She looked up at the imposing front door.

This old life is over.

Again.

Twenty-Nine

Dane read the scrawled note left for him by Miss Deborah Browne. He looked up at Angus Forrestor. 'Port Fairy,' he told the solicitor. 'I had the servants keep me informed. A shilling to sweeten the exchange.'

Angus leaned over his desk and raised his eyebrows. 'We knew. She told Kate as much. What do you suggest?' He pushed a cigar box across the smooth leather top of the bureau to the men opposite him.

Dane declined the offer. 'I'm not preying on a rich young woman, Angus. I want her for my wife, regardless of your brother-in-law's companies. I do admit I want Jacaranda back. This is where my partner, Mr Cawley comes into things.' He indicated the man sitting on his left. Reuben inclined his head, a small smile on his face as he reached for an aromatic cigar.

'Mr Cawley,' Angus acknowledged. 'My wife is a very good friend of your mother's.'

'Yes, sir. I have had the pleasure of meeting Mrs Forrestor at one or two of my mother's many afternoon teas.' Reuben lifted his cigar in a salute.

'Ah yes, the many afternoon teas.' Angus chuckled. 'Actually, I believe the subject of our conversation here today called them

298

"bloody afternoon teas". My sister-in-law is not averse to colour-ful language.'

Dane recalled his own experience. 'She is not.'

Angus took a cigar himself and sat back. 'So, you have a com-pany ready to purchase the Carriers and Jacaranda.'

'A subsidiary of the Cawley Group,' Reuben began, 'Melbourne Lands & Holdings, will purchase the carriers, and Jacaranda will be purchased as a separate entity by Capital Properties. If neces-sary, we can then sell each off at will.'

'I told Georgina I wished to buy the Carriers,' Dane added. 'You told me she agreed. We had not managed to discuss Jaca-randa in time.'

Angus nodded at Dane, tapping his fingers gently on the desk top. 'But you will be buying back your homestead, Dane. I believe no money exchanged hands when the deed was transferred to Conor.'

'I am prepared to buy it back. It is at a much reduced price and I can no longer afford to wait.'

Angus was happy to let him do so, happy that Dane MacHenry would not know from him that Georgina had naively offered it on a deed transfer only. Her girlish suggestion was bad business. The other shareholders would not have agreed to it, he knew.

He pushed the sale contract across the desk. The purchase price listed on one included the Carriers and the office at Echuca. The other, Jacaranda Homestead. The deal would take some time—they would have to contact Georgina, and then have a solici-tor look over the papers for her—but she would sign. Angus was thankful to rid himself of the tiresome burden once and for all.

Damn Conor. Angus wished many times that Conor had willed it all to charity and left Georgina to her own devices. No doubt the silly woman would have forgotten this women's rights nonsense and fallen into MacHenry's arms more than willingly.

Reuben Cawley dipped the offered quill into the inkpot and signed the advance papers on both contracts.

———

Dane and Reuben rode back to the Cawley family home in South Yarra, where they took tea with John and Angeline. John Cawley was especially interested in this new business the younger men had acquired. Neither he nor Angeline were under the impression that it was all for the makings of profit.

'So, the confused and widowed Mrs Foley has flown the coop.' Angeline looked almost gleeful.

'Not for long. She will have to come back.' Dane held his glass up for more rum. *Bloody afternoon teas.* Reuben poured.

'Such confidence,' Angeline commented.

'It is as much a matter of family, as business,' Dane said. 'My family.' He wondered if Angeline found his comment cryptic. He doubted it. He knew by his mother's letter that she and his sister were settled in the lodgings he had found for them in Swan Hill, had found a private tutor for Elspeth to complete her finishing, and that they were comfortable and even happy. Elspeth had met a nice young man, so his mother had said.

His mother had also mentioned the emergence of an old suitor of hers, a Mr O'Rourke. She was keen to have Dane meet him, and wanted to determine a date to do so at his earliest convenience. It sounded as if his mother was quite taken with this Mr O'Rourke. Perhaps it would mean some happiness for her. He must make time soon to travel to Swan Hill.

Especially now he had Jacaranda once more. He would invite his mother back to her home and restore it to its original splendour. He hoped she might lay her demons to rest and enjoy it once again, despite her current aversion. Perhaps Mr O'Rourke would also enjoy it.

'And marriage, I would hope,' Angeline stated flatly, bringing Dane back to the present. 'It is all very well to dally with this girl's affections, as long as you have honourable intentions.'

'I haven't dallied. Of course not. If she had consented already, I'd be organising my wedding now.'

'Nonsense. *I* would be organising the wedding. You, my boy, are just as likely to run her off to an office or some other dreary place.'

Dane laughed. 'I might have to, she might not stand still long enough to attend the wedding of the year.'

'I for one cannot understand why you let her go in the first place—before her marriage to Katie's brother.' Angeline sipped her tea.

'Perhaps it is not our business, my dear,' John Cawley chided gently.

'Perhaps not.' Angeline was still intent on Dane's answer.

'I believed she had played a part in conniving the disappearance of the family fortune.' Dane gave a short laugh at the non-existent MacHenry fortune. 'After some introspection—difficult, to say the least—I transferred the blame to myself. It seemed I had for so long neglected my own family. Inadvertently, I might add in my defence.' He folded his arms. 'I wanted to blame her. I did blame her. I drove her to Foley, of that I'm sure.'

'I don't think so, Dane,' Angeline said, her tone much softened. 'Kate told me her brother had already announced his intention to marry Georgina.'

Dane knew it to be the truth—Georgina had told him so herself. 'Well, at the time I was thinking about marrying her, I had known her one week, if that.' He looked up at his second family. 'It would have been a very strange affair indeed had I married her then.'

'Much too early, my dear.'

John Cawley shook his head. 'You boys can get yourself into some tangles.'

Reuben laughed. 'Not me, Father. I'm as content as an old kangaroo. Amelia is the only one for me, thankfully. I don't want any more of this heartstrings stuff.'

'A reformed rake,' Dane muttered good-naturedly. 'Only the worst kind.'

'Exactly that, my friend. As you perhaps seem to be.'

Angeline cut short their jibing. 'What will you do now, Dane?'

He swallowed the last of his rum. 'Angus Forrestor has drawn up the legals on all of it and by the end of the month, we should be settled.'

'Very satisfactory.' Reuben finished his rum. 'And then, I certainly want to meet this Georgina of yours. She seems to have tamed the raging beast, my old friend.' He waggled his eyebrows.

Dane snorted. 'Unlikely.'

'The meeting or the taming?'

In the following weeks, Angus Forrestor kept Dane informed of the progress made with Georgina, mainly by telegraph. They waited as the original documents travelled back and forth by mail. As hoped, she signed all the relevant papers required to sell to this Melbourne Land & Holdings and to Capital Properties.

He wrote to his mother that he had purchased Jacaranda, and if she so wished, he would install her there.

Jemimah's return letter stated that *Jacaranda was devastated by the violent deaths upon it and I would be hard pressed to make my home there again. Instead, I ask you to purchase a small property in Swan Hill for me where I would be content to live out my life. Elspeth might marry in a year or two, perhaps a monetary wedding gift from you would suffice for her.*

There was no admonition in her words, but he bore the heavy guilt of neglecting her, all the same.

'*As for myself,*' his mother continued, '*I am quite taken by the pleasant and attentive company of Mr O'Rourke. It is my fervent wish that you meet him, Dane. We have to discuss a number of things and Mr O'Rourke must be party to that. Please write with the date of your visit, son.*'

Dane pursed his lips. This Mr O'Rourke was definitely someone he needed to meet.

He hung his head.

Jacaranda. When it was lost, he had made it his goal to return it to his family. Now they didn't want it. But he would make it great again, for himself. For his wife and his family. He would have a home to be proud of.

He had plans. He would crop, farm with new ideas, educate himself about the new irrigation project …

Georgina.

He still expected to hear from her that she was in the family way, but as another month had passed and no screams for help had come by mail or telegraph, Dane surmised she was not with child.

In that case, he would have to take the next careful step in his plan.

Thirty

Georgie idled her way along the little beach over which Port Fairy stood sentinel. Life was peaceful for her here. Her neighbours were kind and not intrusive, and the townsfolk were reserved, although generally suspicious of a single woman in their midst with no apparent male to keep her.

She removed her shoes and stockings, careful not to attract attention, and paddled in the ocean at her leisure. It was cool, the day overcast, but the water invigorated her. Sometimes she wished she could throw off all her clothes and wade in to splash.

That would most certainly *not* do.

Her little house was comfortable, not the kind she would have expected Conor to buy. It was almost a bungalow, a single storey with a separate kitchen room, two comfortably sized bedrooms and a sunny morning room facing the ocean. It was weather-proof, something many other houses hereabouts were not. It had a little garden that she found she enjoyed.

But it wasn't by the river.

Georgie missed living there. Missed the wide plains near Jaca-randa, the tall gums, the screeching birdlife, the pleasant balmy heat in spring and, in early summer, the eucalypt-fragranced breeze skimming across the water. One day, she would buy a house somewhere there, somewhere along the Murray. She would go home.

She'd never given another thought to moving to New South Wales as she'd vowed to do. She was content for the moment, and kept her restlessness at bay by taking long walks on the beach. Deborah had long since ceased to accompany her on these walks. It was too cold, she said, and she would prefer to visit her new friend, a widow named Agnes Story, instead. Georgie was happy for Deborah to have made friends, and something of their old, friendly relationship returned. She was no longer uncomfortable in Deborah's presence, and Deborah had recovered her happy nature again. Georgie suspected Mrs Story's companionship was to blame.

Buttons had sought stock carefully for her but he had secured a position with another gentleman and could not provide his services any longer. She wished him well. Georgie instead discovered stables in the township that belonged to a Mr Caxton. She had approached one day to chat, but his surly rebuttal did not encourage further conversation. Thoughts and plans of horses and stables to put them in would have to wait.

Georgie padded up the grassy slope to her little house, looking left and right to ensure nobody had seen her without her stockings. She ran to her door and rushed inside, her feet suddenly cold, the sand gritty underneath.

The house was cosy. She pulled her skirts up and lifted her foot onto the hall stand to brush away the sand, when a male voice startled her so badly she nearly fell over.

A strong arm gripped her elbow. 'Not showing a pretty ankle about town, are you, Georgie?'

Despite the sudden fright, she steadied herself and snatched her arm away. 'What are you doing here—and in my house?'

Dane took her arm more gently. 'I'm sorry. I didn't mean to frighten you.'

'Didn't you? How could you not frighten me, sneaking into my house and—Let go of me!'

'The door was open and it's brisk outside. Much warmer in here.'

'How did you come? MacNamara?'

'No. He is stabled at the Cawleys's. I took the coach, and walked from the township.' He held out his hand, indicating she should move into the little sitting room. 'It's a very long and uncomfortable journey.'

Georgie padded to a chair closest to the fire. 'I hope you're not intent on staying.' She reached into the wood basket, snatched up a sturdy piece, and threw it into the glowing hearth.

'I am.' He helped himself to whatever was in the decanter on the sideboard, pouring two glasses. 'I trust you are in robust good health.' He handed her a glass, sniffed at the contents of his.

She took the glass and set it on a little table alongside her. 'You didn't come here to enquire of my health. How did you find me?' She folded her arms.

'It wasn't difficult. You had left no instructions that your new place of abode was to remain a secret. It was a simple enough task to find out.'

'And now you're here.' She snatched up the glass then frowned at it.

'Sherry.'

'I know that.' She swallowed it in one gulp, and wondered if she shouldn't have.

He stood by a vacant chair. 'We have much to discuss, and much more to look forward to. I didn't believe you would run away again.'

'I did not run away. There was nothing further for us to discuss; the matter was closed when the sale went through.' She closed her hands into fists and rested them in her lap.

'That is true, if we are speaking only of business.' He eased his tall frame into the chair, his legs stretched out to absorb some heat from her merry little fire. 'Which we are not. I want to visit you, and with good intentions. It's the natural progression of our courtship. I want marriage, so there is still much to discuss.'

'That really is laughable.' She felt her face pinch.

He placed his glass on a side table. 'Where is Deborah?'

'She'll be along soon.'

'When she comes in, dismiss her for the evening.'

'I will not. I happen to be known here as a respectable widow.'

'For God's sake,' he said tiredly. 'It still hasn't occurred to you I might mean what I say.'

'The business is sold. There is no reason any longer to press me like this—'

'I want you to be my wife, Georgina. Tell me I'm wrong in believing you want that as well.'

Instead of her voice, Georgie heard small puffs of breath push out of her lungs. 'I—haven't thought any such thing,' she managed, and then felt heat flame her face.

'I don't believe you.' Dane spoke softly as he stood and reached for the decanter to refill their glasses.

Georgie eyed her glass suspiciously. She didn't touch it. She didn't want to dwell on his proposal, either.

'I don't wish for our meetings to be so strained, Georgie. I seem to remember the pleasure the last time we met.'

'Please.' She pressed her hands to her ears, her face flaming anew.

'We got along extremely well, I happily recall. But my proposal of marriage was left unanswered.'

'And I remember that it was not.'

'I will keep returning until you consent.'

'You presume I will consent.'

'I presume nothing,' he said, removing his coat. He placed his booted feet on the edge of her chair and she moved her legs aside for fear she would not resist his touch.

They heard a door open and close and Dane rose to his feet. 'Ah, Deborah. Nice to see you again.'

Deborah grinned broadly at him. 'Only a matter of time, Mr MacHenry—' she began then had the misfortune of spying her mistress. 'Oh—miss, I can explain … '

Georgina leapt to her feet. 'Out,' she snapped, pointing to the door.

Dane nodded at Deborah. 'Perhaps you have somewhere else to stay for tonight, Deborah. Mrs Foley will be quite all right here. Go on,' he said. Dropping his voice, he added, 'You'll still have your job tomorrow.'

'Thank you, sir,' she said. She ducked out the door without another glance at Georgie.

Dane closed it behind her. 'Both Manning and Deborah have been in my employ as well as yours,' he confessed blithely. 'I needed to know you were in good health, and safe.'

'I have no doubt about their employment, now.' Hands on hips, she faced him squarely. 'I have never in all my life encountered such a man as you.'

'Stop glaring at me that way.' His voice dropped. 'You don't hate me, I know that.' He sat down again. 'I needed to see you, Georgie. You are in my blood, you are in my head, you walk with me daily, which is a distraction I can no longer keep at bay.' He rubbed his hands over his face. When he looked back at her, his eyes were bloodshot and tired. He sighed, and rested back in his chair.

Her life was shifting, as if strings were being pulled, as surely as if she were a marionette. She looked at him at home in her house, languid in the chair, comfortable with a mid-morning glass of sherry. Domestic, charming, secure, but now perhaps just a little vulnerable.

'Despite what you might think, I am glad the Carriers was sold to you as you wished. To meet your needs.'

He smiled wearily. 'The boats are integral to my next venture. I plan to crop, once we have adequate water again. And it means you have more money in your pocket. Jacaranda—'

'I wanted to sign Jacaranda back to you,' she offered quickly. 'I insisted. But this Capital Properties company purchased it as an important part of their—' She stopped when she saw his expression. 'What is it?'

He looked as if he was in shock. He sat there for some moments, speechless. Then, 'You'd have *signed Jacaranda back* to me?'

'Yes, but—'

'—but it was *sold*, instead.'

Georgie nodded, watched the deep frown that formed on his face—a measure of anger, she thought. Clearly, Jacaranda's loss was a nerve still raw. Why had she been so eager to bring it up?

'Well,' he said softly, shaking his head. 'Life does have its twists and turns.' He rubbed a hand over his mouth.

'You are struggling with it. I'm sorry.' Georgie's gaze roved over his face, so close. A lightness overwhelmed her, a heady, sweet, flooding relief. Her heart swelled.

He reached across and steadied her hand with his. 'Truly, that you thought to deed it back to me is enough ... ' His voice trailed away as he sighed heavily. 'But the deeds of some men ... ' He was silent for long moments, frowning again. Then he looked at her and smiled. 'That whole issue can wait. We will discuss it further, but not now ... not today.' He shook his head again. 'Georgie, I'm asking you to marry me.'

She let her hand rest in his. 'Marriage. I have already been there.' She sat up straight, lifted her shoulders, tilted her head. 'I do not want marriage if I'm to be a useless, coveted possession, to be dictated to.'

He dropped his gaze to their joined hands. 'As it should be. We would discuss and agree on any given subject before we go any further.'

'I do not want marriage if I cannot explore the things which mean a great deal to me.'

He nodded. 'You should explore those things. Unless they exclude me totally, that is. I wouldn't allow that.' He dipped his head and his lips brushed the back of her hand.

Warmth tingled through her. 'I do not want marriage if I cannot be a part of my husband's life. Of all of his life.'

Dane looked up at her. 'Naturally.' He waited. 'And is there not another most important thing to want in a marriage?'

Flustered, she removed her hand. 'Well, I—want to love and be loved. Of course.'

'Of course. Thankfully.'

She took a deep breath. 'So, now you have your purchase from the estate, you won't need to … acquire me any longer. In any case, I have just stated I would be altogether too demanding.'

His hand cupped her face, warm fingers toying with a lock of her hair. He left his seat to kneel beside her and kissed her cheek, pressing his face against hers. 'I don't want an acquisition for a wife.'

He scraped his chin against that little spot on her neck he'd discovered not so long ago. Then he pulled back and looked at her, taking her face in his hands to kiss her. 'I want a warm, passionate woman beside me. To light a fire in me, to bring me joy and laughter and maddening frustration and all of the things you already bring to my life.' He looked into her eyes. 'I want the things you want for you. Without them you wouldn't be you. I need you to be those things, for both of us.'

'Is that so? They are pretty words.'

'It is so. And they are more than just words.'

He looked so solemn, so sincere, her heart danced a jig.

Georgie smiled a little then brought her lips to his in a firm kiss. She murmured against him, 'I don't sew, nor do I do any other wifely types of things.'

'I hope you can at least cook an egg.'

'I ride horses.'

'And so very well. You will have your horses. Though I would ask you don't aim the horse or quirt at me too often.' His voice faltered. 'Georgina.' He stroked her cheek again, brushed fingertips over her lashes.

'You would teach me your business?'

'I would. The parts of it you'd want to learn.'

'I have heard that before.'

'But not from me.'

'I'd want to learn everything. Everything. To be a part of all of it.' His fingertips danced down her cheek to her neck, glided down to the swell of her breast. She looked at him, her heartbeat quickening in anticipation. 'Dane, it's so very early in the day … '

'But not too cold here by the fire.'

———

They lay together on the floor in front of the hearth, clothes strewn about them, love sated, and loving beginning. When their stomachs growled, they hurriedly dressed and went to the kitchen.

They ate bread and mutton in her room, naked once more and happy on her bed, laughing as it creaked under their weight. They drank the sherry and made love again, falling asleep in each other's arms, only to wake in the night to love each other again.

In the morning he stood at the end of the bed and dragged on his breeches. He looked back at her as she sat up, blinking sleep away. 'I need to return to Melbourne and I have to leave today, but I think a wedding very soon would suit. I'll leave the timing up to you.' He threw open the curtain. 'I will visit as soon as I am able.'

Sharp daylight pierced her eyes. She clutched the sheet to her chin. 'Oh. There's no need to rush. I want a little more time to think.'

'Don't think too long, Georgina.' He turned back to her, a frown creasing his brow.

'I really do have to think … It's hardly been enough time since—'

'I expect to announce our engagement when I get back to Melbourne, or at least very soon after. You're not going to refuse me, now?' The dark look remained, the shadow of his day-old beard swarthy on his features.

'I will take all the time I need, Dane MacHenry,' she said and answered his glare with one of her own. 'I will not be pushed by a man growling at me in my own bedroom as if I'm a possession.'

He snorted. 'You have never been, nor ever will be, my possession. But you will be marrying me very soon. Make no mistake about that.' He faced her over the end of the bed. 'I suggest you get yourself dressed and see me off.'

Georgie lay down again. 'I intend to sleep some more.'

He continued to dress, shrugging into his shirt and stuffing the tails into his pants. 'I *will* have your answer.'

'You will. But not yet.'

'And it *will* be the answer I expect to have.'

Georgie simply looked at him. She lifted her cheek as he came to kiss her.

'Goodbye for now, Georgie.' He turned and left her room.

Moments later Georgie heard the front door slam. She sat up, swung her legs out of the bed and reached for her nightgown on the floor. She wriggled into it and padded to the window to watch as Dane strode towards the town, no doubt to pick up the return coach to Melbourne.

She wasted no time washing and dressing. There was much she had to do today.

Deborah arrived at the house mid-morning, full of apologies and excuses. Georgie dismissed her with a few coins in her palm.

Manning would be paid off by a note in the mail sent to the Foley residence.

And now, she had a letter to write to Kate and Angus.

———

Kate took the letter into Angus as he sat in his office with the day's newspaper. He glanced up.

'From our sister-in-law,' she said, waving the page at him.

Angus took the pages from his wife, shifting his spectacles further up his nose. He leaned towards the window for better light and read a few lines before harrumphing.

'Now she's on the see-saw again, is she?' Angus said, and shook the letter at his wife.

'Keep reading, darling.'

Georgina apologised for not writing sooner. She wished to visit and to stay at the big house and would arrive in a month's time. She looked forward to seeing them. She added a couple of lines about Dane's visit, and his offer of marriage, which she had not yet considered.

'For pity's sake. If she doesn't voluntarily marry MacHenry this time I shall organise it myself,' Angus grumbled. 'The fellow has been after getting himself between her legs for ages.'

'Angus.'

'She should marry the man,' he said. 'All this—' he thumped Georgie's letter on the table, '—is a bloody sounding board for her—excuse my language, darling—and I won't have a bar of it. I will no longer offer to control her financial affairs, and I damned well won't stand for this rot.'

'Keep your voice down.'

'She's clinging to some idiotic idea that—'

'Angus, she's a young, rich widow and she's been shunted left, right and centre all her life and none the least by this family. Now just be a little more tolerant.'

'I will advise her to marry him the moment I see her.'

'You'll do nothing of the sort, Angus. *I* will. And it won't be friendly advice.'

———

Georgie and Kate were coming back from the garden, heading up the bluestone steps of the big house that marked its entrance. Nothing Kate had said so far had moved Georgie to agree to marry any faster than she intended. She was obstinate. She would take her time to decide.

'And I've been back in this house two weeks with nary another visit from him, so I expect he's actually forgotten all about it.' Georgie glanced at Kate, stopping on the steps as a peculiar palpitation fluttered through her. Perhaps she'd put him off after all, being so free with her affections. Her stomach lurched. That didn't sit well with her. She frowned and ran a hand along her throat.

Kate brought the bouquet of roses and lilies she had gathered to her nose and breathed in the scents. 'Contrarily, it sounds to me you're just a little disappointed he hasn't pressed his suit more ardently.'

The heady perfume reached Georgie and her nostrils filled with overly sweet scents. Her belly rolled. 'Oh dear.' She swallowed once or twice, fearing she was coming down with a fever. She pressed a flat palm across her stomach. 'I don't know, Kate. Marriage ... He is so fierce and so strong.' *And I am so uncomfortable. Am I going to be sick ... ?*

'And so are you.'

'I thought I was.' Georgie looked away, swallowing the bile as it rose in her throat. 'I don't want to make any more wrong choices. I want to be sure, clear-headed. My choices in the past have not been so good.'

But Dane was far away. In fact, she had no idea where he was. He hadn't called on her, so perhaps he really had given up on the idea of marriage.

In any case, her life no longer had the same dreary monotony of the days before Conor's death. She was independent, and financially comfortable. She would direct her energy to something constructive and interesting. She had contacted Miss Goldstein to offer her services to the cause of the suffrage. She had thought to involve herself in a new idea Miss Goldstein had spoken of: a school for the children of women who had fallen on hard times. It was some time off yet, but she had toyed with the idea of a riding school for youngsters.

Georgie had been in contact with Jemimah again. After exchanging long letters, they had agreed to meet, their estranged relationship mended. Perhaps Georgie could visit Swan Hill?

And she was riding every day—

Oh, my stomach—

She ran back down the steps and brought up her breakfast in the rose bushes.

Thirty-One

Kate folded her petit-point in her lap. 'Twice in a row?'

'I've never missed before … and I'm sore here.' She touched her chest. 'I'm vomiting every time I turn around.'

Kate softened. If only Georgina would stop fighting her fate. 'Oh, Georgie, don't do it to yourself. You must call him back to you. You must.'

'He trapped me,' Georgie blurted. Her face contorted.

'How? The man loves you.'

'He knew I would—would become … He asked after my health … '

'Perfectly natural.'

'You know, like *that*,' she said, pointedly. 'He said I *would* marry him.'

'Well, could it be so bad? You have obviously consummated the—'

'Oh no, no, no. Don't say it.'

'When Angus hears of this, there'll be no other way out for you.'

'Angus cannot—'

'He would be relentless in protecting your interests. And believe me, when he hears this baby is Dane MacHenry's—'

'No one will know it's his baby,' Georgie protested.

The embroidery dropped to the floor as Kate jumped to her feet and strode across the room to shake Georgie's shoulders. 'You will not talk of such a thing! It's not a game any longer! You are having Dane MacHenry's baby and I'll not hear another word. You sit right there and write that letter to him and call him back here. Do you hear me? I will not have this nonsense go on any longer.' She wagged a finger under Georgie's nose. 'You will *not* dare to live a life in this society unmarried and with a child. I will *not* have the widow of my brother bringing shame to our name.'

Georgie gaped at her. 'I was not thinking of your—'

'If you do not write this letter, I will personally *deliver* you to Dane MacHenry.' She bent and snatched the petit-point from the floor then crossed to her writing table. 'You will sit here and you will do it now. Your child will have its proper name and you will ensure it is so. You would *not* survive the wrath of society no matter how much money you think you have.'

Georgie swallowed. 'Yes. You're right. The baby must have its proper name.' She stood up and eased her way to the table to write. Tears squeezed out despite her determination not to cry.

As Kate blotted Georgie's face with a napkin, so too did she blot the letter numerous times before Georgie had finished. Kate ordered her to rewrite it without the tell-tale blotches.

'Now, read it back to me.'

'*Dear Mr MacHenry, I accept your offer of marriage. I find the idea more suitable to me now that I am once again residing temporarily in Melbourne and somewhat more settled in my frame of mind. Would you please, at your earliest convenience, communicate with me. Sincerely, Georgina Foley.*'

Kate ignored the jagged sob that caught in Georgie's throat.

Within the hour the letter was despatched to Dane MacHenry, Cawley Residence, South Yarra.

It was another month before a reply arrived. Both ladies fidgeted and fretted in a state of nervous agitation. Georgie believed Dane had deliberately left his letter writing until the last possible moment, most likely because he guessed her reason for writing.

However, his reply letter left her more infuriated than his tardiness. 'That incorrigible, devious, mean-tempered—' Georgie ripped the letter in half and tossed it on the floor

'Now, Georgie,' Kate said. Kate picked up the two pieces of paper and pressed the seething Georgie into a chair. 'Calm yourself.'

Georgie's temper had soured as the days progressed with no answer forthcoming. With Georgie's waist expanding, life was becoming difficult for both of them.

'Read it.'

'*My dear Mrs Foley, your much welcomed communication has unfortunately caught me by surprise—*'

'Liar,' Georgie exploded.

'*—and as I am on the river, I regret to say I cannot come to Melbourne for at least three months due to the pressure of business—*'

'I will be out here,' Georgina wailed and held her hand about two feet from her belly. 'And nearly six months gone, the low scoundrel.'

'*However, I would be immensely pleased if you would consider coming to Echuca to make good our nuptials there at your very earliest convenience.* So, he's been in Echuca all this time, dear,' Kate finished.

'Goddamn him.' Georgie swore very quietly.

'You will have to go there, Georgina.'

'And the sooner the better.' Georgie's condition could not be kept a secret for much longer.

As it was, Kate was beginning to have difficulty hiding the truth from Angus and Angeline, and was desperately trying to hide everything from the community at large. She had tried to interest Georgie in other suitable men, but to no avail. No one appealed to her, she said, and Kate was sure she knew why. 'Georgie, my dear, I really do think you love him.'

'I hate him,' she cried, tasting the creeping nausea at the back of her throat again.

Kate shrugged as if preoccupied. 'That's close enough, I suppose.' Georgie gave her an exasperated look and Kate burst out laughing. 'Oh dear Georgie—do save those fierce looks for Dane MacHenry.'

Georgie tested another scowl, then let slip a laugh at Kate's amused face, despite her lurching stomach.

Another letter went back to Echuca, and two weeks later his return letter informed her he would expect her within the fortnight, that they would be married immediately upon her arrival.

Even as Kate was displeased at that, Georgie would at last be made respectable.

Displeased was not a word Georgie would have used.

Thirty-Two

Dane met her dutifully at Echuca Station. He kissed Georgie's cheek and held her longer than he needed to. His arm went around her and he pressed her body to his.

'I am so very happy to see you, Georgie. And I see you have something to tell me.'

She was about to hiss at him, but he interrupted. 'You must be extremely tired after your journey, but I meant what I said about our being married immediately. Our witnesses and a church man await us now.' He ushered her to a waiting sulky, helped her aboard then flicked the reins over the horse. He headed to his house on the north side of town.

Georgie was scarcely breathing she was so exhausted, and fearful each lungful would cause her breakfast to reappear. Tired as she was, she was pleasantly surprised: the house looked delightful from the outside. Inside, it was sparsely but tastefully furnished, clean and tidy. It was not a grand house, but simple, its stone walls cool and inviting.

He ducked back out to the sulky to retrieve her bags, which he dumped in the vestibule. He helped her out of her coat and led her to the dining room. There, three others awaited them.

Dane's introductions were friendly, and his voice held a smile. 'This is Georgina Foley. Georgina, these are my very closest friends, Reuben and Amelia Cawley. They have graciously accepted the invitation to witness our wedding.'

Georgie nodded at them both. This was Angeline Cawley's son and daughter-in-law.

Amelia gripped both Georgie's hands in hers, giving her a warm smile. The man, Reuben, beamed at her happily and his kind face brought a smile to her lips despite herself.

'And this is the pastor. Pastor Peter McNeill.'

The pastor nodded at her, his round, young-looking face covered by a bushy beard sprinkled with wiry grey hair. His hands clutched a bible.

Georgie nodded back at him and felt a creeping heat come up her middle. This was to be her wedding day, and here she was, four months with child or thereabouts and facing up to a pastor. She bit her lip, returned Amelia's comforting grip and together they walked into the parlour ahead of the men.

Papa Rupert was once again *in absentia*. And Jemimah would miss her son's wedding, too.

Pastor McNeill directed Dane where to stand, and then Georgie, and he began the short ceremony.

Georgie's heart thudded as she said, 'I do.'

Dane slid a heavy gold band onto her finger and planted a chaste kiss on her nose before they toasted with a glass of champagne. Georgie could not bring herself to take a sip.

A photographer hauled in his equipment. Georgie sat for only two photographs because enough was enough. The photographer had barely unpacked before she was done.

Amelia and Reuben stayed only long enough to help finish the bottle of champagne, and then said their goodbyes. Amelia hugged Georgie, as did Reuben. 'My mother will be green she wasn't here … and I swear I'm as happy with this as if I were the groom myself,' he said and then laughed at the look on both Georgie's and Dane's faces.

Amelia took her husband's arm and ushered him firmly out the door, followed by the pastor, who had a large donation tucked deep into his pocket.

Dane watched from the doorway as his friends took their carriage and the pastor made haste on foot back to the main street.

He turned to her standing by the settee in the formal room. 'Would you like to see the rest of the house now or later?'

'I am tired now.'

'Of course. But you look well, Georgie.' She could tell from the expression on his face that he approved of her thickened waistline and larger bosom.

'I am already the size of a cow. I don't know of any other woman this big at this time in her condition and I am not happy.' Georgie found a chair, eased into it, and stared at the gleaming band on her ring finger. 'You knew,' she repeated, tapping her belly lightly.

'Would you have written otherwise? I knew, without a doubt.' He sat opposite her, his gaze direct.

'Without a doubt,' she echoed, lamely. 'And yet you let me sit there worrying—'

'Georgina, I had offered marriage more than twice. I was not going to continue riding all over the colony like a madman just to sleep with you. You had to come to me.'

'Well, you got your wish.'

He reached over and took her hands in his. 'Yes, twofold. I trust you have not been too uncomfortable?'

'I was in a far better state six months ago.'

'It's not the way I wanted it to happen, I can assure you of that.' His tone lowered and he dipped his head to catch her eye.

'For me to be bullied, and harassed—?'

'Hah. That was not the case. Anyway, I'll see you have everything you want and need.' He swept a lock of hair from her forehead. 'Though perhaps not as grandly as you've had before.'

'I have no need of grand.' She withdrew her hands gently and slumped back in her chair. 'And how long are we supposed to have been married?'

'Long enough for you to have mourned your first husband and long enough for anyone to count. I also took the liberty,' he began, taking something from his pocket, 'of buying you a gift for the occasion.' He held a small box out to her.

She didn't move. He took her hand and slipped on a second ring, a large topaz set in gold.

Georgie gazed at it a second or two. 'I have rights as a wife. And I have conditions to discuss.' She held her hand up to the light and gave him the smallest of smiles.

'I believe we already discussed those, my love. I will do my utmost to see they are met.'

The smile dropped and a frown gathered. 'We can't possibly really be husband and wife.'

He barked a laugh. 'We are legally husband and wife, and a husband also has rights.'

She snorted. 'You'd be too frightened of hurting your child,' she said, a possessive hand over her belly.

Dane's eyes closed and he tilted his head. 'Ahh, my child.' His chest expanded.

'You *know* whose child this is. You wouldn't marry me if you didn't.' She glared at him, holding onto her belly to still its flutter.

His eyes popped open and he looked baffled. 'Of course I know whose child it is. It's mine. I know it.' He spread his hands, genuinely perplexed. 'I was not dishonouring you.'

'Oh.' She fell back heavily into her seat, confused by her own emotions. Moreover, the fluttering in her belly had not ceased. She *had* to calm herself.

He squatted beside her chair, his blue eyes intense and moody as they held hers. 'Georgie. Had we known you were having a baby to Conor, and then he died, I would still have wanted to marry you.'

She inhaled a sharp breath. 'Dane.' She covered her face with her hands and wept without sound.

He took her wrists and gently tugged her hands from her face. 'Come, my sweet Georgie. I'll show you where you can rest.'

'I'm so sorry.' She sniffed and looked about for a handkerchief until he produced one. 'My brains have gone. I'm quite sure they've been heaved out of me this last month.'

'Apparently a common affliction.' He helped her to her feet and guided her to her own rooms in the house. He opened the door to her bedroom.

The bed beckoned, simply furnished with a thick quilt and a deck of pillows. 'I would like to sleep.'

Dane was careful not to touch her in any other way than by a steadying hand at her elbow. He saw to it that she was comfortable, and bounded downstairs to grab the rest of her bags.

———

Time moved slowly for Georgie. Daylight was misery. She now had morning sickness every waking hour. Morsels of food to tempt her would only turn her stomach.

By day, Dane went to the wharf to work. By night, she sat in relative silence trying to stem her roiling stomach while he held her hand and told her of his day. She tried to be pleasant and interested but all she wanted to do was retch. She was grateful that he slept in a separate room, opposite hers.

One evening, he pressed a packet of peppermints into her hands. Her eyes watered at that, and she gratefully savoured a chip of peppermint lolly under her tongue.

She excused herself early once again, and slept almost as soon as she felt the pillow under her head.

MacNamara was stabled behind the house. At every opportunity she visited him, if Dane had not taken him out. The great horse would eye her knowingly, and nuzzle her, sometimes stamp his feet, demanding to be ridden. But she would not. She rested her head against his and apologised. For the first time in her life, riding did not have any appeal.

A week after her arrival, she woke close to tears yet again, but thankfully not bilious. The hourly purging had stopped. She dressed and sat on the edge of her bed as tears poured down her face. She couldn't stop them coming. She groped inside her bodice for a handkerchief and wept hard into it for some moments before it stopped. A few hiccups escaped.

She must get a grip. Other mothers-to-be she'd met at *those* afternoon teas had said their brains were often mad early in their term. It was surely the problem. *It is this stupid baby mischief that makes me someone I'm not. No more tears!*

She sniffed and stretched her back, a hand on the nagging pain there again. She would have to tell someone soon. She didn't know what it could mean.

Georgie wiped more tears. She worried for her baby. Their baby ...

And Dane. So patient, so careful with her and her baby-mischief emotions. If she could trust in their marriage just a little bit, she would enjoy living a good life with him.

She set to weeping again, not because she knew it wouldn't be a good life, but because she knew it would.

———

Dane, after gentle discussion with his wife, employed Mrs Anita Baker, a stout local woman versed in midwifery, as a housekeeper. Every morning, bright and early, Mrs Baker would come to clean and to chat, and to sit with the subdued Georgina until conversation was coaxed from her. It was from Mrs Baker that Dane discovered all was not well with his wife.

'A good day, Mrs Baker?' Dane came in from long hours on the wharf as Mrs Baker, coat on her arm, was about to leave.

'Mr MacHenry, your wife complains of a nagging pain in her lower back, and it's the worry of it that's wearing her down. She won't let me call the doctor.' She changed her coat to her other arm and shifted her weight. 'However, what with her being out of sorts so badly and this little pain every day, it just might be something not quite right with the baby.' Mrs Baker took a deep breath. 'I also believe Mrs MacHenry might be a lot further along than she thinks.'

Dane felt the thud of that in his gut, but he pushed that thought away. *Not possible.* The baby might not be well and that could mean Georgina's life, too, was in danger. He thanked Mrs Baker for her care.

Without calling upstairs to see Georgie, he took a short ride to Dr Wilson's house, requesting a visit the next day.

When Dane returned, he bounded upstairs to her room and knocked on the door.

For the first time in the couple of weeks Georgina had been married to him, she answered without delay. When she saw him standing in the doorway, she simply opened her arms.

He gathered her to him, lifted her and carried her across to the bed. He sat her on his lap, and kissed her face and her neck, holding her close.

'Oh Dane, my brain is always so woolly,' she said and tucked her head under his chin. 'I am worried for our baby. I don't know what these things mean.'

His heart swelled and his breath became short. All he managed to say was, 'The doctor will come tomorrow.' He was glad when she nodded. They sat, and he was happy just to be close once again. When she began to drift off to sleep, he shifted her onto the bed.

Her eyes opened. 'Help me get out of these clothes and under the covers ... ' She turned so he could pull the bow at her throat, and the bed jacket slipped off.

He reached out and undid the buttons on her smock, edged her closer so he could pull it over her head. Georgina covered her breasts with an arm and slid under the coverlet.

'Come in with me, Dane. I've missed you so.'

He had a day's sweat and grime on him but he stripped off and climbed in beside her, tucking her against his chest and murmuring how much he loved her. She nestled closer. He eased her further under the covers, inhaled the faint perfume of soap, and slid his hands over her velvety skin.

'Georgie.'

She stirred sleepily against him, his erection pressing hard on her bottom. He pushed between her legs.

Her full breasts were warm, the large rosy nipples darkened with the pregnancy. Her rounded belly mesmerised him and her heavier hips and buttocks filled his hands.

He groaned and buried his face against her shoulder. 'I don't want to hurt you,' he whispered.

She shook her head. 'You won't.'

Georgina guided him inside her and he moved gently until he could no longer resist the urge to let go. He cupped the heavy breasts, squeezed gently, rubbed the nipples and sank into her body, no longer in control. When he cried out, she reached back and caressed his face, their bodies still cleaved, his glistening, hers glowing in the aftermath of lovemaking.

They woke in the late morning to more lovemaking and a sweetness between them they had not known before. Georgina clung to him as if discovering her love for the first time. He was careful again, but the struggle to contain himself was proving far too great. She matched him with fervour and when at last they lay exhausted but happy, she told him, 'I love you, Dane MacHenry.'

He whooped his delight.

Mrs Baker was astonished at the change from one day to the next as the house became a happier place. She made her approval known, especially to Georgina, who, after all, carried the greater burden.

When Dr Wilson arrived, he instructed Mrs Baker, in her capacity as midwife, to conduct the examination on Georgina. When done, she helped Georgina to dress. Mrs Baker relayed her information to the doctor, whose eyebrows raised. He would take over now. Mrs Baker departed as the doctor went in to see Georgina. He carried a large ear trumpet.

Moments later, Dane heard a yelp he assumed was from Georgina, then a resounding, '*What?*' and then a long wail.

He waited in the front room for the doctor to appear, his hands wringing the closest antimacassar he could grab.

Dr Wilson met with Dane, dropping his bag at his feet. He groped in his waistcoat and pulled out a smoke. 'Her mood is normal for some women in this stage of her condition,' he assured Dane. 'She says the daily sickness has eased, luckily for her. Some don't have that pleasure.' He stuck the cheroot between his teeth and didn't attempt to light it. 'So, has she complained of this pain in her back for only a week or so?'

'Thereabouts.' Dane stood, stiff and formal, at the mantle. The frown deepened. What had Georgina yelled about? He cast about for another antimacassar.

The doctor waved a dismissive hand, then pulled the smoke from his teeth. 'I'm surprised she hasn't said anything before now. I don't think it's serious, probably a group of muscles stretching to make room.' He frowned then raised his eyebrows. 'She's a first-time mother, after all, and it is typical to be worried. Perhaps keep your conjugal distance for a while.'

Dane hollowed. To hear this now just after their reconciliation …

At the stricken look on Dane's face, the doctor amended, 'But only if she's overly uncomfortable. I believe it's more to do with the fact that twins are on the way and she is feeling every bit of the burden of carrying two babies.'

'Two—?' Dane's voice stuck in his throat. Then he managed to croak, 'Twins.' He looked at the doctor as if seeing him for the first time. '*Twins?*'

'Yes, twins, my man. You didn't know? Are they in the family?'

Dane could not speak. His mouth moved silently and he shook his head until the words came out. 'I didn't know. I don't know. I'll write and ask my mother.'

'Right.' The doctor bent to retrieve his bag. 'She is as far along as she says and if all goes well, they'll arrive safely, though perhaps earlier than she expects. That's more often the case when there's two. We will be keeping a watchful eye on her. We should not be alarmed.' He thumped Dane on the shoulder. 'Any questions?'

Dane shook his head. He couldn't think of anything. Except twins.

As he reached the door, the doctor turned back to him. 'However, if she begins to haemorrhage, or they stop moving, then you must find me immediately. Good day.'

'Good day, Dr Wilson. Thank you.' He saw the doctor out then sank, dazed, onto the front steps of the house.

He began to laugh, thought better of it as he recalled Georgie's anguished yell earlier, stood and leapt back inside to go to his wife.

———

Dane bounded in from the wharf waving a letter in his hand. He handed it to Georgie then went back to the door and pulled off his boots. 'It's a telegram from Ma,' he called from the step of the back door. 'I wrote as soon as we heard we had twins on the way and she insists we visit immediately. Immediately. And a telegram, no less.'

He padded inside in his stockinged feet. 'Are you up to it, Georgie?' He brushed his lips over hers. 'We could take a boat downriver to Swan Hill. Much easier than a carriage ride.'

Georgie held her growing roundness with one arm. 'The sooner the better ... I'm sure a small trip will be all right.' The news that twins were arriving had settled slowly. Dane had assured her, on the day they'd learned of it, between laughing his delight and soothing her anguished cries, that they would more than adequately cope with two babies.

'I still have my foggy brain, but I'm sure all will be well. I feel very well.' She smiled, and winced.

'Another kick?'

She nodded and gave a little laugh.

They agreed the plans for horses and stables would wait until the birth was behind them. Until then, she would be content to make more paper plans.

'We could even sail on to Jacaranda afterwards. The boys working there have made great headway, I'm told.' Dane had sent working parties to Jacaranda to begin much needed repairs and renovations.

'By ourselves?'

'I doubt my mother will want to visit yet. We will have to vastly change and improve it before I get her to venture there again.'

True to his word, Dane was including Georgie in his day-to-day business. He sat at a lamp-lit table by night entering figures into his cashbook, which he left for her in the morning. If she had questions, he would take her through each process in the evening until she was happy.

'Our funds are growing,' he said one night.

'We have plenty,' she replied. 'You should not be surprised.'

He looked at her and smiled. 'Our funds, independent of yours.' He squeezed her hand. 'I meant that kindly. The business can start to repay the Cawleys' loan I took for Jacaranda.'

She laid her hand on his arm. 'Perhaps we should have challenged Angus and his deceit about that.'

They both knew there was no point attending to it with another solicitor; the end result—Jacaranda back in Dane's hands—was all that mattered.

He shook his head, inhaled, scowled then let the emotion drop. 'Angus was protecting your interests, Georgie, or Conor's, or that's what I choose to believe ... *have* to believe. It was only Reuben who stopped me from going to his office after that visit to Port Fairy to—But it doesn't matter any more. I bought my own station back and I can rightfully call it mine. Ours,' he corrected with a quick grin. 'But I hope never to see Angus Forrestor again.' His brows furrowed. 'And he should feel the same about me.'

'It's hard on you, Dane, having to pay off the Cawleys when—'

'It's my pleasure after all they've done for me. Reuben paid me out of my share in the Captain's Cabin, so it was easy to repay in part the Jacaranda loan with those proceeds. And it's not as if I haven't put my back to it before.' He rolled his shoulders. 'Just got soft awhile. I still have much to do—'

'*We* still have much to do.'

'Yes, *we* do, my love.' He dipped his head to her hand and kissed it. 'And the sun shines on me every day.'

Georgie watched as he bent to the light to scratch more figures on his book. Receipts and invoices were logged, inventory items checked. He'd started his freight hauling despite a slower movement in river trade. The boats also carried passengers from Echuca to Goolwa, the mouth of the mighty Murray, for a reasonable fee that undercut his competitors. He kept his boats clean. The passengers were happy; Mr Finn was happy; the men were happy.

Ultimately, the plan was Dane's boats would carry only his own freight, decreasing his costs from the homestead to the railway station. He would reduce the number of boats when it was necessary.

'We should visit Jemimah in a week's time,' he said as he closed up his ledger for the night. 'What do you think?'

'I am very much looking forward to that.'

Thirty-Three

A quick thrill of excitement rushed through Georgie when the short carriage ride from their home brought the Echuca wharf into view. With Dane's help, she alighted and stood at the top of the grassy slopes of the riverbank.

Dane hired a driver who would deliver the carriage back to their house.

The *Lady Goodnight*, freshly painted and resplendent, gleamed in the dock.

In fact, both Conor's boats, now Dane's, shimmered in the morning light. The ladies *Goodnight* and *Mitchell*. The boats certainly did not remind her of happy days, just days gone by. She fought down a peculiar tightness in her throat when she recalled the frantic run to the wharf that eventually took her to Conor.

She stood awkwardly, hand on her hat as she swivelled, looking for Dane.

Her gaze turned back to the wharf. The *Sweet Georgie*, Dane's prized boat, the boat he intended to keep if he had to reduce his holdings, was lined up behind the ladies. Dane jogged on the wharf deck above her gleaming hull, shouting orders to the men unloading her.

She followed him with her eyes. A rush of affection and relief rolled through her in waves. Georgie had run to the mighty river looking for life and love with another. She was only lucky she found it with this man, her handsome, much-loved husband. Her heart lifted. The little lives within her fluttered as if they also recognised her love.

Dane strode towards her. 'The *Sweet Georgie* will take us downriver, sweet Georgie,' he said and his eyes crinkled as he laughed. 'I am a happy man.'

She was a happy woman.

Travelling at a sturdy eleven knots until some miles out of Echuca, the *Sweet Georgie* and her passengers made an overnight tie up to the bank just before dark. A simple meal on board and Georgie and Dane retreated to their bunk room. Carefully, tenderly, they renewed the spark ever present between them.

He moulded her fuller breasts in his hands, cupping their silky weight. He pressed his solid chest against her back and slipped himself inside her ready body. They rocked with the ebb of the tide and fell asleep in their embrace.

She wore a simple cotton housedress over her growing form and a wide brimmed hat to sit out on deck in a good sturdy chair the following morning. She lifted her face to the sun, heard the call of the magpies over the rhythmic chug of the steamer. The low banks seemed endless, but that didn't matter to Georgie. She saw little evidence of civilisation. A station or two, though one appeared abandoned, and the small township of Koondrook passed in moments. Barely a rise of hills to be seen on either side. A hint of eucalypt drifted past. She brushed away the flies and watched the glide of the water.

Only once did she see people. A small family of black people squatted by a fire on the southern bank. She stood and
lifted a hand to wave. A young woman, clearly with child, waved
back.

The boat pushed downstream.

The river had called again and this time she was coming home.
Had she been away so long? She tried to add on her fingers the
months passed, the people she'd encountered; the deaths; the
treachery; the lies. The love and the new life. So many events
crowded into a short space of time.

Dane leaned out of the wheelhouse and smiled at her. The
swarthy shadow of his day-old beard lent him the look of a rogue.

Her heart tripped a beat. It still alarmed her how easily she
might have missed being part of his life. He was no longer the
angry, driven man she'd met on the banks of the river—oh, was
it aeons ago? Their lives were full of promise and love and life on
the mighty river.

She held her belly, felt a faint kick and then another on the
other side. She smiled gleefully. She, who had believed she didn't
want children.

———

They reached Swan Hill late in the afternoon and decided to stay
aboard until the morning, when Dane would find a carriage to
hire. His mother had taken a little house on the edge of town, and
though the town itself was small—barely four hundred people—
in her letter she directed them past the brick water tower which
was on the west side.

As Dane pulled the old farmer's cart to a halt, he glanced at
Georgie. 'Ready, Georgie?'

'I cannot wait to see Aunt Jem.'

'No riding astride or stout language today,' he advocated and stepped off the cart.

She laughed. 'Of course not.' She began to climb off the cart and by the time he'd come to her side she was halfway down the little step. 'I'm heavier by the minute, Dane. I don't know how much more I'll grow before—'

Aware her husband stood rigid beside her, she glanced at him, her hand gripped in his, the solid mass of his body stock-still. 'What is it?'

Then she followed his gaze to the veranda where his mother stood. She saw her beautiful Aunt Jemimah once again and a smile of delight spread on Georgie's face.

'Aunt Jem!'

Beside Jemimah stood a man of stature. He had a head of black hair shot with silver. A man with blue eyes, dark brows and Dane's face, though he was much older. Mr O'Rourke.

The air crackled around her. Georgie carefully moved off the precarious step of the cart and settled her feet on the ground. Her husband had not let go of her hand.

The man on the veranda focused only on Dane. His mouth opened, his nostrils moved, but he made no sound nor gesture. His intense gaze locked with Dane's.

Dane, himself transfixed, returned O'Rourke's stare. His breath came in gasps, and his free hand pressed at his chest. When he doubled up Georgie released his hand and gripped his shirt front. She pushed at him.

'Dane.'

He lifted his head. He gazed at her only a moment before his eyes returned to the man on the veranda. His brow puckered, and a realisation descended; Georgie could see it come over him.

Jemimah ran down the steps. She pressed Georgie in a quick embrace then took her son's face in her hands. 'Dane, my boy. I know he is a great shock to you, but you are not a shock to him.'

Dane straightened slowly. He took his mother's hands gently and slipped them from his face. He blinked once, twice, and his breathing eased.

He looked back at O'Rourke and straightened to his full height.

Then he reached for Georgie's hand on his shirt. 'My wife, Ma.' His voice shook. 'We should get her inside. A cool drink perhaps.'

———

Dane couldn't control his chest rapidly rising and falling as great draughts of air dragged in and pushed out. His heart banged against his ribs and his head filled with fog.

Liam O'Rourke.

I see my face in his. No mistake. His hands are mine, but bigger. I have his height, his build …

Good God, do I sound like him? Surely not, I have no Irish accent.

He glanced at his wife. Georgie sipped at the wine Mr O'Rourke had opened for them, watching him. She seemed engrossed.

'An old red from vines planted near Bendigo during the gold rush in the fifties,' he said, the tell-tale lilt of brogue still present in his voice.

'You were there?' Dane asked, his fingers on the stem of a fine crystal glass. He tried to relax in his seat at Jemimah's table, and stretched out his legs. Inside, turbulent and confused emotions, well guarded from his mother, he hoped, threatened to give way. His eyes never left O'Rourke.

Liam O'Rourke nodded. His gaze rested on the grown man who was his son. 'My da and ma came out before the Potato Famine—we were lucky. So my twin brother Lorcan and I worked on the fields, saw the rush done, then had to look for more work.

We grew fruit and vegetables where we could for nearly ten years, sold it off.'

'Where is Lorcan?' Georgie asked.

'Renmark now, South Australia. I hear, from time to time. He has—'

'And you met my mother how?' Dane rested his glass on the table. He felt a pulse in his throat so strongly he thought it would easily be seen by the others. 'What is the story?'

'I was a young girl, all the way from England, visiting my worldly brother in Bendigo,' Jemimah answered. She looked into her glass of wine. 'I had gone to the street for some provisions. Liam was unloading his cart.'

Dane looked back at Liam O'Rourke. 'You made your presence felt, apparently.' He hadn't meant to sound as if he were judging—

'And so did I, Dane,' his mother said clearly, firmly. 'But my brother and Liam's father would not have it, something to do with the old wars between the English and the Irish. Ridiculous.' She coloured quickly. 'We met often, in hiding, and for more than a year we were … Then I found I was with child, with you.'

Dane returned her stare, unblinking. He felt something in his chest give way, as if some new knowledge came to him and he could understand a little …

Impossible! How could he ever know that terror a woman might feel, with child but without a husband—

'We went to your uncle Rupert and my da, but they wouldn't have it.'

Jemimah took a breath. 'I was trying to find Liam to tell him, to beg that we run away, when Tom MacHenry drove past me in his wagon. He stopped for me, a crying young woman dragging her feet in the rain, on her way to find her love. He picked me up, turned the wagon around and took me home to my brother.' She sipped and glanced at O'Rourke. 'Rupert kept me through my confinement and after. I refused to give you up and he was my staunchest ally. So I agreed to marry Tom. By then, you were nearly three and I was a tarnished woman well and truly.'

Tom had taken her in with her small child. A huge burden for any man at the time. At any time.

I remember his face when I was so young, always laughing. He taught me to shoot, to trap, to build a fire ...

A great sorrow burrowed down. His father had forsaken almost everything to take on a woman who had lain with a man not her husband and who had borne that man's child.

Would someone else have done that for Georgina had he not intended to marry her? The thought crushed him. He had no answer.

A muscle flicked in his jaw. He clenched his teeth. God, what a mess it would have been back then, and no better now.

He studied Jemimah. Her face serene. No sign of the anguish of years past ...

He bowed his head a moment and let the breath rush out.

'Tom was my pa,' he said and flicked a glance at the older man.

O'Rourke nodded. 'Yes, he was. I couldn't be. And I will be forever in his debt for it. But,' he spread his hands, 'I decided if I couldn't be married to your mother, I would never let her out of my sight, so to speak. I stayed in Bendigo, but I visited Swan Hill often, hoping for a glance when you'd come to town. Until one day someone said to me how much Tom MacHenry's boy had the look of me. I had to be more careful for your mother's sake, so I could only see you from a distance. When it got too much, I risked going to the homestead, more than once.' He leaned back and looked at Jemimah. 'A very selfish thing to do. But I couldn't help it.'

Jemimah took O'Rourke's hand. Dane glanced between the two, then at Georgie, who watched him keenly.

His head was woolly. The tale unravelled as one of loss. For his mother and for Liam. And, it seemed, for Tom. His pa must have known that Jemimah loved another. He must have.

Dane recalled their talk by the river when he'd first answered Tom's call for help. *'But let that story be for now. It's your mother's to tell.'*

'You never married?' Dane asked, aware the silence fell on him. He drained his glass. O'Rourke shook his head. 'What is it you do?'

'I am a fruiterer in Bendigo. Seemed right.'

Dane chinked his glass against the bottle. 'An excellent drink, thank you, sir.'

'Liam,' his father said.

Dane nodded. Words failed once again.

The pressure in his chest had not let up. He had to go. Leave. Take Georgina and get to the boat. Take the river run downstream and order his thoughts. Get to Jacaranda.

He stood, cleared his throat. 'If you don't mind, Ma, Liam, we will continue on to Jacaranda this afternoon.'

He nodded at Georgina, who frowned a little, but didn't rise.

Jemimah gave a rueful smile. 'Of course. It's not far to go.' She stood up and walked around the table to Georgina, hugging her where she sat. 'Elspeth would love to see you both. She was going to come tomorrow after the ... introductions.'

'We will press on for the night.' Dane's voice sounded tight to his own ears. 'Georgie.' He held his hand out for her.

Georgina took his hand and rose. Then she released Dane and offered both her hands to O'Rourke, who stood, towering over her. 'I am very pleased to have met you.' She pressed his hands in hers. 'You will be an important part in our children's lives.'

He nodded, clutched her hands and shook them, but did not speak. He sucked his cheeks, his eyes shimmering. Jemimah came to his side, unshed tears in her eyes also.

'Georgie.' Dane had to get out, to breath more easily. 'We will call in on the way back,' he told his mother, 'but I am unsure when that will be. A few days, a week.' He directed Georgie to the door. Then he stopped and turned back, holding O'Rourke's gaze. 'Will you be marrying my mother this time?'

'Yes. Soon.'

Dane nodded, his jaw working as he clenched his teeth. Then he said, 'Good.'

He drove the cart back to the river in silence for fear his torment would erupt. His hands gripped the reins until his fingers hurt and his forearms ached.

Thirty-Four

Georgie stood behind her husband as he sat on the steps of Jacaranda. He looked out across the dusty yard.

'We will bring MacNamara here again,' he said.

'The stables look very fine, as if someone's kept them.' She remembered long, devoted hours cleaning stalls, polishing saddles, grooming her beloved horses. It would be a joy to have MacNamara on Jacaranda again. Douglas would be returned from the Cawley's stables as soon as they were settled.

'Probably Joe and Watti. I got the boys to employ them again once I started the repairs.' He turned and frowned. 'Was it a mistake—coming back, wanting to rebuild?'

Georgie shook her head and came to stand by him. 'It's not a mistake. It's your home. Our home.'

'It will be a long road, Georgie. There are hard times to come. The old men say another drought, too.' He held his hand out to her. 'I cannot promise any fine dresses or balls for you to attend.'

She laughed. 'I don't need such things, if I ever needed them. Besides, it might take a while before I can fit into anything other than these tents I have to wear.' She stepped closer, the warmth of him against her leg. 'I wish I could sit on the steps with you but I'm not sure I'd get up again.' He hauled himself up and Georgie linked her arm with his. 'We had a very subdued run from Swan Hill, my love. You have not said too much about Mr O'Rourke.' She hadn't pressed him for his thoughts in the few hours they travelled.

'My mind is still bent over it.' He scratched the back of his head. 'I never knew. I never had a sense of it, not ever.' He peered out at the afternoon sky. 'It will take some getting used to.' He slipped an arm around her shoulders and squeezed. 'It's all I have thought of these last hours.'

'I liked him.' Georgie thought Mr O'Rourke seemed a wonderful man. The light in his eyes when he looked at Jemimah warmed her all over. And when he looked at Dane, she thought her heart would break for all the untold regret and love she saw in his eyes. He would make her children a fine grandfather.

'There will be unkind talk, Georgie. About my mother. Me. You. Even our children.' He checked his hands as if to ensure they were steady.

'We need not suffer it,' she replied and smiled. 'Do you remember saying that to me?'

He nodded and looked at her upturned face. 'I do.' She felt his arm around her relax a little. 'But all I've thought since meeting him … I am an illegitimate son. I cannot inherit this place.' A tremor moved through him and he checked his hands again.

Alarmed, she turned to face him. 'Dane—'

'When people learn of it, the law will move to prevent me from keeping Jacaranda. I worked, slaved all those years—'

She shook him then. 'You are forgetting our very clever friend, Angus Forrestor. He made you *buy* Jacaranda from its legal owner.'

A moment passed.

'Angus Forrestor. You're right.' Dane scuffed his boots and barked a laugh. 'I haven't thought straight since seeing Liam O'Rourke on Ma's veranda.'

'You did not inherit.' She wrapped her arms around him and rested her head on his chest. 'No one can take it away from you, now.' She looked up. 'No one. It could be said that Angus did you a favour.'

'I should thank him.'

'In a fashion.' Georgie followed his gaze out to the distant crowded avenue of gums that lined the winding river. Some things she could thank Forrestor for, others she could not.

'And O'Rourke himself,' he muttered. 'It's too much for my head. I need to visit Tom.' He offered her his hand. 'Come with me?'

They walked out of the dusty house yard across a long paddock to the fenced-off plot, still marked only by a crude cross of timber. 'A headstone next.' He linked his arm again through hers and looked skywards once more. 'I know it will one day take its place in my life, but I can't help but recall the terrible events of his death. Here. In the yard beyond.' He gestured behind him. 'And Foley's death,' he said, but didn't look at her.

Georgie squeezed his arm and remained silent.

It never was Foley's rightful place and she didn't want to discuss him here. She thought again about her decision not to visit his grave in Swan Hill. Perhaps she would one day. When she could understand; when she could forgive.

She turned back. She would not think of him any longer here.

Jacaranda had been her home for four long, bewildering years, and yet the comfort and the welcome she felt being back here overwhelmed her. To think that in those four years, and the many months since she left, she had come to love the place so fiercely that it was now a part of her very being. The smell of the baked dirt underfoot, the warming scent of eucalyptus on a breeze, and the mighty river's gentle lapping on sandy banks not far away had called her home.

Jacaranda was home. The river was home.

She looked towards the homestead; a shell of itself, waiting. Work had begun and the house sat there surrounded by the saw-horses, the laid-out timbers ready for new fences and a new veranda, the smithy's lean-to with its sturdy block and fire pit. Newly crafted bricks were stacked close to the refurbished stables ready for refitting to the main dwelling.

This would be home again, hers to love and to be loved in it. They would rebuild together and make it well again.

The sun reached for the horizon and the shadows of the gums lengthened.

'We still have about an hour or more of light yet,' Dane said, 'but we should sleep on the boat. The house is not anywhere near ready.' He blinked rapidly as he looked back at the wooden cross. 'Tom had a big heart, taking my mother and me in as he did.'

Georgie felt the old affection for her step-uncle. 'I saw a good man in him before he let his—'

'If Liam O'Rourke hadn't come to Jacaranda that one last—'

Georgie pressed her husband's arm. 'Or if Jemimah hadn't gone to Bendigo as a girl and met him, or if Tom wasn't driving past on that day she was utterly distraught, or if Rupert hadn't met my mother, and if I hadn't come here … or—or any one of the people who crossed each other's paths.'

Dane cast her a look.

'You can go round and round … Jemimah told me she chose survival, and now I see she meant for you as well as her. Tom MacHenry was that choice.' Georgie turned and leaned on the rail. Too much emotion welled inside and her belly fluttered. She glanced sideways at him. 'Aunt Jem and I went to Bendigo not long after Mr O'Rourke visited Jacaranda.'

'You met him?' Dane stood upright.

'No, no. I saw him, from a distance. It was hard to forget the sight of the two of them, arguing it seemed. Then she sent him away.' She turned her hands up. 'Maybe Aunt Jem wanted to go to Bendigo after that, for more than one reason. She said at the time she wanted to show me my mother's old house, where I was born.' Georgie's brows creased, remembering. 'But then we saw this woman in the street, destitute, yet someone you could tell had been gentle born. She looked awful at the time, not a good advocate for being independent. She spoke of the rights of women—'

'So, she is the one I should give a good talking to.' Dane smiled and leaned back on the rail.

'—that society should help with their plight if they were displaced from family. Like Jemimah had been, I suppose.' She scraped the baked earth with her boots. 'So we came back to Jacaranda and all seemed well again.' Georgie leaned into his shoulder, solid and protective. 'Till the day you arrived and Jem told me she and Uncle Tom would have to find me a place to go.'

He rested his head on hers. 'And I was a part of that for you. I'm sorry, Georgina.'

'Seems so long ago.' She patted his arm. 'And she reminded me of that poor woman then and what she stood for. Jem told me at the time to make clear choices for my survival.'

'I see you did that.' His glance held a frown.

She nudged him in the ribs. 'I did the best I could with what was on offer.' She closed her eyes to the sun on her face. How she had missed the warm sunshine of home. 'To think clearly. She said that to fight for my rights was better than to be independent. I was frightened then. I didn't want to show it, or sound it.'

'You didn't, my love. You were impressive in your eloquence.'

She laughed. 'And survive I did. Though at times I wonder at my luck along the way. How much of it did I ride, trip, fall, slide, take a *dunking in the river*.' She gave him a pointed glare. 'Not much of it was thinking clearly.'

He took a breath as if to say something then stopped.

'Tell me,' she said.

'If Conor hadn't been killed—'

Georgie hadn't wished anyone dead, but if her first husband was still alive ... Her heartbeat skittered. She tapped a finger to his lips. 'We never need to think of that. Ever.'

'And Liam O'Rourke brings more confusion ... Jacaranda is my home.' He stared towards the homestead in the near distance. 'I dreamed to build it up for my family, for my mother and father ... ' He glanced down at her. 'For my wife, one day. My own family.' He placed a hand over her firm belly. 'I couldn't imagine life without you, Georgie. Not from the moment I set eyes on you. You must know that.' Then he rubbed his hands vigorously in his hair.

Worried now, she stilled his hands. 'I do know—'

'So my thoughts spin. I can't understand how he could've let her go. It would drive me to madness thinking of that loss.' He looked at her, his eyes red-rimmed. 'When I'd had nothing but myself to worry about, nothing mattered. Now I have you, Georgie, and a family to look after ... '

Alarmed, she held her hand against his chest. 'Stop. Your heart is racing.'

Dane's eyes watered. 'If Liam felt for my mother as I feel for you, I don't know how he survived what happened. It would break me to lose you, to lose our children.'

Georgie touched his face with her fingertips. Her heart glowed. 'It won't happen to us.' She turned and tucked herself against his chest, let her arms dangle over the rail. 'Perhaps it did break Liam. He never married, he said. Didn't mention other children. Perhaps when Jem went to Bendigo with me, she went to look for him, maybe to run away finally. Maybe it nearly broke her.' She brushed at flies and tilted her head to look at him, squinting against the sun as it shone lower. 'But with Elspeth at home, and

Tom, and perhaps after seeing that woman in the street, she had to continue on her path.'

'If it were us—'

'But it's not.' She turned around, her belly pressing against him. She gripped his hand, and looked into his eyes. 'And I am happy for her now. For them. They clearly love each other. Probably always did.'

'You saw a lot in a few short hours.'

'And did you not? It takes only a moment to see and you know it, Dane MacHenry. Besides, I know my own heart well enough now to know what love looks like.' She felt the surge of emotion press against her ribs. 'Yet I could have lost it.'

'Not mine, Georgie.' He grabbed her left hand and held it up, the rings gleaming in the late afternoon light. 'You're part of me and I will never let you go. Ever.' He drew her hands into his chest. 'Besides, you're about to begin our dynasty with my two babies.'

'Please. I can't forget that.' Georgie bumped him gently with her belly. 'I am heartily glad we will have three generations of family when these two are born.' She looked towards the trees. 'At least we have one mother between us. I wonder about my own parents at times. Especially now. I never knew my real father at all.'

Dane reached over and squeezed her hands. 'Perhaps we'll find relatives of yours in Bendigo after the babies are born.'

She shrugged and smiled at him. 'One day we'll go looking. Perhaps these two will want to know.' She smoothed a hand over her round bump. 'But I don't miss what I never knew, or barely remember. Besides, we will have too much to do building our life here to look elsewhere. So,' she said and tapped his chest, 'be calm, my love. You have it all, and it will all be very good.'

He dipped his head. 'If you love me, I have it all. If not, nothing I have means anything to me.'

She touched his cheek and reached up to press her lips to his. 'I will be at your side forever and together, our family will build a majestic line of horses that will outshine our MacNamara.' She waved a hand to encompass all of Jacaranda. 'We will have a magnificent run, and our river will flow with gold.'

His gaze was intent on her face. 'I want that in writing.'

'In writing. With witnesses.' Georgie smiled. 'And I will do all the business books.' She felt very pleased with herself.

Dane laughed. 'And so, do you love me?'

'Oh, yes.'

He drew her closer and rested his hand on her belly.

A sturdy kick thrust from within her. 'Dane, they are strong, and lively.' Georgie covered his hand with hers to feel another kick. She laughed delightedly up at him, her other hand resting over his heart. 'Like us, my love.'

His chest swelled and for a moment words seemed to lock in his throat. 'I dare not speak for fear my voice will break like a lad's.'

Georgie felt her eyes glisten. His love was safe, and new life inside her, new life they'd made together, was coming. Soon.

She looked down at her hand over his, and felt the strong warmth beneath.

It would all be very good.

Acknowledgements

Writers are often in solitude, but they are never solo on their journey.

My heartfelt gratitude to:

Meredith Whitford, Nicola Boss and Annie Seaton, all of whom took on my earlier works – and published them. Thank you for that faith in me.

The Romance Writers of Australia Inc. Without my association with this wonderful band of writers I would never have pitched a thirty-three year old/reworked a thousand times over manuscript in 2015 to Harlequin Mira's Sue Brockhoff – and got my big break.

Susi Parslow, my beta reader. I have no stronger writing ally.

Amy Andrews of WordWitchery. Your compassionate direction and insight is invaluable.

Melody B Research for Writers. What a journey we've taken in the nineteenth century, Mel!

Shirley Durden and the Swan Hill Genealogical & Historical Society, and Heather Rendle and the Echuca Historical Society for your meticulous research and your warm reception.

My supportive community here on Kangaroo Island. You've come along for the ride and you've been great company.

Family and friends for everything. Just everything.

Sue Brockhoff and my Harlequin Mira team – Jo Mackay, Annabel Blay, Laurie Ormond, Rachael Donovan, editors Kylie Mason and Kate James, and cover designer Christa Moffitt of Christabella Designs. Just superb.

The mighty River Murray herself and to all who continue to take care of her.

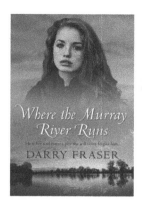

Turn over for a sneak peek.

Where the Murray River Runs

by

DARRY FRASER

Available now

One

Bendigo, Victoria, mid–1890s

Linley Seymour stared at the sleeping baby in his crib.

He stirred in his firm swaddling, his sweet face reflecting a happy sleep, a dream floating across his features. His little mouth pouted, ruby-red lips working as if he needed to say a few words.

He is so beautiful.

Something surged deep inside her, shifted in her chest, a force of emotion, and a yawning chasm opened at her feet. She stepped back, the shock of it making her heart race. A moment, a beat later when it slowed, she leaned cautiously over the cradle again.

Solemnly, his wide-open eyes stared back at her. He frowned a moment and let it go, drifting back to sleep.

'You are so beautiful,' she whispered to him. 'And I love you with all my heart.'

But this tiny creature, this serene-looking infant, had, through no fault of his own, created havoc from the moment he was conceived.

She stopped herself short. What was she thinking? Her Aunt CeeCee wouldn't let a thought like that creep in. CeeCee didn't judge anyone. In her work she offered refuge to mothers and babies like this one, not judgement. She wouldn't blame a little child for the sins of his mother.

Or his father.

That was another matter. The bristling needled up Linley's back. She put a hand to her throat as heat crept over her neck, and herded her thoughts back to her aunt. A few townsfolk knew how CeeCee kept herself occupied. Certainly, some did pass judgement, but there were others who were very happy someone offered refuge, just as long as it wasn't asked of them.

Linley rubbed her arms. At times she despaired for CeeCee and their work. Of course it was important, and sometimes dangerous, so it had to be clandestine. The few folk who did know thought they were foolhardy, not brave or enlightened. It kept Linley on her toes to go about their business as quietly as possible.

That meant life with CeeCee was lively and engaging, if a little unsettling at times. Yet it seemed that the nature of her vocation had not had the slightest impact on her aunt's bearing. At just over forty, she was still dark-haired, slim and elegant, vibrant, and certainly not solitary. Linley was none of those things. She often joked that she and Aunt CeeCee were perhaps not related. CeeCee assured her that was not true—they were definitely related by blood: aunt and niece.

Of course, Linley didn't know enough of her father's side to attest to hair colour or any other attributes. She didn't remember him, and he was certainly never spoken of, ever. Perhaps it was all his fault, her freckles and her dark copper hair.

The baby's tuft of black hair caught Linley's eye. Idly, she wondered if her hair colour and her green eyes would appear in a baby of her own if she married a certain black-haired man—

Stop that nonsense right this minute!

She focused. The baby. Concentrate only on the baby in his crib. This beautiful baby ... Take a deep breath.

So, now that she had at last decided on a name for him, she should announce it. She was sure that this last month she'd driven everyone mad with her ponderings and musings. Mary Bonner, the baby's mother, had had only a few hours with him before she died, and hadn't given him a name. Yet she had made sure that in the event of her death, Linley would be the one to make that decision, not her husband.

Though why on earth Mary hoped I would take on her child and rear him as my own, I don't know ... Do I?

She'd shied away from that very thought, hour by hour, day by day. Ever since Miss Juno first placed the poor neglected, wretched little soul in her arms at that terrible house. Miss Juno was from the solicitor's office, and had nominated herself to be Linley's agent. The day Mary had died, Miss Juno had accompanied CeeCee and Linley to get the baby from Gareth Wilkin's house.

It was best not to keep wondering why Mary did anything because Linley was only deluding herself. She knew the reason behind Mary's decision, even if the words of it lay unspoken, buried deep in her heart.

Gazing down at the baby, she had a sudden, urgent desire to pick him up, to snuffle into that new-baby smell of him. She puffed involuntarily, resisting the urge until it eased. It was harder than ever to do and lately she'd found herself not resisting one bit. His was a comfortable and familiar weight in her arms these days. She looked forward to it, craved it at times, and it soothed a relentless longing. She'd gotten to love the way her body moved when she held him and quieted him, as if she had, at some other time, been a mother with her own babe and knew what to do.

Very bewildering.

This baby—*oh, for goodness sake, Linley, use his new name ...* how could he possibly be hers to keep? Yet Mary had given him to her. How would she, with her job in the tea-rooms, manage to look after him? But without her job, how would she manage to keep him? Of course she had CeeCee's continued support, but what would everybody think?

What everybody thinks is not a priority, Linley Seymour. She heard CeeCee's voice as clearly as if her aunt was in the room and had spoken to her.

CeeCee was staunch in rallying to the cause. Of course she was. Had she not rallied when Linley herself was a needy child? Besides, the wet nurse would still come for the baby, or Linley would take him to the nurse. At least that sort of feeding was taken care of, although she had no clue how long it would last. She should ask.

The baby stirred again and this time when he looked at her, Ard O'Rourke sprang to mind. A blush warmed her cheeks.

Ard O'Rourke. Had her scalding letter to him blistered his fingers when he read the news, the terrible, *terrible* news of Mary's death? That, and the fact that Linley knew Mary's husband, Gareth Wilkin, wasn't the baby's father.

She pressed a hand to her forehead and squeezed her eyes shut. Time and time again she'd agonised over why she'd rushed to put her furious words on paper. What had possessed her? Why had she marched with one-eyed determination to the post office and mailed the letter? Why had she marched all the way home then instantly, horribly regretted it?

She'd run back to the post office in a desperate fever hoping to retrieve the letter and tear it to bits. Only to see the mail coach charging around the corner, out of reach then out of sight.

———

Linley called to mind that day of the picnic by Lake Weeroona. The day he left. She remembered clearly. It had started out like she always hoped it would, full of easy laughter with friends, and the chance to finally wander off to be close to Ard. Perhaps today would be the day he'd ask her to let him court her.

Ard, leaning against a tree, as she stood inches in front of him.

Her clothes felt tight. Her voice stuck in her throat, and that peculiar heat pounded through her veins like an exhilarating flutter of a thousand butterflies. And yet ... and yet how madly euphoric and exciting the thrill of it.

Those black eyes of his had watched her, a small quirk at his mouth deepening a line in his face. It wasn't a smile, more that a thought had crossed his mind and had vexed him. His dark brows furrowed a little. The beard stubble roughened his cheeks and neck—perhaps two days without a shave—and the blue-black of his wavy hair crept at the back of his collar.

And none of that old-fashioned, silly-looking moustache and stringy beard thing for Ard O'Rourke. One day he had two days' growth and a mop of dusty, sweat-grimed hair, the next he was clean-shaven, with his hair silky-washed and thrust back from his forehead in a long sweep, the loose dense curls waiting for her shaking hands to reach. He had a certain air about him, a leonine grace, as if nothing fazed him or got in his way. A big man, not so tall, but elegant in his movements—

Elegant...?

But he was. Supple. Fluid. And he well knew his worth. Aunt CeeCee had once commented he was more gentlemanly than the gentlemen she'd observed in Melbourne.

Ard had let her gaze trawl over him, his only movement a resting of his shoulders back against the tree trunk.

Then he spoke. 'All I have is some beef jerky.' He held up a ragged piece, then took a bite, a quick clamp and tug of teeth. He held her gaze only a moment then looked away.

Her blush rushed to deepen, and her heartbeat thudded in every pulse point of her body. Something was not right.

She stood, transfixed, waiting. Would he reach out and hold her?

Damn and bother. It didn't appear that he would. After all these years. They were finally adults, and still he would not gather her to him and declare …?

They'd grown up together. For long years they'd glanced furtively at each other, touched hands or fingers, almost as if in a game since they were children. Trailed each other from classroom to paddock to stream, and to their respective families' sitting rooms. Though nothing was formalised between them, Linley had expected that she and Ard would soon step out as a couple, and court, and finally be married. But no, he was so determined to find his way in the world first. Well, she would wait, hard as it was.

She was losing sleep because of him. Going mad because of him, with thoughts and feelings and needs she couldn't explain … Languid, heavy warmth tingled between her legs, softened her. A delicious fear of something she couldn't name rippled inside.

He stood without moving. Her hand rose and rested on the wall of his chest and she felt a muscle jump beneath. A quick glance at his face revealed nothing, just the immoveable stare. Suddenly, he was not all cool and masculine grace, but heat and power and—

She snatched her hand back, but too late. He'd snapped it within his and wouldn't let go, as unbreakable a bond as if she were bound in steel.

But then his bewildering words. They were uttered without so much as a change in his expression—except for a light in his eyes, which, for an instant, were like glistening onyx.

'I'm going away, Linley. To Renmark, where my parents are, to help out there, try to make something of my life. I'll get wages at last, maybe prove I can support a wife. But I don't know when I'll be back. This depression steals everything, and I—' He dropped her hand. 'My uncle Liam can look after the orchard here. Don't wait for me to come back. I can't promise anything.' He'd lowered his head. 'I never could.'

Her face burned anew. Her cheeks would now be as red as her hair—that much her aunt used to tell her.

She snatched her hand away. 'Don't wait?' She began to sputter. 'I don't care how much money you have.'

He pushed off the tree. 'I shouldn't even be here now, Linley. I've no right. I've nothing to offer, nothing to give you. Whatever was there is gone.' His frown was a deep scowl and a dimple in his cheek worked as if by itself. His mouth was downturned, his stare flinty.

'But I—'

'I'll come back, sometime. Sometime when I've made something of myself.' He looked despairing. 'But don't wait for me. I can't give you what you want. I can't be who you need me to be. Not yet.'

Words rushed out. 'That's rubbish, Ard O'Rourke. We can start now, with nothing. I don't mind.'

'I do. I won't be talked around.'

'That's just pride. We could live at the orchard. I could try and ask for more work at Mrs Tilley's shop.'

Ard's frown deepened. 'Aye, a woman supporting a man. I'll not do it, Linley. If I can't support my wife, I'll not be taking a wife.' He straightened abruptly. 'I never courted you properly, Linley, because there was no prospect of ever ...'

Linley gaped at him. 'You've already made up your mind. You never once said that you'd go away.'

He threw the jerky to the ground. 'Things have just got worse and worse here. I can't stay. There's no money, no jobs.'

'But not to discuss anything, just to announce you're going off somewhere?'

'I can't sit around here any longer and wonder if I'll ever earn a living.' He stood so close, seemed so angry.

Linley knew she was losing the fight, knew she wouldn't be able to change his mind. Her life, her hopes of a life with Ard, were slipping away.

She gripped his arms. 'Ard, I could come, too. We could …' She hesitated only a moment, a desperate, pleading moment. 'I don't need to be married if that's what you're—'

He shook off her hands, his black eyes flashing and his mouth set. 'Don't ever say that to me. Ever.' He turned his face away, rubbing his eyes. 'I've already made up my mind. I need to have work. It's been too long already.' He let out a ragged breath. 'I'll go to Renmark.'

'No!'

He leaned in a little and she thought her heart would give way. He only let his cheek warm the air beside hers, a quick touch of his fingers on hers, a sweep of his gaze over her face. And he turned and walked away.

Ard O'Rourke walked away.

Linley could only stand there, staring. If she ran after him, what could she do? He was not a man to change his mind. And she would not beg again.

Ard.

Her cry was silent then, but walking home along the edge of the lake, alone, with not a word to the others at the picnic, she whispered his name over and over.

That had been months and months ago. And now, if she ever saw Ard O'Rourke again she would take him to the authorities. She would brand him a scoundrel and a shirker of his right and proper duty and—

And what? Never talk to him again? Shun him? Refuse to invite him for tea?

As for Mary! Carefree, always with her skirts held high as she ran through the dusty paddocks at the back of the town ... Seems like she'd held her skirts high once too often ... with Ard O'Rourke.

Linley's blush flared again. She'd warned Mary about being too frivolous and light-hearted with the boys who'd been her childhood friends.

'But we are only friends, Miss Linley,' Mary had said, waving off the well-meaning concerns. 'I've been friends with them all since we were born almost. Do not worry about the prattle and the gossips. I can take care of myself.' There'd been a gleam of high excitement in her eye.

Gleeful in life, she was. Appearing unconcerned about society's mores, she was free with her affections, and with no thought to any consequences. *Silly, silly girl.* Her old aunt had often scolded her, but had always protected her.

Linley shut out Mary's pixie-like face laughing at her from the afterlife. Mary had thought this life was a fun game. However, without a doubt, the end days of her life were nothing like fun at all.

You were a foolish girl, Mary Bonner, but you didn't deserve your type of death.

She checked the baby once more and again he stared at her, wide-eyed, fascinated. He squirmed in the firm swaddle and when she reached out and touched a finger to his cheek, he smiled with a toothless happiness that shot a bolt of pleasure through her.

Her heartbeat thudded in her throat. She reached down and scooped him up, hugging him to her chest. Something familiar stirred, yet not. Something deep inside, but not what she recognised as belonging to her. It was in a place she hardly dared explore.

Ard O'Rourke. He makes me feel hot and melting and sad and bursting with rage ...

And I'm holding his baby close to my heart.

talk about it

Let's talk about books.

Join the conversation:

 on facebook.com/harlequinaustralia

 on Twitter @harlequinaus

www.harlequinbooks.com.au

If you love reading and want to know about our authors and titles, then let's talk about it.